17 = 6/10
18 - 2/14

1-1-26
2/19

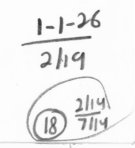

18   2/14
     7/14

LITTLE,
BROWN

1837

LARGE
PRINT

ALSO BY JOSEPH WAMBAUGH

FICTION
Hollywood Station
Floaters
Finnegan's Week
Fugitive Nights
The Golden Orange
The Secrets of Harry Bright
The Delta Star
The Glitter Dome
The Black Marble
The Choirboys
The Blue Knight
The New Centurions

NONFICTION
Fire Lover
The Blooding
Echoes in the Darkness
Lines and Shadows
The Onion Field

HOLLYWOOD CROWS

A NOVEL

JOSEPH WAMBAUGH

LITTLE, BROWN AND COMPANY
LARGE PRINT

Little, Brown and Company
Hachette Book Group USA
237 Park Avenue, New York, NY 10017
Visit our Web site at www.HachetteBookGroupUSA.com

First Large Print Edition: March 2008

The Large Print Edition published in accord with the standards of the N.A.V.H.

ISBN-10: 0-316-02671-9
ISBN-13: 978-0-316-02671-0
LCCN: 2007934863

10 9 8 7 6 5 4 3 2 1

RRD-IN

Printed in the United States of America

ACKNOWLEDGMENTS

Once again, special thanks for the terrific anecdotes and wonderful cop talk goes to officers of the Los Angeles Police Department:

Mike Arminio, Richard Blue, Tom Brascia, Ken Brower, Joe Bunch, Vicki Bynum, Paula Davidson, Francesca Flores, Maggie Furmanski, Beatrice Girmala, Brett Goodkin, Maria Gray, Craig Herron, Art Holmes (ret.), Jeff Ingalls, Roger Jackson, Jim Jarvis, Alisha Jordan, Richard Kalk (ret.), Mike Kammert, Al Lopez, Kathy McAnany, Julie Nony, Ed Pandolfo, Danny Pesqueira, Ralph Sanchez, Armen Sevdalian, Jeritt Severns, Mike Shea, Bill Sollie, John Washington, Jerry Wert

And to officers of the San Diego Police Department:

Don Borinski, Andra Brown, Joel Bryden, Rob Burlinson, Henry Castro, Kim Collier, Joe Cristinziani,

Reggie Frank, Robin Hayes, Ken Impellizeri, Nick Kelbaugh, Charles Lara, Noel McElfresh, Wende Morris, Gib Ninness, Tony Puente (ret.), Joe Robertson, Dave Root, Adam Sharki, Jerry Stratton, John Tefft, Roxie Vigil, Judy Woods, Kelly Yatch, Randy Young

HOLLYWOOD CROWS

★ ONE ★

"DUDE, YOU BETTER drop that *long* knife," the tall, suntanned cop said. At Hollywood Station they called him "Flotsam" by virtue of his being a surfing enthusiast.

His shorter partner, also with a major tan, hair even more suspiciously blond and sun streaked, dubbed "Jetsam" for the same reason, said, sotto voce, "Bro, that ain't a knife. That's a bayonet, in case you can't see too good. And why didn't you check out a Taser and a bean-bag gun from the kit room, is what I'd like to know. That's what the DA's office and FID are gonna ask if we have to light him up. Like, 'Why didn't you officers use nonlethal force?' Like, 'Why'd that Injun have to bite the dust when you coulda captured him alive?' That's what they'll say."

"I thought you checked them out and put them in the trunk. You walked toward the kit room."

"No, I went to the john. And you were too busy ogling Ronnie to know where I was at," Jetsam said. "Your head was somewheres else. You gotta keep your mind in the game, bro."

Everyone on the midwatch at Hollywood Station knew that Jetsam had a megacrush on Officer Veronica "Ronnie" Sinclair and got torqued when Flotsam or anybody else flirted with her. In any case, both surfer cops considered it sissified to carry a Taser on their belts.

Referring to section 5150 of the Welfare and Institutions Code, which all cops used to describe a mental case, Flotsam whispered, "Maybe this fifty-one-fifty's trashed on PCP, so we couldn't taze him anyways. He'd swat those darts outta him like King Kong swatted the airplanes. So just chill. He ain't even giving us the stink eye. He just maybe thinks he's a wooden Indian or something."

"Or maybe we're competing with a bunch of other voices he's hearing and they're scarier," Jetsam observed. "Maybe we're just echoes."

They'd gotten nowhere by yelling the normal commands to the motionless Indian, a stooped man in his early forties, only a decade older than they were but with a haggard face, beaten down by life. And while the cops waited for the backup they'd requested, they'd begun speaking to him in quiet voices, barely audible in the unlit alley over the traffic noise on Melrose Avenue. It was there that 6-X-46 had chased and cornered him, a few blocks from Paramount Studios, from where the code 2 call had come.

The Indian had smashed a window of a boutique to steal a plus-size gold dress with a handkerchief hemline and a red one with an empire waist. He'd squeezed into the red dress and walked to the Paramount main gate, where he'd started chanting gibberish and, perhaps prophetically, singing "Jailhouse Rock" before demanding admittance from a startled security officer who had dialed 9-1-1.

"These new mini-lights ain't worth a shit," Jetsam said, referring to the small flashlights that the LAPD bought and issued to all officers ever since a widely viewed videotaped arrest showed an officer striking a combative black suspect with his thirteen-inch aluminum flashlight, which caused panic in the media and in the police commission and resulted in the firing of the Latino officer.

After this event, new mini-flashlights that couldn't cause harm to combative suspects unless they ate them were ordered and issued to new recruits. Everything was fine with the police commission and the cop critics except that the high-intensity lights set the rubber sleeves on fire and almost incinerated a few rookies before the Department recalled all of those lights and ordered these new ten-ouncers.

Jetsam said, "Good thing that cop used flashlight therapy instead of smacking the vermin with a gun. We'd all be carrying two-shot derringers by now."

Flotsam's flashlight seemed to better illuminate the Indian, who stood staring up white-eyed at the starless smog-shrouded sky, his back to the graffiti-painted wall of a two-story commercial building owned by Iranians, leased by Vietnamese. The Indian may have chosen the red dress because it matched his flip-flops. The gold dress lay crumpled on the asphalt by his dirt-encrusted feet, along with the cut-offs he'd been wearing when he'd done the smash-and-grab.

So far, the Indian hadn't threatened them in any way. He just stood like a statue, his breathing shallow, the bayonet held down against his bare left thigh, which was fully exposed. He'd sliced the slit in the red dress clear up to his flank, either for more freedom of movement or to look more provocative.

"Dude," Flotsam said to the Indian, holding his Glock nine in the flashlight beam so the Indian could observe that it was pointed right at him, "I can see that you're spun out on something. My guess is you been doing crystal meth, right? And maybe you just wanted an audition at Paramount and didn't have any nice dresses to wear to it. I can sympathize with that too. I'm willing to blame it on Oscar de la Renta or whoever made the fucking things so alluring. But you're gonna have to drop that *long* knife now or pretty soon they're gonna be drawing you in chalk on this alley."

Jetsam, whose nine was also pointed at the ponytailed Indian, whispered to his partner, "Why do you keep saying *long* knife to this zombie instead of bayonet?"

"He's an Indian," Flotsam whispered back. "They always say *long* knife in the movies."

"That refers to us white men!" Jetsam said. "We're the fucking *long* knives!"

5

"Whatever," said Flotsam. "Where's our backup, anyhow? They coulda got here on skateboards by now."

When Flotsam reached tentatively for the pepper-spray canister on his belt, Jetsam said, "Uncool, bro. Liquid Jesus ain't gonna work on a meth-monster. It only works on cops. Which you proved the time you hit *me* with act-right spray instead of the 'roided-up primate I was doing a death dance with."

"You still aggro over that?" Flotsam said, remembering how Jetsam had writhed in pain after getting the blast of OC spray full in the face while they and four other cops swarmed the hallucinating bodybuilder who was paranoid from mixing recreational drugs with steroids. "Shit happens, dude. You can hold a grudge longer than my ex-wife."

In utter frustration, Jetsam finally said quietly to the Indian, "Bro, I'm starting to think you're running a game on us. So you either drop that bayonet right now or the medicine man's gonna be waving chicken claws over your fucking ashes."

Taking the cue, Flotsam stepped forward, his pistol aimed at the Indian's pustule-covered face, damp with sweat on this warm night, eyes rolled back, features strangely contorted in the flashlight beams. And the tall cop said just as quietly, "Dude, you're circling the drain. We're dunzo here."

Jetsam put his flashlight in his sap pocket, nowadays a cell-phone pocket, since saps had become LAPD artifacts, extended his pistol in both hands, and said to the Indian, "Happy trails, pard. Enjoy your dirt nap."

That did it. The Indian dropped the bayonet and Flotsam said, "Turn and face the wall and interlace your fingers behind your head!"

The Indian turned and faced the wall, but he obviously did not understand "interlace."

Jetsam said, "Cross your fingers behind your head!"

The Indian crossed his middle fingers over his index fingers and held them up behind his head.

"No, dude!" Flotsam said. "I didn't ask you to make a fucking wish, for chrissake!"

"Never mind!" Jetsam said, pulling the Indian's hands down and cuffing them behind his back.

Finally the Indian spoke. He said, "Do you

guys have a candy bar I could buy from you? I'll give you five dollars for a candy bar."

When Jetsam was walking the Indian to their car, the prisoner said, "Ten. I'll give you ten bucks. I'll pay you when I get outta jail."

After stopping at a liquor store to buy their meth-addled, candy-craving arrestee a Nutter Butter, they drove him to Hollywood Station and put him in an interview room, cuffing one wrist to a chair so he could still eat his candy. The night-watch D2, a lazy sensitivity-challenged detective known as "Compassion-ate" Charlie Gilford, was annoyed at being pulled away from shows like *American Idol*, which he watched on a little TV he kept con-cealed in the warren of work cubicles the size of airline restrooms, where he sat for hours on a rubber donut. He loved to watch the panels brutalize the hapless contestants.

The detective was wearing a short-sleeved, wrinkled white shirt and one of his discount neckties, a dizzying checkerboard of blues and yellows. Everyone said his ties were louder than Mötley Crüe, and even older. Charlie got fatigued listening to the story of the window smash on Melrose, the serenade to the guard at

Paramount Studios' main gate, the foot chase by the surfer cops, and the subsequent eerie confrontation, all of which Flotsam described as "weird."

He said to them, "Weird? This ain't weird." And then he uttered the phrase that one heard every night around the station when things seemed too surreal to be true: "Man, this is fucking Hollywood!" After that, there was usually no need for further comment.

But Charlie decided to elaborate: "Last year the midwatch busted a goony tweaker totally naked except for a pink tutu. He was waving a samurai sword on Sunset Boulevard when they took him down. That was weird. This ain't shit."

When he spotted the acronym for American Indian Movement tattooed on the prisoner's shoulder, he touched it with a pencil and said, "What's that mean, chief? Assholes in Moccasins?"

The Indian just sat munching on the Nutter Butter, eyes shut in utter bliss.

Then the cranky detective sucked his teeth and said to the arresting officers, "And by the way, you just had to feed him chocolate, huh? This tweaker don't have enough speed bumps?"

To the Indian he said, "Next time you feel like breaking into show business, take a look in the mirror. With that mug, you only got one option. Buy a hockey mask and try singing 'Music of the Night.'"

"I'll give you twenty bucks for another Nutter Butter," the Indian finally said to Compassionate Charlie Gilford. "And I'll confess to any crime you got."

Nathan Weiss, called Hollywood Nate by the other cops because of his obsession, recently waning, to break into the movie business, had left Watch 5, the midwatch, eight months earlier, shortly after the very senior sergeant known as the Oracle had died of a massive heart attack there on the police Walk of Fame in front of Hollywood Station. Nothing was the same on the midwatch after they lost the Oracle. Hollywood Nate had been pulled out of trouble, usually involving women, and spared from disciplinary action more than once by the grizzled forty-six-year veteran supervisor, who had died just short of his sixty-ninth birthday.

Everyone said it was fitting that the Oracle had died on that Walk, where stars honoring Hollywood Division officers killed on duty were embedded in marble and brass just as they were for movie stars on Hollywood Boulevard. The Oracle had been *their* star, an anachronism from another era of policing, from long before the Rodney King riots and Rampart Division evidence-planting scandal. Long before the LAPD had agreed to a Department of Justice "consent decree" and gotten invaded by federal judges and lawyers and politicians and auditors and overseers and media critics. Back when the cops could be guided by proactive leaders, not reactive bureaucrats more fearful of the federal overseers and local politicians than of the street criminals. The day after the Oracle died, Nathan Weiss had gone to temple, the first time in fifteen years, to say Kaddish for the old sergeant.

All of them, street cops and supervisors, were now smothered in paperwork designed to prove that they were "reforming" a police force of more than ninety-five hundred souls who ostensibly needed reforming because of the actions of half a dozen convicted cops from both incidents combined. Hundreds of sworn officers had been taken from street duties to manage the paper hurricane resulting from the massive "reformation." The consent decree hanging over the LAPD was to expire in two more years, but they'd heard that before and knew it could be extended. Like the war in Iraq, it seemed that it would never end.

The Oracle had been replaced by a university-educated twenty-eight-year-old with a degree in political science who'd rocketed almost to the top of the promotion list with little more than six years of experience, not to mention overcoming disadvantages of race and gender. Sergeant Jason Treakle was a white male, and that wasn't helpful in the diversity-obsessed city of Los Angeles, where fifty-five languages were spoken by students in the school district.

Hollywood Nate called Sergeant Treakle's roll call speeches a perfect meld of George Bush's garbled syntax and the tin ear of Al Gore. During those sessions Nate could hear cartilage crackling from all the chins bouncing off chests as the troops failed to stay awake and upright. He'd hated the rookie sergeant's guts the first time they'd met, when Sergeant Treakle criticized Nate in front of the entire assembly for referring to Officer Ronnie Sinclair as a "very cool chick." Ronnie took it as a compliment, but Sergeant Treakle found it demeaning and sexist.

Then, during an impromptu inspection, he'd frowned upon Hollywood Nate's scuffed shoes. He'd pointed at Nate's feet with an arm that didn't look long enough for his body, saying the shoes made Nate look "unkempt," and suggested that Nate try spit-shining them. Sergeant Treakle was big on spit shines, having spent six months in the ROTC at his university. Because of his knife-blade mouth, the cops soon referred to him as "Chickenlips."

Hollywood Nate, like his idol, the Oracle, had always worn ordinary black rubber-soled shoes with his uniform. He liked to needle the cops who wore expensive over-the-ankle boots to look more paramilitary but then experienced sweaty feet, foot fungus, and diminished running speed. Nate would ask them if their spit-shined boots made it easier to slog through all the snow and ice storms on Sunset and Hollywood Boulevards.

And Hollywood Nate had given up suggesting that field training officers stop making the new P1 probationers call them sir or ma'am, as most did. The more rigid and GI of the FTOs seemed to be those who'd never served in the military and they wouldn't think of letting their probies wear the gung-ho boots before finishing their eighteen-month probation. Nate would privately tell the rookies to forget about boots, that their feet would thank them for it. And Nate never forgot that the Oracle had never spit-shined his shoes.

Before the midwatch hit the streets, every cop would ritually touch the picture of the Oracle for luck, even new officers who'd never known him. It hung on the wall by the door of the roll call room. In the photo their late sergeant was in uniform, his retro gray crew cut freshly trimmed, smiling the way he'd always done, more with his smart blue eyes than with his mouth. The brass plate on the frame simply said:

The Oracle
Appointed: Feb 1960
End-of-Watch: Aug 2006
Semper Cop

Hollywood Nate, like all the others, had tapped the picture frame before leaving roll call on the first evening he'd met his new sergeant. Then he'd gone straight downstairs to the watch commander's office and asked to be reassigned to the day watch, citing a multitude of personal and even health reasons, all of them lies. It had seemed to Nate that an era had truly ended. The Oracle — the kind of cop Nate told everyone he had wanted to be when he grew up — had been replaced by a politically correct, paper-shuffling little putz with dwarfish arms, no lips, and a shoe fetish.

At first, Hollywood Nate wasn't fond of Watch 2, the early day watch, certainly not the part where he had to get up before 5 A.M. and speed from his one-bedroom apartment in the San Fernando Valley to Hollywood Station, change into his uniform, and be ready for 0630 roll call. He didn't like that at all. But he did like the hours of the 3/12 work shift. On Watch 2, the patrol officers worked three twelve-hour days a week during their twenty-eight-day deployment periods, making up one day at the end. That gave Nate four days a week to attend cattle calls and harangue casting agents, now that he'd earned enough vouchers to get his Screen Actors Guild card, which he carried in his badge wallet right behind his police ID.

So far, he'd gotten only one speaking part, two lines of dialogue, in a TV movie that was co-produced by an over-the-hill writer/director he'd met during one of the red carpet events at the Kodak Center, where Nate was tasked with crowd control. Nate won over that director by body blocking an anti-fur protester in a sweaty tank top before she could shove one of those "I'd Rather Go Naked" signs at the director's wife, who was wearing a faux-mink stole.

Nate sealed the deal and got the job when he told the hairy protester he'd hate to see *her* naked and added, "If wearing fur is a major crime, why don't you scrape those pits?"

The movie was about mate-swapping yuppies, and Nate was typecast as a cop who showed up after one of the husbands beat the crap out of his cheating spouse. The battered wife was scripted to look at the hawkishly handsome, well-muscled cop whose wavy dark hair was just turning silver at the temples, and wink at him with her undamaged eye.

To Nate, there didn't seem to be much of a

story and he was given one page of script with lines that read: "Good evening, ma'am. Did you call the police? What can I do for you that isn't immoral?"

During that one-day gig, the grips and gaffers and especially the craft services babe who provided great sandwiches and salads all told Nate that this was a "POS" movie that might never reach the small screen at all. After she'd said it, Nate knew that his initial impression had been correct: It was a piece of shit, for sure. Hollywood Nate Weiss was already thirty-six years old, with fifteen years on the LAPD. He needed a break. He needed an agent. He didn't have time left in his acting life to waste on pieces of shit.

On the morning after the midwatch surfer cops busted the wooden Indian, Nate Weiss was assigned to a one-man day-watch report car known as a U-boat, which responded to report-writing calls instead of those that for safety reasons required a pair of officers. At 8:30 A.M. Nate did what he always did when he caught a U-boat assignment: He went to Farmers Market at Third and Fairfax for a coffee break.

The fact that Farmers Market was a couple of

blocks out of Hollywood Division didn't bother him much. It was a small peccadillo that the Oracle would always forgive. Nate loved everything about that old landmark: the tall clock tower, the stalls full of produce, the displays of fresh fish and meat, the shops and ethnic eateries. But mostly he loved the open-air patios where people gathered this time of morning for cinnamon rolls, fresh-baked muffins, French toast, and other pastries.

Nate ordered a latte and a bagel, taking a seat at a small empty table close enough to eavesdrop on the "artistes' table." He'd started doing it after he'd overheard them talking about pitching scripts to HBO and getting financing for small indie projects and doing lunch with a famous agent from CAA who one of them said was a schmuck—all topics of fascination to Hollywood Nate Weiss.

By now, he was almost able to recognize them from their voices without looking at them directly. There was the features director who, due to Hollywood ageism, complained that he couldn't even get arrested at the studios. Ditto for three former screenwriters who were regulars at the table, as well as for a former TV producer. A dozen or more of these would come and go, all males, the average age being seventy-plus, far too old for the youth-obsessed entertainment business that had nurtured them.

A formerly famous painter and sculptor, wearing a trademark black beret, wasn't selling so well these days either. Nate heard him tell the others that when his wife asks him what he wants for dinner, his usual response is, "Get off my back, will ya?" Then the painter added, "But don't feel sorry for us. We're getting used to living in our car."

A former TV character actor wearing a safari jacket from Banana Republic, whose face was familiar to Nate, stood up and informed the others he had to leave and make an important call to a VP in development at Universal to discuss a script he'd been deciding whether or not to accept.

After he'd gone, the director said, "The poor schlemiel. I'll bet he gets a 'Please leave a message' recording from the VP at Universal. That's who he discusses the project with — a machine. Probably has to call back a hundred and thirty-five times to get his whole pitch into the VP's voice mail."

"I've suspected he's calling the number for highway information when he pretends to be talking to HBO," the painter said, clucking sadly.

"He never was any good, even in his prime," the director said. "Thought he was a method actor. They'd run out of money doing retakes. Twenty tics a take on average."

"If he had more of a name, they could paint him like a whore and let him do arthritis and Geico commercials, like the rest of those has-beens," said the has-been TV producer.

"And women?" one of the screenwriters said. "He thinks we believe his daffy seduction stories. Instead of another face-lift, the old bastard should have his balls stapled to his thigh to keep them from dropping in the toilet."

"He could do it without anesthetic," said the oldest of the screenwriters. "At his age it's a dead zone down there."

All of the geezers, who tended to talk over one another in multiple conversations, went silent for a moment when a stunning young woman paused to look into a nearby shop that sold glassware and candles. She wore a canary cotton jersey accented by hyacinth stitching, and $400 second-skin jeans, and stood nearly six feet tall in her Jimmy Choo lilac suede pumps. She had a full, pouty upper lip, and butterscotch blonde hair so luxurious it fanned across her shoulder when she turned to look at a glass figurine and then fell back perfectly into place when she continued walking. Her amazing hair gleamed when spangled sunlight pierced the covered patio and provided honey-colored highlights.

The codgers sighed and snuffled and did everything but drool before resuming their conversations. Nate watched her walk out toward the parking lot. Her remarkable body said Pilates loud and clear, and he could see she wasn't wearing a bra. There in Hollywood, and even in Beverly Hills, Nate Weiss had not seen many showstoppers like her.

By then, Nate was ready to go back to work. It was getting depressing listening to the old guys railing about ageism, knowing in their hearts they'd never work again. He'd noticed that always around 9:30 A.M., they'd get up one by one and make excuses to leave, for important calls from directors, or for appointments with agents, or to get back to scripts they were polishing. Nate figured they all just went home to sit and stare at phones that never rang. It gave him a chill to think that he might be looking at Nathan Weiss a few decades from now.

Nate strolled to the parking lot thirty yards behind the beauty with the butterscotch hair, wanting to see what she drove. He figured her for a Beverly Hills hottie in an Aston Martin with a vanity license plate, compliments of a bucks-up husband or sugar daddy who drove a stately Rolls Phantom. It was almost disappointing when she got into a red BMW sedan instead of something really expensive and exotic.

Impulsively, he jotted down her license number, and when he got back to his black-and-white, ran a DMV check and saw that she lived in the Hollywood Hills, off Laurel Canyon Boulevard in the development called Mt. Olympus, where realtors claimed there were more Italian cypress trees per acre than anywhere else on earth. Her address surprised him a bit. There were lots of well-to-do foreign nationals on Mt. Olympus: Israelis, Iranians, Arabs, Russians, and Armenians, and others from former Soviet bloc countries, some of whom had been suspects or victims in major crimes. A few of the residents reportedly owned banks in Moscow, and it was not uncommon to see young adults driving Bentleys, and teenagers in BMWs and Porsches.

Around the LAPD it was said that mobbed-up former Soviets were more dangerous and cruel than the Sicilian gangsters ever were back in the day. Just five months earlier, two Russians had been sentenced to death in Los Angeles Superior Court for kidnapping and murder. They'd suffocated or strangled four men and one woman in a $1.2 million ransom scheme.

Mt. Olympus was pricey, all right, but not the crème de la crème of local real estate, and Nate thought that the area didn't suit her style. Luckily, it was in Hollywood Division and he'd often patrolled the streets up there. He figured it was unlikely that this Hills bunny would ever need a cop, but after finally getting his SAG card, Hollywood Nate Weiss was starting to believe that maybe anything was possible.

At 6 P.M. that day, after the midwatch had cleared with communications and was just hitting the streets, and Nate Weiss was an hour from end-of-watch, the electronic beep sounded on the police radio and the PSR's voice said to a midwatch unit, "All units in the vicinity and Six-X-Seventy-six, a jumper at the northeast corner, Hollywood and Highland. Six-X-Seventy-six, handle code three."

Hollywood Nate in his patrol unit — which everyone at LAPD called their "shop" because of the identifying shop numbers on the front doors and roof — happened to be approaching the traffic light west at that intersection. He'd been gazing at the Kodak Center and dreaming of red carpets and stardom when the call came out. He saw the crowd of tourists gathering, looking up at a building twelve stories high, with an imposing green cupola. Even several of the so-called Street Characters who hustled tourists in the forecourt of Grauman's Chinese Theatre were jaywalking or running along the Walk of Fame to check out the excitement.

Superman was there, of course, and the Hulk, but not Spider-Man, who was in jail. Porky Pig waddled across the street, followed by Barney the dinosaur and three of the Beatles, the fourth staying behind to guard the karaoke equipment. Everyone was jabbering and pointing up at the top of the vacant building, formerly a bank, where a young man in walking shorts, tennis shoes, and a purple T-shirt with "Just Do It" across the front sat on the roof railing, a dozen stories above the street below.

In the responding unit were Veronica Sinclair and Catherine Song, both women in their early thirties who, as far as Nate was concerned, happened to be among the better cops on midwatch. Cat was a sultry Korean American whose hobby was volleyball and whose feline grace made her name a perfect fit. Nate, who had been trying unsuccessfully to date her for nearly a year, loved Cat's raven hair, cut in a retro bob like the girls in the 1930s movies that he had in his film collection. Cat was a divorced mother of a two-year-old boy.

Ronnie Sinclair had been at Hollywood Station for less than a year, but she'd been a heartthrob from the first moment she'd arrived. She was a high-energy brunette with a very short haircut that worked, given her small, tight ears and well-shaped head. She had pale blue eyes, great cheekbones, and a bustline that made all the male cops pretend they were admiring the shooting medals hanging on her shirt flap. The remarkable thing about her was that her childless marriages had been to two police officers named Sinclair who were distant cousins, so Flotsam and Jetsam called her Sinclair Squared. Most of the midwatch officers over the age of thirty were single but had been divorced at least once, including the surfer cops and Hollywood Nate.

The two women were met at the open door of the vacant building by an alarm company employee who said, "I don't know yet how he got in. Probably broke a window in the back. The elevator still works."

Ronnie and Cat hurried inside to the elevators, Nate right behind them. And all three stood waiting for the elevator, trying to be chatty to relieve the gathering tension.

"Why aren't you circling the station about now?" Ronnie said, looking at her watch. "You're almost end-of-watch and there must be a starlet waiting."

Nate looked at his own watch and said, "I still have, let's see, forty-seven minutes to give to the people of Los Angeles. And who needs starlets when I have such talent surrounding me?"

When Nate, whose womanizing was legendary at Hollywood Station, shot her his Groucho leer, Ronnie said, "Forget it, Nate. Ask me for a date sometime when you're a star and can introduce me to George Clooney."

That caused Hollywood Nate to whip out his badge wallet and proudly remove the SAG card tucked right underneath his police ID, holding it up for Ronnie and Cat to see.

Ronnie looked at it and said, "Even O.J. has one of those."

Cat said, "Sorry, Nate, but my mom wants me to date and marry a rich Buddhahead lawyer next time, not some oh-so-cute, round-eyed actor like you."

"Someday you'll both want me to autograph an eight-by-ten head shot for you," Nate said, pleased that Cat thought he was cute, more pleased that she'd called him an actor. "Then I'll be the one playing hard to get."

During the ride up in the elevator they didn't speak anymore, growing tense even though the location of the jumper call, here in the heart of Hollywood tourism, made it likely that it was just a stunt by some publicity junkie. The three cops were trying their best not to take it too seriously. Until they climbed to the observation deck encircling the cupola and saw him, shirtless now, straddling a railing with arms out-stretched, tennis shoes pressed together, head slightly bowed in the crucifixion pose. This, as tourists, hustlers, tweakers, pickpockets, cartoon characters, and various Hollywood crazies were standing down below, yelling at him to stop being a chickenshit and jump for Jesus.

"Oh, shit!" Cat said, speaking for all of them.

The three cops walked very slowly toward him and he turned around on the railing to face them, wobbling precariously, making onlookers down below either scream or cheer. His sandy, shoulder-length hair was blowing in his face, and his eyes behind wire-rimmed glasses were even more pale blue than Ronnie's. In fact, she thought he looked a lot like her cousin Bob, a drummer in a rock band. Maybe it was that, but she took the lead and the others let her have it.

She smiled at him and said, "Hey, whadda you say you come on down here and let's talk."

"Stay where you are," he said.

She held up her hands, palms forward, and said, "Okay, okay, I'm cool with that. But how about coming down now?"

"You're going to kill me, aren't you?" he said.

"Of course not," Ronnie said. "I just wanna talk to you. What's your name? They call me Ronnie."

He did not respond, so she said, "Ronnie is short for Veronica. A lot of people see my name somewhere and think I'm a guy."

Still he did not respond, so she said, "Do you have a nickname?"

"Tell them to go," he said, pointing at Nate and Cat. "I know they want to kill me."

Ronnie turned around, but the others had immediately retreated to the door when they heard his demand, Cat saying, "Be careful, Ronnie!"

Then Ronnie said to him, "See, they've gone."

"Take off your gun belt," he said. "Or I'll jump."

"Okay!" Ronnie said, unfastening her Sam Browne and lowering it to her feet, close enough to grab for it.

"Step away from the gun," he said. "I know you want to kill me."

"Why would I kill you?" Ronnie said, taking a single step toward him. "You're getting ready to kill yourself. You see, that wouldn't make sense, would it? No, I don't wanna kill you. I wanna help you. I know I can if you'll just get down from that railing and talk to me."

"Do you have a cigarette?" he said, and for a few seconds he swayed in the wind, and Ronnie sucked in a lungful of air, then let it out slowly.

"I don't smoke," she said, "but I can have my partner find you a cigarette. Her name's Cat. She's very nice and I bet you'd like her a lot."

"Never mind," he said. "I don't need a cigarette. I don't need anything."

"You need a friend," Ronnie said. "I'd like to be that friend. I have a cousin who looks just like you. What's your name?"

"My name's Randolph Bronson and I'm not crazy," he said. "I know what I'm doing."

"I don't think you're crazy, Randolph," Ronnie said, and now she could feel sweat running down her temples, and her hands felt slimy. "I just think you're feeling sad and need someone to talk to. That's why I'm here. To talk to you."

"Do you know what it's like to be called crazy? And schizophrenic?" he asked.

"Tell me about it, Randolph," Ronnie said, walking another step closer until he said, "Stop!"

"I'm sorry!" she said. "I'll stay right here if it makes you feel better. Tell me about your family. Who do you live with?"

"I'm a burden to them," he said. "A financial burden. An emotional burden. They won't be sorry to see me gone."

After six long minutes of talking, Ronnie Sinclair was fairly certain that the young man was ready to surrender. She found out that he was nineteen years old and had been treated for mental illness most of his life. Ronnie believed that she had him now, that she could talk him down from the railing. She was addressing him as "Randy" by the time backup arrived on the street, including a rescue ambulance and the fire department, whose engine only served to clog traffic. Still no crisis negotiator from Metropolitan Division had arrived.

And the first supervisor to show up at the scene was Sergeant Jason Treakle, who'd been on a suck-up mission to buy two hamburgers and an order of fries for the night-watch lieutenant. Sergeant Treakle had gotten a brainstorm the moment he'd heard the call. The idea actually made him say "Wow!" aloud, though he was alone in the car. Then he looked at the bag of burgers next to him, turned on his light bar, and sped to the location of the jumper call.

The young sergeant had recently read about an attempted suicide where a jumper had been talked down by a crisis negotiator who'd bought him a sandwich that they shared while talking at length about the people, real and imagined, who were tormenting him. The crisis negotiator had gotten her photo in the *L.A. Times* and had done several TV interviews.

When the midwatch supervisor ascended to the tower, carrying the bag of burgers, and brushed past Cat Song and Hollywood Nate, Cat said, "Sergeant Treakle, wait! Ronnie's talking to the guy. Wait, please."

Hollywood Nate said, "Don't go out there, Sergeant."

The sergeant said, "Don't tell me my job, Weiss."

Nate Weiss, who had several years in age and job experience on his former supervisor, said, "Sergeant, nobody should *ever* bust in on a suicide standoff. This might be Hollywood but this is not a movie, and there's no air bag down there."

"Thanks for your wise counsel," Sergeant Treakle said with a chilly glance at Nate. "I'll keep it in mind if you ever become my boss."

Ronnie turned and saw him striding confidently along the deck and said, "Sergeant! Go back, please! Let me handle —"

The anguished moan from Randolph Bronson made her spin around. He was staring at the uniformed sergeant with the condescending smile and the bulging paper bag in his hand, into which he was reaching.

The boy's pale eyes had gotten huge behind the eyeglasses. Then he looked at Ronnie and said, "He's going to kill me!"

And he was gone. Just like that.

The screams from the crowd, a gust of wind, and Cat's and Nate's shouts all prevented Ronnie from hearing her own cry as she lunged forward and gaped over the railing. She saw him bounce once on the pavement. Several bluesuits immediately began holding back the most morbid of the boulevard onlookers.

A few minutes later, there were a dozen more uniforms in the lobby of the building who observed Ronnie Sinclair, eyes glistening, yelling curses into the face of Sergeant Jason Treakle, who had gone pale and didn't know how to respond to his subordinate.

Ronnie didn't remember what she'd yelled, but Cat later said, "You started dropping F-bombs and it was beautiful. There's nothing Treakle can do about it, because now he knows he was dead wrong. And now that kid is just plain dead."

When they got out to the street, they were amazed to see that Randolph Bronson's wire-rimmed glasses were still affixed to his face and only one lens was broken. He had not blown apart, as some of them do, but there was a massive pool of blood.

Cat put an arm around Ronnie's shoulder, squeezed it, and said, "Gimme the keys to our shop. Let me drive us to the station."

Ronnie handed Cat the car keys without objection.

Compassionate Charlie Gilford, who never missed a newsworthy incident, especially with carnage involved, arrived in time to observe them picking up the body, and he offered his usual on-scene commentary.

The lanky veteran detective sucked his teeth and said to the body snatcher driving the coroner's van, "So, one of our patrol sergeants thought he could keep this looney tune from a back flip by feeding him a meal, right? Man, this is fucking Hollywood! Everybody knows you can walk a couple blocks to Musso and Frank's and dine with movie stars on comfort food. And Wolfgang Puck's got a joint right inside the Kodak Center with some of the trendiest eats in town. But what does our ass-wipe sergeant do to cheer up a depressed wack job? He brings the dude a fucking Big Mac! No wonder the fruitloop jumped."

Later that night, Compassionate Charlie Gilford saw Ronnie Sinclair in the report room massaging her temples, waiting for the interrogation from Force Investigation Division, knowing that this one would be handled just like an officer-involved shooting.

The detective said merrily, "I hear you really carpet bombed Chickenlips Treakle, Ronnie. Hollywood Nate told me you wouldn't hear *that* many 'motherfuckers' at a Chris Rock concert. Way to go, girl!"

★ TWO ★

IT WAS A FEW WEEKS after the jumper incident that Ronnie Sinclair decided she'd had enough of the midwatch and Sergeant Treakle, who had only received an official reprimand for barging into her crisis negotiation and, in Ronnie's opinion, causing the demise of young Randolph Bronson. She'd discussed her situation with an old sergeant for whom she'd worked at Newton Street Division, now officially called Newton Street Area, since the current LAPD brass had decided that *division* sounded too militaristic. The working cops said the brass were full of shit, and they kept right on referring to police divisions even in the LAPD union's monthly newspaper.

Ronnie's former sergeant suggested that in these repressive times, supervisors like Treakle were harder to get rid of than Rasputin and jock itch. He thought she ought to have a talk with the boss of the Hollywood Division Community

Relations Office, or CRO, pronounced "Crow" by the cops. "CRO is a good job, Ronnie," he told her. "You've done enough hard-core police work for a while. Being a senior lead officer in CRO will give you a leg up when you take your sergeant's oral."

It had surprised Hollywood Nate to learn that Ronnie Sinclair was seeking the job that had opened up at the Community Relations Office, a job that Nate coveted. The CRO was composed of eighteen cops and two civilian workers led by a twenty-two-year sergeant. Eleven of the officers, both men and women, were senior lead officers, or SLOs, pronounced "Slows," and were given a pay bump and wore two silver chevrons on their sleeves with a star beneath them. The SLOs acted as ombudsmen or community liaisons for the Hollywood Division captain. Five were Hispanics and could translate Spanish as needed, and three others were foreign born and could communicate in half a dozen other tongues, but that was only a fraction of the languages spoken in Hollywood. The coppers called their bailiwick Babelwood Division.

The Community Relations Office was housed in a one-story rambling old structure just a wedge shot across the police parking lot. It was dubbed Hollywood South by the troops in the main station, to which the Crows referred as Hollywood North, and which, like all LAPD police facilities, had the architectural charm of a parking garage in Watts.

Among other duties, Crows handled calls from chronic complainers and Hollywood loons, and they could pretty well set their own ten-hour duty tours in their four-day work week. The major efforts of these cops were directed at quality-of-life issues: chronic-noise complaints, graffiti, homeless encampments, abandoned shopping carts, unauthorized yard sales, and aggressive panhandlers. Crows also had the job of overseeing the Police Reserve Program and the Police Explorer Program for teenagers and directed the Nightclub Committee, the Homeless Committee, the Graffiti Committee, and even the Street Closure Committee.

In 2007, the city of Los Angeles's love for committees was almost as overpowering as its lust for diversity and its multicultural mania, and it would be hard to imagine anywhere with more social experimentation involving the police than LAPD's Hollywood Division. African Americans were the only ethnic group underrepresented in Hollywood demographics, but young black males arrived on the boulevards in large numbers every night, traveling on the subway or in cars from South L.A., many of whom were gang members.

The Crows also had to organize events such as the Tip-A-Cop fund-raiser, the Torch Run for the Special Olympics, and the Children's Holiday Party, and were tasked to help police the antiwar demonstrations, the Academy Awards, and all of the red carpet events at the Kodak Center. In short, they were doing jobs that caused salty old-timers to shake their heads and refer to the CRO as the sissy beat. Crows were often called teddy bears in blue.

They were also called much worse, but there was some envy involved in all of the pejoratives aimed at the Crows, because these officers of Hollywood South had relative freedom and the choice of wearing uniforms or street clothes depending upon the assignment, and they almost always did safe, clean work. Crows generally chose to stay in the job for a long time.

Ronnie had beaten out Hollywood Nate for the first opening in the Community Relations Office and was sent to senior lead officer training at the recruit training center near LAX. An unexpected retirement occurred a month later, and Nate Weiss ended up following Ronnie to the CRO, thinking he had found the spot where he might remain happily until retirement or until he attained show business success, whichever came first. By early summer, he had worked on two more TV movies, with a line of dialogue in each, the plots being for people who watch daytime TV. He was sure that the last one might make it to Spike TV because at the last minute they'd included lots of gratuitous blood and gore for high-school dropouts.

By July 2007, all of the Crows were future millionaires — in theory. One of them had been born in Iraq and had come to the U.S. as a child. He'd touted the wisdom of buying Iraqi dinars to his Crow partner now that the country was in chaos and its money nearly worthless. Through a currency broker, the partner bought one million dinars for $800 U.S. As the broker explained it to them, when Iraq eventually was able to get back to one dinar for one dollar and started being traded in all of the exchanges, "You'll be millionaires!"

So two other Crows bought a million dinars. Three bought half a million each. Another bought one and a half million, figuring to buy a yacht when he retired. Ronnie Sinclair was very hesitant, but thinking of her aging parents, she bought half a million dinars.

The week after he'd been assigned to the CRO, Nate had one of his vigorous iron-pumping workouts in the high-tech weight room at Hollywood South. After the workout and a mirror examination of his impressive pecs, lats, and biceps, Nate entered the CRO office, sat down at a desk, and carefully studied an Iraqi dinar that one of the others had given to him. Looking at it under a glass and holding it against a lamp, he examined the horse in the watermark as though he knew what he was doing.

"Check it with a jeweler's loupe, why don't you?" said Tony Silva, one of the Hispanic officers. "It's not counterfeit, if that's what you're thinking."

"No, but I read in the paper that counterfeiters are bleeding out the ink on these things,"

Nate said, "and using them to make U.S. currency with laser printers."

"Aren't you gonna buy while you have the chance?" Samuel Dibble, the CRO's only black cop, asked Nate. "What if Bush's troop surge works and the dinar stabilizes? We'll all be rich. How about you?"

Nate only smiled, trying not to look too condescending, but later said privately to his sergeant, "Cops are such suckers. Anyone can sell them a bill of goods. They'll invest in anything."

His sergeant said to him, "Yeah, I'm in for one million."

Later, after the new commanding general in Iraq gave a major TV interview and said that the troop surge had a very good chance of success, Hollywood Nate Weiss secretly made a transfer from his savings account, called the currency broker, and bought *two* million dinars without telling any of the others.

Of course, Hollywood Nate's former colleagues, the midwatch officers of Watch 5, were not dreaming of being millionaires. They were just trying to cope with young Sergeant Treakle, whose administrative spanking for bringing the Big

Macs to the rooftop standoff had not dampened his zeal or ambition. They knew that Hollywood Division was as shorthanded as the rest of the beleaguered LAPD, so before a supervisor like Sergeant Treakle could get a suspension without pay, he would have to do something *really* terrible. Such as saying something politically incorrect to a member of what had historically been considered a minority group. At least that was the thinking of the midwatch, according to all of the bitching heard around the station.

On one of those summer nights under what the Oracle used to call a Hollywood moon, meaning a full moon that brought out the crazies, Flotsam mentioned the rooftop incident to Catherine Song and said, "Why couldn't the jumper have been black or Hispanic? That would've pushed Treakle's off button."

"What about a Korean female?" Cat said back to him. "We're not potential PC victims?"

"Negative," Flotsam said. "You people have got too rich and successful for victimhood. You and me're in the same boat. We could jump off a roof and who cares?"

Sergeant Treakle had teamed them up arbitrarily for one night, assigning Jetsam to ride with a Hispanic probationer whose field training officer was on a sick day. Jetsam didn't like working with a boot, but Flotsam wasn't complaining, and Cat knew why. She was very aware that he had eyes for her, but so did most of the other male officers on the midwatch.

That was when the PSR's radio voice said, "Six-X-Thirty-two, a four-fifteen fight, Santa Monica and Western, code two."

"Why can't we get a call in our own backyard once in a while?" Flotsam grumbled as Cat rogered the call. "Doomsday Dan's working sixty-six with a probie partner. They should be handling it."

"Dan probably had to run over to the cyber café to rent a computer and watch his foreign stocks tumble," Cat said. "Doesn't matter how good the market's doing. He's a great anticipator of international disasters."

When they got to the location of the call, which turned out to be a bit east of Western Avenue, Cat said, "Doomsday Dan sure would break out the gloves for this one."

Four onlookers, two of them Salvadoran gang members, along with a pair of white parolees out looking for some tranny or dragon ass, were watching the disturbance. Transsexuals were preferred by the ex-cons in that all of their hormone treatments and surgery made them more like women, but in a pinch the parolees would settle for a drag queen. The onlookers were watching what had been a pretty good fight between a black drag queen and a white man in a business suit, which was now down to a screaming contest full of threats and gestures.

When the cops got out of the black-and-white, four observers walked quickly away, but a fifth stepped out of the shadows from a darkened doorway. Trombone Teddy was a transient, known to Flotsam from prior contacts. He was a street person nearly eighty years old who panhandled on the boulevards.

Teddy had stayed at the fight scene to watch the denouement, knowing he was drunk enough to get busted but too drunk to care. He wore a Lakers cap, layers of shirts that were now part of him, and nearly congealed trousers the color and texture of just-picked mushrooms. Looking at Teddy made you think fungus.

"I'm a witness," Trombone Teddy said to Flotsam.

"Go home, Teddy," the tall cop said, putting

his mini-flashlight under his arm, cursing because the little light wouldn't stay there.

"I am home," Teddy replied. "I been living right here in this doorway for the last few days. The cops rousted us outta our camp in the hills. Up there we could hear the concerts at the Hollywood Bowl. I was a real sideman in my time, you know. I could blow better than any I ever heard at the Bowl. Back when I was a real person."

That made Flotsam feel a little bit sad, Trombone Teddy reminiscing about having been a real person. Back in the day.

With the police there as protection, the black dragon, wearing a mauve shell and a black double-slitted skirt, hauled off for one last shot, swinging a silver purse at the white businessman, until Flotsam stepped in and said, "Back off! Both of you!"

Reluctantly, the dragon stepped back, blonde wig askew, one heel broken off the silver pumps, makeup smeared, panty hose shredded, and yelled, "He kidnapped me! I barely escaped with my life! Arrest him!"

Flotsam had already patted down the other combatant. He was portly and middle-aged with a dyed-black comb-over that shone like patent leather. A trickle of blood dripped from his nose and he wiped it with a silk handkerchief from his breast pocket.

He handed Flotsam his driver's license and said, "My name is Milt Zimmerman, Officer. I've never been arrested for anything. This person stole my car keys and took off running to here, where I caught her. My car is two blocks west in an alley. I want her arrested for attempted car theft."

"Ask this guddamn kidnapper how we got in the alley! Jist ask him!" the dragon cried.

"Step over here with me," Cat said to the slender drag queen, who listed to starboard on the broken silver pump.

When the combatants were separated, Trombone Teddy staggered back and forth from one pair to the other so as not to miss any of the good parts, and he heard Cat say to the dragon, "Okay, now give me some ID and tell me what happened."

The drag queen produced a driver's license bearing the name of Latrelle Johnson, born in 1975, from the silver purse. Cat shined her light on the photo, taken when Latrelle was without eyebrows and lipstick and wig, and Cat decided that the dragon was far better-looking as a man than as a woman.

Cat said, "Okay, Latrelle, tell me what happened."

"Please call me Rhonda," the dragon said. "That's my name now. Latrelle don't exist no more. Latrelle is dead, and I'm glad."

"Okay, Rhonda," Cat said, thinking that sounded kind of sad. "So what's the story here?"

"He picked me up from the corner two blocks down Santa Monica and offered to take me to a club for some drinks and a dance or two. Me, I'm stupid. I believed him."

"Uh-huh," Cat said. "You just happened to be on this corner waiting for someone to go dancing with?"

"I ain't hookin'," said Rhonda, then after a few seconds added, "Well . . . I admit I got busted a couple times for prostitution, but tonight I happened to be jist makin' a call at the public phone here by the liquor store." Rhonda pointed to the phone box behind them.

"Okay, then what?" Cat said, deciding that there would be no kidnapping report and maybe no reports at all, except for a couple of field interrogation cards.

"I thought maybe he was takin' me out to the Strip, but we only got a couple blocks and he whips into an alley and forces me to commit a sex act. I was scared for my life, Officer!"

Milt Zimmerman heard part of that and yelled, "She's a liar! She wanted it! Then she grabbed my car keys and ran off with them!"

"Okay, pay attention to me, not to them," Flotsam said, taking Milt Zimmerman by the arm and walking him several steps farther away, while Trombone Teddy drifted toward Cat and Rhonda because their conversation sounded juicier.

Milt Zimmerman said to Flotsam, "She's lying! I told her I wanted a blow job and she gave it up willingly. Then when she's done she wants an extra twenty. I said no way, and she grabs my keys from the ignition and starts running back here, where I first picked her up. My Cadillac's still back there in the alley!"

"Thing is," Flotsam said. "She's a him. You might call her a 'shim.'"

"I didn't know!" Milt Zimmerman said. "She looks like a woman!"

"This is Hollywood," Flotsam said, "where men are men and so are the women."

Back by the liquor store Rhonda was starting to reveal more details, causing Trombone Teddy to shuffle closer, his hearing not what it used to be. When Cat came on the Job, she was trained by old male coppers who scorned latex gloves, which cops didn't have back in the day. But looking at Trombone Teddy made Cat glad she was carrying a pair tonight.

She said to the old eavesdropper, "Get your butt away from here. Now!"

"But I always liked soap opera," Trombone Teddy said.

Cat reached in her pocket and said, "Don't make me glove up. If I do, you're going to jail."

"Yes, ma'am," Teddy muttered and walked back toward Flotsam, where he knew it wouldn't be nearly as entertaining.

"So what exactly went on in that alley?" Cat asked Rhonda. "The details."

Rhonda said, "At first he seemed real nice. He stopped the car the second we was in the alley. He turned off the motor and started kissin' me. Hard. I said somethin' like, 'Easy, baby, give a girl a minute to breathe.' Next thing I know, the pants came off."

"Yours?"

"His. Then he made me do something that I would never do. He said if I didn't do it, he'd get violent. He had very strong hands and I was afraid. When he said it, he reached under my skirt and pulled my panty hose down and my thong clear off!"

"Was it anal sex? Did he bugger you?"

"No! He made *me* bugger *him!* It was humiliatin'. I was so scared, I done it. I don't know how I managed, but I did. And I didn't have no condom neither."

"I see," Cat said. "Then what?"

"Then, when I was through, he said he wanted more and I said no way and tried to get outta the car. And he started cussin' and said he oughtta run over me with his Cadillac. So I jist grabbed his keys, got out, and ran while he was tryin' to pull his pants back up."

Rhonda took out a tissue and wiped at her mascara then, and Cat wasn't sure if it was for her benefit or if Rhonda was really getting weepy.

Cat said, "Rhonda, don't make us do a lot of paperwork for nothing here. Tell me the truth. Was there money involved in this incident?"

Rhonda put the tissue back in the purse and said, "He offered me thirty-five dollars." Then Rhonda quickly added, "I didn't ask him for it. He jist offered to give it to me. Not for sex, but like a gift, sorta."

"If you went dancing with him?"

"Uh-huh," Rhonda said, sniffling again.

"Stay right here."

Seeing Cat walking toward him, Flotsam told Milt Zimmerman to stay put, and he met Cat halfway, where they could talk in whispers. Trombone Teddy tried to sidle closer, but when Cat gave him a look, he scuttled away to his doorway bed, muttering, "I been scared to death of them ever since Pearl Harbor."

"She's Korean, Teddy. You're safe," Flotsam informed him.

"North or South?" Teddy asked anxiously.

When Cat and Flotsam were huddled, Flotsam said, "He claims he picked up the dragon in front of the liquor store by the phone booth. The dragon offered sex for fifty bucks but said okay to thirty-five. They drove to the alley, where he got his steam released from a head job, then the dragon demanded twenty more. He refused and the dragon up and grabbed his keys and ran back to the liquor store."

"Did he say why Rhonda wanted twenty more after it was over?" Cat asked.

"No, why?"

"If Rhonda's telling most of the truth, it's because the guy wanted something that the more fem dragons like Rhonda are seldom asked to do."

"Dragons and trannies do anything you want," Flotsam said, "which is why they got every kind of plague and pestilence. So what was it?"

"Anal sex," Cat said.

"So? The dragon found that peculiar?"

"Milton was the catcher, not the pitcher."

Flotsam said to Cat, "Lemme track this. You're telling me that Milton ended up being Rhonda's bitch?" He turned to gawk for a moment at the outraged businessman impeccably clothed by Armani, then said, "Sometimes it gets way too confusing out here."

All that was left to do was to mollify both of the complainants. The two cops walked over to the businessman, and Flotsam said, "Mr. Zim-merman, do you really wanna make a crime report? Before you answer, lemme tell you that the person over there in the torn skirt says that you paid to be..."

"Buggered," Cat finished it abruptly. "That doesn't mean you can't be a victim of an attempted car theft, but it might get embarrass-ing for you and your family if it went to court. Of course, we could disprove Rhonda's allega-tions by taking you to Hollywood Presbyterian and having a doctor swab your anus for DNA evidence. Whadda you think?"

After a long hesitation, Milt Zimmerman said, "Well, I'm okay with just forgetting the whole thing and getting the hell away from that lunatic."

Flotsam said, "Just stand by for a minute until we see if the other party is satisfied with this outcome."

When they walked back to the liquor store, Rhonda was hanging up the receiver on a public phone attached to the wall. Cat said, "Rhonda, you might wanna think this over before you insist on reports for kidnapping or sexual assault. You see, there *was* money involved here, regardless of whether he decided to give it or you asked him for it. Sex and money usually means prostitution."

"And after all, he's the one that got boned," Flotsam said to Rhonda. "So even if we arrested him for assaulting you, his defense lawyer would say he took it in the chute, not you. That this is just a case of tit for tat."

"Okay," Rhonda said with a sigh. "But I will always know that I was the victim, not that freak. And my tits had nothin' to do with it!"

While Milt Zimmerman walked to the alley with the car keys that Cat had retrieved, Rhonda removed the broken silver pump and hobbled down Santa Monica Boulevard in the other direction, disappearing into the night.

"No such thing as rape in Hollywood," Cat said to Flotsam. "Just a lot of business disputes."

Flotsam had the last word, two words, actually. It was what was always said by officers in that unique police division, there in the very heart of Los Angeles. He shook his head in utter bewilderment and said, "Fucking Hollywood!"

Just then the public phone rang. Cat was heading for their car but Flotsam said, "They're all afraid of cell phones from watching *The Wire* on TV."

Flotsam picked it up and in a voice as close to Rhonda's as he could manage said, "Heloooo."

As expected, a male voice said, "Is this Rhonda?"

"It certainly is," Flotsam said in falsetto.

"I'm the guy who had a little party with you at my apartment three weeks ago," the caller said. "Lance. Remember?"

"Ohhhh, yes," Flotsam said. "Remind me of your address, Lance."

Before he hung up, Cat heard him say, "Get ready to shed those pants, Lance!"

"What's going on in that water-logged brain?" Cat asked with a sloe-eyed glance.

At eleven-thirty, 6-X-32 pulled up in front of an apartment building on Franklin, an upmarket neighborhood where Flotsam and Cat wouldn't have expected a dragon streetwalker to have an outcall date.

Flotsam said to Cat, "I thought we'd find the guy somewhere like that building near Fountain and Beachwood. That's where a lotta trannies and dragons do business. My partner and me call it Jurassic Park."

"Why?" Cat asked.

"Because of the occupants. We don't know *what* the hell they are."

Flotsam shined his spotlight along the second-floor balcony until he spotted Lance's apartment number, then got on the PA and said, "Attention, Lance! Miss Rhonda regrets she is indisposed and unable to keep her date with you tonight. It's her recurring prostate infection."

★ THREE ★

RONNIE WASN'T SURE how she felt about working at the CRO. It surely wasn't police work, and yet she couldn't stop thinking about how she'd felt when her mother and father and married sister had ganged up on her. It had happened when she'd mentioned her new job to them during a family dinner at her parents' home in Manhattan Beach, where her father owned and operated a successful plumbing-supply business.

"I don't even like what they call us," Ronnie said to them.

"Crows?" her mother said. "That's cute."

"How would you like to be called a crow?" Ronnie said.

"I'm too old to appreciate it," her mother said. "But on you it's cute."

Ronnie had felt exceptionally tired that evening, and while her mother and her sister Stephanie were preparing a dinner of roasted halibut and wild rice, Ronnie was sprawled on the sofa with her niece Sarah sitting on her stomach. She'd tried without much success to enjoy a glass of pinot while Sarah prattled on, bouncing incessantly.

After the meal, Ronnie's mother urged her just to relax and listen to her mom's favorite Sting CDs and her father's Tony Bennett albums while the others tidied up. She should have been suspicious of the extra solicitude. Then they all entered the living room and sat down, her mother and sister with a glass of wine each, her father with a beer. And they started in on her.

"The Community Relations Office is where you belong, Ronnie," her father began. "You should stay there until you make sergeant. It's a good stepping-stone and there's no reason for you to leave."

Her mother said, "You've done your share of dangerous work, honey."

Stephanie said, "Do a year or two as a community relations officer, study, and get promoted. I know you think being a street cop is more fun, but you gotta think of the future."

Her sister had assured her own future by marrying a computer geek who made three million dollars from selling his start-up company and investing it in another computer business, which was soaring.

"What is this, an intervention?" Ronnie said. "When did you all decide to do good-cop, bad-cop on me?"

"We've been talking about you, it's true," her mother said. "We know you're not thrilled with your new job, but you're smart. You can climb the ladder and end up—"

"In a safe desk job somewhere," Ronnie said, ruefully. "Build them a desk and they will sit, right?"

Stephanie, who bore a family resemblance to her older sister, said, "I'll never understand your fascination with being a cop anyway. What's it got you except two failed marriages to other cops?"

"But they were both Sinclairs, so I didn't even have to change my driver's license," Ronnie said with a smirk, pissed off as she always was when Sanctimonious Stephanie spouted off about Ronnie's bad choices. Both Sinclair husbands had fooled Ronnie at first, but she felt she hadn't gotten enough credit for dumping each of them quickly, as soon as she discovered that one was a secret drinker and the other a philanderer.

"Give your new job a chance," her father said.

"You might start liking it," her sister said. "Making your own hours to suit your own schedule."

"And I could quit worrying about you," her mother said.

After that evening, Ronnie decided to give it all she had at the CRO, especially since the sergeant had teamed her with an experienced senior lead officer, Bix Ramstead, to whom Ronnie had been drawn instantly.

Forty-five-year-old Bix Ramstead was thirteen years her senior, on both the Job and the calendar. At six foot one, he was fit and good-looking, with a warm and kindly smile. He had a head full of curls the color of pewter, and smoky gray eyes, and though Ronnie had never dated a man his age, she would have jumped at a chance with Bix. Except that he was married with two children he adored, a sixteen-year-old girl named Janie, and Patrick, who was twelve. Their photos were on his desk and he talked of them often, worrying about whether he'd have enough for their college tuition when the time came. Because of that, he worked as much overtime as he could, and the citizens in his area liked him.

When Ronnie had mentioned Bix to Cat, she'd said, "Yeah, I was teamed with him a few times, maybe six years ago, when he was working patrol. A complicated guy who never wanted to make sergeant. Not as much fun as some of the gunfighters when you're working the streets. Back then I was always happier with carnivores than with grazers, but I don't need kick-ass partners anymore. Now he'd probably suit me fine. Plus, he's very cute."

When Ronnie said it was too bad that Bix was married, Cat said, "He's a little too old for you, and besides, didn't you learn your lesson marrying two cops? I learned from marrying one. Do like me and look for a rich attorney next time. Hang out in lawyer-infested bars. Shysters are all over the place, like Starbucks cups."

The first appointment Ronnie took with Bix Ramstead was at "The Birds," as the cops referred to the Doheny Estates, in 6-A-31's area. It was late morning as they cruised up the hills, surrounded by seven-figure homes on streets named Warbler Way, Robin Drive, Nightingale Drive, Thrush Way, and Skylark Drive. Many movie and rock stars owned high-dollar houses in the Hollywood Hills, some of them serving as occasional homes when their owners were in L.A. Many had great open views, some were on secluded properties. The showbiz residents were fearful of stalkers, burglars, and paparazzi.

"Occasionally, we do burglary walk-throughs," Bix Ramstead explained to Ronnie while they drove the streets. "We just point out all the vulnerable places that need protection."

"Quality of life," Ronnie said, repeating the CRO mantra.

"You got it," Bix said with a grin. "The quality-of-life calls we get up here in the hills are a bit different from the quality-of-life calls in East Hollywood, you'll notice."

Ronnie looked at the luxury surrounding her and said, "Their quality is a lot different from my quality, for sure." She was silent for a moment, then said, "We still look like police officers, still think like police officers, but we aren't doing police work."

Bix Ramstead said to her, "When I was a cop, I spoke as a cop, I understood as a cop, I thought as a cop. But when I became a Crow, I put aside cop-ish things."

"Who's line is that?" Ronnie said.

"St. Paul to the Corinthians. More or less." Then he said, "This is a good job, Ronnie. You'll see. Don't fight it."

The call to the Community Relations Office that had come from The Birds was from a drummer in a rock band who was definitely on his way down. At one time he'd been hot and mentioned in the same breath with Tommy Lee, but internal dissension between the singer and the lead guitarist, who wrote their material, had broken up the group. The drummer lived with a singer whose career had taken a similar dive. She was known on the Strip as a very bad drinker whose cocaine addiction had gotten her arrested twice.

When they rang the bell, Bix said to Ronnie, "Look for *Scarface*. He's an icon."

"Who?" Ronnie said.

It took the rocker a minute to come to the door, and when he did, he looked pale and puzzled. His ginger ringlets hung in his face.

He had a week's growth of whiskers, and the wispy, dark soul patch under his lip was plastered with dried food. He wore a "Metallica" T-shirt and battered designer jeans that Ronnie figured had cost more than the best dress she owned. His arms were covered with full-sleeve tatts and he appeared malnourished.

"Oh, yeah, thanks for coming," he said, stepping back in bare feet, obviously just recalling that he'd called the police the day before.

When they entered, Ronnie saw his singer girlfriend sprawled in a huge wicker chair inside a garden room just off the foyer. She was listening trancelike to speakers built into the walls on each side of the chair. Ronnie figured it was her voice on the CD singing unintelligible lyrics. Behind her on the wall was a framed one-sheet movie poster of *Scarface*, starring Al Pacino.

The rocker didn't invite them in any farther than the foyer, and Bix Ramstead said, "How can we help you?"

"We're scared of getting trapped in a fire," the rocker said, scratching his ribs and his back, even his crotch for a moment, until he remembered that one of the cops was a woman. "It's the pap. They come around with scopes and watch us from vacant property on the hilltop. And they smoke up there. We're scared they'll start a brush fire. Can you chase them away?"

"Are there any up there now, or do you not know?" Bix asked.

"I don't know. We see them watching us. Always watching."

"We'll take a drive up the hill and check it out," Bix said.

"Stop back and let us know," the rocker said.

"Sure, we'll be back in a little bit."

When they got in their car and drove up the hill, Ronnie said, "He's a poster boy for 'Just Say No.' He's thirty years old, going on eighty. And speaking of posters, how did you know *Scarface* would be there?"

"Rocker plus cocaine plus Hollywood equals *Scarface,*" Bix said. "The cocaine set loves that movie, especially that dopey scene where Al Pacino's so buzzed he falls face-first into a snowdrift of coke. You can usually find *Scarface* somewhere in all their cribs."

Ronnie said, "The first time I drove up to the Hollywood Hills, I saw these homes and figured these were the kind of people who listen to music I never hear on K-Rock. Now I find out there're people here who download tunes from Headbanger's Heaven."

"Big bucks don't change human nature," Bix said.

He didn't waste much time on the paparazzi search. Bix drove to the area where homes had not yet been built on the steeper slopes, looked around perfunctorily, then drove back down to the rocker's address and parked in front, where the man was waiting for them in the doorway.

"Well?" the rocker said.

"You were right," Bix said. "There were four of them. They had telephoto cameras on tripods. And there were three more driving up while we were talking to the other four. You're a very popular target, it seems."

"What'd you tell them?" the rocker asked anxiously.

"I told them that I know they're just doing their jobs but that there could be serious repercussions for stalking famous people."

"I understand they gotta make a living," the rocker said.

"I reassured them that you understand. That celebrities like you need them and they need you. A reciprocal arrangement, so to speak."

"Yeah, exactly," the rocker said. "Just so they don't start a fire. That's all we're worried about."

"They promised me that there'd be no smoking up there in the future unless it was done in their van with cigarettes extinguished in the ashtray."

"They had a van?" the rocker said with a little smile.

"Yes, sir," Bix said. "They come prepared for someone like you." Then he added, "And your lady, of course."

The rocker's smile widened and he said, "Yeah, because of the pap, she's afraid to get in the Jacuzzi without wearing something."

"The price of fame," Bix said, nodding sympathetically.

"Well, thanks, Officers," the rocker said. "Anything I can do for you, let me know. We played a gig one time for the Highway Patrol."

"We'll keep that in mind, sir," Bix said. "We'd be thrilled to hear you play."

When they were driving back down toward Sunset Boulevard, Bix said to Ronnie, "We get a lot of those. I never tell them the truth. They're miserable enough in their failed lives without finding out that there's no paparazzi. That nobody gives a shit anymore."

Hollywood Nate was supposed to be doing similar CRO work that day, but he took a drive up into the Hollywood Hills on his own, to a neighborhood farther east. On an impulse, he cruised up to Mt. Olympus, sipping a cup of Starbucks latte as he remembered the young woman with butterscotch hair. He hadn't been able to forget her since the day he wrote down her license plate number at Farmers Market.

Nate parked a block from her home on her very winding street. It was obvious that on her side of the street, there was a good city view. He told himself that he wasn't going to sit there long, only long enough to finish the latte.

Hollywood Nate couldn't understand why he was there in the first place. That is, until he remembered the way she'd moved. Like an athlete, or a dancer, maybe. And the way her hair itself had danced when she'd turned abruptly. He couldn't forget that either. In fact, he was ashamed of himself for doing this, but as long as nobody would ever know, what the hell. He just wanted to see her one more time, to see if she measured up to the image in his memory.

Then Nate thought, What am I, a high-school kid? And he tossed the empty cup on the floor of the car, started the engine, and was just about to head back down, when the garage door opened and the red Beemer backed out. The car turned and drove down the hill with Hollywood Nate Weiss following behind, but far enough to be out of mirror range.

Nate's heart started pumping faster and he knew it wasn't the caffeine. He'd never done anything like this before, had never had the memory of a beautiful woman affect him in this way. Hollywood Nate Weiss had never had to pursue any woman, not in his entire life. And it made him think, I've turned into a goddamn stalker! Now Nate was experiencing something altogether unique for him. Not just shame, but a trace of self-loathing had entered his consciousness.

He said aloud, "Fuck this!" and was about to abandon this silliness when they were a few blocks from Hollywood Boulevard. But then he saw her car rolling through a boulevard stop without so much as a tap on the brake pedal.

Suddenly, Nate Weiss was no longer in charge. Something took him over. It was like he was watching himself on a movie screen. Without completely willing it, Nate stepped on the accelerator and got close behind her, turning on the light bar and tooting his horn until she glanced at her rearview mirror, pulled over, and parked.

When he got to her driver's-side window, she looked at him with amber eyes that matched her hair and said, "Ditzy Margot didn't come to a complete stop back there, did she?"

Her cotton jersey that stretched tight over her cleavage was a raspberry shade. Her skirt was eggshell white and was halfway up her suntanned thighs. Those thighs! She *was* an athlete or a dancer, he just knew it.

Nate's hand trembled when he took her driver's license, and his voice was unsteady when he said, "Yes, ma'am, you ran the stop sign without even trying to stop. Your brake lights didn't glow at all."

"Damn!" she said. "I've got so much on my mind. I'm sorry."

He read the driver's license: Margot Aziz, date of birth 4-13-77. She was six years younger than

Nate, yet he felt like a schoolboy again. Stalling for time in order to pull himself together, he said, "Could I see your registration, ma'am?"

She reached into the glove box for the leather packet containing the owner's manuals, removed the registration and insurance card, handed them to Nate, and said, "Please don't call me ma'am, Officer. I recently turned thirty, as you see, and I'm feeling ancient. Call me Margot."

Her lipstick was a creamy raspberry to match her jersey, and her perfect teeth were probably whiter than nature intended. Nate blurted, "I won't call you ma'am if you don't call me Officer. My name is Nate Weiss."

She had him and she knew it. The smile widened and she said, "Do you patrol this area all the time, Nate?"

"Actually, I'm what the other cops call a Crow. I work the Community Relations Office. I don't do regular patrol."

"You don't look like a crow," Margot Aziz said. "More like an eagle, I would say."

He couldn't remember the last time he'd blushed, but his face felt hot. He said, "Yeah, I do have a bit of a beak, don't I?"

"No, my husband has a beak," she said. "Your nose is barely aquiline. It's very strong and manly. Actually, quite...beautiful."

He wasn't even aware that he'd handed her back her license and registration. "Well," he said, "drive carefully."

Before he could turn to leave, she said, "Nate, what does a Crow do?"

He said, "We deal with quality-of-life issues so that the officers on patrol don't have to. You know, stuff like chronic-noise complaints, graffiti, homeless encampments up near where you live. Stuff like that."

"Homeless encampments!" she cried, like calling a winning Bingo. "This is an amazing coincidence because I was going to call Hollywood Station about that very thing. I can see them from my patio. They make noise up there and they light campfires. It's terrible. How lucky to run into you like this. Sometime I'd like you to come by my house and let me point them out. Maybe you can do something about it."

"Sure!" Nate said. "Absolutely. When, today?"

"Not today, Nate," she said quickly. "Can I have your phone number?"

"Of course," Nate said, reaching for his business cards. "I can come and talk to you — and to your husband — anytime up to eight P.M., when I usually go home."

"My husband and I are separated, in the middle of a divorce," Margot Aziz said. "You'll just be talking to me when you come."

Nate Weiss couldn't give her the card fast enough. He had ordered a custom-made business card with the Hollywood sign across the front of it, alongside an LAPD badge. And under that was his name, serial number, and the city phone number he'd been assigned by the CRO sergeant.

He hesitated for only a few seconds, then wrote his private cell number on the back of the card and said to Margot Aziz, "It might be better for you to call me on my cell. Sometimes we don't pick up the calls on our city line right away, but I always pick up my private cell."

"Good," she said. "Let's keep it personal, Nate." And she showed that gleaming smile again, then turned her head to look for eastbound traffic. Her amazing hair caught another sunbeam and danced for Nate Weiss. And she drove away.

A few minutes after he was back in his car, Nate thought, That Hills bunny just flirted her way out of a ticket that I was never going to write in the first place, and I feel like a chump. Separated from her husband? She'll show that card to him tonight over dinner and they'll both have a laugh. On Nate Weiss!

Then he thought about her surname, Aziz. Some kind of Middle East name. She was married to an Arab, maybe. It didn't feel good for a Jewish cop to think of this fantastic woman married to a rich Arab. Nate Weiss wondered how that might have happened.

After leaving Hollywood Nate, Margot Aziz drove to a nightclub called the Leopard Lounge on Sunset Boulevard. It was a strip club but topless only, so liquor could be sold. Her estranged husband also owned a totally nude strip club, but in that one, no alcoholic beverages were allowed by the state. In that nightclub, Ali Aziz had to make money from hugely overpriced soft drinks, minimums, and cover charges. He spent most of his time in the Leopard Lounge but frequently drove to the other club to pick up the cash from his manager.

Margot had made a phone call to be sure that Ali would not be at the Leopard Lounge at this time of day, and she avoided the Mexican employees preparing for the early-evening business, heading for the dressing room. It was not a typical strip club with dim lights and dark colors. Not like Ali's totally nude nightclub, which had faux-leather banquettes, faux-granite columns, and faux-walnut soffits. That one was claustrophobic, with nude prints in gilded frames that Ali thought would provoke fantasies and erections. Margot had been in that kind of strip club often enough.

She'd designed the Leopard Lounge interior herself, despite her husband's complaints about how much money she was spending. This one featured woven-leather chairs surrounding the stage, with terra-cotta walls and a sandy tile pattern cutting through chocolate brown carpeting that Ali had insisted on because he'd gotten it cheap. This club had a more open feeling, more inviting to female patrons. At least that was Margot's intent when she did the interior design.

She opened the dressing-room door without knocking, and a lovely Amerasian, twenty-five years old, wearing a terry robe and sitting at the makeup table applying eyeliner, looked up.

"What time's he coming back, Jasmine?" Margot asked.

She walked up behind the young woman and swept Jasmine's long black hair onto one of her surgically enhanced breasts, whose nipples and areolas were rouged. Then she massaged the dancer's neck and shoulders, kissing the right shoulder lightly.

"About seven, seven-thirty," Jasmine said, placing her delicate fingers over Margot's. "Not so hard," she said. "I strained my shoulder on that goddamn pole last night." Then she asked, "Have any luck with your friend? Will he be visiting again soon?"

"Not as soon as I'd like," Margot said, stopping the shoulder rub and sitting on a chair next to the makeup table. "He gets attacks of remorse. I think I can pull him out of it, but how soon, I can't say."

"Shit!" Jasmine said.

"Don't be discouraged," Margot said. "I had a lucky break today."

"Yeah, what kinda break?" Jasmine said listlessly.

"A cop stopped me for a ticket," Margot said. "Of course he didn't write it. A handsome, horny cop with no wedding ring on his finger."

"So what? It's not too hard for someone like you to talk a cop out of a ticket. I've done it myself."

"There was something about this one," Margot said. "I think it could work with him."

"A substitute?"

"If a second-stringer is needed," Margot said. "But let's not give up on our number-one draft pick. He's perfect."

"Did today's cop try to make a date?"

"I have his cell number," Margot said. "If we need it."

"Tell me something about your husband that I gotta know," Jasmine said.

"What's that?"

"Does that fucking Arab asshole *ever* get enough blow jobs?"

★ FOUR ★

WATCH 5 HIT THE STREETS with a bang that evening. The bang came from a twelve-year cop with a sporty blonde haircut, rosy dumpling cheeks, and just a hint of makeup, whose Sam Browne belt was rumored to be a size 44. Gert Von Braun had recently transferred to Hollywood from Central Division, where she'd been in an officer-involved shooting that cops refer to as a "good" shooting. Gert had encountered an armed bandit running out of a skid row liquor store, loot and gun in hand, at the same moment that Gert, working alone in a report car, was pulling up in front. Steering with her left hand, Gert had fired one-handed through the open passenger window and hit the parolee-at-large with four out of five rounds, killing him instantly, thus making herself a celebrity gunslinger at Central Station.

But Gert was sick of all the skid row derelicts and the smells associated with them: urine and feces, vomit and blood. And, worst of all, the unbearably sweet, sickly smell of decaying flesh from corpses that had lain dead under bridges and in cardboard shelters. Some had been there for so long that even the flies covering them were dead. At least those corpses didn't smell. And the living weren't much better off, derelicts with their legs and feet covered with clumps of maggots that were eating them alive while the wretches ate whatever they could beg at the back doors of downtown eateries.

The watch commanders were always calling for acid washes at Central Station. They had an air-deodorizing machine going most of the time and burned incense sticks in the report room. Cops would come on duty, sniff the air, and say, "Is it a three- or four-stick day?"

Finally, Gert Von Braun had decided that Central Division smelled like one huge tennis shoe and she couldn't get the odor out of her uniforms or her nostrils. Hollywood Station was closer to her home in the Valley and smelled much better, even though she knew it was a lot weirder than Central. She'd asked for a transfer and had gotten it.

Coppers at Hollywood Station noticed that

Gert carried everything but a rocket launcher in her war bag, which was not actually a bag but a huge black suitcase on wheels. And the cops at Hollywood Station discovered quickly that Gert had "ETS," which was what they called explosive temper syndrome, especially when she'd come puffing out of the station into the parking lot, red faced in the summer heat, dragging her load while her partner lagged behind with a beanbag shotgun as well as the Remington 870 one-shot-and-you-rot model.

It wasn't a good time to start hacking on her, but nobody ever said the surfer cops were founts of wisdom. They always referred to big war bags on wheels as "wimpy bags for airline employees." Jetsam nodded toward her nylon suitcase, winked at Flotsam, and said to Gert, "Excuse me, miss, but is our flight on time?"

Taking the cue, Flotsam said, "Can we have a beverage before takeoff? And extra peanuts?"

Gert Von Braun, who was only five foot six but outweighed Jetsam, if not the much larger Flotsam, said, "Shove your peanuts up your ass, you surfboard squids."

"Oh, that's scandalous," Flotsam whispered to Jetsam.

"I'm so appalled," Jetsam whispered back to Flotsam.

Still giving the surfer cops the stink eye, Gert hefted her equipment into the trunk of her shop, closed the lid, and began testing her Portable Officer Data Device System, which she'd checked out at the kit room.

The PODD, pronounced "pod" by the cops, was one of the instruments of torture encouraged by the monitors of the federal consent decree. It was a handheld instrument resembling a large BlackBerry. In it were the FDRs, or field data reports, which LAPD officers had to fill out for every contact with a suspect that was not the result of a radio call, that is, any stop of a suspect initiated by an officer. On it they had to list the gender, descent, and age of a suspect, and the reason for the stop, also indicating whether there was a pat-down or a more complete search of the suspect's person or car.

The purpose of the FDR was to monitor whether or not cops were engaging in racial profiling, but like everything else connected with the federal consent decree, it discouraged proactive police work. With the mountains of paperwork they already had to endure in order to please their monitoring masters, this one was cumbersome and insulting, and it encouraged otherwise honest cops to dishonestly "balance out" their legitimate suspect stops of blacks and Latinos by creating nonexistent Asians or white Anglos. And it just generally pissed off everybody connected with it and resulted in yet more cops being taken off the streets to deal with the PODD information.

And at that moment nobody was more pissed off than Officer Gert Von Braun, who checked her PODD and placed it on the deck lid of her shop, trying to ignore the surfer team who were watching her and chortling. Because she was mad at the surfers, and at the PODD, and at herself for transferring to Hollywood Station, her mind had been elsewhere when she loaded the magazine tube of her shotgun. The loading protocol was designed to make the gun "patrol ready," that is, four in the magazine and none in the chamber, with the safety on until the gun is ready to be taken from the car and used. Then a final round was to be taken from the butt cuff to top off the magazine.

Probably because she was so hot and distracted by the smirking surfers, and had such a famously short fuse in the first place, she forgot that she'd just loaded the magazine. And she decided to test the action as she usually did before loading any rounds into the gun. Of course, that racked a live round into the chamber, with the safety off.

Gert realized at once what she'd done, and cursing the surfers under her breath for dissing her, she was about to unchamber the round after placing her cell phone beside the PODD on the deck lid of the car.

"Dude, I think we better get our wheels up," Flotsam said to his partner. "Gert has locked in on us with lips drawn, fangs bared, and a shotgun in her paws."

"Bro, that swamp donkey can shoot with either hand," Jetsam agreed, eyeing Gert's Distinguished Expert shooting medal on her left pocket flap over her extra-large bosom. "And her heart pumps Freon to her veins."

Still glaring at the surfer cops, and trying to think up some crack she could make about their dumb-looking, bleached-out spiky hair, Gert saw that the PODD had bumped the cell phone and it was sliding clear off the deck lid of the car.

She said, "Shit!" and tried to catch it with her left hand before it hit the asphalt, but she touched the PODD and it started sliding. Now she was trying to catch both instruments with her left hand. And she accidentally touched the trigger with her right.

The evening began with a bang, all right. A big one. Doomsday Dan Applewhite yelled like he'd been shot. He'd been bent over the open trunk of his shop and leaped back from the explosion, twisting clumsily and falling down on his hip. His P1 partner, young Gil Ponce, who was one month from completing his eighteen-month probation, instinctively crouched and drew his Beretta.

Officer Von Braun's shotgun had been pointed skyward, so the explosion did no damage, except to the psyche of Officer Applewhite. Within a minute, there were three supervisors running into the parking lot, including the lieutenant and Sergeant Treakle. Gert Von Braun was scared, mortified, and greatly relieved when she saw that she'd not blown away a cop, though she knew she'd be facing disciplinary action for the accidental discharge.

"You okay?" the lieutenant asked the senior

field training officer, whose face had gone white.

"I think so," Dan Applewhite said. Then he added, "I'm not sure. I better run over to Cedars and get MT'd. I went down hard."

To the supervisors of Dan Applewhite, it went without saying that he'd go for medical treatment, since his retirement date was nearing. A paper cut could send him to Cedars-Sinai or Hollywood Presbyterian, demanding a tetanus shot. He was determined to have recorded on paper any injury he'd suffered while on duty as an active cop in case some disability popped up during his retirement years, as he was sure it would.

Gert Von Braun followed the supervisors into the station to give her statement for the 1.28 personnel complaint while the surfer cops jumped into their shop and cleared for calls, hoping they wouldn't somehow get blamed for harassing, enraging, and distracting a recognized gunfighter who wore a size 44 Sam Browne. They needn't have worried, though. Gert was told she'd probably end up with an official reprimand, and she took it like a man.

After the supervisors and Gert Von Braun

were gone, Dan Applewhite's twenty-two-year-old boot turned to his shaken partner and said, "Want me to drive tonight?"

Wordlessly, the older cop handed Gil the keys to their shop. Phantom pains were already burning Dan's left hip and running down into his femur. He wondered if this would lead to eventual hip replacement. He'd heard horror stories of staph infection that crippled patients after hip surgery, and he got a terrifying mental picture of himself trying to negotiate the steps to his apartment with a walker.

Unhappily for the older cop, but happily for his young P1, the ER was jammed with patients who had real injuries that needed treatment. LAPD officer or not, Dan Applewhite was told that he'd have to wait an hour, maybe more, before a doctor could see him.

"How're you feeling now?" Gil asked his partner, whose lean body was twisted gingerly onto his good hip as he sat contorted.

A six-year-old Latino boy whose mother was experiencing contractions was watching Dan Applewhite. Finally he said to the wiry cop, "Why do you sit down so funny? You look like a blue grasshopper."

Dan Applewhite ignored the kid but said to Gil Ponce, "Let's get the hell outta here. But if anything happens as a result of this, I want you as witness. I'm in pain from my hip..."

"To your lip," Gil said, then with his FTO glaring at him added, "Sorry. Just trying to cheer you up. Let's get you a cup of coffee."

Like Hollywood Nate, Doomsday Dan was one of the Starbucks cops and would rather endure severe caffeine deprivation than ever set foot in a 7-Eleven for a cuppa joe. Gil Ponce couldn't understand that, given the price of Starbucks coffee, but his field training officer was a partner who would often buy coffee for both of them, and sometimes even a meal at Hamburger Hamlet or IHOP. Generosity was one of Dan's saving graces that everyone appreciated, and it made working with him tolerable when he was in a dark mood. Gil figured that maybe it was his FTO's way of compensating.

Dan Applewhite was called Doomsday Dan by the other cops because he lived in constant anticipation of calamity, with permanent frown lines and an inverted smile on his lips. He could be assertive and fearless, but after the fact he'd lapse into a funk and imagine the horrors that might befall him for his actions. He'd reach ungloved into a resisting doper's mouth to pull out a five-gram stash of rock cocaine but later conclude that if he was lucky, he'd only contract staph from the encounter, instead of the AIDS virus. He was forty-nine years old and had one year to go before retirement, but he was morbidly convinced he'd never make it. Or if he did, the stock market would crash and bankrupt him, and there he'd be, a retired cop, begging for quarters on Hollywood Boulevard.

"I heard that Donald Trump carries a sterilizer for when he has to shake hands with lots of people," Flotsam had said to Gil Ponce. "If I had to work with Doomsday Dan all the time, I'd buy him one. It gets embarrassing when he's on a real downer and you go for a Fat Burger and he gloves up to spritz the table and scrub it down with paper napkins."

Gil Ponce had hoped that a supervisor would move him to another training officer, but being a P1 with so little time left on his probation, Gil had resigned himself and felt lucky when deployment considerations put him with other partners. Despite Doomsday Dan's pathological pessimism, the older cop had taught Gil a lot, and the twenty-two-year-old boot never doubted that Doomsday Dan was dependable and instructive.

More than once the older cop had lectured Gil on ways to take advantage of his Hispanic status in the diversity-conscious LAPD, especially now that the city of L.A. had a Mexican American mayor with political topspin.

"You're Hispanic," Dan had reminded him. "So use it when the time comes."

"But I'm really not," Gil Ponce finally said to his partner one evening when they were cruising the side streets in East Hollywood, looking for car prowlers. "Let me explain."

Gil Ponce had been named after his paternal grandfather, who had immigrated with his parents to Santa Barbara, California, from Peru. All of their children, including Gil's grandfather, had married Americans.

Gilberto Ponce III told Dan that he wished his mother, whose ancestry was a mix of Irish and Scottish, had named him Sean or Ian, but she said it would have dishonored his grandfather, whom young Gil loved as much as he loved his parents. Yet Gil had always felt like a fraud, especially now, when this FTO kept harping about the diversity promotions that a name like his could facilitate in Los Angeles, California, circa 2007.

"Having a Hispanic name is bogus," Gil finally said that night to the senior officer.

"Read the nameplate on your uniform," Dan Applewhite retorted. "You're Hispanic. That means something today. Look around Hollywood Station. Except for the midwatch, white Anglos are in the minority. Half of the current academy class is Hispanic. L.A. is on the verge of being reclaimed by Mexico."

"Okay, look at it this way," the probie said. "What if my Peruvian grandpa had come from neighboring Brazil, where they have Portuguese names and don't speak Spanish? Would I still rate diversity points?"

"Don't make this too complicated just because you been to college," Dan said. "It's all about color and language."

Gil said, "I know about as much Spanish as you do, and my skin is lighter than yours and my eyes are bluer. If you wanna work out the math, I'm exactly one-fourth Peruvian, and I don't think any of that is mestizo in the first place."

"You overanalyze," Dan Applewhite said, wishing this college boy wouldn't debate every goddamn thing, thinking it really was time for him to retire.

Gil said, "And if I had the same Peruvian DNA on my mother's side with no Hispanic surname attached to me, we wouldn't be having this discussion. And should Geraldo Rivera's kids rate diversity points? How about Cameron Diaz when she has kids? Or Andy Garcia? Or Charlie Sheen, for chrissake. He's as much Hispanic as I am!"

The conversation was forever ended when Doomsday Dan pulled their shop to the curb, put it in park, and, turning to face his young partner, said, "This ain't the city of angels, it's the city of *angles,* where everybody's looking for an edge. There're hundreds of languages spoken right here in Babelwood, right? It's all about diversity and preferences and PC. So if the lottery of life gave you an edge, you're gonna accept it and be grateful. Because even though you're a nice kid with potential, I'm telling you right here and now that if you don't shut the fuck up and act like you *been* somewhere, as your FTO I'm gonna decide that you're too god-damn stupid to be a cop and maybe shouldn't even make your probation! Are you tracking?"

Then Dan Applewhite started to sneeze and had to grab his box of tissues and his nasal spray. "See what you did," he said, sniffling. "You stressed me out and activated my allergies."

When the older cop got his sneezing under control, his young partner thought things over, looked at his training officer, and said in English-accented high-school Spanish, *"Me llamo Gilberto Ponce. Hola, compañero."*

Wiping his dripping nose, Doomsday Dan said, "That's better. But you don't have to overdo it. You Hispanics always tend to gild the lily."

Leonard Stilwell was a thirty-nine-year-old crackhead with a mass of wiry red hair, a face full of freckles, and large, unfocused blue eyes that would have looked believable on a barnyard bovine. He had served two relatively short terms for burglary in the Los Angeles county jail system but had never been sentenced to state prison. The last conviction resulted from Leonard's having tossed his latex gloves into a Dumpster after successfully completing his work. The cops later found the gloves, and, after cutting off the fingertips, the crime lab had successfully treated the inside of the fingertips and got good latent prints. After that conviction, Leonard Stilwell began watching *CSI*.

The county jail was so overcrowded that nonviolent prisoners like Leonard Stilwell could usually get an early release to make room for rapists, gangbangers, and spouse killers. So Leonard had benefited from all the crime that everyone else was committing and got squeezed out of the county jail onto the streets like toothpaste from a tube. Whenever he was free, he would hurry to old companions to try talking them into an advance against his cut from the next job, then he'd go on a rock cocaine binge for a few days to smoke the miseries of county jail from his memory bank before going back to work. But that had been when he was teamed with master burglar Whitey Dawson, who'd died from a heroin overdose six months earlier, his last words being "It don't get any better!"

Leonard Stilwell had proved reasonably adept at breaking into liquor storage rooms, which had been Whitey Dawson's specialty, and also showed some competence in refilling empty bottles of premium brands with the cheap stolen booze, then affixing a believable stamp to seal the cap. Twice he'd sold several of the doctored bottles, mixed with legitimate ones, to Ali Aziz of the Leopard Lounge, who had never caught on.

Now with Whitey Dawson gone, Leonard Stilwell was reduced to taking a job. It was the first time in fifteen years that he'd actually drawn a paycheck and he hated every minute of it. He was the only gringo at a second-rate car wash, and when the owner wasn't yelling at him, the other workers were. One of the Mexicans was an old homeboy named Chuey, who sometimes had some decent rock to sell. Chuey never carried the rock on his person and he lived in a cottage in East Hollywood, where Leonard had to drive to if he wanted the dope.

Leonard drove there just after sunset and found Chuey's door wide open. He yelled and finally entered but couldn't find Chuey anywhere. Then he walked into the backyard and found him. Horrified, Leonard ran back inside, picked up Chuey's phone, and called 9-1-1, reporting what he'd found in what he considered to be Spanish-accented English but which was almost indecipherable.

Before he left the cottage, he sublimated his horror long enough to ransack the bedroom until he found Chuey's wallet. He stole $23 from the wallet and got the hell out of there.

Their "unknown trouble" call came a couple of hours after Dan Applewhite's allergy attack had quieted. Unknown trouble usually meant that somebody had phoned while drunk or hysterical, or sometimes in a language that was unintelligible. But it could mean anything and made cops a bit nervous and more alert.

That part of Hollywood was gang territory, but not the turf of the Salvadorans. This was where older cruisers lived, Mexican American *veteranos* of White Fence. Recent reports identified 463 street gangs in Los Angeles with 38,974 members. But how the LAPD had managed to count heads so precisely was anybody's guess.

"Bring the shotgun," Dan said to Gil Ponce,

who removed the Remington from its barrel-up bed between the seats and racked one into the chamber, topping off the magazine with an extra round.

It was a wood-frame cottage, white paint faded and peeling, the tiny yard full of weeds. A smell of salsa and frying lard was coming through the open door.

"Police!" Dan Applewhite said at the doorway. "Did somebody call?"

No answer. He took the shotgun from Gil and used the muzzle to push the door farther open. The house was dark but there was light coming from the kitchen. Somebody had eaten at the table recently. The single bedroom was vacant and the bed was made carelessly, a worn bedspread pulled up over a single pillow. A man's clothes were draped over a chair and hanging in the closet, the meager wardrobe consisting of two pairs of khaki trousers, several white tees, and a gray sweatshirt with cutoff sleeves.

The back door was open and Gil shined his light outside into a small rear yard, where he saw a child's tricycle and a plastic wading pool, although the house interior bore no signs of a child living there. On a cheap dresser in the bedroom, he noted four pictures of a smiling Latino boy, and said, "He's got a son living somewhere, if not here."

The young cop walked to the back porch of the cottage and noticed that the rear gate was hanging open, facing onto an alley. Across the alley was a firetrap of an apartment building, defaced by gang graffiti, known to house Latino illegal immigrants. The proof of their occupancy was all of the bean and tomato plants in the common areas, where there was an erstwhile flower planter or a patch of earth. It wasn't very late and only a few windows showed light in that three-story building, whose westside owner had been cited for fire code violations.

Gil Ponce walked through the yard and out to the alley, and there he found the object of their call. He was hanging by what appeared to be nylon rope from a climbing spike on a telephone pole between the cottage and the house next to it. He was wearing white cotton briefs and that was all. He was shoeless and there were drizzles of feces running down his legs and over his feet. His neck was stretched a third more than normal and his face had gone from its normal olive tone to purple and black. His torso, arms, neck, and even the side of his face, were decorated with colorful body art, much of it gang tatts. A stepladder was tipped over onto the alley floor a few feet from the dangling corpse.

"Partner!" Gil yelled.

When the older cop saw the dangling corpse, he said, "Somebody from that apartment building must've put in the call."

Never having seen a suicide victim before, Gil said, "Whadda we do now?"

Dan Applewhite said, "Mostly we worry about this dude's head coming off and rolling down the alley."

When the coroner's crew arrived, a floodlight was set up. One of the body snatchers said he'd go up the ladder to remove the noose if his partner and a cop could lift the corpse to give the rope some slack. By then several residents of the apartment building had their windows open and were gawking down at the macabre spectacle.

Gil gaped in horror at the feces-caked legs of the dead man, and Dan Applewhite said, "My young pard is big and way stronger than me. He'll help you."

"I can smell him from here!" Gil cried.

"We'll wrap a sheet around him when we lift," the body snatcher said. "We never untie the knots. The coroner wants his knots intact. Hold your breath. It'll be all right."

"Gross!" Gil Ponce murmured, gloving up.

By the time the stepladder was in place, and the lights and voices in the alley had caused several more illegal immigrants to pop their heads out of windows, D2 Charlie Gilford had arrived, pissed off for having to leave his TV just because some old cruiser did an air dance. One of the talent show contestants, a fat girl, had begun blubbering, and the killer panelists were pouring it on just as the phone rang.

Dan Applewhite said to the detective, "Just an over-the-hill homie. Which means a middle-aged guy that never filed a tax return."

Charlie gazed at the dangling man's full-torso and full-sleeve colorful gang tatts, then at young Gil Ponce walking disconsolately toward the stepladder as though to his own hanging. Finally, the detective sucked his teeth and smirked. Dan Applewhite noticed and said, "I know what you're thinking, Charlie, but those people up there can hear you. It's obvious, so don't say it!"

But the night-watch detective was nothing if not obvious. Squinting at pale and queasy Gil Ponce, Compassionate Charlie Gilford yelled, "Hey, kid, find me a fucking stick! *This* is what I call a piñata!"

FIVE

FLOTSAM AND JETSAM caught an early-evening call that they felt should have been referred to the CRO the next day. A Guatemalan woman who lived in Little Armenia complained that she couldn't drive out of her alley early in the mornings because of all the cars parked at an auto body repair business owned by a man who she thought was Armenian. She needed to get downtown to her sweatshop job in the garment district by 7:30 A.M., but the south end of the alley was often blocked. The north end had apartment buildings on both sides filled with Latino gang members, and everyone was afraid to drive or even walk in that direction.

"This is a quality-of-life issue," Flotsam said to the mother of five, whose English was better than most.

"I do not understand," she said.

"We got officers who deal with this kind of

thing," Flotsam said. "They work in the Crow office."

"Like the bird?"

"Well, yeah, same name," Jetsam said. "See, they warn people and then write citations if they do stuff like blocking alleys in the neighborhood."

"I can sympathize," Flotsam said. "I mean, you can't even use the alley because of thugs. Your kids have to bob and weave their way to school just to get through yellow tape."

She understood the allusion to yellow tape. She'd seen plenty of it strung across crime scenes since migrating to Los Angeles.

"How do I call to this crow?" she asked.

"I'll tell one to call you tomorrow when you get home from work," Flotsam said. "You can tell them about the problem."

When they cleared from that call, Jetsam decided to drive to the alley and have a look. The body shop was closed and there was only one security light on in the front of the building. Those at the rear were burned out or had been broken by vandals.

Jetsam pulled the car up near a chain-link

fence where cars were stored, awaiting repair. He got out and shined his light around, lighting up empty oil drums, wooden crates, a Dumpster, and hopelessly damaged car tires and wheel rims.

"These fucking mini-lights!" he said. "If I ever get chalked because I couldn't get enough light, it's gonna be the police commission and the chief who really killed me. Remember that, bro, and seek revenge." Jetsam shined his light up at the window eight feet above the alley floor and began looking for something to stand on.

"What're you looking for anyways?" Flotsam asked, not bothering to get out of their black-and-white.

"That woman said there were lots of cars blocking the alley and I noticed that the shop didn't seem big enough to do that kind of business."

"So?"

"So I was wondering about the rest of the businesses in this little strip. Like, the place next door has no sign on it. I was thinking the body shop might use that part of the place to work on the cars. If they use stuff like welding torches and flammable cylinders in a space that's only separated by a plasterboard wall from some dwelling units, there might be a fire ordinance that could be cited to close them down. See?"

"Lemme lock in on this shit," Flotsam said, genuinely perplexed by his partner's behavior until the answer came to him. After a moment he said, "I get it!"

"You get what?" Jetsam said, as he stood on a wooden box and then on top of an empty oil drum to shine his light into the window of the building next to the shop.

"This is all about Ronnie Sinclair!" Flotsam said. "She's working Hollywood South now. You wanna run over there tomorrow and get some face time with the Crow sergeant and show how you're all obsessed about quality-of-life crap. So maybe he'll consider you next time there's an opening. And then, if dreams really do come true, you might even get to be Ronnie's partner. And she eventually might not find you as repulsive as she does now. Like, I'm on it, dude!"

Jetsam would have been really steamed by Flotsam's accurate assessment of his motives, but he was too busy being surprised by the business at hand. He said, "Bro, climb on up here and look what's inside."

"Don't keep me in suspense," Flotsam said, not budging. "Enlighten me."

"This whole place is a wide-open storage and repair area. There must be a couple thousand square feet of floor space in there."

"So?"

"So I'm looking at six SUVs. New and almost new. A Beemer, a Benz, a Lexus, and, let's see, I can't tell what the others are. It's too dark."

"Dude, this is a body shop. Did you expect these Armenians to be storing olives and goat cheese in there, or what?"

"I'm just sayin'," Jetsam mumbled, still peering in the window. Suddenly, he turned and said, "Bro, they ain't Armos."

"Okay, so what are they?"

"I can see a newspaper on a workbench right down below this window. I think it's in Arabic. I think they're Arabs."

"Now I know why you don't have the word *detective* on your badge, dude. News flash: We got thousands and thousands of camel fuckers in L.A. So what?"

"I know what they're up to, bro."

"Lemme guess. They're al Qaeda operatives?"

"They're repainting and selling hot SUVs. I'm calling the auto theft detail tomorrow morning soon as I get up."

"Why don't you go all radically *CSI* on me and start looking for stuff with DNA on it? I don't mind sitting here while you sleuth around. Maybe you'll find O.J.'s knife or Robert Blake's gun."

"Do you think they really *could* be al Qaeda?" Jetsam said.

While Jetsam was annoying his partner with his sleuthing, Ali Aziz was counting the crowd at the Leopard Lounge and ranting at his black bartenders, his white cocktail waitresses, and even his Mexican dishwashers. Ali wasn't worried about his rant upsetting his customers. All of them were men whose rapt attention was focused on a pair of topless dancers in G-strings, writhing around metal poles while music blared from a sound system that had cost Ali $75,000, even though he'd gotten a special discount from a customer who'd needed cash prior to beginning a prison sentence for fencing stolen property.

Ali Aziz had employed all manner of bartenders, both male and female: whites, Asians, Mexicans, now two black men whom he was going to fire next week, and even a man from the Middle East. They were all thieves, Ali Aziz believed. Ali's bartenders and his cocktail waitresses wore starched white shirts, black bow ties, and black trousers, but Ali always said that if bartenders served drinks completely naked with a manager watching them, they would find a way to steal from him.

Of course, Ali also thought that the U.S. government stole from him, as well as the state of California, as well as the city of Los Angeles. He fought back by keeping two sets of books for both nightclubs he owned, one with the real income, the other for IRS auditors. Whenever possible in years past, Ali had bought liquor from the addict burglar he knew as Whitey Dawson, whom he had met shortly after coming to America thirty years earlier, when Ali was twenty-two years old. He'd gotten word that Dawson had overdosed on heroin and died, and Ali was prepared to deal with Daw-son's protégé, Leonard Stilwell. But soon even Leonard had stopped coming.

Of course, a prosperous businessman like Ali Aziz did not trust the late Whitey Dawson or Leonard Stilwell any more than he trusted his bartenders, and far less than he trusted his estranged wife, Margot, the thought of whom filled him with rage. Ali had always made sure that any liquor that came from thieves like Whitey Dawson was picked up by a friend or an acquaintance of one of Ali's Mexican busboys. Or by someone else not directly connected to Ali or to his businesses.

"You, Paco!" Ali yelled at a Mexican who was busy cleaning the table at the largest ban-quette.

The Mexican, whose name was Pedro, not Paco, had been employed by Ali for six months and said, "I come, boss."

"Where is my goddamn key? My key ain't on my desk!"

"I don'...I don'..." Pedro couldn't remem-ber the English word for *comprendo,* his brow knitting into furrows. He kept his eyes low-ered, fixed on Ali's diamond pinkie ring and on his huge gold watch as Ali shook a finger in the Mexican's face.

"Do not be so stupid!" Ali said. "Key. *Llave.*" Then Ali muttered, "Goddamn Mexican. I speak in Spanish. I speak in English. Goddamn stupid Mexican."

At last Pedro understood. "Boss!" he said. "Joo not geev to me. Joo geev to Alfonso."

Ali stared at Pedro for a moment, then said, "Go back to work."

Ali stormed back into the kitchen to scream at the sweating dishwasher, whose arms were submerged in soapy water, his head enveloped in a mist of steam. After retrieving the key to the storage room from the apologetic Mexican, and after threatening to fire him and withhold wages for incompetence, Ali returned to the bar to check the crowd again.

He grudgingly had to admire the job that Margot had done with her interior decor. The room was first-class, and well designed to accommodate as many customers as the fire inspector allowed. Ali had balked at the price she'd paid for the wallpaper, with its wine-colored swirls bleeding into earth tones. And the wine-colored carpet she'd wanted would have cost more than the silver Rolls-Royce he'd test-driven last week, so he'd overruled her and bought chocolate brown carpet at a discount price. Now that his business had improved and customers seemed happy with the refurbishing, he was glad he had listened to Margot. And he had to admit that the bitch had many talents. But he still wished that she were dead.

Leonard Stilwell had gotten fed up and quit his short-lived job at the car wash, and he hadn't been able to set up a sting of any kind since Whitey Dawson had died. Security had tightened everywhere and Leonard Stilwell needed rock cocaine. He was lapsing into severe depression in the rat hole of a two-room apartment he rented by the week in East Hollywood. It was what the manager called a "studio apartment." There was a room with a hide-a-bed that closed up against the wall so he could enter the kitchenette without walking across the bed. And the kitchenette was so small, an anorexic tweaker couldn't squeeze through it without turning sideways. To make matters worse, a biker and his biker bitch were living in the apartment next door, and they'd be outside working on their chopper at all hours, revving the engine so Leonard couldn't sleep. The dude didn't wear any biker colors or have shit logos attached to his leather jacket, but he was big, hairy, and ugly, and Leonard was scared to say anything to him. At times like this Leonard almost wished he were back in jail.

In fact, he was so desperate he decided to go out that evening and try to game some chump at the ATM in the shopping mall. There was a market there that he'd burglarized on two occasions back when Whitey Dawson was alive and not so heroin crazed. Whitey could disarm most of the alarms they'd encounter, and he was a master with lock picks. Leonard was no good at any of it but had always been available to Whitey. Now Leonard had fallen on very hard times and been forced to become resourceful.

He'd tried an ATM trap four times and each attempt had failed, but he'd learned a few things through failure. This time Leonard made sure he had strips of black film that would be undetectable when pressed against the black slot reader at an ATM. He folded over the ends of the film and attached glue strips on the folded portions. What he'd failed to do last time, he corrected by cutting slits on the film so the card didn't get kicked back out the slot by the mechanism.

It was getting close to the hour when most of the stores were closing in Hollywood, so he didn't waste time. He dressed in a clean Aloha shirt, reasonably clean jeans, and sneakers, in case he had to beat feet in a hurry. He drove his old Honda to the mall parking lot, leaving the car near enough to the ATM for a fast exit but not so close that a witness would see him jumping into it. He strolled to the ATM and pretended to be inserting a card to make a transaction. Instead he inserted the trap into the slot and pressed hard on the glue strips on the upper and lower lip of the card reader. Then he retreated and waited.

An elderly woman approached the ATM holding a child by the hand, probably the woman's grandson, by the looks of them. They appeared to be Latinos, and Leonard cursed his luck. If they were illegal aliens who didn't speak enough English to give up the PIN, it wasn't going to work. But on second thought, they were too well dressed to be illegals, and it gave him hope.

The woman inserted her card, but nothing

happened. She punched in her PIN and waited. Still nothing happened. She looked at the boy, who Leonard guessed was about ten years old. Then Leonard strolled closer and heard them speaking a foreign language that wasn't Spanish.

Leonard pulled out an old ATM card he carried for this game, made sure that they saw it, and said, "Excuse me, is there something wrong with the machine?"

The boy said, "The card is stuck inside. It won't come out."

"Lemme try it," Leonard said. "I've had this happen to me."

The woman looked at Leonard and he gave her his biggest freckle-faced, blue-eyed, reassuring smile. She said something to the boy in that strange language and the boy answered her.

Up close, while he was trying to sell Leonard Stilwell to them, she didn't look so old, maybe the same age as his mother, who would be fifty-eight if she were alive. And up close this woman looked smart. And wary.

"Where're you from?" Leonard asked the boy.

"My grandmother is Persian," the boy said. "I am American."

He should've known. They were all over

Iran-geles. And he'd never met a poor one, so he was feeling pretty stoked when he said, "See, I know what to do to get your card back. You punch in your PIN number at the same time that I press 'cancel' and 'enter.' Then the card should just pop out."

The boy spoke again to the woman, and she reluctantly moved aside for Leonard, who stepped up and put his fingers on the "cancel" and "enter" keys. She looked at him and he smiled again, trying not to swallow his spit. When he did that, his oversized Adam's apple bobbed, a sure sign of nerves.

"We have to time this right," he said to the boy. "Tell her she has to put in her PIN number now."

Instead, it was the boy who moved next to Leonard. He said, "I can do it. I'm ready."

"Go," Leonard said, and he watched the boy punch the five digits as Leonard pressed the "cancel" and "enter" keys.

And then Leonard stepped back, scratched his head theatrically, making dandruff flakes appear on his bird's nest of rusty red hair, and said, "I'm sorry, it's always worked before. Can't help you, I guess."

Leonard shrugged at the woman and, lifting his hands palms up, turned and walked toward the parked cars, where he crouched behind the first row and watched them. The woman and boy conversed for a moment and then went inside the store while Leonard sprinted to the ATM machine, carefully lifted the folded tips of the film, gently pulled, and captured the ATM card. Then he punched in the PIN, took a chance on asking for $300, the maximum daily withdrawal allowed by the bank whose name was on the card, and jackpot!

Fifteen minutes later, Leonard Stilwell was parking in the pay lot closest to Grauman's Chinese Theatre on Hollywood Boulevard, not even pissed off by the exorbitant parking fee because he had three bills in his kick. He was looking for Bugs Bunny, not the tall Bugs Bunny who often showed up on Friday night, but the short Bugs Bunny who always kept a stash of rocks inside his bunny head as he hopped around in his rabbit suit with a big foam-rubber carrot in his paw, saying, "What's up, doc?" to every tourist with a camera who got within ten yards of him.

The Street Characters were always out in

numbers on soft summer nights like this one. He saw Superman, Batman, Porky Pig, and SpiderMan, one of several, in his predatory pose with one knee raised, looking more like a bird than a spider. Summer nights like this, when the smog conditions created a low sky, cutting heaven down to size, made people feel that paradise could be found right here on Hollywood Boulevard. They made this a magical place for anyone with hopes and dreams.

Leonard Stilwell, who knew something about Hollywood magic, watched an intent tourist with a purse dangling from a strap over her shoulder snap a photo of her husband, who was posing with Catwoman. This, while a lean and nimble teenage boy expertly opened her purse and removed her wallet, disappearing into the crowd before she'd even asked Catwoman to pose for one more.

When it was time to pay the amazon for the photo, the woman said, "Oh, Mel! Melvin! My wallet's gone!"

Leonard hoped he'd never have to resort to the risky trade of purse and pocket picking, and as he sidled through the throngs, he heard Catwoman say, "I hope you don't think I dress up and pose for free, Melvin. Nobody got *your* wallet, did they?"

When Leonard saw the Hulk, he was hopeful. He knew that the Hulk was a pal of Bugs Bunny because he once saw them leave together in the same car. But the Hulk was very busy at the moment with no less than six Asian tourists lining up to take photos with him. Ditto for Mr. Incredible, Elmo, and even Count Dracula, whose blood-dripping leer was too scary for photos with little kids.

Then Leonard spotted him. Bugs Bunny was doing a double shoot with the Wolf Man, both of them sandwiching an obese, fifty-something woman wearing a sequined "I Love Hollywood" baseball cap, her chubby hands caressing the heads of both Street Characters.

When Bugs had collected his tip from the woman, Leonard approached him and whispered in a two-foot ear, "I need some rock."

"How much you got?" Bugs said.

"I can spend two bills. You good with that?"

"Good as gold, dude. I got some rock, and some ice-that's-nice if you wanna do crystal. Wait one minute and follow me into the Kodak Center. I gotta take care of Pluto, then you."

When Leonard looked back on that moment later in the evening, he thought it must have been his sixth sense as a burglar that saved him. All those years watching, waiting, studying people. Asking himself things like, Is that greaser looking at me the way one of the 18th Street crew would look at me? Or the way an undercover cop would look at me? Or, why is that nigger hooker working this corner tonight, when I never saw her or any hooker here before? Did that fucking little junkie from Pablo's Tacos tell the cops that I'd be taking off his boss's store tonight with the alarm code he gave me? Is that sneaky whore really a cop, or what?

Leonard did not like the look of the fat tourist in a new white tee with the Hollywood sign emblazoned across the front and back. Leonard didn't like his L.A. Dodgers baseball cap either. It was too well worn to belong to an out-of-towner. The bottom-heavy guy looked like he was trying too hard to appear touristy, and he wasn't quite fat enough for Leonard to say he couldn't be a cop.

Leonard stayed far back and was one hundred feet away when he spotted Bugs Bunny and Mickey Mouse's dog Pluto, their huge heads under their arms, standing outside a restroom. He saw the buy go down. And he saw the fat guy take off his Dodgers cap. And Leonard knew that was a signal, for sure.

The fat guy ran straight at them, and three other undercover cops came at them from other directions. Bugs Bunny tried to dump the meth from his head by tipping it upside down. Pluto took the rock cocaine he'd bought and threw it backward across the floor.

The fat guy pulled a pistol from under his tee and yelled, "Police! Drop your heads and raise your paws!"

So far, Ronnie Sinclair and Bix Ramstead had experienced an uneventful ten hours. In furtherance of their quality-of-life mission, they'd been involved in crackdowns on some of the nightclubs on Sunset and Hollywood Boulevards that were generating numerous complaints from other businesses and residents in the area. Nightclub customers parked wherever they found curb space, ignoring the color of curbs or whether portions of their cars might extend into the driveways of residential property. The nightclub patrons, especially those who frequented the topless clubs where booze was sold, also urinated and vomited on sidewalks and in planted areas and threw trash anywhere that was handy.

Those who preferred all-nude dancers would emerge with more sobriety, since ordinances prohibited booze to be served in those clubs, but the more enterprising customers found ways to flavor their soft drinks and setups with secreted containers of liquor. Some of the customers went so far as to make frequent trips to the restroom, where they'd withdraw plastic bottles of spirits from under their clothing and fill their mouths before returning to their tables, then spit it into their half-empty soft drinks. Bolder ones just poured it under the table into the setups. Still others just forgot about booze and ingested or snorted other drugs, which did the trick well enough.

The vice unit would work these clubs and cite or arrest for all sorts of violations, from prostitution to alcoholic beverage violations, but Ronnie and Bix were attending to the needs of the neighbors. In the short time she'd been a Crow, Ronnie was already getting to know the roster of chronic complainers by name. One of these was Mrs. Vronsky, who owned a twenty-nine-unit apartment building near the Leopard Lounge, one of the clubs that used the word *class* in all of its commercials.

"Officer Ramstead, thank you for being so prompt," the old woman said in slightly accented English when they found her standing in front of her building. She was in her mideighties, short, still full-figured, her white hair coiffed, and she wore slacks with a matching jacket that Ronnie thought would exceed her own budget.

"Of course, Mrs. Vronsky," Bix said. "I'd like you to meet one of our new community relations officers. This is Officer Sinclair."

"Very nice to meet you, dear," Mrs. Vronsky said, then turned to Bix. "I have asked that man Mr. Aziz a thousand times to tell his employees not to park in our spaces here, but when they see a parking space open, they grab it. And then my tenants come home at midnight after getting off the swing shift, and what happens?"

"You have to call Hollywood Station to have them cited or towed," Bix said sympathetically. "I do understand, Mrs. Vronsky."

"I've been patient, Officer Ramstead," she said, her pale eyes watery. "But the man ignores my calls."

"We'll just have to keep citing and towing, won't we?" Bix said, patting the old woman gently on the shoulder. "But for now we'll go have a talk with him."

"Thank you, Officer Ramstead," she said. "The next time I see you I shall have some of my homemade piroshki. Just the way you like it."

"Oh, thank you, Mrs. Vronsky," Bix said. "Officer Sinclair is in for a treat."

When they were walking toward the front door of the Leopard Lounge, Ronnie said, "The look that old lady was giving you said, If only I were forty years younger. As it is, she'd gum you to death given half a chance."

Bix smiled and said, "It's just as easy to be patient with them. Last year she donated a thousand dollars to the L.A. Police Memorial fund along with a thank-you to 'that nice Officer Ramstead at Hollywood Station.' The boss gave me an attaboy for that. Wait'll you meet Mrs. Ortega. She's Puerto Rican and always makes me sit down and eat some baked fish and rice.

And she never fails to suck the eyeballs out of the fish head."

"Yikes!" Ronnie said, then followed Bix through the darkened doorway into the night-club, finding the Leopard Lounge to be more posh than she'd imagined.

A burly Latino bouncer nodded at the uni-formed cops and stepped aside when they entered. There were three bartenders pour-ing drinks with both hands, and a busboy was running trays of dirty glasses through swing-ing doors into the kitchen. The place was dark, but light enough that all customers and their tableside activities could be monitored by undercover cops as well as by the bouncer. The banquettes looked comfortable and the table-tops were clean, thanks to Latino busboys in white shirts and bow ties, working hard.

Ronnie was surprised by how pretty the cocktail waitresses were, and the two girls dancing onstage were knockouts. One of them looked to be part Asian and part white, her glossy hair hanging down nearly to her G-string as she gyrated under strobe lights.

A busty cocktail waitress walked toward the cops, smiled, and said, "Table for two, Officers?"

"I gotta warn you, I don't like tropical toys in my mai tais," Bix said, smiling back at her. "Is the boss around?"

"He's in his office. Just a minute, I'll tell him you're here."

She was gone for a moment, returned, and said, "You can go in."

Ronnie noticed the cocktail waitress giving Bix the big eye when they squeezed passed her in the narrow corridor leading to the office, but he didn't seem to notice. Ronnie had decided by now that Bix was the elusive Monogamous Male Cop, a creature she thought was extinct, if it had ever existed in the first place.

Ali Aziz was sitting at his desk, which was covered with file folders, bills, and photos of prospective dancers, most of them topless. He was yelling in Arabic at someone on the phone. When he looked up at them, he forced a polite smile and motioned them to the two client chairs.

Ronnie thought the office was very nice, not at all what she'd expected. The wall coverings were subtle, mostly pale colors that complemented the earth tones in the carpeting, and drapes that concealed the single small window facing the alley. The only bling was on the person of Ali Aziz himself, who wore a creamy silk blazer with a monogrammed pocket, a black shirt and matching black trousers, a gold Rolex, and pinkie rings on both hands. He was middle-aged, balding, swarthy, and wasn't likely to get invited to the Jonathan Club downtown, she thought. But he'd fit in okay on the Nightclub Committee of the Community Police Advisory Board.

When Ali Aziz hung up the phone, he stood and reached across the desk to shake hands with both cops. He was several inches shorter than Bix and looked up with all of the cordiality he could muster, saying, "Welcome, Officers. I hope there is nothing wrong? We are friends of Hollywood Station. I am knowing your captain well, and each year I give from my heart to the Children's Holiday Party and the Tip-A-Cop fund-raiser."

"It's the same complaint, Mr. Aziz," Bix said.

"Parking?" With his accent he pronounced it *barking*.

"Yes, parking."

"Fucking Mexicans!" Ali Aziz said, then looked at Ronnie and said, "Sorry. I am sorry,

Officer. I have so much anger with my Mexicans. I shall fire them. They do that illegal parking. I am sorry for my rude mouth."

Ronnie shrugged and Bix said, "We wouldn't like to get anybody fired. We just want your employees to stay out of the parking places belonging to the apartment building across the street. Even though the spots look empty, people who work late hours come home to find your employees' cars in their spaces."

"Yes, yes," Ali said. "The old Russian lady, she is right. She calls me all the time. I have police coming here all the time. I do not mind. I wish for my customers to see the police here. They know this is a respectable club. But I am sorry for you to waste your time. I shall fix this problem. I am going to send flowers to the old Russian lady. Do you need money for anything? I shall give you some cash for the — how you call it? — Pals Program." He turned the *p* into a *b* again.

"No cash," Bix said, standing up. "If you like, you can make a donation by check to the Police Activity League."

"I shall do that tomorrow, god willing," Ali said, standing to shake hands.

Ronnie was looking at the framed photos on a shelf over a big-screen TV. Three were studio shots of a beautiful boy, one taken when he was about two and another when he looked to be about five years old, wearing a suit, white shirt, and necktie in both photos. The third studio photo was of the boy posing next to his mother, he wearing a blazer and tie, she a basic black, V-neck dress with only a string of pearls hanging at her throat. She was a striking beauty, with hair the color of, what? Golden chestnut, maybe, full and heavy hair that any woman would die for.

Ronnie carefully touched the frame and said, "Your family is very beautiful."

"My little son," Ali said, smiling genuinely for the first time. "My heart. My life. My little Nicky."

"Your wife should be in movies," Ronnie said. "Don't you think, Bix?"

"Uh-huh," Bix said, hardly glancing at the photo.

Ali's smile turned sour then and he said, "We are in a divorce battle."

"Oh, sorry," Ronnie said.

"No problem," Ali said. "I shall obtain my son

from her. I have the best divorce lawyer in all Los Angeles."

They said their good-byes, and when they left the nightclub, Bix said, "So what's your opinion of Ali Aziz?"

"I wouldn't wanna work for him," she said.

"Butter wouldn't melt in his mouth when he's talking to cops," Bix said.

"Please," Ronnie said, "make that nonfat yogurt."

As they were getting in their car to go end-of-watch, she said, "He won't be a problem for long. That dude's so golded up, he'll probably drown in his pool someday if he goes in the deep end."

And that's how their uneventful watch would have ended if they had not driven to the station by way of Sunset Boulevard. Traffic was only moderate that evening, but Sunset was blocked at Vine Street by a confusing flare pattern that a motorist had placed. They saw a black-and-white that had been speeding north on Vine Street come screeching to a stop at the intersection. Bix turned on the light bar and drove west in the eastbound lane, turning south on Vine, and there it was: a major traffic collision.

"The TC must've just happened," Ronnie said, as two cops from Watch 3 were running from their shop to a flattened old Chevy Caprice that had rolled more than once after having been slammed broadside by a two-ton flatbed truck that had blown the traffic light while racing southbound, driven by a teenage driver with a cell phone glued to his ear. The kid was bleeding from facial lacerations and was leaning against a door that was folded like a wallet from the force of the collision.

Bix leaped out and ran to the old car, Ronnie following. And one of the young Watch 3 cops yelled to them, "Two RA's on the way! There's a woman and kid in there! They're bleeding bad and we can't get them out!"

The other cop, a bigger man, was kicking at the jammed rear door of the Caprice where they saw a child's head inside, gashed open from the crown to the forehead, blood running across her face from deep channels that had been opened to the bone.

"God!" Ronnie said. "God almighty!"

And she began kicking the door also, after

the big cop stopped and drew his baton. He tried using it as a pry, trying to muscle open the door while yelling to his partner, "Get me a tire wrench! Anything to pry with!"

Bix could see through the shattered glass that the Asian woman behind the wheel was dead. Her chest had been crushed by the steering column and she stared lifelessly at the black sky through what was left of the roof.

Ambulance sirens were getting closer and Bix heard several voices shouting, and then he saw something move. He shined his light inside and realized that another child had been in the backseat of the car.

"There's another kid in there!" he yelled, just as the big cop succeeded in prying the rear door open, and Ronnie saw clearly that the little girl's shattered skull was attached to her neck only by a few shredded knots of red, slimy tissue.

"God almighty!" she repeated and ran around the car to Bix and the other child he had found, hoping that this one was alive.

Bix, his mini-flashlight on the asphalt, was down on his knees, crawling under the car, trying to lift the portion of wreckage that had the child pinned. Ronnie could hear him grunting and saw him lifting with his back, and when she shined her light under the car, she lit the face of a four-year-old girl who turned out to be the second daughter of young Cambodian immigrants who had been in Hollywood for nearly five years.

The child's body was twisted and bloody, but her face and head were unmarked. She had a delicate, very pale beauty, and Ronnie crawled under the wreckage to help Bix try to lift the twisted metal.

It was then that the thing happened, the thing that Ronnie knew she'd remember for the rest of her career. Perhaps for the rest of her days. The little girl opened her eyes and looked directly into the straining face of Bix Ramstead, who had at last raised the chunk of wreckage high enough for Ronnie to pull her free.

Just before Ronnie grabbed her, the child said to Bix, "Are you my angel?"

Controlling his labored breathing, Bix managed to say, "Yes, darling, I am your angel."

When they got back to Hollywood Station, Bix changed out of his uniform much faster than

Ronnie did. When she left the women's locker room she saw him sprinting across the parking lot to his minivan, and she was pretty sure she knew where he was going.

After Ronnie arrived at work the next morning, she learned that the child had survived the ambulance ride to Hollywood Presbyterian Medical Center but died in the ER moments before her angel came running to her side.

★ SIX ★

ONCE A MONTH every patrol division of the LAPD was required to hold a CPAB meeting, pronounced *see-pab*, for Community Police Advisory Board. Hollywood Division held its CPAB meeting on the last Tuesday, the idea being to bring together community leaders, neighborhood watch captains, the City Attorney's Office, the Department of Transportation, the L.A. Fire Department, and others, all to discuss crime and quality-of-life issues in the respective police divisions. The meeting was run by the division captain along with the CPAB president, whoever that might be.

The problems began almost immediately for the Hollywood Division CRO because, according to unofficial reports to the office of the chief of police, Hollywood was not like anywhere else. In fact, the unofficial report referred to Hollywood as "America's kook capital." Because it was a community meeting, residents of Hollywood could not be segregated or excluded due to irrational behavior, unless the behavior turned dangerous. Many of the same people showed up regularly at the meetings for free coffee and donuts. And, more often than not, havoc ensued.

Special arrangements had to be made to accommodate the Hollywood Division CPAB meetings, and it was decided that a second meeting would be held the day after the official CPAB meeting. The names and addresses of the more peculiar and troublesome residents were culled from sign-in sheets at the CPAB meetings, and letters were sent telling them that their meetings would now be held on the last Wednesday of the month. The Wednesday gathering was officially renamed the "Hollywood Community Meeting." But the cops unofficially referred to it as the "Cuckoo's Nest."

Crows would say to one another, "Are you going to CPAB or Cuckoo's Nest?"

The Cuckoo's Nest meeting was not run by the captain or any member of the command staff. Sometimes even the CRO sergeant wasn't in charge, preferring to leave it to one of the senior lead officers. The Crow would try to arrange for interesting guest speakers, such as a narcotics detective or a gang officer or a vice cop. In order to entice speakers, the Crow told them that this was a very low-key community meeting that the speakers would find enjoyable. Once the speakers discovered the truth, they never came back.

Ronnie Sinclair was tasked to assist at her first Cuckoo's Nest meeting the day after Jetsam became convinced that he might have stumbled onto an al Qaeda cell operating in Hollywood. Jetsam had phoned the auto theft team the moment he woke up that morning, but they were in court or otherwise occupied and away from the station. When one of them finally returned his call, the detective, whom Jetsam didn't know personally, was less than enthusiastic.

After hearing Jetsam's terrorist theory based upon spotting one Arabic newspaper at a body shop that worked on expensive SUVs, the detective said to him, "Do you know Arabic from Farsi?"

"Well, no," Jetsam had to admit.

"The newspaper could have been left there by an Iranian," the detective suggested.

"All the more reason to check it out," Jetsam

said. "Remember the case last year where LAPD and the FBI popped those Chechens who had a racket where they got people to report expensive cars stolen and collect insurance payoffs? And then the cars were smuggled in big shipping containers to their country to help Muslim terrorists? Remember that one? Well, these SUVs were too newish and expensive to be worked on in a repair joint in East Hollywood."

The detective was silent for a moment and then said, "Are you saying you think these people are Chechen terrorists?"

"No, but maybe they're copycats pulling the same scam, and they're gonna smuggle hot SUVs to places like..."

"Baghdad?"

"Or like..."

"Tehran?"

"Aw, shit," Jetsam said.

"You have my blessing if you wanna check it out yourself," the detective said. "But you catch 'em, you clean 'em. Right now I'm due in court, so I gotta run."

After hanging up, Jetsam said to the phone, "And we thank you for your call. Fuck you very much."

Detective indifference and condescension is what brought Jetsam and his reluctant partner to the Cuckoo's Nest meeting on Wednesday night. Of course it was a bonus for Ronnie Sinclair to observe a meeting conducted by an experienced Crow. The sergeant told Ronnie that Tony Silva would be a good one to emulate because he was patient and had a calming effect on most of the regulars if things turned violent.

"Violent?" Ronnie said in astonishment, but her sergeant only shrugged and walked away. She thought he must be kidding.

Twenty minutes before the Cuckoo's Nest was to start, Ronnie was surprised to see Jetsam enter the meeting room and wave her outside.

"What's up?" she said, walking with him to the black-and-white, where Flotsam sat behind the wheel.

Flotsam looked out at her and said, "Don't blame me for this, Ronnie. Watch five only has three cars in the field tonight and he's got me beached. If Treakle finds out, he'll have us castrated."

"I got something for a Crow to check out,

Ronnie," Jetsam said, giving her a piece of notebook paper with the address of the auto body shop and the address and phone number of the Guatemalan woman who phoned about their cars blocking the alley.

"What's all this?" she said.

"It's a quality-of-life deal," Jetsam said. "And it's an opportunity for you to go to this body shop and maybe, just maybe, end up with something pretty big."

"It's Osama bin Laden," Flotsam said. "My pard thinks he's there, pounding out dents on Beemers and Benzes."

"Dude, can you stop hacking on me for two minutes?" Jetsam said to his partner. "You're spiking me like you spiked those barneys at Malibu this morning."

Ronnie, who knew that Flotsam and Jetsam surfed almost every day before going on duty, said, "Spiking? Barneys?"

Flotsam said, "He thinks I shouldn't do surfboard self-defense on four squids that flipped us off and stole my juicies when I was rippin'. They thought it was cooleo till one of them caught my log upside his head when I snaked him on the next wave."

"What?" Ronnie said.

"All I said was," Jetsam said to Flotsam, "you should cap the little surf Nazi if you wanna turn him into part of the food chain. Not torpedo him till he's almost dead in the foamy."

"There's just too damn many languages spoken in this town," Ronnie said rhetorically. "Did you bring me out here for today's surfing highlights, or what? I got a meeting inside."

"Take a few minutes tonight or tomorrow night," Jetsam said quickly. "Phone the woman about the Arabs at the repair shop. They got the joint vacuum-packed with some slammin' SUVs. I think they gotta be hot. You could warn them about blocking the alley and maybe take down some license and VIN numbers."

"I'm not a detective," Ronnie said. "Call the auto theft detail."

"Been there," Jetsam said. "They're about as lazy as Compassionate Charlie Gilford. A blocked alley affects everybody in the apartment house. I need a quality-of-life cop to get this thing kick-started."

"That's not my area," Ronnie said.

"You're the only Crow I know real well," Jetsam said, "except for Hollywood Nate. This is a job for a real cop. They couldn't have morphed you into a teddy bear already. If you want, we could meet you tomorrow at the body shop as backup, say around sixteen hundred hours? Right before they close."

"*You* can meet her," Flotsam said to his partner. "I go on duty at seventeen-fifteen."

"Dude . . . ," Jetsam said in exasperation to his partner.

"This one ain't on my desktop," Flotsam explained to Ronnie. "Him and me, we're close, but we ain't Velcro close. I ain't down for this one."

"Okay, okay!" Ronnie said, relenting. "I'll give her a call later tonight and maybe I can stop by the body shop tomorrow afternoon. If I can, I'll give you a call on your cell. Will you be hanging ten at Malibu or remaining on dry land?"

"I'll be home," Jetsam said. "And ready to jam."

After Ronnie went back inside, Flotsam said, "You know you wouldn't be doing any of this if Ronnie was a yuckbabe instead of totally mint. Get over yourself, dude. She ain't never gonna be your fuck puppet."

"This might be too much for you to download, bro," Jetsam said, "but this ain't about hose cookies. This is about what the Oracle always said to us: Doing good police work is the most fun we'll ever have in our entire lives. I know there's something going down in that repair shop. And whadda you got to do tomorrow except crawl along the sand and sniff around some salty sister whose whole life is smoking blunts and chugging coolers?"

Flotsam thought it over and said, "Okay, dude, you're totally frenzied. I guess we better stop there on the way to work. Just to get it outta your system."

"You're down?" Jetsam said.

"I'm down," Flotsam said, with no more enthusiasm than Jetsam had heard from the auto theft detective or from Ronnie Sinclair.

After they were back cruising their beat, Jetsam said dreamily, "Dude, ain't there something about Ronnie that's like...like being all flattened in dead water, and, like, here comes a beautiful peel breaking so clean from the top? And next thing, you're flying down the lane smelling that Sex Wax, and you get the blood surge? Know what I'm saying, bro?"

"You could LoJack that chick and still not

park her in your crib," Flotsam said. "Look for a date on MySpace. She's too tall for you."

"We're about the same height."

"She puts on sky-high stilettos, then what? You'll look like Sonny and Cher."

"But she's, like, smokin' hot," Jetsam said. "I bet that girl and me could put some antic in romantic! I'll bet she could make me harder than Gramma's biscuits!"

"You two would look like Tom Cruise and every babe he marries," Flotsam said dryly.

Officer Tony Silva got the meeting off to a good start with his soothing and reassuring manner. He'd instructed Ronnie to maintain a "calm and professional smile," no matter what happened. But he was getting close to the hazardous part of the meeting, when questions from the floor were permitted.

One of the eldest of the regulars, who couldn't get to the bathroom fast enough at the prior meeting, was responsible for a rules change. Tony Silva's Crow assistant, Officer Rita Kravitz, whose trendy eyeglasses said "I am smarter than you," was asked by Tony Silva to help with the cleanup last time, but she said to him, "Instead of you sitting up there popping bubble wrap while you look calm and professional, go find yourself a goddamn mop!"

Cuckoo's Nest Rule 1 was enacted: "No punch is to be served at Wednesday meetings."

Ronnie was warned about "Deputy Dom," always the first to arrive and the last to leave. He was in his sixties, with a fringe of gray hair, and always wore an odorous, food-stained security guard uniform.

"Dom was absent for the first time last week," Tony Silva told Ronnie. "He was in jail, but the City Attorney's Office decided not to prosecute. He tried to pepper spray an entire Laotian family: father, mother, four kids, and a grandma. He said none of them were carrying passports, and that made them security risks."

Ronnie learned that the cross-eyed guy in a bowling shirt with "Regent Electrical Supply" across the back and "Henry" over the front pocket was the one they'd dubbed "Henry Tourette." He was an unintentional disrupter, because he'd yell out "Fucking-A-Bertha!" to every single statement offered by anyone. It was worrisome in that it provoked angry retorts from other borderline personalities.

Unfortunately, there wasn't much that the Crows could do about any of it, not in the land of diversity, where all behavior that was not overtly criminal must be understood and respected. Where people were *never* to be considered "sick," but only "different."

The sole "weapon" that the Crows found somewhat effective was the Community Service Completion Certificate. The CRO sergeant first encountered it when a young man who had attended meetings for three months without ever uttering a peep approached the sergeant and presented him with a folded document, saying it was given to him by a motorcycle officer.

"The officer wrote me a jaywalking ticket on Hollywood Boulevard," the young man explained. "My mother paid the ticket, and then the officer stopped me again a week later in the same place."

"For jaywalking?" the sergeant asked.

"Yes, but this time I told him about the voices."

"What voices?"

"The ones that tell me when to cross the street."

"What did the motor officer say about that?"

"He said, 'Why don't the voices ever tell you to cross on a *green* light?'"

"That sounds like Officer F.X. Mulroney," the sergeant said. "Did he write you another ticket?"

"No, he gave me this certificate and told me that I would have to attend every Wednesday night Hollywood Community Meeting for ninety days, and to stay away from Hollywood Boulevard. And if I did it, you'd sign my certificate."

Thus, a tradition was started. The CRO sergeant signed the "certificate" and announced to the entire assembly that the young man had completed three months' community service for jaywalking, and the other members at the meeting gave him a standing ovation.

Things started well at Ronnie's first meeting. Everyone seemed calm, even bored. They ate copious amounts of donuts, and Ronnie later wondered if elevated blood sugar had something to do with what happened later. Things started going sideways when one of the homeowners, a meticulously groomed gentleman with a dyed transplant, stood and said, "I'd like something done about the gay men who park in front of my house after the bars close and commit sex acts."

One of the trannies, the best-dressed person at the meeting, said, "If they're on the street, it's public property. Are you jealous?"

"Yeah," said a woman wearing a lip ring, an eyebrow spike, and a tongue stud. The face jewelry seemed peculiar in that she was seventy-five years old if she was a day. "Just stay in your house, and that way you won't know there's people blowing each other in this world."

"Fucking-A-Bertha!" Henry yelled.

That set off the one they called "Rodney the Racist," a fiftyish Nazi wannabe, whose shaved skull was decorated with a backward swastika that he'd created with a mirror and Magic Marker.

Rodney raised his hand, and when Tony Silva acknowledged him, he stood and said, "It's all these goddamn illegal aliens causing the problems."

A burly senior citizen who resided in Little Armenia and was said to have made a few bucks before alcoholism rotted his brain stood and said, "Immigrants make America great!"

The play Nazi said, "What're you, an illegal alien?"

"I come to this country legal, you son of bastard!" the Armenian yelled.

"Yeah, through a drainpipe at the Tia-juana border!" a homeless transient yelled back.

"Order, please!" Tony Silva said from the front of the room. "Please, folks! Let's stay on point and take turns!"

"He is Nazi and he eat shit!" the Armenian yelled.

"Spoken like a goddamn illegal Mexican!" the play Nazi shot back. "Get a green card!"

"I am not Mexican!" the Armenian hollered, pointing to Officer Tony Silva. "He is Mexican! I dare you call Officer Silva filthy names, you pig-shit Nazi."

Widening his smile to no avail, Tony Silva said, "Actually, my family is from Puerto Rico."

A stick-thin woman looking slightly Goth with a hedge-clipper do turned and said to Ronnie, "My little love dumpling claims my hemorrhoids look like Puerto Rico. Or is it Cuba?"

Tony Silva tried levity then. Sweat beads popping, he stood and said, "To quote the ex-convict philosopher and celebrity thug Rodney King, can't we all get along? Can't we just get —"

He didn't get a chance to finish. The Armenian geezer made as though to attack the play Nazi but was easily restrained by Bix Ramstead, who'd been sitting quietly in the back row. That officially ended the Wednesday night meeting, and the distracted cops never saw the homeless transients stealing all of the remaining donuts, stuffing them under their grimy layers of clothing.

After locking up, Ronnie and Officer Tony Silva were standing in the shadows of the parking lot when she said to him, "Tony, those people weren't just sitting there spouting designer slogans and trendy complaints. That was truly a cuckoo's nest. Some of those people are seriously crazy!"

"Crazier than Kelly's cat," Tony Silva responded with his calm professional smile frozen in place.

"Fucking-A-Bertha!" a voice yelled from the darkness.

Meanwhile, some unusual police action was about to take place on Hollywood Boulevard, and Leonard Stilwell was present to witness it. He had placed himself directly in front of the Chinese Theatre because there were more tourists than usual meandering around the theater forecourt on this warm evening, looking at the movie star handprints in cement. If desperation was forcing him to try his hand as a purse pick, this seemed like the place to do it.

Of course, Leonard was streetwise enough to have spotted a few hooks waiting by the entrance to the subway station, young black guys ready to hook up customers to partners holding crack or crystal. The hooks liked the subway for quick retreat back to South L.A., where they resided. When the foot-beat cops or the bike patrol appeared, the hooks would vanish.

Leonard was hoping to see that skinny kid who had lifted the wallet from the tourist's purse while she was snapping pictures. The kid had moves, and if Leonard spotted him, he was going to offer him $20 just to give Leonard some tips. Leonard smoked half a dozen cigarettes while he watched and waited, feeling his palms dampen whenever he spotted a likely purse dangling from the arm or shoulder of a preoccupied tourist. He figured they were all wise to the jostling gag and would reach for their purses if someone bumped into them. That was the thing about the kid. He didn't touch her. He just drifted in like a ghost and was gone, leaving the purse hanging open and the wallet missing.

What Leonard failed to see was the start of an incident that did not make the *L.A. Times* but did rate a column in one of the underground sheets beneath a provocative headline and a story yammering about "warrior cops." The warrior cop in question was Officer Gert Von Braun, but it all got started by a sharp-eyed rookie.

Probationer Gil Ponce was teamed with Cat Song in 6-X-32 because Dan Applewhite was on days off. Gil was ecstatic to get away from his moody field training officer, and being teamed with someone as cool as Cat Song was definitely a bonus.

When Gil had occasion to work with a P3 or even a P2 whom he didn't know personally, he'd always address them as "sir" or "ma'am." He still had a few weeks to go on his probation and he wasn't going to risk any negative comments from anyone.

When he got to their shop after roll call, she said, "I'm driving, you're booking, okay?"

"Yes, ma'am," he said to Cat.

"How old're you?" she asked after they were in their car.

"Twenty-three," he said. "Almost."

"I'm thirty-three," she said. "Almost. But if you call me 'ma'am,' I'll get feeling so matronly I'll have to kill you and blame it on hormonal hysteria. My name's Cat."

"Okay, Cat," Gil said.

When she wrote his name in the log, she said, "If we need it, can you translate Spanish, Gil?"

"No, sorry. My name's Hispanic but…"

"No need to apologize," Cat said, raising a slender hand with manicured nails the same color as her lipstick. "Somebody's always calling on me to translate Korean and all I can say is *kimchi* because I grew up eating the stuff."

Later in the evening Gil Ponce was starting to mentally play How much would I give to trade Dan Applewhite for Cat Song? when they got the call to meet the foot-beat team at Hollywood and Highland.

It wasn't much. The foot beat had a plain drunk in tow and they needed a team to transport him to jail. He was a transient who'd been begging for change in the Kodak Center and apparently had been very successful.

"He's annihilated," the older cop said to Gil, who wasn't sure if he should glove up or not. He knew that some of the older cops scoffed when the young ones drew the latex gloves, but there had been roll call training about the prevalence of staph, along with some grisly photos of cops who'd picked up horrible lesions on their hands and arms and even their legs.

There was plenty of light from street lamps and headlights, and plenty of neon there on Hollywood Boulevard, but Gil shined his flashlight beam on the guy. He saw that the transient had a long string of snot dangling from one nostril and his cotton trousers were urine soaked. So Gil put on the gloves, glad to see that Cat did the same. Just before he took control of the reeling drunk, the guy started moaning, leaned forward, and vomited.

All four cops leaped back a few paces and Gil said, "He's chunking all over his shoes! Oh, gross!"

It was this part of police work — the smell of the hanging body leaking feces or a drunk reeking from urine and vomit — that Gil Ponce feared he might never learn to accommodate. The blood and hideous trauma of every kind he could handle, but not the odors. And just as he was about to lead the drunk at arm's length to their shop, he was saved. He looked at the mob of tourists half a block away on the Walk of Fame and spotted a young guy with shoulder-length dark hair, a red tee, baggy jeans, and flip-flops, walking fast, a brown leather purse tucked under his arm.

"Hey!" Gil said. "Look! A purse snatcher!"

Gil instantly started running south, and when the guy, who'd been glancing behind himself, turned and saw a strapping young cop sprinting his way, he wheeled and ran across Hollywood Boulevard, nearly getting creamed by an MTA bus. Four Street Characters in full costume began shouting encouragement when Gil had to stop for the fast-moving, westbound traffic.

An older woman, obviously the victim, was standing next to the Characters, screaming, "My purse. He's got my purse!"

"Move your ass!" Conan the Barbarian shouted

at Gil. "He's running in sandals with his butt crack showing, for chrissake!"

"I'm paying your taxes!" Superman shouted. "Get it in gear!"

"Zigzag through the traffic, you big chicken-shit!" the Lone Ranger shouted, minus Tonto, who was in jail.

Even Zorro chimed in, and with his bogus Spanish accent said, "*¡Ándale, hombre!* Don't be such a wienie!"

And Gil Ponce, perhaps subconsciously spurred by the taunting of the superheroes, did just that.

Cat Song saw him nearly get hit by a Ford Taurus whose driver was busy checking out the freak show in front of the Chinese Theatre before jamming on his brakes to keep from killing the young cop.

Cat jumped in their shop and slowed traffic with her light bar and siren, turning the corner and driving west in the eastbound number one lane, stopping car traffic in front of the Kodak Center. She was broadcasting a description of the suspect and location of the foot pursuit, when a van full of tourists caused her to brake and blast them into awareness with her siren. The tourist van skidded sideways and screeched to a stop, gridlocking traffic in both directions.

Gil Ponce was amazed by the purse snatcher's foot speed. Of course, the guy wasn't wearing all of the gear on his belt that Gil was, but the thief was running in flip-flops. And Gil, who was in the best shape of his life, couldn't gain on the guy, who ran a broken field pattern through and around the hordes of pedestrians on the boulevard. Gil could see the long hair floating and the head bobbing. Otherwise, he wouldn't have known where in the hell the guy was.

Then he saw more heads bobbing their way through the crowd a block away, and he knew that some cops were running his way. Short-haired bobbing heads were chasing a long-haired bobbing head like a zany board game on Hollywood Boulevard, with Gil Ponce leaping high to see over the crowds, hoping the eastbound bobbing heads would meet the westbound bobbing head and gobble him up like Pac-Man. But suddenly, the whippet in flip-flops was gone.

The decision that the thief made to zip around the corner, running south on Orange

Drive, turned out to be unwise. Because after following the foot pursuit on the radio, several cops were fanning out and trying to guess where the thief would run, and one had figured correctly that it would be through the parking garage.

Some of the foot pursuit information was broadcast by Cat Song, her shop still trapped in traffic while she boiled in frustration, cursing everything, including tourism in general. Yet the more her siren howled and her light bar winked, the more confused the out-of-town motorists became, and the gridlock grew more impenetrable. The other foot pursuit information came from five cops who'd parked west of the Chinese Theatre and were broadcasting on their rovers while running through the crowds.

The one copper who had everything doped out perfectly was Gert Von Braun. There were lights all over the parking structure, but there were dark places where a wide person dressed in a navy blue uniform could hide. She was behind a concrete wall when he ran to the structure, puffing and panting, looking behind himself, the purse in his hand now.

He never slowed and never saw Officer Von Braun holding her PR-24 baton in a rising-sun samurai pose before she stepped out from the shadows and whirled in a 360-degree whip with amazing agility for a woman in a size 44 Sam Browne. She was holding her baton in a Barry Bonds two-handed baseball grip when she swung for the bleacher seats. The baton struck the purse snatcher across the chest, and he might as well have slammed into the side of a bus. His right flip-flop continued hurtling forward, along with his left eye. It popped from its socket and rolled, clicking across the pavement, scooting off the curb, and coming to rest against the tire of an illegally parked car.

The first to arrive at the scene of arrest was Gil Ponce. The purse snatcher was proned out, hands cuffed behind his back, making creaking raspy sounds as he sucked at the air but couldn't get enough of it. His empty eye socket glistened in the neon glow from the boulevard.

Gert Von Braun handed the purse to Gil Ponce, who was still wearing the latex gloves he'd donned when asked to take charge of the putrid drunk. Gil looped the purse strap over his arm and was putting his baton back in the ring when the surfer cops pulled to the curb and parked.

The surfers alighted from their shop, and Flotsam looked at Gil, saying, "You need somebody to accessorize you, dude. That purse does not match your shoes and gloves."

Gil quickly peeled off the gloves and stuffed them in his pocket, and Jetsam removed the cap and straw from a cup of Gatorade he'd been drinking and said, "Here, bro. Rehydrate before you pass out."

Gil took a gulp of Gatorade and handed it back to Jetsam while Flotsam and Gert Von Braun, each holding an arm, lifted the purse snatcher to his feet.

"My eye!" he said, wheezing. "I lost my goddamn eye!"

Flotsam shined his flashlight beam on the thief's face and said, "You did lose it, dude. There's just a hole in your face now. Stuff it with toilet paper before you get to the slam or those jailhouse meat packers will add a whole new meaning to eye-fucking."

"Do you know what that eye cost!" the thief yelled, his baggy jeans and boxers now down so low his penis was exposed.

Taking out her handcuff key, Gert Von Braun uncuffed his hands, saying, "You missed a belt loop. In fact, you missed the whole belt. Do me a favor, put that thing away while we look for your eye."

Shining his flashlight beam around the pavement, Gil Ponce said, "There it is. Under the tire of that car. Gnarly!"

"Pick it up, will ya?" the purse snatcher said to Jetsam, who was sitting on the fender of his shop, looking down at the glass eyeball, sipping his Gatorade.

"I ain't picking up nobody's eyeball," Jetsam said. "You can pick up your own fucking eyeball, bro."

"Get gloved up again, boy," Flotsam said to Gil Ponce. "And pick it up. Every man's got a right to his own eyeball."

"Why did I transfer to this lunatic division?" Gert Von Braun asked rhetorically and strode across the sidewalk. "There's not a real man on the midwatch."

And she squatted, shined her light under the car, picked up the glass eyeball, ungloved, and then strode over to Jetsam and dunked the dirty eyeball into the surfer's drink. And swished it around.

"My Gatorade!" Jetsam cried in disbelief to all present. "She dunked an eyeball in my Gatorade!"

"Girlie men," Gert Von Braun muttered, and she handed the eyeball to the purse snatcher, saying, "Stick this in your head, dude."

There were two civilians watching the action from a hundred feet away. One was Leonard Stilwell, who then had decided that purse picking wasn't for him. Along with him was a young guy who looked like a transient but was a stringer who wrote pieces for the underground rags. The stringer was thinking he might submit this piece to the editors at the *L.A. Times,* who were always harping about LAPD's "warrior cop" ethos. He'd already decided on his headline: "The Eyes Have It with Warrior Cops."

Gert Von Braun said to Gil Ponce, "I'll see you at the station."

"I think maybe there is one real man on the midwatch," Flotsam said, watching Gert get in her shop. "At least we didn't get spit at."

Finally having negotiated her way through

the traffic on Hollywood Boulevard, Cat Song double-parked across from the parking structure and trotted over to the group of cops, where she saw the purse snatcher wipe something on the front of his T-shirt and then use both hands to do something to his face.

But her mind was on her young boot, who had nearly gotten himself killed, and she was very mad when she pulled Gil Ponce aside and said quietly, "You almost got pancaked by that head-up-ass tourist in the Ford. You were very lucky. Dumb and lucky."

"I misjudged his speed," Gil Ponce said.

"Listen, man of steel," she said, "you can play Russian roulette, date Phil Spector, or otherwise self-destruct on your own time, but not on mine. There's no place for a kamikaze kid in my shop."

"I'm sorry, Cat," Gil said. "But we got him. We got the guy!"

Jetsam walked over to Cat Song and pointed at Gert Von Braun driving away. "She dunked an eyeball in my Gatorade!" he said. "And swished it around!"

"What?" said Cat Song.

★ SEVEN ★

THE NEXT DAY was one where all the watches had to listen to roll call training prepared by the LAPD's Behavioral Science Services about recognizing suicidal behaviors. The California Highway Patrol, which was a much smaller law enforcement agency than the LAPD, had been experiencing a frightening suicide cluster. Eight of their officers of both genders had committed suicide in the prior year alone, the rate being five times higher than the national average for law enforcement. Suicide was a subject that cops did not wish to talk about. It was disturbing to think about and unnatural that far more cops murder themselves than are murdered by criminals. And that if they stay on the Job long enough, they will have worked with or around some cop who does it.

They preferred to treat it much like others in high-risk jobs treat death, the way fighter pilots treat the deaths of colleagues by blaming nearly all air crashes on pilot errors that they themselves would not have made.

Cops would say, "He probably got into massive debt and couldn't find a way out."

Or, "She probably was into drugs or booze and it all got to be too much."

Or, "He probably had some bipolar shit in his DNA and just went mental. So why didn't he just hang out at UCLA and shoot law students before they metastasize?"

The first question that a cop asked the sergeant who read the material at day-watch roll call was "Why the CHP? They got it made. Like working for the auto club. Triple A with guns. How hard is that? Why should they be capping themselves?"

And another cop said, "What if they had to live under a federal consent decree like we do? Along with a police commission full of cop-hating political hacks? They'd be setting themselves on fire like Buddhist monks."

The training bulletin was meaningless to the young coppers at the various roll calls. Why were they being briefed about it? Whatever drove those poor bastards to bite it had nothing to do with *their* young lives.

The senior sergeant, who recognized the defense mechanisms and knew that the BSS shrink assigned to Hollywood Station was the loneliest underworked guy in the division, said, "Yeah, I guess reading this material is a waste of time. It could never happen to us tough guys, could it?"

That morning, before Ronnie and Bix Ramstead could tend to their many calls for quality-of-life service, they were to assist two other Crows with Homeless Outreach, that is, cleaning out the transient encampment in the Hollywood Hills. The other Crows on that assignment were Hollywood Nate Weiss and Rita Kravitz, neither of whom wanted to be there.

Their task was to roust the transients and write citations for trespassing in a mountain fire district. They called it "hitting the billy goat trail," and for this one, even Nate wore boots and BDUs, the black battle-dress uniform favored by SWAT officers. The encampment was behind the Hollywood Bowl, in the hills and canyons where one could see the lighted cross on the promontory overlooking the John Anson Ford Theater's parking lot. That parking lot was where older Hollywood cops used to go after night watch for a brew or two, sometimes with a few badge bunnies joining in the fun. That was before the former chief of police, whom they called Lord Voldemort, put a stop to it and to most other activities that provided any enjoyment whatsoever.

Rita Kravitz started complaining the moment they parked their Ford Explorer and started up the steep hillside. She slipped twice and had to grab at some brush and tumbleweed, getting thorns in her hand and breaking an acrylic nail.

"Goddamnit!" she muttered after the second fall. "Now a scorpion will probably sting me."

"Or you might step on a rattlesnake," Nate said, climbing behind her. "They say the babies are the deadliest."

"Shut up," Rita said.

Then Bix Ramstead slipped and skidded down the slope a few feet until he grabbed a handful of brush and pulled himself upright.

"I'm too old for this," he said.

Ronnie, who wasn't having an easy time

either, said, "Everybody's too old for this. How the hell do the homeless geezers do it?"

"They must have a helicopter stashed somewhere," Hollywood Nate said, wiping sweat from his brow. "This is steeper than a dinner tab at the Ivy." Then he added, "Where I happen to be going next week with a director pal of mine." Nate was disappointed that everybody was too tired and grumpy to give a shit.

When they finally got to the encampment, there were only three little tents in place, made from blue tarps that had probably been stolen from a construction site. A homeless transient was cooking a hot dog over a small fire pit dug into the dry earth.

"Morning, Officers," he said when he saw them.

He looked seventy, but he could have been fifty. His clothing was typical: a sweatshirt over a T-shirt over another T-shirt, even on this hot, smoggy day. And a pair of baggy dungarees, none of it having been dipped in soapy water for several weeks. Or months.

"I recognize you," Bix Ramstead said. "I thought we told you to leave last time I was here."

"I did leave," he said.

"But you're still here," Bix said.

"That was then. This is now."

"You weren't supposed to come back."

"Oh," the guy said. "I didn't know you meant forever."

"Why don't you go to the homeless shelter?" Bix said.

"Too many rules," the transient said. "A man's gotta be free. It's what America's all about."

"I'm getting all choked up," Rita Kravitz said. Then she looked in the second makeshift tent, where a fat woman was snoring, surrounded by empty cans of Mexican beer. Rita kicked the bottom of her filthy bare feet until she sat up and said, "What the fuck?"

Hollywood Nate went to the third tent and heard more snoring. Powerful chainsaw snores, along with wheezes and whistles and snuffling.

"Hey, dude!" Nate said. "Rise and shine!"

The snoring continued, rhythm unbroken. Nate grabbed the tent and started shaking it.

"Earthquake!" he yelled. "Run for your life!"

Still there was no change in the pattern of snores or the whistling snuffles.

Nate grabbed the tent in both hands and shook it violently, yelling, "Get your ass up!"

And it worked. A deep voice from within the tent bellowed, "I'll kill you, you motherfucker! I'm armed! If I come out, you're a dead man, you son of a bitch! Hear me? Dead!"

Nate leaped back and drew his Glock, tripping on a loose chunk of sandstone and falling flat on his ass, tumbling backward several feet down the hillside.

Ronnie drew her Beretta and so did Rita Kravitz. Bix Ramstead pulled his nine and his baton, just in case deadly force was not in the cards. And they all started yelling.

"Crawl out!" Rita Kravitz ordered. "Hands first!"

"Let's see your hands!" Ronnie ordered. "Your hands!"

"Now!" Bix Ramstead ordered. "Crawl out now!"

As Hollywood Nate scrambled to his feet and advanced on the tent, looking for cover if the guy should come out shooting, the tent flap was thrown open and four guns were deployed diagonally, leveled at the tent.

A wizened transient with a wild white beard halfway down his puny bare chest popped his head out, holding his "weapon," a piece of broom handle, and saw the four cops pointing pistols at him.

He offered an apologetic, toothless smile and said, "I'm just not a morning person."

Things were getting desperate for Leonard Stilwell. Nothing was working out in a world where trust was eroding. The old burglary targets had gotten harder what with more sophisticated alarms and window bars. His short flirtation with purse picking had terrified him after seeing what happened to the long-haired guy in flip-flops. He'd tried the ATM scam for three nights straight and never again was able to score the way he had with the Iranian woman. One of the chumps figured it out right away and threatened to call the cops.

He had no rock left, no crystal meth, not even a blunt to mellow him out before he hit the streets, contemplating a degrading life as a common shoplifter. Then he thought of old customers to whom he had sold stolen cases of liquor. He thought of Ali Aziz.

It was late afternoon by the time he arrived at the Leopard Lounge on Sunset Boulevard.

The nightclub would not be open yet, but he knew workers would be there cleaning and setting up. This was the hour when he used to drive up to the back door with Whitey Dawson and get his prearranged cash payment from Ali. Leonard banged on the front door and was admitted by a Mexican busboy who recognized him. Ali was in work clothes behind the bar, checking the stock.

"Ali!" Leonard said, slapping palms with the nightclub owner.

"Leonard!" Ali said with a grin, displaying the gold eyetooth that Leonard figured was a status symbol in shitty sand countries.

"Can we go in your office and talk?" Leonard asked. "Just for five minutes?"

"For my old friend Leonard, yes," Ali said.

And Leonard was glad he'd worn his only clean T-shirt and freshly laundered jeans. His sneakers were worn out, but he felt that he didn't look as poor and desperate as he really was.

When they got inside the office, Ali said, "You got some liquor for me, Leonard?"

"Well, no, not yet. But I'm working on it."

Ali turned sullen. He didn't ask Leonard to

sit. If this thief wasn't selling liquor, what could he possibly want?

"So?" Ali said, sitting on the corner of his desk.

"I got this deal in the works, Ali," Leonard began, "but I need an advance. Not much, but enough to pay a guy to give me an alarm code."

"Advance?" Ali said, and he started fidgeting with one of his gold pinkie rings, the one with a big white stone that Leonard doubted was real.

"Maybe . . . five hundred?"

"You wish to borrow five hundred dollars?" Ali said, incredulous.

"As an advance against my fee when I deliver the stock."

"You are going crazy," Ali said, standing up. "Crazy, Leonard."

"Wait, Ali!" Leonard said. "Two hundred. I think I could shake the alarm code loose for two hundred."

"You waste my time," Ali said, checking the face on his huge gold watch.

"Ali," Leonard said, "we done lots of business in the past. I can still help you out. I got several plans in the works."

Ali Aziz glanced at the photos on the shelf over the TV. Then at Leonard, then back at the pictures. He went around his desk and sat in his executive chair and motioned Leonard to the client chair.

Leonard's legs were shaky and his hands were sweating now. He needed some rock bad. Perspiration was running down his freckled cheeks from his rusty hairline, and sweat beaded under his sockets, beneath the vacant blue-eyed stare. But he was full of hope and he waited.

Nearly a minute passed before Ali spoke. When he did, he said, "Leonard, you are a good thief, no?"

"I'm the best," Leonard Stilwell said, trying to look confident. "You know that. We never had no trouble when Whitey and me sold you liquor. No trouble at all."

"No trouble," Ali said. "That is so. But now Whitey is dead."

"And if I just had the alarm code that this guy said he'd..."

Ali shook his head, waving his hand palm down, and Leonard shut up.

"You are giving me a big idea," Ali said.

"About the alarm code. You enter and steal from business buildings many times," Ali said. "You also can enter and steal from a house, no?"

"Yeah, sure, but why would I want to? There's nothing in most houses. Even the big houses up where you live. People don't keep cash laying around no more. Everything's done with credit cards. And a lot of that fancy jewelry you see at red carpet events? It's fake."

"How you know where I live?"

"You told me one time," Leonard said. "Up in the hills. Mount Olympus, right?"

Ali nodded. "Okay, but I do not live there no more. My bitch wife is living there with my son. We are in a very big divorce fight. The house is sold and we must wait for escrow to close up."

"Sorry to hear that," Leonard said, unable to concentrate fully. Thinking how fast he was going to drive his Honda to Pablo's Tacos or the cyber café and score something to smoke, wondering how much he could get out of this Ay-rab.

"I am thinking that I need for you to enter my house on a Thursday. At four o'clock in the day. There is something I must have for my divorce fight."

"What something?"

"Bank papers. Very important."

"Can't you just ask for them? Or have your lawyer do it?"

"Impossible," Ali said. "My bitch wife is not going to give them. She wishes to use the documents against me."

"Are they in a safe? I never done a safe."

"No, just in a desk drawer."

Now Leonard was perspiring even more. This didn't sound right. He didn't like the way Ali was explaining it. There was too much hesitation, like he was making it up as he went along. If he'd only smoked one little blunt to mellow him out, he could think better.

Finally he said, "Another reason I never did much housebreaking was 'cause there's always a chance somebody will walk in on you. I'm not into violence, Ali."

"No violence," Ali said. "That is why Thursday is the correct day. My wife does the exercise that afternoon. The maid finishes housecleaning at four o'clock. She sets the alarm, she locks doors, she goes. Her grandson collects her in front. Then you enter my house and get the bank papers for me."

"I don't know, Ali," Leonard said. "It ain't that easy. How about the alarm? You got the code?"

"I am sure that my bitch wife changes all locks so my key is no good. And she also changes the regular alarm code. But I do not think she can change the code for the maid. Lola is a most stupid Mexican who cannot see good up close. Stupid old woman cannot find most of dirt in the house neither. I want to fire her, but my wife says that Lola is very good with my Nicky. Okay, Lola many times forgets her correct code and many times she sets off alarms. My wife is not changing the code for Lola, no way. That code I give to you."

"Lemme lock on this," Leonard said. "I break in through one of the access doors that's alarmed, right? A door that's used for entering and leaving, so there's no panic at the alarm company? Not as long as I enter the maid's code within a minute or so, right?"

"Absolutely correct," Ali said with a reassuring smile.

"You could do the same," Leonard said warily.

After a short hesitation, Ali said, "No, I cannot. Number one reason: I cannot permit for someone to see me doing such a thing. My lawyer would explode like...like..."

"An IED in Baghdad."

"Precisely. Number two reason: I do not know how to enter a door that has the lock in place without making big damage."

"Why is that important? When she finds the papers're missing, she'll know somebody broke in and stole them."

"No, no," Ali said, and after a thoughtful pause he continued. "She must not learn that the papers are of so much value and she must not know they are missing. You see, there are many other documents there."

Now Leonard was certain that something was wrong and that Ali was winging it. But at least it didn't involve violence, so Leonard said, "Windows are out of the question. And I'm sure you got a motion detector. Is there an attached garage?"

"Yes, the garage attaches to the house."

"Do you think she changed the code on the garage door opener?"

Ali thought for a moment and said, "I do not

think so. The gardener has a door opener and so does Lola."

"Do you have one? I mean besides the one that's probably built into your car."

"Yes, I have the old one."

"I'm sure the front door has a dead bolt and probably the other doors, but how about the door leading to the garage? A dead bolt? The kind you have to turn?"

"Dead bolt?" Ali pondered. "Yes."

"And another lock, right? One on the door-knob or handle that locks by itself when the door closes unless you turn a little thumb-turn on the inside?"

"Yes, that is correct. On the doorknob. It is a very old lock."

"And is the alarm pad right inside that door?"

"Yes."

"Okay," Leonard said. "Here's the deal. Most people don't bother to throw the dead bolt on the access door from the garage to the house. They feel comfortable that two doors are between them and the street. And besides, they're always bringing something in or out of the car to the house. Do you think your maid might lock the dead bolt on that door when she sets the alarm and leaves?"

"Absolutely no," Ali said. "When I was living there, I always drive into the garage and use my key for only the doorknob lock. But when my wife is home, no knob lock. No nothing."

Leonard thought, if he was going to lie, he should lie large. He had to have this job. He said, "I can pick any ordinary lock, so your wife won't know it's happened. I'll need your garage door opener and an exact idea of what papers I'm looking for and where to find them. And I'll need your maid's alarm code."

"And you are very certain nobody will know you enter into the house?"

"Not unless your wife is paranoid and calls the alarm company to see if her maid came back for some reason. But would she?"

"No, my bitch wife will not do that," Ali said.

"If your garage opener don't work or if the dead bolt is thrown on that access door, I'm outta there," Leonard said.

"Is okay with me," Ali said.

"So where do I find the bank papers, and what do they look like?"

"Look for the brown folder. Big one. With the year two thousand and four on the outside. You shall find it when you open the bottom drawer in the white desk. It is in the office room next to the kitchen. Other brown envelopes are there too, but do not touch. Leave other papers. You understand?"

"I guess so," Leonard said. "So how much do I get for this job?"

"I give you the two hundred dollars you say you want."

"Fuck that!" Leonard said. "That was an advance. This is housebreaking and it's dangerous and takes special talent."

"Okay, okay," Ali said. "I give you four hundred dollars after you give me the bank documents."

It was the biggest gamble that he'd taken in a long time, but he decided to go for it. Leonard said to Ali Aziz, "Two hundred now. One thousand more when I give you the papers."

"You crazy, Leonard," Ali said. "No way."

Leonard was fully prepared to back down, but he gambled again. Standing up, he said, "I'm outta here. Good luck, Ali."

"Okay, okay," Ali Aziz said. "I agree."

Now Leonard quickly swiped at his face to stem the rivulets of perspiration and said, "But what if the papers ain't there? I still risk state prison. I still want the thousand."

"But how shall I know if you go in there and try?"

"Tell me something that's in the house that your wife won't miss. Some little thing."

"Napkin," Ali said. "She have very special cocktail napkins. Look inside baskets on the countertop in the kitchen. Has her initial printed in gold on every napkin. Bring one to me if you don't find no bank papers. I see that napkin, I pay you."

"You'll give me the thousand anyways? No argument?"

"Yes, I shall not argue."

Leonard put out his hand. Ali looked as though he didn't want to touch it but did. "We got the deal," Ali said.

"Call me on my cell when you're ready. I'll stop by here same time as today. Have the garage door opener and the alarm code for me. Now I'll need the two hundred."

Ali reluctantly pulled out his wallet and peeled off four $50 bills and handed them to Leonard Stilwell.

"One thing more," Ali said. "When you finish with the job, you meet me down where you see the Mount Olympus sign. I shall be there in my car. Black Jaguar."

"That's weird," Leonard said. "Why don't I bring them here?"

Ali hesitated yet again. "Maybe I look at the papers and don't find the certain document I need. Maybe I ask you to go back, look somewhere else."

"No fucking way!" Leonard said. "I go in one time and that's it. What're you trying to pull?"

"Okay," Ali said quickly. "If the correct document is not there, is okay."

"Are we finished here?"

"You leave that door with no lock on the knob. Very important. No lock."

Now Leonard was totally confused. This thing was going sideways before it started. "Unlocked? But you said you didn't want your wife to know anybody had busted in her house. If she gets outta her car and finds the knob lock ain't set, what's she gonna think?"

"She shall think the stupid old Mexican maid forget to lock the doorknob again. No problem."

"This ain't right, Ali," Leonard said, brow wrinkling. "There's something wrong here."

"I wish for her to fire the stupid Mexican maid," Ali explained. "My bitch wife says Lola is good for my son. I do not think so. My wife finds the door unlocked again, maybe she decides to fire Lola. That shall be good for my Nicky."

"Look, why don't you and me just do the job together?" Leonard said. "All I gotta really do is pick that lock and let you in. That way, you could look around anywheres you want. You could check her underwear drawer and sniff her panties if you want. And I could leave you in there and go about my business. Don't that make a lotta sense?"

"No, Leonard. I shall never go inside the house, no way. Not till my divorce is finish. I must not take a foolish risk. Someone see me go into the house, what do you think happens to my divorce fight? Do the job like I tell you and I pay, no problem. Okay?"

"Okay, but you still wanna meet me there in your neighborhood rather than right here?"

"By Mount Olympus sign, Leonard."

Leonard felt the four President Grants in his pocket and thought, if he could smoke a little rock, this whole thing might clear up in his mind. Maybe then he could figure out what this goat fucker was really up to.

"I'll come here when you call me," Leonard said to Ali Aziz, using the desk notepad to write down the number of his throwaway cell phone. "By the way, what's the address?"

When Ali recited his Mt. Olympus street and house number, Leonard wrote it down on a second notebook sheet.

"No, Leonard," Ali said, watching him. "You write down the wrong number. Last two are not correct numbers."

Leonard showed Ali his knowing smile and said, "That's a little trick I learned from Whitey Dawson. "I always subtract two from the last pair of numbers in the address of a job I'm gonna be working. That way, I don't have to memorize nothing. Guys forget stuff when they gotta memorize things. If the cops stop me and find the address, it ain't gonna mean shit to them."

"Very clever, Leonard," Ali said. "I think you are a clever man."

"You gotta do your homework," Leonard Stilwell said, thinking about the rock he'd be smoking that night. Figuring he had lots of time to see his Fijian neighbor and learn how the hell to pick a lock.

★ EIGHT ★

LATE THAT DAY, after the Homeless Outreach had been concluded and the hills behind the Hollywood Bowl were encampment free for the time being, Ronnie kept her appointment with the surfer cops. She arrived with Hollywood Nate at 4 P.M. and parked in front of an auto body repair business in East Hollywood that was ostensibly diminishing the quality-of-life for a few hundred Hispanic people at the other end of their shared alley. Bix Ramstead was at the station catching up on paperwork and "constant caller" phone messages that he'd been postponing. It was estimated that about 30 percent of all CRO complaints were from the same callers.

The surfer cops were already there, standing by Flotsam's pickup truck in their normal street attire of T-shirts and jeans.

"Thanks for coming," Flotsam said, glancing

uneasily at Nate, whose expression said to him, Are you an innocent bystander, or what?

"So why don't you come in with us and make sure I do it right," Ronnie said to the surfers.

Jetsam followed Ronnie inside, and Flotsam trailed, whispering to Nate, "The game's afoot, dude. He think he's Holmes, but I ain't no Dr. Watson."

The proprietor of Stan's Body Shop was not an Arab, not an Iranian, nor an immigrant from any foreign country. He was a fifty-year-old white Anglo native of Los Angeles named Stan Hooper, and he was very surprised to see two cops in uniform and two other guys who looked like cops enter his place of business.

Ronnie said, "Good afternoon, sir. We're from Hollywood Division Community Relations Office. Here's my card."

While Stan Hooper looked at the card, she said, "We have a complaint from residents at the other end of the alley that cars from your shop are often blocking the alley early in the morning, and apartment residents can't get their cars out when they need to go to work. In fact, I noticed three cars parked there now with barely enough room for a VW Bug to squeeze by."

Stan Hooper wiped the grease from his hands and said, "We'll move them right away, Officer. I'm sorry. This place is too small for us but it's all we can afford right now. I'm looking for more space. I try to keep the alley clear, but sometimes customers park there before I can tell them not to."

"Business must be good," Ronnie said, looking toward the open door leading into the main room, where body work was in progress on a white Lexus SUV that was taped and primered.

"Too good, but I shouldn't complain," he said, looking at the surfers, wondering why it took four cops to deliver the warning. "I don't want no tickets. I won't let it happen again."

Jetsam said, "Nice rides you got in there." And he strolled into the large open area, where the work was being done.

"He's one of our officers," Ronnie said to Stan Hooper. "He likes cars."

Stan Hooper followed Jetsam into the work bay and said, "Two of those are for sale. My customer said I could sell them if someone wants to buy. I wouldn't take no commission if an officer from Hollywood Station wanted one of them. The Mercedes is really nice and the price is pretty good."

The surfer cop began writing down license numbers and VIN numbers, and Stan Hooper said, "Something wrong, Officer?"

Jetsam said, "We got a few reports about hot SUVs being repainted and having license plates switched. It's just routine."

"I never been in trouble in my life!" Stan Hooper said. "You can check. I got a reputation with insurance companies for doing honest work at an honest price, and we specialize in SUVs. We can even straighten bent frames if they're not too bad. Insurance companies refer SUV owners to us all the time."

At this point the other three cops knew that Jetsam was just trying to save face when he said, "I wasn't thinking of you. I was thinking of the owners of the SUVs. Do you know them personally?"

"I know two of them from way back. I've worked on their cars for ten, fifteen years. The other two I don't know. One's an old guy, lives in Los Feliz district. The other's a woman. Drop-dead gorgeous. Lives in Hollywood Hills some-wheres. One of my guys drove her home."

"Are any of your workers from the Middle East? Arabs maybe?"

"Arabs? No. Three're Mexican, two're Salva-doran. One's an Okie. That's about it."

Jetsam looked sheepishly at the other cops, and Stan Hooper said, "The woman customer has a name that sounds like maybe an Arab name, but she's American. Her SUV was full of old magazines and newspapers written in a Middle East language. They were laying around the shop last time I looked. I wish she'd come and pay me and pick up her car, but she hopes I can sell it for her."

Stan Hooper handed the repair estimates to Ronnie, who glanced at them perfunctorily just to help Jetsam gracefully exit, and she saw the name Margot Aziz.

"Aziz," she said. "Would this customer be related to Ali Aziz who owns a nightclub on Sunset?"

"You got me," Stan Hooper said, shrugging.

Hollywood Nate suddenly got very inter-ested. He looked over Ronnie's shoulder and saw the familiar address on the work order, and he memorized the phone number.

"How much does the lady want for the SUV?" Nate asked casually.

"It's three years old but has very low mileage. It had some body damage but nothing major. Somebody smacked into her in the parking lot at Farmers Market, she said. She'll take twenty-eight."

"Twenty-eight thousand," Nate said. "That's a little high, isn't it?"

"Maybe she'll come down," Stan Hooper said.

"Keep the alley clear, please," Ronnie said, turning toward the door.

When the four cops were back outside, Ronnie said, "A Mercedes SUV? And you recently bought a Mustang, I believe. Are you on the take, Nate?"

"Nice ride. I always admired these Mercedes SUVs."

"See you guys," Ronnie said. "I'll leave you to run license and VIN numbers if you wanna stay on this case."

When the surfer cops got back in Flotsam's pickup to drive to Hollywood Station, Flotsam said, "Dude, I know Ronnie rocks your libido, but this kinda move ain't gonna help you become a Crow."

Jetsam said, "At least I got it right about the Arabic newspaper."

When they arrived back at Hollywood South, Ronnie found Bix sitting at a desk with his BlackBerry in front of him, still making tedious phone calls. And Nate seemed in a hurry to make a few calls of his own, but not in the office, where the others were working. Nate walked outside and dialed the number on his cell, surprised at how cotton mouthed he was when she answered.

"Hello...Margot?" Nate said.

"Yes. Who is this?"

"It's Nate Weiss. The police officer you met?"

"Oh, yes," she said. "How'd you get my number?"

"You won't believe what a coincidence this is," Nate said. "But today I had occasion to be at Stan's Body Shop and I saw your SUV there and learned it's for sale."

"Yes, it is," she said.

"I'd like to talk to you about it," Nate said. "I might be interested."

"I'm asking twenty-eight thousand."

"Would you be willing to negotiate?"

After a few seconds she said, "I might."

"Could I come by and talk to you about it?"

"When?"

"Oh, after I get off work this evening?"

"What time would that be?"

"I could get to your house as early as eight o'clock."

"My au pair is not available tonight," Margot said. "I'm afraid I'll be occupied with my five-year-old son. It'd be better if you come tomorrow night."

"Tomorrow night at eight?"

"That'll be fine," Margot Aziz said. "One question, Officer Weiss."

"Call me Nate. What's the question?"

"That's my dinner hour and I'm not a bad cook. How about sharing some homemade pasta and mango chicken salad with me?"

When Hollywood Nate Weiss closed his cell phone, he actually felt giddy.

After Margot Aziz hung up her house phone,

she used her pay-as-you-go cell phone and rang another go cell that she'd bought for a beautiful Amerasian topless dancer.

"It's me," Margot said when Jasmine answered. "I can't wait any longer for the number one draft pick. Remember the other one I mentioned to you? He's coming here tomorrow night. I'll see how it goes. He might work out."

"I'm getting sick and tired of this," the dancer said. "If something don't happen soon, I'm pulling outta the whole thing. It's too nerve-racking."

"Be patient, honey," Margot said. "We've worked hard getting into the man's head. We've got him primed. It'll just be a little while longer."

Since there wasn't a full moon, the watch commander hoped for a quiet night. A full moon over Hollywood meant that anything could happen and usually did. Most of the things were not the sort that the police discussed with the business community at meetings of the Community Police Advisory Board.

Dan Applewhite was using up some of his accumulated overtime days, so young Gil Ponce had been assigned to ride with Gert Von Braun.

They hadn't been out on the streets more than thirty minutes after sunset when 6-X-66 got a call in Southeast Hollywood regarding a silent burglar alarm at a furniture store. When they arrived and did a routine check of windows at the store, Gert's new eight-inch flashlight began blinking. She tapped it a few times and the light went out.

"Goddamn this piece of shit!" she said. And she tapped it again and switched it off and on a few times.

And then Gil Ponce got a firsthand look at Gert's EST, the explosive temper syndrome that other cops talked about privately.

"Motherfucking political hacks!" she snarled. And hurled the flashlight against the block wall at the rear of the furniture store, debris flying.

Gil just watched but said nothing, and she turned to him, saying, "We're gonna stop at a drugstore and buy a goddamn flashlight that works!"

It sounded to Gil Ponce like a challenge, so he swallowed and said, "Yes, ma'am. Okay."

"Don't call me ma'am, goddamnit!" she said, getting into their shop, squeezing her bulk between the steering wheel and backrest.

"No,...Gert," Gil said, slipping into the passenger seat as quickly and quietly as possible, keeping his eyes on the streets.

An hour later, Compassionate Charlie Gilford was once again called away from one of his favorite reality shows to meet 6-X-66 at the scene of a possible homicide, where the body was missing and a baby was dead. It was the kind of location that the committees that were dedicated to the beautification and renewal of Hollywood liked to think was so far off the boulevards that one needn't consider it a Hollywood neighborhood at all. But it was.

It happened at a Brentwood slumlord's three-story Hollywood apartment building. There was an outside stairwell under the roof at the rear of the property, which was used by various homeless transients as temporary housing. They slept, drank, urinated, and even defecated there, belying the adage about not shitting where one sleeps. All outdoor metal piping had been stripped and stolen long ago, and before brass hinges were replaced with steel, at least one transient was stabbed while kicking down the door of an empty apartment just to get the shiny treasure. Hispanic children did not dare walk barefoot for fear of discarded syringes.

One of the Honduran residents of the building, who had passed the stairwell from the parking lot on his way to the transient-free staircase at the front, spotted what appeared to be bloodstains on the concrete walkway where the trash bins were located. He poked his head inside the stairwell area, holding his breath against the stench, and saw more blood. He followed the trail to the corner under the stairwell and there saw thick viscous chunks of blood, and something that looked like raw oysters, but he just didn't want to know. There was dried spatter on one wall and a Rorschach pattern on the concrete floor beside a blanket stiff from blood drenching, as well as articles of discarded clothing. The Honduran thought the scene was so horrible that rats would flee from it. But he was wrong. There were rats.

And under a cardboard box in the other corner he found a dead baby. Not a fetus, but a full-term baby with the cord still attached. It was a boy but he could not tell any more about it. He knew that he should not disturb this scene and ran to his apartment to call the police. When he told his wife about what he had found, she returned with him to the stairwell to await the police officers' arrival.

Despite her husband's protests, she went back to their apartment and fetched a bath towel, refusing to let the body lie on the dirty concrete floor. She picked up the dead baby, who was not stiff, rigor mortis having come and gone, and placed the body on the third step, folding the towel over the tiny body.

"Pobrecito," she said, and offered a prayer for the baby and for the mother if she was still alive, but the Honduran woman did not think that the mother could have lived. All that blood!

When 6-X-66 arrived at the scene, Gert Von Braun said to Gil Ponce, "You better do the talking here. They probably don't speak English any better than George W. Bush."

Here we go again, Gil Ponce thought, and he said, "I'm sorry, Gert. I don't speak Spanish."

She gave him a doubtful look and muttered the familiar refrain: "Fucking Hollywood. Nothing's ever the way you expect."

The Honduran man directed his remarks to

young Gil Ponce. "Very bad thing happen," he said in passable English. "Blood ees all over. We see thees dead baby."

He led them to the stairwell and pulled back the towel. Gert shined the beam from her new flashlight onto the body and said, "Looks like it's been here awhile. Wonder where Momma went."

The Honduran said to Gil, "Much blood over there." And he pointed to the blood-caked blanket.

When Gert shined her light on the wall, she said, "That looks like spatter. This might be more than a homeless woman giving birth. We better treat this as a homicide scene. Call the night-watch detective. Tell him we got something that looks like pizza topping without the crust."

"We stay here?" the Honduran said to Gil Ponce.

Gert Von Braun said, "I'm ten years older than him. Talk to me, why don't you?"

"Sorry?" the man said, not understanding.

Gert said, "Never mind. Talk to him." She was used to it with people from male-dominated cultures.

"Go to your apartment," Gil said. "But a detective will come and speak to you soon. Okay?"

"Okay," the man said.

Compassionate Charlie got there well before the coroner's crew. He spoke with Gert and Gil, looked at the spatter and the vast blood loss someone had suffered, and got the Homicide D3 at home, telling her what they'd found. The D3 said she'd phone the detectives who were on call and get back to him.

And that was when the fattest transient any of the cops had ever seen staggered onto the scene. He was a homeless alcoholic who'd been arrested many times on the boulevards where he panhandled tourists. He was a middle-aged white man, perhaps a few years older than Detective Charlie Gilford, but very much larger. He wore a battered fedora, a patched, dandruff-dusted sport coat, and a greasy necktie over a filthy flannel shirt, perhaps his attempt to retain a drop of dignity.

When he lurched unsteadily toward the stairwell, the neck of a wine bottle protruding from his coat pocket, he didn't even see the cops until Gert Von Braun lit him with the beam from her new flashlight.

Charlie Gilford said, "Jesus! This double-wide juicer must weigh three bills easy."

"Uh-oh," the fat man said when he saw them. "Evening, Officers."

Gil Ponce gloved up and patted him down, removing the wine bottle as the man looked at it wistfully, his breath like sewer gas, facial veins like a nest of pink worms. The fact that his face had color and had not turned lemonade yellow was a testament to his still-functioning liver.

"What's your name?" Charlie Gilford asked him.

"Livingston G. Kenmore," the man said, lurching sideways until Gil Ponce steadied him.

"Whadda you know about this?" Charlie Gilford asked.

"About what?"

"The blood. The dead baby."

"Oh, that."

The cops looked at one another and back at the drunk. Finally, Charlie Gilford said, "Yeah, that. What happened here?"

"About the blood or the baby?"

"Let's start with the baby," Gert said.

"It belongs to Ruthie. It's dead."

"We know it's dead. Who's Ruthie?"

"She was sleeping here," he said. "She was big as a house, but she still was doing guys for ten bucks. Ruthie didn't get too many takers at the end. Her belly was out to here." He patted his own enormous belly then.

"Where's Ruthie now?" Charlie asked.

"She went to the homeless shelter two days ago," the fat man said. "You can find her there now. She wasn't feeling too good after she had the baby. Poor thing. It was dead before it came out. She bled a lot."

"Did you help her have the baby?" Gert asked.

"Her friend Sadie did," he said. "She went to the shelter with Ruthie. You can go there and ask them about it. I tried to stay outta their affairs. They're businesswomen, if you get my meaning."

"Are you telling us that all this blood came from Ruthie?" Charlie Gilford said.

"No, some of it came from Ruthie," the man said, looking at Charlie like he was stupid or something.

"Did some of it come from Sadie?" Charlie asked.

"No," the fat man said. "Some of it came from me."

"From you?" Gert said. "Where from you?"

"From my schwanze," he said. "See, I been having lots of trouble peeing, so I went to the clinic a few weeks ago and had some surgery. A doctor put a catheter clear up my willie with one of those balloons inside my bladder to hold everything in place. But the other night after I drank a couple forties and a quart of port, I got mad at it and ripped it out. Blood squirted everywhere."

Both Charlie Gilford and Gil Ponce involuntarily uttered painful groans from stabs of sympathy pain. Gil doubled over a bit and Charlie grabbed his own crotch while Gert sneered at the two of them. Gil already knew she thought they were all just a bunch of pussies, so he stood up straight, took a deep breath, and told himself to maintain.

Gert said to the drunk, "You mean your thingie bled that much?"

"You can't imagine," the big man said. "I almost called nine-one-one. Wanna see it?"

Both Charlie Gilford and Gil Ponce said, "No!" But Gert Von Braun said, "Yeah, whip it out."

He did. And while Charlie Gilford and Gil Ponce got busy looking in other directions,

Gert shined her beam on the fat man's penis and said, "Whoa, that's gnarly! You gotta have a doctor stitch it up. That thing looks like the pork sausage my mom used to make."

The detective said to Gert and Gil, "How about you two driving Mr. Kenmore here to the shelter and grabbing Ruthie and Sadie. In case they used different names, he can point them out. Treat this like a possible homicide. They coulda killed the baby."

"Oh, no!" the fat man said. "She was going to adopt it out. She thought she could get maybe two thousand bucks for it if it was white. And sure enough it was. She cried when she saw it was dead. She wouldn't hurt the baby. It was stillborn. I'm a witness. I put it in the corner and covered it with a box. We wouldn't throw it in a Dumpster or anything like that. They were gonna come back and take care of the body like responsible citizens."

"We gotta corroborate everything you told us and we'll need you to help us do it," Charlie Gilford said.

That was Gert's cue, and she headed out to the front street to get their car and drive it around to the parking lot so they didn't have to walk so far with the fat drunk.

"Just find the two women," Charlie Gilford said to Gil Ponce. "Bring them to the station and we'll let the Homicide team decide how they wanna handle all this."

Gil said, "If the women don't wanna come, do we place them under arrest?"

"Absolutely," Charlie Gilford said. "We got a dead baby. This is a crime scene until somebody tells us different."

"Nobody committed a crime," the fat man said, reeling again and grabbing the corner of the concrete wall. "Ruthie woulda been a fine mother."

Charlie Gilford said, "Yeah, well, that's heartwarming, but I doubt that our Crows will wanna share this tearjerker the next time they meet the folks from the Restore Hollywood project."

And while Charlie Gilford was dialing the Homicide D3 again to tell her about the new developments, and Gil Ponce was watching the detective, eager to ask more questions about his further duties, nobody was watching Livingston

G. Kenmore. He just couldn't stay upright any longer. He staggered a few steps over to the darkened stairwell and saw a pad of some kind on the third step and sat down on it.

"Holy shit!" Gil Ponce yelled. "Get up! Get up! Get the fuck up!"

It all happened just as the D3 on the other end of the line said to Charlie, "Is there any obvious trauma to the dead baby?"

"Oh, yeah," said Compassionate Charlie Gilford after turning toward the commotion. "There is now."

★ NINE ★

THE CROWS HAD a recurring problem and it had to do with the Nightclub Committee's complaints about hot dog vendors. The prior evening, the vice unit, working in concert with the Crows and night-watch patrol, initiated Operation Hot Dog.

The night-watch and midwatch patrol officers had been too busy and too short staffed to deal with the vendors, and things had gotten out of hand. On Hollywood and Sunset Boulevards, where so many nightclubs were springing up — clubs whose purported ownership changed nearly as often as the tablecloths — Latino hot dog vendors were setting up carts to catch nightclub customers coming and going during the wee hours. On the night of Operation Hot Dog, there had been more than fifty vendors cited for illegal sidewalk sales, and their carts had been impounded. Now the station parking lot was jammed with carts and rotting hot dogs, and everyone was wondering if the "wienie sweep" had been a bit overzealous.

Ronnie got relieved of any responsibilities for Operation Hot Dog when she and Bix Ramstead were asked to meet 6-A-97 in Southeast Hollywood. The Crow who usually took care of calls in that neighborhood was on a short leave due to a death in his wife's family. There were not many black residents living in Hollywood Division, and the absent Crow, a black officer, had established rapport with some of them.

Six-A-97 had responded to a complaint regarding shopping carts, five of them, that were lying around a wood-frame cottage rented to a Somalian couple. When Ronnie and Bix arrived, the older of the two waiting cops nodded to Bix Ramstead.

"We're not trying to kiss this one off," he said, "but you Crows deal with chronic-noise complaints and quality-of-life shit, right?"

"And 'quality-of-life' covers a lot of territory," Bix said wearily. "What's the deal?"

The cop said, "The woman who called us says the people who live in that little house are from Somalia and the husband doesn't like black people, so she can't talk to them."

"Somalians *are* black people," Bix said.

"Yeah, but he doesn't like American black people. So she wants us to talk to the guy and tell him that in this country, you can't just walk off the market parking lot with shopping carts. In fact, she says the Somalian even jacked a cart from her teenage son when he tried to take it back to the market. She says the guy just doesn't get it about shopping carts."

"So did you try talking to the guy?" Ronnie asked.

"He won't answer," the cop said, "but the woman swears he's in there. Can you take over? We got some real crime to crush."

There it was, Ronnie thought. They were real cops, the Crows were something other.

"Okay," Bix said. "What's her name?"

"Mrs. Farnsworth." The cop was obviously happy to dump this one on the Crows, since patrol officers believed that Crows never did a day's work anyway.

Mrs. Farnsworth was a stout woman with straightened gray hair combed in a Condi Rice flip. Her bungalow, across the street from the Somalians', had a geranium garden in front and was freshly painted. She invited the cops in and asked if they'd like a cold drink, but they declined.

"I'd like to handle this my own self," she told them, "but that Somali man is mean. He has a big scar down the side of his face and he never smiles. His wife is very sweet. I talk to her when she passes on the way to the market. She's about twenty years younger than him, maybe more. And she left him once. I didn't see her for maybe three weeks and I don't know where she went. Then a week ago she came back."

"We'll have the shopping carts picked up," Bix said. "Any idea why he keeps taking different ones?"

"I think he's plain crazy," she said. "I tried to ask him to turn down his music one night and he screamed at me. Called me a nigger. I said, 'Whadda you think *you* are?' He didn't answer."

"Anything else you can tell us about him? Something that makes you think he's crazy?"

"I talked to his wife a couple times when he had a big party with some Somali friends on New Year's. She said they just chew something called *kaat* and eat their spicy food and gamble all the time. Every one of them has their birthday on New Year's, that's why their party lasted for three days."

"Why New Year's?" Ronnie asked.

"They're so damn backwards, they don't know when they were born. They just pick any year they want for the immigration papers, and make the birthday fall on New Year's so it's easy to remember. That's what she told me. They're that ignorant. And he has the gall to call *me* a nigger."

"What's his name?" Ronnie asked.

"Omar," Mrs. Farnsworth said. "I found out they're all named Omar, or Muhammad. I don't know his last name."

"Are you sure he's home now?" Bix asked.

"He sure is," she said. "And she is too. That damn music was blaring an hour ago and then it went off and he ain't left the house. I been watching it. He just don't wanna talk to the police, is all."

"We'll knock and see if he'll open the door," Bix said. "And we'll call the store and get the carts picked up."

"I can tell you this," Mrs. Farnsworth said. "His wife is scared of him. You can see that. I'm surprised she come back to him, but maybe she just didn't have no money and nowhere else to go."

They crossed the street and Ronnie knocked at the door of the cottage while Bix stood to the side, trying to peek into the window through a rip in what looked to be muslin curtains. No answer.

She knocked louder and said, "Police officers. Open the door, please."

They could clearly hear some movement inside and then an accented voice said, "What do you want?"

"We just need to speak to you for a minute," Ronnie said.

The door opened, and a tall, very dark man with the chiseled facial structure often seen in the Horn of Africa stood in the doorway. He wore only black trousers and tennis shoes, and he was unmistakable by virtue of the pale scar running from his hairline down the right side of his jaw to his throat. His irises were gun-metal blue.

Ronnie said, "We've received complaints about loud music and about the shopping carts in your yard. Do you know it's against the law to take shopping carts home from the market? That's theft."

"I will take them back," he said with a rumbling voice from deep inside him.

"What's your name?" Ronnie asked.

"Omar," he said.

"And your last name?"

"Omar Hasan Benawi," he said.

"Why do you take so many carts, Mr. Benawi?" Bix asked.

The man stared at both cops for a moment and said, "If they steal one cart I have more."

"If who steals one cart?" Bix asked.

"Them," he said.

"Who?" Ronnie asked. "Neighbors?"

"Them," he said without elaborating but looking off vaguely in the distance with those gunmetal eyes.

"Is your wife home?" Bix asked.

"Yes," he said.

Ronnie said, "Let us see her. Now, please."

The Somalian turned and mumbled something, and a bony young woman wearing a maroon head scarf, pink cotton dress, and sandals came to the door. She wasn't as dark as her husband, but like him, she had sharply defined features, and large, velvety eyes.

"Do you speak English?" Ronnie asked.

She nodded, glancing up at her scowling husband.

"Did you hear what we said to your husband?"

"Yes," she said. "I hear."

"Do you understand that you cannot play loud music at night and that you cannot take shopping carts home from the market?"

"Yes," she said, looking at her husband again.

"Are you all right?" Bix Ramstead asked.

"Yes," she said.

"I'd like to talk to you about the shopping carts. Can you step outside, please?" Ronnie said.

The young woman looked at her husband, who hesitated and then nodded. His wife walked onto the porch and followed Ronnie to the front yard, where Ronnie put an overturned cart upright.

Then in a quiet voice, while Bix kept the husband busy by getting names, phone number, and other information, Ronnie said, "Is there something wrong with your husband?" Ronnie pointed to her head and said, "Here?"

The young woman glanced back at the house and said, "No."

"What is your name?" Ronnie asked.

"Safia," the young woman said.

"Don't be afraid to tell me the truth, Safia," Ronnie said. "Has he hurt you in any way? If he has, we can take you to a shelter, where you'll be safe."

"No, I am fine," Safia said.

"And your husband," Ronnie said. "Is he fine? Up here?" And she pointed to her head again.

"He is fine," Safia said, eyes downcast.

"Does he have a job?" Ronnie asked.

"No, not now," Safia said. "He look for job. I look for job also. I clean houses."

"How old are you?" Ronnie asked.

"Twenty-one," she said. "I think."

"Do you really want to stay with your husband?" Ronnie asked. "Is he kind to you?"

"I stay," the young woman said, looking at Ronnie now. "My father give me to Omar. I stay."

Bix left the Somalian on the porch and approached Ronnie and Safia then, saying quietly, "You do not have to stay with him."

Speaking slowly and articulating carefully, Ronnie said, "This is America and you are a free woman. Would you like to get your clothes and leave with us? There are people who can help you."

"No, no!" the young woman said emphatically. "I stay."

Ronnie pressed a business card into the young woman's hand and said, "Call if you need help. Okay?"

The young woman hid the card in her sleeve and nodded.

Bix Ramstead went back to see Mrs. Farnsworth and gave her one of his business cards, writing his personal cell-phone number on the back of it. "If you suspect anything really bad is going on over there, I want you to call me. I can be reached at this number anytime."

And that's how it was left. Bix and Ronnie stopped by the market two blocks away and notified the kid who picked up shopping carts abandoned in the neighborhood that there was a jackpot in Omar's yard. They went about their business, hoping it was the last they'd hear of Omar Hasan Benawi.

Half an hour later, while driving to Hollywood South, Bix Ramstead said, "I have a very bad feeling about that Somali couple."

"So do I," Ronnie said.

Los Angeles experienced a rare summertime thunderstorm at twilight. The rain came down hard for twenty minutes and then it stopped, and a gigantic rainbow appeared over the Hollywood Hills. It was a magic moment, residents said. And the rain led to an incredible moment that would be remembered in LAPD folklore for years to come. It occurred moments after the midwatch hit the streets, and the surfer cops were there to see it.

The Gang Impact Team, called GIT, had made arrangements with the watch commander to use two of the midwatch cars and two from the night watch on a surprise sweep of the 18th Street gang. GIT had the highest felony filing rate at Hollywood Detectives and loved to jam the street gangsters, but morale had been suffering ever since the U.S. district judge overseeing the federal consent decree wanted all six hundred LAPD officers assigned to gang and narcotics units to disclose their personal financial records as part of the anti-corruption crusade. However, since that information could be subpoenaed, a cop's bank account information, Social Security number, and much else could end up in the hands of lawyers for street gangsters. Cops were threatening to quit their present assignments rather than let that happen, and their union, the L.A. Police Protective League, was waging a battle on their behalf. It was another of many oppressive, paper-intensive skirmishes during the dreary years of the federal consent decree.

The information that GIT had was that the 18th Street crew were going to cruise south in their lowriders into Southeast L.A. to help other Hispanic gang members mete out street justice to some black gangsters who were suspected of shooting a Latino. More than half of the Los Angeles homicides in the prior calendar year were gang related. The informant indicated that the 18th Street homeboys would be waiting by a chain-link fence next to an apartment house in Southeast Hollywood, where most of them lived. When the cops arrived, eleven of the cruisers were perched on the top of the fence or leaning on the portion that was pulled from the posts and rolled in a tangle of steel wire.

At a prearranged signal on the police tactical frequency, the patrol units swooped in, led by two teams of Hollywood gang cops.

None of the homies had seemed particularly disturbed and nobody ran. Several who were smoking cigarettes continued smoking. Nobody tried to toss any crystal or crack. They kept chatting among themselves as though the cops were putting on a good show for their benefit. The crew were not proned out on the ground due to the deep rain puddles that had formed under and around the fence, so the usual commands were modified:

"Turn and face the fence!"

"Interlock your fingers behind your head!"

"Do not move or talk!"

Then the cops began patting down each homie and pulling them aside to write FI cards. The gang cops took various members of the crew to their cars for more private conversations, but all in all it was a disappointment. The consensus was that the information had somehow leaked and the crew were expecting to be jacked up. The gang cops were mad and embarrassed.

During the first twenty minutes of the episode, when a few of the crew were copping attitudes, a cruiser dressed homie-hip in a baggy tee and khakis — with the usual face tatts consisting of spiderwebs and teardrops — turned to his crew and grinned, proudly displaying two gold caps. Like several of the others, he wore a red-and-white bandana around his shaved head.

He said, "Yo, this ain't right," to one of the Hispanic gang cops who'd arrested him in the past.

"What ain't right, *ese?*" the gang cop said.

"We're just hangin', man. Ain't no law being broke around here."

"Homes, I would never accuse you of law breaking," the gang cop said.

The cruisers were all grinning at one another, and the gang cops became more certain that somehow they had anticipated this sweep.

Flotsam wasn't the least bit surprised and said to Jetsam, "Dude, have you ever heard of a cop keeping a secret?"

"Might as well give it to *Access Hollywood*," Jetsam agreed. "You want it out there? Telephone, telegram, tell-a-cop."

The surfer cops were waiting for the gang

unit to give them the okay to clear, when a motor cop pulled up. He wasn't just any motor cop. He was Officer Francis Xavier Mulroney, a hulking, craggy, old-school veteran who still wore reflector aviator sunglasses and black leather gloves. He had thirty-seven years on the LAPD, thirty of it riding a motorcycle. He was usually assigned to the Hollywood beat, where his nickname "F.X." seemed wildly appropriate. He stepped off his bike and walked through the standing puddles, boots splashing any cops who didn't get out of his way.

With his helmet and those boots and his paunch and those glasses, he looked to Jetsam like the guy that played General Patton in that old World War II movie. In fact, he even sounded like the guy, kind of gravelly.

What's this cluster fuck all about?" he said to the nearest of the two Hispanic gang cops.

The gang cop shrugged and said, "Nothin' much, looks like."

Then the motor cop said, "Why ain't these *vatos* facedown in the fucking water instead of standing around giggling like girls? What, you don't prone out these hanky heads when it's rained?"

The gang cop smiled agreeably and said, "Roger that message, F.X. I wish we could still do things like back in the day."

Referring to the May 1 immigration rally in MacArthur Park, which got negative national attention when the LAPD used force on demonstrators and reporters, F.X. Mulroney sneered and said, "This is May Day all over again. Like, oh, dear me, let's not rough people up. Shit! Sister Mary Ignatius tuned us up worse than that when I was in the third fucking grade!"

"Roger that," the gang cop said patiently.

The motor cop said, "When I came on the Job, we were taught, 'When in doubt, choke 'em out.' This is why when I retire next year, I'm driving my bike onto the freight elevator at Parker Center and I'm running it right up to the sixth floor and leaving it in front of the door to the chief's office. With a sign addressed to all LAPD brass, the police commission, and the mayor. A sign that says, 'Put this crotch rocket between your legs. You got nothing else there.' That's what I'm gonna do."

Clearly, nobody doubted him. Then one of the cops from the night watch turned toward his car to stow his beanbag shotgun.

The old motor cop snorted and said, "Beanbags. When I came on the Job, beanbags were used by little kids to throw at cutout clowns. That's what they've turned LAPD into, a bunch of clowns!"

"Roger that too," the gang cop said with a sigh. "We hear you, F.X. Loud and clear."

Now the other cops were even more eager to get away from there, what with F.X. Mulroney on the scene. But the homeboys perched on the fence or leaning against it were giving the old motor cop the stink eye. A few of them actually laughed at him. And then a big mistake was made.

The homie with the gold teeth said in a stage whisper to one of his crew, loud enough for F.X. to hear, "He's so old they should have training wheels on his baby hog."

All of the 18th Street cruisers chortled at that one.

The motor cop took three big strides in those black, shiny boots toward the night-watch cop standing by the open trunk of his shop, where he was putting away his beanbag gun.

"Lemme borrow this for a minute," F.X. said, and he pulled the cop's Taser from his Sam Browne.

"Hey!" the cop said. "Whadda you think you're doing?"

"We only got those bulky old piece-of-shit Tasers in our saddlebags. This is the new one, ain't it?"

"What're you doing?" the cop repeated.

The old motor cop showed the young night-watch cop what he was doing.

"Homes," the motor cop said to the banger with the gold teeth, and to all the other food-stamp homeboys in their $200 Adidas, "don't ever keep an electric appliance around your bathtub. And don't *ever* stand in a rain puddle and lean on a chain-link fence. A bolt from heaven could strike."

And he fired a dart that was attached to the gun by a twenty-one-foot copper wire, right into the tangle of fencing.

When the prongs bit and hooked onto the wet steel, fifty thousand volts made a crackling sound and arced a blue dagger like in Frankenstein's lab. And the cops watched in astonishment as the homies started doing the Taser dance.

Two dropped off the fence and three fence leaners fell ass-first in the rain puddles. The rest leaped clear after experiencing shocks, mostly imagined, and everyone began screaming and cursing.

"He fucking electrocuted me!"

"I'm suing!"

"All you cops are witnesses!"

"I got a burn on my ass!"

And F.X. Mulroney joined in the chorus, crying out, "But I was only doing a spark check! Shit happens!"

"*Pinchi* cop!" Gold Tooth yelled. "He shocked us! You saw it!"

"My lawyer!" a homie yelled. "I'm calling my lawyer!"

Flotsam and Jetsam stared as Officer Francis X. Mulroney spread his arms wide, looked up at the darkening sky, and cried, "God knows I'm innocent! Even Bill Clinton had a premature discharge!"

"I'm fucking suing!" Gold Tooth yelled.

F.X. Mulroney bowed his head then and murmured, "Oh, the horror. The horror!"

Flotsam whispered to Jetsam, "F.X. always goes over the top. He's, like, way dramatic."

Jetsam whispered back, "In Hollywood everybody's an actor."

All the drama caused Flotsam and Jetsam to walk quietly to their shop, start the engine, and drive away before anyone noticed they were gone.

Most of the other bluesuits were doing the same, and the gang cop pulled Gold Tooth aside and said, "Homes, I think you better forget all about this . . . accident."

"Accident, my ass!" the homie said.

The gang cop said, "Can you imagine what'll happen if this story gets out? That crazy old motor cop can retire anytime. You can't hurt him. But everybody'll be laughing like hyenas. At you, dude. At your whole posse. MS Thirteen will laugh. White Fence will laugh. *El Eme* will laugh. All the Crips and Bloods from Southeast L.A. that done your people wrong, they'll laugh the loudest. You'll hear fucking laughter in your sleep!"

Gold Tooth thought it over and huddled with his crew for a minute or two. When he returned, he said, "Okay, but we don't want nobody to know about this, right? All your cops gotta keep their mouths shut."

"If there's one thing cops can do, it's keep a secret," the gang cop said.

★ ★ ★

When they were two blocks from the scene, Flotsam said, "Dude, do you realize we were a witness to Hollywood history being made? That old copper just brought down a whole crew with one fucking shot!"

"We didn't see nothing, bro," Jetsam said. "We were already gone when history was being made." After a pause, he said, "When he's ready to pull the pin, do you think that loony old motor cop will really, like, drive his bike up to the chief's office and leave it there with a sign on it?"

"What motor cop?" Flotsam replied.

★ TEN ★

IT WORRIED RONNIE SINCLAIR that her partner, Bix Ramstead, was so troubled by the encounter with the Somalians. They were at Starbucks on Sunset Boulevard, both doing some paperwork before going end-of-watch. Bix, never garrulous, had been unusually quiet all day.

The third time he brought it up he said, "Sometimes I think being a copper turns you into an animal in more ways than one. The hair on my neck hasn't settled down since we first laid eyes on that scar-faced Somali. That guy's fifty-one-fifty, for sure."

"He's way out there, no doubt," Ronnie said, "but what could we do about it? There was no evidence of violent behavior. I gave her every chance to walk outta there and she flat-out refused. What could we do?"

"Nothing, I suppose," Bix said. "But wasn't

your blue radar blinking? That dude's gonna hurt that girl."

"He's probably hurt her already," Ronnie said. "Lots and lots of times. He owns her, according to their customs. You know we couldn't pick her up and bundle her out on the basis of blue radar, Bix."

"Of course," he said, "but it still bothers me."

"The way I look at stuff like that is, it's not my tragedy. I have to see it, but I don't have to take it home with me. I let it go."

"My wife's told me that for years," Bix said. "That's one of the reasons I got into CRO. Her telling me I was bringing too much shit home with me for too many years."

"She was right," Ronnie said, thinking that every once in a while she'd run into a cop like Bix Ramstead, someone who didn't have the right temperament for the Job. Somebody who couldn't let it go.

He suddenly looked a bit embarrassed, as cops do when they indulge in uncoplike self-revelatory talk. He turned the conversation to her. "You ever gonna get married again, you think?"

"I'm not in the market," Ronnie said. "I've proven to be a bad shopper. Besides, I'm concentrating on passing the sergeant's exam. But if I ever get married again, it will *not* be to another cop."

Bix smiled and said, "Smart girl."

And Ronnie thought, If you weren't already bought and paid for, buddy, I might make an exception. She was surprised by how much she liked Bix. Those sensitive, dusky gray eyes of his could make a girl's knees tremble.

She said, "Will you be staying on the Job until the bitter end?"

"Until I'm fifty-five, at least," he said. "I've got a couple of teenagers who'll have to get through college, and my daughter is talking about becoming a physician. I won't be retiring anytime soon, that's for sure."

Ronnie almost suggested that he might consider an inside job somewhere, one that would keep him from the likes of Omar Hasan Benawi and his pitiful wife, but she thought she shouldn't be offering career advice to a veteran like Bix. Besides, the Community Relations Office was the next best thing to an inside job.

How much real police work would they ever have to do as Crows?

She said, "A couple of us are heading up to Sunset after work for a few tacos and a tequila or two. Wanna come?"

Bix hesitated, but he obviously trusted Ronnie and could confide in her in ways he might not to a male officer. He said, "I'd better not join you. I have a bit of a problem."

"Problem?"

"I haven't had a drink for almost a month, and I'm reluctant to go places where everyone else is powering them down."

"Sorry, I didn't know," Ronnie said.

"It's nothing major," Bix said. "I've been dealing with it for years. On the wagon, off the wagon. I deal with it."

"I hear you," Ronnie said. "My first ex was an alcoholic in denial. Still is."

"I'm not an alcoholic," Bix said quickly. "I just don't handle booze very well. When I drink, my personality changes. My wife, Darcey, put me on notice last month when I came home hammered, and I'm grateful she did. I feel a lot better now. Getting too old for that nonsense."

Ronnie didn't know what else to say, and Bix obviously thought he'd said too much. They finished their cappuccinos and their reports silently.

Hollywood Nate Weiss could not wait to log out at 7:30 P.M. He'd changed from his uniform into a pricey white linen shirt, and black jeans from Nordstrom's. He'd thought about really dressing up but figured it might make him look like some schmuck who'd never had a private supper at the home of some flaming hot, bucks-up chick in the Hollywood Hills. Which was the case exactly.

While driving to Mt. Olympus he thought of half a dozen opening remarks he could say to her, but rehearsing aloud made them sound dumber than they did in his mind. He almost parked on the street in front but decided that as a guest he was entitled to pull into the bricked motor court. The lot was quite expansive for a view site in the hills, where land was scarce, and the motor court was large enough for an easy U-turn. The house itself was deceivingly large, with a Spanish-tile roof, white plaster walls, exposed beams, and lots of arches, a style that realtors liked to call "early California." A cinch to sell, especially to non-Californians who found it romantic.

Nate was very happy to see that there were no other cars in the motor court. He'd been worried that the babysitter might have decided to stay with the kid at Margot's house. Or that maybe Margot had invited somebody else to her pasta supper. He attempted to stay calm, trying on the affable but poised mini-smile he'd used successfully in his last piece-of-shit movie, and rang the bell.

Margot showed him that dazzling smile when she opened the door. She too was wearing jeans, low-cut designer jeans, and a yellow tee that stopped six inches before the jeans began. His eyes went from her eyes directly to that tan, muscular belly. She'd pulled back her heavy butterscotch hair and pinned it with a tortoiseshell comb.

Extending her warm, dry hand, she took his and said, "Officer Weiss. You look so different in civilian clothes."

"The uniform makes the man, huh?" He tried to keep the tremble out of his voice, needing one drink to mellow out.

Seeming to read his mind, she said, "What can I get you to drink? And to answer your question, you don't need a uniform. In fact, you look much younger now."

Nate tried on a broader smile and said, "Wine?"

"Name your flavor."

"Whatever you're having."

"Pinot grigio it is," she said. "I'm not a wine snob. Just give me an honest California pinot and I'm happy as a lark in the park. Come in and pour while I finish the pasta."

Nate entered and was drawn at once to the living room, with its view of Hollywood and beyond. Blankets of lights, some twinkling, some still, and the summer smog hanging low and dark against the golden glow of sunset actually calmed him. The view wasn't as good as some he'd seen from houses in the Hollywood Hills farther west, but this would do. He couldn't imagine how many millions a home with a view would cost around there.

As far as the furnishings, it looked a trifle overdone, like many of the westside living rooms he'd seen in *Los Angeles* magazine and the *L.A. Times.* An unpleasant image of the Arab ex sitting on one of those plush sofas smoking a hookah flashed and faded. Nothing could spoil it for him. It all smelled like big bucks to Hollywood Nate Weiss.

"You know," he said, "from here even the smog looks beautiful."

Margot chuckled and he thought it sounded charming and warm. Everything about her was warm.

She said, "Come on, boy, let's away with us to the kitchen, where you can pour us some grape. I need to let my hair down whenever my five-year-old stays over with our au pair."

Nate followed her into a very large gourmet kitchen with two stainless-steel side-by-side refrigerator-freezer combinations and a commercial gas range and oven, also done in stainless steel. There were three steel sinks, and he wondered which she'd choose when she drained a pan of pasta. Too many choices!

He picked up the corkscrew and the bottle of pinot grigio and tried to peel off the neck seal and extract the cork like he'd seen sommeliers do it on those occasions when he could afford to take a date to an expensive restaurant. He had some trouble with the cork, but she didn't seem to notice.

"Have you been a police officer long, Nate?" she asked.

"Yeah, almost fifteen years," he said.

"Really?" Margot said. "You don't look old enough."

"I'm thirty-six," he said. Then he added, "You don't look old enough to have a five-year-old child."

"I could have one a lot older, but I'm *not* telling you my age," she said.

"I already know," Nate said. "Your driver's license, remember?"

"Drat!" she said. "I forgot."

Nate poured wine into the glasses and put one on the drain board by Margot.

"Does your son stay with your nanny often?" Nate asked.

"Only on very special occasions," Margot said, and there was that coy smile again.

He took a big swallow then but told himself to slow it down, way down. He began thinking of acting tricks, such as pretending that this was a movie starring Nate Weiss. Trying to get himself into character but uncertain whom the character should resemble. Hollywood Nate Weiss simply had no frame of reference for a date like this one.

"So are you really interested in the Mercedes?" Margot said.

"Of course," Nate said nervously. "Why else would I have called?"

She stopped slicing the mango. Repressing a grin, she glanced at him before saying deadpan, "I can't imagine."

Nate felt his face burning. He *was* like a kid around this woman! "Am I lame or what?" he finally said. "Sure, I love the Mercedes, but I just bought a new car last year. You should kick me right outta here."

Margot brought the wine bottle to the bar counter, topped off his glass, and said with sudden seriousness, "I was glad you called, Nate."

"Really?"

"Really," she said. "To tell you the truth, I've been frightened about something and I was thinking about talking to the police."

"Frightened of what?"

"Let's have supper and then we'll talk," Margot said.

★ ★ ★

Gert Von Braun was teamed with Dan Apple-white for the first time after he returned from his days off. The other cops figured that putting Doomsday Dan with someone as explosive as Gert would produce a match made in hell. The surfer cops had bets on how long Gert could listen to Dan talking about the worldwide Muslim calamity on the horizon, or the imminent collapse of the world financial markets, before she threw a choke hold on him. What they didn't know was how much Dan and Gert's mutual loathing of Sergeant Treakle would produce a bond that nobody could have predicted.

It began when Sergeant Treakle informed Gert that the accidental discharge of the shotgun was going to result in an official reprimand for certain, the first in her eleven-year career. She was ready for it, of course, but not in the way the information was delivered.

Sergeant Treakle, who rarely bothered to learn any cop's first name, called her into the sergeants' room and said, "Von Braun, you will be getting an official reprimand for your carelessness with the shotgun."

"I figured," Gert said and prepared to leave.

"Furthermore," he said, and she paused at the doorway, "it will result in a serious penalty if such a thing should ever happen again."

Gert's rosy complexion went white around her mouth and she said, "You think it's ever gonna happen again, Sergeant?"

"I'm just giving you a word to the wise," the young sergeant said, looking away nervously. Gert's collar size was larger than his, and it was rumored that she had embarrassed a male cop at Central Division when he'd boozily arm wrestled her at the Christmas party.

She forced herself to stay calm and said, "Thanks for the words of wisdom." And again she tried to leave.

But Sergeant Treakle said, "Part of the problem could be your physical condition."

That stopped her cold. In fact, she took a step toward his desk and said, "What about my physical condition?"

"Your weight," he said. "It must be hard to move around quickly enough when something unexpected happens. Like your cell phone falling and you trying to grab it, and accidentally hitting the shotgun trigger. Police officers must be ready to think and act quickly. Like athletes, as it were."

Gert dead-stared Sergeant Treakle for a moment and then said very softly, "I've passed every physical since I came on the Job. And I was first in the agility test for women in the academy. And I've competed twice in the Police Olympics. Now I have a question for you. Have you ever heard of EEO laws?"

"Equal Employment Opportunity?"

"That's right, Sergeant," she said. "It's all about discrimination in the workplace. And I'm giving you a gift right now by forgetting about this conversation. Because you're *offending* me in a very personal way."

Sergeant Treakle blanched and said, "We'll talk later. I've got some calls to make."

By the time Gert Von Braun joined Dan Applewhite in the parking lot, the grim set of her jaw told him that it wasn't the time to tell her that staph infections had stricken several officers in neighboring divisions and an outbreak was imminent.

She drove in silence for five minutes, and

when she spoke, she said, "Have you had any personal dealings with Treakle?"

"Once," Dan Applewhite said. "He told me I had a sour expression when talking to citizens and that my attitude needed improving. He said he was sure I could improve my outlook on life by attending Bible study with him. He's a born-again and got baptized in a pond somewhere, with people singing on the bank."

"He told you that?"

Dan Applewhite nodded. "I told him I'm a Unitarian. I could tell he didn't know what that was."

"Neither do I," Gert said, then added, "we had a sergeant like him at Central Station. Things started happening to that guy."

"What kind of things?"

"Mostly to his car. If he forgot to lock it, he'd find a string tied from his light-bar switch to the door. Or he'd find the plastic cord-cuffs hanging from his axle making noise while he was driving. Or he'd find talcum powder in his air vent. It'd make his uniform look like he was caught in a blizzard."

"That's kid stuff," Dan Applewhite said.

"Once when a truck got jacked that was hauling huge bags of popcorn and candy to a chamber of commerce holiday party, we recovered it and somebody filled the sergeant's private car with popcorn. I mean from the floor to the roofline. You looked inside his windshield and all you could see was popcorn."

"That's kid stuff," Dan Applewhite repeated.

Gert said, "Then one night somebody paid a skid row derelict ten bucks to do some asphalt skiing. The cop who did it borrowed an old piece of plywood roofing from one of the makeshift lean-tos where the transients sleep. And tied a piece of rope to it and attached the rope to the sergeant's car while he was inside a diner. And the derelict was promised another ten if he'd hang on for a whole block. He did, but it was pretty gnarly. Sparks were flying and the derelict started yelling and it pretty much all went sideways. People on the street were shocked, and the captain's phone rang off the hook the next day. IA investigated the night watch for a month but never caught the culprit. All the derelict would say was, the guy who hired him was a cop and all cops look alike when they're in uniform. The sergeant got ten days off for not looking after his car."

"Well, that's not childish," Dan Applewhite said. "It's much more mature when you can get an asshole like that a ten-day suspension."

It was less than a half hour later that Sergeant Treakle himself rolled on a call assigned to 6-X-66. Dan Applewhite groaned when he turned and saw the young supervisor pull up in front of an apartment building in Thai Town that was occupied mostly by Asian immigrants.

"Chickenlips is here to check on us," he warned Gert, who was knocking at the door.

The caller was a Thai woman who looked too old to have a twelve-year-old daughter but did. The girl was crying when the cops arrived, and the mother was furious. The girl's auntie, who was a decade younger than the mother, had been trying to calm things. The auntie spoke passable English and translated for the mother.

The trouble had started earlier in the day when the local clinic informed the mother that her twelve-year-old daughter's bouts of vomiting were the result of an early pregnancy. The mother wanted the culprit found and arrested.

Of course, the cops separated the kid from her mom, Gert walking the child into a tidy bedroom, talking to her gently, saying, "Wipe your eyes, honey. And don't be afraid."

The child, who was all cheekbones and kewpie lips, had lived in L.A. since she was eight, and her English was good. She stopped sobbing long enough to say to Gert, "Will I be taken to juvenile hall?"

"You won't be taken anywhere, sweetie," Gert said. "All of this can be handled. But we must find out who put the baby in you."

The child dropped her eyes and asked, "Am I in trouble?" Then she began sobbing again.

"Now, now," Gert said. "There's no need to do that. You're not in trouble with us. We're your friends." Then sensing someone behind her, she turned and saw Sergeant Treakle standing there watching.

Gert tried but failed to suppress the sigh that popped out of her, then said to the sergeant, "I wonder if you'd mind letting us females talk about this in private."

Sergeant Treakle arched an eyebrow, grunted, and returned to the kitchen, where Dan Applewhite was getting a list of potential suspects for the follow-up by detectives. The child had no siblings, but there were uncles, cousins, and neighbors who were possibles.

Sergeant Treakle looked at his watch a couple of times, and when Gert left the girl in the bedroom and came back to the kitchen, he said, "Who's the daddy?"

"I don't know," Gert said. "The sex crimes team will have to talk to her."

"All that time and you don't know?" Sergeant Treakle said.

Her voice flat as a razor, Gert said, "The child says she doesn't know how it happened."

Sergeant Treakle guffawed loudly and said, "She doesn't *know?*"

Knowing his religious views, Gert Von Braun said, "Tell me, Sergeant Treakle, what if the young girl's name was Mary? And the baby inside her was gonna be named Jesus, would you still scoff? After all, Mary didn't know how the hell it happened either. *Did* she now?"

The sergeant's jaws opened and shut twice, but nothing came out. He started to say something to Dan Applewhite, but nothing happened there either. He left the apartment and hurried to his car to make a negative entry in his log.

When they got back to their shop and started driving, Dan Applewhite took a good look at Gert Von Braun. He was a lot older and knew he wasn't much to look at. And he couldn't seem to keep a wife for very long, no matter how much money he spent on her. But he was starting to develop feelings he hadn't had for a while. Despite her bulk and scary reputation, Gert Von Braun was starting to grow very attractive.

"What say we stop at Starbucks, Gert?" he said impulsively, then added something that usually interested other female partners. "I'd love to buy us a latte and biscotti."

Gert shrugged and said, "I'm not much for sissy coffee, but I wouldn't mind an In-N-Out burger."

And *zing* went the strings of his heart! He grinned big and said, "Okay! One In-N-Out burger coming up!"

"With grilled onions and double the fries," Gert added.

He was back at an ATM that night, a different one this time, on Hollywood Boulevard. Leonard Stilwell had worked diligently to set the film trap with the glue strips in place. He couldn't sit around his room waiting for the job with Ali. The advance that Ali had given him was gone, smoked up in his pipe and lost on those goddamn Dodgers after he was stupid enough to make a bet with a sports book who'd beaten him 90 percent of the time.

Despite his prior misgivings and fear of all the cops he'd seen around the Kodak Center, the area offered an irresistible attraction in the persons of all those doofus tourists. So after casing carefully, he'd decided that a certain one of the ATMs wasn't quite as dangerous as the others because it was in a dark corner and provided an easier escape route to the residential street several blocks away where he'd parked his old Honda. Now he was watching that ATM. Several Asians with cameras dangling from their necks almost bit. They'd be no good to him unless they spoke enough English to accept his "help."

The ATM customer who finally stopped was the one he wanted. The guy was at least seventy years old and so was his wife. He was carrying a bag from one of the boulevard souvenir shops and she was carrying another one. They wore walking shorts and tennis shoes and their baseball caps had pins all over them from Universal Studios' tour, Disneyland, and Knott's Berry Farm. Her brand new T-shirt said "Movies For Me" across the back. Just looking at them made him imagine the heavenly smoke filling his lungs.

The guy put his card into the slot but nothing happened. He punched in his PIN and looked at his wife. Then he looked around, presumably for help, just as a younger man with hair the color of an overripe pumpkin, a wash of freckles, and a howdy-folks smile walked to the machine, holding his own ATM card in his hand.

"Are you finished with your transaction, sir?" Leonard said.

"There's something wrong with the machine," the tourist said. "My card won't come out and the dang thing doesn't work."

"Golly," Leonard said, as syrupy as he could manage. "I've run into this before. Do you mind if I try something?"

"Help yourself, young man," the tourist said. "I sure don't wanna be calling my bank and canceling my card. Not when we just got to Hollywood."

"Don't blame you," Leonard said. "Let's see."

He stepped forward, put his fingers on the "enter" and "cancel" keys, and said, "Way it was explained to me is, you punch in your PIN number at the same time you hold down 'cancel' and 'enter,' and it should kick out the card. Wanna try it?"

"Sure," the tourist said. "Let's see, I hold down which two keys?"

"Here, lemme help," Leonard said. "I'll hold the two keys down and you just go ahead and punch in your PIN number."

"I'll hold down the keys," a deep voice behind Leonard said.

He turned and saw a guy his age. A tall, buffed-out guy looking him right in the eye. Leonard's Adam's apple bobbed.

"This is my son," the tourist said. "There's something wrong with the machine, Wendell. This fellow's helping us."

"That's nice of him," Wendell said but never took his stare from Leonard's watery blue eyes, not for an instant.

Leonard said, "Go ahead and punch in your PIN number." But he didn't dare look at the keyboard. In fact, he made it a point to look away.

"Nothing," the tourist said. "Not a goldang thing happened."

"Well, guess you'll have to cancel it," Leonard said. "It was worth a try. Sorry I couldn't help you."

As he was sidling away, he heard the woman say, "See, Wendell, there's lots of real nice, polite people in Hollywood."

Leonard felt like weeping by the time he'd walked several blocks to his car. He needed crack so bad he couldn't think of anything else. He wasn't even hungry, although he hadn't eaten a real meal for two days. And to make matters worse, there was a police car parked behind his car with its headlights on, and two cops were giving him a goddamn ticket!

"Is this your car?" Flotsam asked when Leonard approached, keys in hand.

"Yeah, what's wrong?" Leonard said.

"What's wrong?" Jetsam said. "Take a look where you're parked."

Leonard walked around to the front of the car and saw that he was halfway across a narrow concrete driveway belonging to an old two-story stucco house that was crammed between two newer apartment buildings. He hadn't noticed the driveway when he'd parked, not after he'd circled the streets for twenty minutes, looking for a parking place where he wouldn't get a goddamn ticket like this.

"Gimme a break!" Leonard said. "I'm between jobs. And even if I wasn't tapped, I couldn't give my ride to those goofy wetbacks at the pay lot. They'll back your car right up onto the fanny pack of the first tourist dumb enough to take a shortcut through the parking lot, and then what?"

"Too late," Flotsam said. "It's already written. Lucky you came back, though. The guy in that house wanted your car towed."

"No mercy," Leonard said. "There ain't a drop of mercy and compassion in this whole fucking town."

Jetsam had his flashlight beam close enough to Leonard's face to see the twitching and sweat. He raised the light to check Leonard's pupils and said, "Got some ID?"

"What for?" Leonard said. "I haven't done nothing."

"You drive this car," Jetsam said. "You have a driver's license, right?"

Leonard reached in his pocket for his wallet. "Not a drop of mercy or compassion for a fellow human being," Leonard said, taking the parking citation from Flotsam and handing Jetsam his driver's license.

Jetsam took the license and walked back to their shop and sat down inside it.

"Aw, shit," Leonard said. "What's he doing, calling in on me?"

"Just routine," Flotsam said, giving Leonard a quick pat-down.

"That's what they always say," Leonard whined. "Do you guys ever give a person a break? I mean ever?"

"Whadda you been arrested for?" Flotsam asked.

"You're gonna find out in a few minutes," Leonard said. "Couple of small-time thefts is all. I learned my lesson. I'm just a working stiff now. Between jobs."

When Jetsam came back, he said to his partner, "Mr. Stilwell here has two priors for burglary and one for petty theft."

"The burglaries were reduced to petty theft,"

Leonard said. "I pled guilty and I only got county jail time. The petty theft was for shoplifting when I had to steal some groceries for an elderly neighbor who was sick. Jesus! Can't a guy get a second chance?"

By then, both cops figured him for a crackhead or maybe a tweaker, and Flotsam said, "Mr. Stilwell, you wouldn't object if we took a look in your car, would you? Just routine, of course."

"Go ahead," Leonard said. "If I said no, you'd find an excuse to do it anyways."

"Are you saying no?" Jetsam said.

"I'm saying just do what the fuck you gotta do so I can go home. I give up. There ain't a drop of mercy and compassion and charity left in this whole fucking city. Here."

He pulled the keys from his pocket and tossed them to Jetsam, who opened the door and did a quick search for drugs in the glove box, under the seats and floor mats, and in other obvious places. All he saw was a note behind the visor with an address on it. He recognized the street as one on Mt. Olympus near the house where a multiple murder involving Russian gangsters had occurred. He jotted the address down in his notebook.

When he was finished, he nodded to Flotsam and said, "Okay, Mr. Stilwell, thanks for the cooperation."

By then Leonard was shaking his head in disgust, and when he got into his car, he was mumbling aloud about the merciless, pitiless, fucking city he lived in.

"Let's drive up to Mount Olympus for a minute," Jetsam said when they were back in their shop.

"What for?"

"That guy had an address behind his visor. What would a loser like that be doing up on Mount Olympus? Except casing a house, maybe."

"There you go again," Flotsam said. "Dude, you are determined to go all detective and sleuthy on my time. Maybe the guy's looking to become a gardener or something. Did you think of that?"

"He's the wrong color. Come on, bro, it'll just take a few minutes."

Flotsam headed for the Hollywood Hills without another word and, finding the winding street, followed it up to the top.

Jetsam checked addresses and said, "This number don't exist."

"Okay," Flotsam said. "You satisfied now?"

He turned around just as Jetsam spotted a familiar car in a driveway a few houses away from where the street address should have been.

"That's Hollywood Nate's ride!" he said.

"That Mustang?"

"Yeah."

"Dude, there's lots of Mustangs in this town."

Jetsam grabbed the spotlight and shined it on the car. "How many with a license plate that says SAG4NW?"

"What?"

"Screen Actors Guild for Nate Weiss. How many?"

"So?"

"Maybe we should stop and see if the resident knows a Leonard Stilwell."

"Look, dude," Flotsam said. "We already dragged Hollywood Nate into one of your wild goose chases. We ain't gonna interrupt whatever he's doing in there with another of your clues. And knowing him, whatever he's doing in there involves pussy, that much is totally for sure. So he is not gonna be happy to see us, no matter what."

"Bro, this could be something he should know about."

"It's the wrong goddamn address!" Flotsam said. "You can tell Nate all about it tomorrow. That thief we just shook ain't gonna be killing no residents on this street tonight. You good with that?"

"I guess I gotta be," Jetsam said.

"Tomorrow you can call Sleuths R Us if you get more brainstorms."

"Bro, do you think you could stop ripping on me about that?" Jetsam said. "So I made a mistake about the SUVs. Can't you just step off?"

Flotsam said, "I'm off it. Somebody's gotta prove there's a drop of mercy and compassion in this whole fucking city. Are we gravy, dude?"

"Gravy, bro," Jetsam said. "Long as you don't mention it again."

"I'm off it forever," Flotsam said. "And that's the truth, sleuth."

★ ELEVEN ★

OF COURSE, Hollywood Nate didn't know anything at all about the surfers' debate taking place out on the street in front of the Aziz home. He was sitting at the dining room table, sipping wine and looking into the amber eyes of Margot Aziz, who kept topping off his wineglass and trying to persuade him that she made the best martinis in Hollywood.

Finally he said, "I'm just not much of a martini guy. The wine is great and the pasta and salad were sensational."

"Just a simple four-cheese noodle," she said. "Your mom called it macaroni and cheese."

"I should help you with the dishes," he said. "I'm good at it. My ex-wife was dishwashing obsessive and turned me into a kitchen slave."

"No dishes for us, boyo," she said. "My housekeeper will be here in the morning, and she gets mad when there's not something extra for her to do." Then she said, "Did you have kids with your ex?"

"That was the one good thing about my marriage. No kids."

"Can be good or bad," she said. "Nicky is the only good thing about my marriage, which will soon be officially over, praise the lord."

Nate looked around and said, "Will you get to keep this house?"

"We're selling it," she said. "Which is sad. This is the only home Nicky's ever known. Did your wife get to keep your house?"

"It was an apartment," Nate said. "More or less a pots 'n' pans divorce. She came out of it way better than I did. Married a doctor and now lives the way a Jewish princess was meant to live. Her father hated it when she married a cop. She shoulda listened to him. I shoulda listened to him."

Margot said, "My Nicky is five years old and deserves to keep the lifestyle he's always had."

"Sure," Nate said. "Of course."

"I worry a lot about him, and that's part of what I need to talk to you about."

"Okay," Nate said. "I'm listening."

"I've become afraid of his father." Then she

stopped, took another sip of wine, and said, "Sure you won't have a martini? I've just gotta have one when I talk about my husband, Ali Aziz."

"No, really," Nate said. "You go ahead."

Margot Aziz got up and walked out of the dining room and into a butler's pantry, then to the kitchen, where Nate could hear her scooping from an ice maker. He got up and joined her, watching her make the cocktail.

"I'm not a big-city girl," she said. "I'm from Barstow, California. Where desert teens spend Saturday night dining at the historic Del Taco fast-food joint and getting deflowered at the prehistoric El Rancho Motel. I dreamed of being an entertainer. Danced and sang at all the school assemblies and plays. I was Margaret Osborne then, voted the most talented girl in the senior class."

She was quiet for a moment, and when they reentered the dining room, she said, "A James Bond vodka martini. Shaken, not stirred. Can't I tempt you?"

"No, really, Margot, I'm feeling just perfect." He wondered if "tempt" was meant as a double entendre, hoping it was.

She tasted the martini, nodded in satisfaction, and said, "The problem was, when I came to Hollywood and started looking for an agent and attending cattle calls and auditions, I discovered that every girl here was the most talented girl in her school. Changing my name from Margaret to Margot didn't glam it up much." She gave a self-deprecating shrug.

"I suspected you were a dancer," Nate said. "Those legs."

"Since turning thirty I've gotta work harder to keep things in place." She sipped again, put the martini down, and said, "I wasn't born to all this. My dad worked for the post office, and it almost broke my parents to put my older sister through college. Lucky for them, I didn't want that. I wanted to dance, and I decided I was going to give it all I had. And that I did for nearly four years. I did waitressing to buy food and keep my car running. And then I did other things."

Nate thought he'd heard this story before. Or seen it in just about every movie ever made about showbiz wannabes. He waited while she lowered her amber eyes as if ashamed, and he finally said, "Other things?"

"I became a topless dancer at some of the clubs on the boulevards. It was good money compared to what I'd been surviving on. Sometimes I made five hundred dollars a night on tips alone."

She looked at him as though awaiting a response, so he said, "A girl's gotta make a living somehow. This is a tough town."

"Exactly," she said. "But I never danced at the totally nude clubs. Those no-liquor joints that do totally nude attract servicemen and other rowdy young guys. I'd never take all my clothes off."

"I understand," Nate said, but he was wondering how big a difference a G-string made. He remembered a screen-writing class he'd taken at UCLA. Reductive. This freaking story was reductive.

"And then I got a job at the Leopard Lounge," Margot said, "and I met Ali Aziz."

"Your husband," Nate said.

She nodded and said, "He owned two clubs. I danced at the Leopard Lounge for more than two years and made quite a lot of money, by my standards. I moved into a very nice condo, and Ali kept taking me on dinner dates and buying me expensive presents and behaving like a real gentleman. And he kept begging me to move into this house with him, but I refused. And finally he convinced me that he would be a kind and loving husband. Fool that I am, I accepted his proposal and married him, but only when he agreed to a proper marriage with no prenuptial. By the way, have you ever heard of my husband?"

"The name's familiar," Nate said. "We have a Nightclub Committee that's run by our Community Relations Office. I think maybe I've seen the name."

"He makes sure he donates to all of the Hollywood police charities. You may have run into him at police events. He's chummy with lots of the officers at Hollywood Station."

"Yeah, I do think I've heard of Ali Aziz," Nate said, wondering how chummy Ali would be with the Jewish cops at Hollywood Station.

"My parents were not thrilled when I told them about Ali, but I took him home to Barstow just before the wedding and they were very impressed by his good manners. He even assured my mother that if we had children, they would be raised Christian." This time when she paused, she took another sip from the martini and yet again topped off Nate's wineglass.

"Back then it was peachy, huh?" Nate said, thinking, she was the most exciting woman he'd ever shared a meal with in his entire life, but this sappy story was killing his wood!

"For sure," Margot said. "The honeymoon was in Tuscany and he bought me a little Porsche for a wedding present, and of course I never had to set foot in the Leopard Lounge again, except to help him with the books. The last real work I ever did in that place was when I talked him into a major refurbishing and he let me do the design."

Nate sneaked a look at his watch. It was 10:30 and they weren't even close to getting naked. And all the goddamn wine was making him gassy. Pretty soon he'd be farting!

He said, "So after a few years of marriage, what? He was no longer a gentleman?"

"He's a fucking pig!" Margot said it so viciously it startled him.

"What happened?"

"Women. Cocaine. Even gambling. And the

scary thing, he kept talking about leaving Hollywood. Leaving America. Going back to the
Middle East with Nicky and me."

"Nice," Nate said. "I can just see you in a
burka, or one of those other beekeeper outfits."

"He said I'd like Saudi Arabia. Claimed he
had connections there, even though he's not a
Saudi. I said I'd die first, and that he wasn't taking my son anywhere."

"And that started the fireworks?"

"Definitely," she said. "And it resulted in my
filing for divorce and starting a really big-time
dispute over the division of property. But that's
another story."

Nate finally decided that even if all this was
gospel, it was hard to feel sympathy for rich
people. He offered an official police response,
saying, "Has he hurt you or threatened you in
any way?"

"That's why I wanted to talk to you tonight,"
she said. "He *has* threatened me, but in very
subtle ways."

"Like how?"

"Like when he comes to pick up Nicky for his
visit. He'll say things like, 'Enjoy this while you

can.' Or, 'A boy needs his father, not a mother like you.' Then he makes signs."

"What signs?"

"He points a finger at me like a gun. Once he mouthed the word *bang*. Things like that."

"That's not much in the way of a threat. And it'd be his word against yours."

"That's what the other officer said."

"What other officer?"

"I've talked to another of your officers about it. An officer I met last year with my husband at one of the Tip-A-Cop fund-raisers. I can't remember his name. I told him what was going on, but he said that I should talk it over with my divorce lawyer. He said that so far, my husband hadn't done anything criminal that I could prove."

"Took the words right outta my mouth," Nate said.

"But last week when Ali brought Nicky home, he said something that made my blood run cold."

Nate remembered his screen-writing professor saying that no screenplay should ever contain those last three words. "Yeah?" he said, trying to muster enthusiasm.

"He said if I didn't agree to sign certain business documents, something very bad would happen."

"What documents?"

"Documents pertaining to the businesses, the stock portfolio, and properties we own."

In a minor way Nate had an understanding of divorce law, and at last something piqued his interest. He said, "You mean you're an owner right along with him of everything?"

"Yes, of course," she said.

And now Hollywood Nate started getting a woody once again. This Barstow babe must be a world-class piece of ass to have rigged a deal like this with a dude from the Middle East! Nate said, "He wants you to sign off on certain things?"

"On certain things I can't even talk about. Signatures I agreed to give so that he could avoid certain tax liability, as well as others of his dealings I can't discuss."

"Back to the very bad thing that would happen," Nate said. "Did he describe what might happen?"

"He's too smart for that," Margot said. "But he drew his finger across his throat."

Here we go again, Nate thought. Finger across the throat. Every time she said something he was ready to buy into, she came up with lines that could have come from the piece-of-shit movies he'd appeared in.

Nate said, "Did you tell your lawyer about it?"

"Of course," she said. "But he told me Ali would deny it, and just to change my locks and alarm code. Which I had already done."

"Anything else by way of a threat?"

"Yes. One night last week I saw him standing on the street when I came home from dinner with a girlfriend. He was half a block down behind a parked car. He ducked when I drove past, but I'm sure it was him. When I got in my driveway, I saw taillights driving down the hill."

"Did you call the police?"

"Yes. I called Hollywood Station and talked to an officer at the front desk. I told him I wanted a car to patrol my street, and if they found my husband, to stop and investigate. The officer said he would tell the area car to be on the lookout for Ali prowling around. I insisted that he make a record of my call. My lawyer advised me to be sure that there is official verification of every incident."

"So you've told the cop you met at the fund-raiser, and you called Hollywood Station, and now you're telling me. Any other police officers know about this?"

"Yes, last Saturday night I was sure I heard footsteps beneath the bedroom balcony at about eleven P.M., and I called Hollywood Station again. And two officers arrived, along with a sergeant. They didn't find anything."

"Do you remember the sergeant's name?"

"Let's see...no, but he was young and officious. He issued a lot of orders to the officers."

"Did he have lips?"

"What?"

"Was his name Treakle?"

"That's it. Sergeant Treakle."

Well, Nate thought, she's done everything but put it on MySpace and send up smoke signals. Help! Ali Aziz is threatening me, but I can't prove it.

"Does your husband still see your son?" he asked.

"Oh, yes. I had to agree to reasonable visitation rights. Ali has a luxury condo in Beverly Hills and a full-time housekeeper and au pair. There was nothing I could do about it."

Nate felt his woody withering again, especially when she said, "Won't you let me make you a vodka martini? It's a wonderful mood enhancer."

And yet hers wasn't half finished. This chick was way more interested in pouring booze into him than into herself. What about *her* mood? It occurred to Hollywood Nate Weiss that wealthy people could be very perplexing.

He once again declined a martini and said, "If you're really scared of him, have you considered moving away?"

"I have," she said, "and I will. But in the meantime I went to a gun store in the Valley where they have a pistol range and I took a shooting lesson. The gun store owner said I'm a fast learner. I'm thinking of buying a pistol. Do you like the Glock or the Beretta?"

"Whoa!" Nate said. "Are you *that* scared?"

"I am," she said. "I'd have bought a gun already, but with Nicky getting into every nook and cranny in this house, I've been afraid to do it. The alternative is more expensive but might be wiser."

"And what's that?" Nate said.

"I've been thinking about hiring someone

from a security firm to stay here in the house until it closes escrow. Oh, did I tell you that I sold it already?"

"No, you didn't," he said.

"Well, I did. With the agreement of my husband and his attorney. And with proceeds to be shared. I'll just need someone here for forty more days, maybe less if the buyer can close early. We have bedrooms and bathrooms we've never used. But then I thought, Who knows what kind of person might be employed by those security firms? And I got to thinking, there might be a police officer from Hollywood Station who'd be interested in a very nice room-and-board arrangement for a month or so. I think I could feel safe with a real police officer being here. Is that feasible, do you think?"

Now Nate was so baffled by this woman that he decided to test her. He said, "I might be interested."

"I was hoping to hear that, Nate," Margot said with a little sigh. "I'm truly scared for my safety and for my son's."

"Where're you moving to?" he asked.

"Haven't decided yet," she said. "That's

another thing our lawyers are fighting about. He doesn't want me to take Nicky out of Los Angeles, but we're trying to show the court that Ali's business environment does not make this the ideal place to raise Nicky. Ali knows I love San Francisco and New York. But until that's settled, I'll rent a condo for Nicky and me right here in L.A."

"Good luck with your battle," Nate said.

She took another tiny sip from the martini glass, her voice sultry now, and said, "What do you drink besides wine? Let's take a pair of fresh cocktails out onto the balcony and talk about this further."

And then it kicked in: the cop's survival instinct, honed by all the years of playing Guess What I'm Really Thinking with countless miscreants on the streets. She had drunk far less wine than he had, and she'd hardly tasted her martini. And those eyes — the color of good whiskey, Jack, maybe, or Johnnie Black — were mesmerizing, but Nate's response to more drinking was dictated by blue radar, not raging hormones.

He said, "Okay, I'd love to talk about it further.

But I'm just not that much of a cocktail drinker. I'll hang on to my wineglass. You go ahead and have another James Bond special."

He saw the immediate disappointment on her face. And then he heard a cell phone chime from the butler's pantry. Margot excused herself, went to the pantry, and picked up her go cell from the countertop.

"Yes," she said and listened. Then she closed the pantry door and whispered, "No, honey, he won't do." She listened for a moment and said, "He's not a drinking man." She listened some more and said, "Please, baby, don't say that. I'm going back to number one. I'm going after him very hard. Please. Give me a week."

While Margot Aziz was in the butler's pantry, Hollywood Nate Weiss made a very tough decision. He was going out on that balcony for more talk, but he was going to make a serious move on her to see where all this was going. And if she resisted and tried one more time to pour booze down his throat, he was outta there. This is Hollywood, he thought, and there are extremely unusual people around these parts — gorgeous, scary people who could turn smoking male wood into a steaming pile of sawdust.

Nate didn't get a chance to execute his strategy. When Margot came out of the butler's pantry and back into the dining room, she said, "Nate, I'm terribly sorry. That was my au pair. Nicky's got a fever and she's worried. I've gotta drive over there right now and pick him up."

"Sure," Nate said, not as disappointed as he might have predicted. "Anything I can do?"

"No, I'll call you tomorrow. I have your number."

When Hollywood Nate was walking out the door, it occurred to him that he should get her cell number too. He started to ask for it but thought he'd better leave. She had a sick kid to deal with. And anyway, he wanted to see if this stunning, rich, very strange woman *would* call him tomorrow. The amazing thing was, he'd been so bowled over that he hadn't done what he always did when he met a likely babe. He hadn't even told her about his SAG card and that he'd appeared in two TV movies.

As he was driving home that night, he remembered what his first field training officer had said to him when he was a boot, fresh out of the academy: "Son, that badge can get you pussy, but pussy can get your badge."

Jasmine was scowling when she stormed out of the dancers' bathroom into the dressing room, wearing only her yellow G-string and red stiletto heels. She put her throwaway go cell in her locker, where she kept her street clothes.

One of the stage-sharing dancers that evening, a broad-shouldered redhead called Tex, was sitting in a recliner, looking at photos in a fan magazine. Tex was top heavy from saline overload and was wearing a G-string, a cowboy hat, a short sequined cowgirl vest, and white cowboy boots.

Tex said, "What's wrong, Jasmine? Boyfriend trouble?"

"Yeah, boyfriend trouble," Jasmine said, her face darkened by rage and frustration.

"If we could invent a vibrator with a twenty-word set of responses, we'd never need them," Tex said. "What is he, a gambler, an addict, or a boozer?"

"This guy's definitely not a boozer," Jasmine said. "Which is too fucking bad."

Tex was about to ask what Jasmine meant by that, when Ali Aziz popped his head in the door without knocking, and said, "Jasmine, I got to see you."

"My next set's coming up, Ali," Jasmine said.

Ali was dressed for the evening in a blue double-breasted, raw-silk blazer, a blue silk tie, and a white shirt with monogrammed cuffs. He said, "Tex can take your set. Come."

Tex rolled her eyes and said, "This job sucks in more ways than one."

When Jasmine entered the office, Ali closed and locked the door, sat in his desk chair, and poured himself a glass of Jack Daniel's. Jasmine stood and waited. Lately, he'd call her in there just to rant, especially if he'd been drinking, so maybe if she was very lucky, it wasn't for a hummer after all.

"Fucking bitch!" he said. "Cunt bitch!"

It could only be one person he was talking about. "Margot?" she said.

"Fucking bitch!" he said. "She don't do nothing my lawyer says. Nothing I say. She always tries to keep my Nicky away from me. She only gives him to me when the judge makes her. She requires me to spend lawyer money for everything. Every week more lawyer money. Fucking bitch!"

Ali took a big gulp of Jack and said, "You have been knowing her for three years. You helped her to decorate this place. You are her friend. I need for you to be my friend. I need for you to help me more."

"Help you even more?" Jasmine said.

"Watch out for my Nicky. The house will be in the close of escrow soon and she will move to a condo. That is what she says to my lawyer. But now I want you to watch."

"Ali," Jasmine said, "I already am sort of watching out for Nicky, just like you said for me to do. Sort of. But I only get to see Margot, what? Once a week? She lives on Mount Olympus. I live in Thai Town. Jesus, Ali, gimme a break."

"She says to me that she is going to take Nicky away from California when the house is finish with the escrow and the divorce is over. She says to me that her lawyer is going to make this happen. She says to me that she has a boyfriend and this is none of my business. She says to me all of this on the phone yesterday. I am going insane, Jasmine! My Nicky! He is my life!"

"Okay, Ali, I'll tell you something I didn't wanna mention. The last time I phoned her, I was sure she was all weirded out on something. Probably coke. And Nicky was there, because she yelled at him real mean."

Suddenly, Ali Aziz started sobbing boozily and pulled a red handkerchief from the pocket of his blazer.

Jasmine watched and waited, and before he stopped she said, "I guess I could pay her a personal visit twice a week. Maybe take her some of the Chinese cookies she loves. I might be able to find out if the boyfriend's staying at the house. And maybe I could ask her straight out if she's doing coke again."

Ali stopped weeping then and said, "I ask her, I beg her, I say, 'Please, Margot, whatever happens, do not go back into the life of cocaine. You must take care of our Nicky.' When I first met her, she was spending all her money on cocaine. A beautiful, young dancer who was doing so much cocaine. Soon I was more than her boss. I was her friend and she quit the cocaine. Then pretty soon I was her husband."

"Yeah, you told me," Jasmine said, thinking how she hated taking the last set. But now she'd have to take it for Tex while she listened to this shit for the hundredth time.

"Jasmine, I want for you to see Margot and to tell me what is what. I shall pay for it. Do not worry, I shall pay you for the time you use. I must know what is in her head. Is she truly wishing to take my Nicky away to a different state? Maybe to do cocaine again with this new man? Without my Nicky I shall die, Jasmine!"

"I'll do what I can, Ali," Jasmine said. Then she added, "Tell me, Ali, what happens to your situation if Margot dies?"

"Margot die? God willing!" Ali said. "I shall have my son then. But do not think that I can make such a thing happen. I am a businessman. I am a loving father. I am no killer."

"Of course you're not," Jasmine said. "But I'm curious about your deal with her. About how you got all your holdings so tangled up with her."

"Fucking lawyer! Fucking accountant!" Ali said. "I got rid of them, but too late. They said to me I can escape from taxes if she is on the deeds and licenses for certain things. Stupid bastards! Now I must suffer for it."

"What if you die?" Jasmine said. "Who gets your piece of the money and property?"

"You talk too much of death, Jasmine," Ali said suspiciously.

"You want me to spy for you? Okay, but I gotta know what's going on. I don't wanna be part of any violent plots."

"No! No violence!" Ali said quickly. "I am not a violent man!"

"So tell me, when you die, who gets all your wealth?"

"Nicky, of course. My lawyer is, how you say, executor. But all goes to Nicky. I weep to think of my Nicky with no daddy and only his bitch cunt mother to take care of him."

"It's hard for me to figure how a smart businessman like you married without a prenup in the first place," she said.

Ali said, "You did not know her when she was a young girl. The most beautiful dancer in all Los Angeles. A young girl with eyes that make you go dizzy. So smart she could make me act stupid. She always refuse to give me the blow job. She refuse to even give me kisses more than a few times. She made me to believe she is a virgin. She made me so stupid I run out and buy her a very big diamond ring. She still will not give me sex even one time. I say we sign a business contract and we get married. She say to me no marriage with a business contract. I was the most stupid man in Los Angeles because she made my brain sick. I make her my wife. No contract, no nothing. Two years after that, I listen to my stupid lawyer and stupid accountant, who get her name mixed up in everything. I save some tax money, but look where I arrive to today!"

Jasmine grinned then and said, "How were the blow jobs after all that?"

"Okay," he said. "But not like the ones you give to me."

"If you were to die, it'd be real nice to be Nicky's mother," Jasmine said. "There'd be ways his mother could cut into Nicky's fortune."

"Why do you talk like that, Jasmine?" Ali said. "Stop! You make me feel sick."

"I'm only saying what you must be thinking," Jasmine said. "If I'm going into the spy business in the middle of a very bitter divorce involving...how many millions?"

"Please, Jasmine, stop now!" Ali said.

"I'm just saying. I just have to be careful what I'm getting into, is all. She might have very bad friends who could see the tremendous advantage to her if you would pass away suddenly. And as your agent I might find myself in serious trouble. Whadda you know about this new boyfriend, for example?"

Ali was holding his head in his hands now, getting a headache. "Nothing. I know nothing."

"How do you know he's not some coke dealer from her younger days? How do you know what the two of them are scheming about? He might be a very dangerous man."

"I beg you to stop," Ali said.

"I just hope it all works out for you, Ali," Jasmine said. "For your son's sake."

Ali said, "When Nicky is older, I think he shall see his mother is a cunt bitch. And he shall want to come and live with Daddy. That is what my new lawyer says. He tells me I must have very much patience."

"Okay, I'll do more undercover work for you, Ali, but I'll need serious compensation for it."

"Yes, yes," Ali said. "If she is doing cocaine with this man, you must tell me very fast. Then I can tell my lawyer and we maybe can go to the judge to get back my son. This country have very insane laws."

"You mean I might have to give a deposition

or something?" Jasmine said. "I wouldn't like that."

"I shall pay you, Jasmine," Ali said. "You shall not be sorry."

"To betray my friend?" Jasmine said. "And to maybe run the risk of her new pal finding out about it? That's gotta be worth a lot."

"I shall pay you plenty," Ali said. "Nicky is my life."

"Okay, I'll see what I can do," Jasmine said.

"Thank you, Jasmine, thank you," Ali Aziz said. "Now, please come here and make me feel like a man once more."

"Not again," Jasmine muttered but nevertheless got down on her knees in front of Ali's chair while he unzipped his fly, wishing he'd taken Viagra.

TWELVE

THE FOLLOWING MONDAY AFTERNOON, an extraordinary photo was taken by Officer Tony Silva in Laurel Canyon. A drunken porn producer in a Ferrari, coming from an all-day shoot at his studio on Ventura Boulevard in the San Fernando Valley, swerved head-on into a pair of eucalyptus trees, doing damage to the front end of his car but not activating the air bag.

The Crow had just dealt with another in the endless complaints about peeping paparazzi from one of the second-rate actors who lived in a rented house in the hills, when he came upon the accident, which a nearby resident had called in. However, Tony Silva was the second cop to arrive, the first being Officer F.X. Mulroney.

The LAPD motorcycle was parked twenty feet behind the Ferrari, whose engine was still running, and the driver, who would later blow an astonishing .37 on the Breathalyzer, was casting panicky looks over his left shoulder.

The porn producer was concentrating on what he thought was the road in front of him but was really open space between the two trees, where his car was wedged and immobile.

With his decades of experience in such matters, F.X. Mulroney immediately understood that as far as this motorist was concerned, he was still negotiating the curves on the canyon road, no doubt with double vision. And by the time Tony Silva got out of the CRO's Ford Explorer, F.X. Mulroney had already been at it for a while and was short of breath from his "pursuit" of the Ferrari.

Tony Silva later said that with a video camera he could have had himself a huge hit on the Internet, but all he had was his cell-phone camera. The grainy still photos he shot were of F.X. Mulroney, in full motor cop regalia, running in place beside the Ferrari, his black boots pumping up and down while he shouted, "Pull over! Pull that fucking car over!" to the porn producer, who was gunning the engine and looking back, desperate to speed away from the relentless motor cop who, as in a dream — or in his case, a nightmare — seemed to be pursuing him on foot!

"I don't wanna have to shoot ya!" F.X. Mulroney yelled. "Pull to the curb and turn off your engine!" Then, as always, F.X. Mulroney went totally over the top and yelled, "Watch out for the woman and baby! Pull right! Pull right!"

For a moment the high-performance engine revved to full rpm, the wheels turning sharply, and this allowed the car to climb a foot or so up the trunk of the larger of the eucalyptus trees, tires smoking, engine roaring. But then it settled back down, coughing, sputtering, and dying when the engine finally blew.

F.X. Mulroney noticed Officer Tony Silva for the first time then, but he couldn't speak. He had to bend forward with his hands on his knees to catch his breath after such a long "chase." Then F.X. stood tall, removed his mirrored aviator sunglasses, and said to the camera, "Am I glad this asshole finally pulled over. I was just about outta gas."

The porn producer looked up at the old motor cop standing beside his car. And with eyes at half-mast, he opened the door and said, "My compliments, Officer. I thought I lost you a couple times, but you caught me fair and square."

★ ★ ★

Ronnie felt that Bix Ramstead had seemed different for most of the day. He was uneasy, agitated, nervous. They'd spent several hours knocking on doors, dealing with the myriad calls from the constant complainers who were so well known at the Community Relations Office. It was tedious work, and on past occasions Bix had seemed temperamentally perfect for the assignment. But not today. He wasn't as patient as usual. His practiced responses didn't seem as sincere. He looked at his watch when people were pouring out their troubles, most of which the cops could do nothing about. The fact was, the callers were lonely and wanted attention from officialdom, but all they had were the Crows from Hollywood South.

On the last call they did together, Ronnie and Bix were standing in the kitchen of an eighty-year-old white-stucco bungalow, listening to the complaint of an elderly Salvadoran immigrant whose children hadn't been to visit her in three months. Her English was good enough that they came to understand that her life was being made miserable by her next-door neighbor's frequent yard sales, which attracted a bad element who threw trash on her property and urinated in her driveway in broad daylight.

When she stopped long enough to answer the phone in her bedroom, Bix went to the sink and helped himself to a glass of water. In the corner of the kitchen he spotted a mouse in a glue trap. The mouse, firmly stuck by its belly, feet, and legs, looked up with eyes both frightened and sad, as though the creature knew it was hopeless.

Ronnie heard Bix Ramstead say to the mouse, "Sorry, buddy, I'd help you if I could, but I can't even help myself."

When the Salvadoran woman returned to the kitchen, she picked up the trap and drowned the rodent in a bucket of water on the back porch. Then she continued reciting her many complaints about her neighbors.

After completing that visit, Bix said, "Let's go back to the office and get another car. I think we should split up and deal with as many calls as we can for the rest of the day. We've gotta get our backlog caught up."

Ronnie agreed but couldn't help wondering what Bix had meant when he'd spoken those words to a doomed mouse.

* * *

In recent years, Alvarado Street in Rampart Division had come to resemble a commercial thoroughfare in Tijuana. Most of the shops and businesses displayed goods that spilled out onto the pavement, and those sidewalks were mobbed by Spanish-speaking pedestrians at all hours of the day and most of the evening. The sights and sounds and smells were all from beyond the imaginary line that marks the southern boundary of the United States of America.

There was a particular *farmacia* in that neighborhood that had been frequented by Ali Aziz since 9/11, when he had had to give up his trips to Tijuana. Prior to that catastrophe, he'd found it well worth a drive across the international border for all the prescription diet drugs, tranquilizers, and stimulants required by his dancers. But after 9/11, he got sick of being directed to the secondary inspection area every time he was coming back and subjected to interrogations and searches the moment he answered the question "Where were you born?"

On the last occasion, the prescription drugs he'd bought in Tijuana were confiscated by a U.S. Customs officer who rightly doubted the legitimacy of Ali's prescriptions issued on the spot by Tijuana doctors who worked with the *farmacias*. After that, Ali talked with his Mexican employees and was directed to the Alvarado Street pharmacy owned and operated by Jaime Salgando, who would sell anything without a prescription to Ali Aziz for three times what a legitimate pharmacy would charge. Prescriptions required expensive office visits to physicians by his entire stable of dancers, and Ali did not want to pay for those, especially when they wouldn't prescribe large enough quantities of the drugs that the dancers needed.

So far, Ali had never been turned down by Jaime Salgando, but today would be a test of the pharmacist's loyalty, and of his greed. Ali had with him a single capsule, something he had stolen from the medicine cabinet in his former Mt. Olympus home. That theft had occurred on the day that he had removed all of his clothes and personal property under the humiliating scrutiny of a security guard hired by Margot to see that he took only what they had agreed upon through their respective lawyers.

When the guard was not watching, Ali had impulsively removed a single magenta-and-turquoise

50-milligram capsule from Margot's vial of sleeping aids. This was shortly after he'd read a news account in an Arabic-language newspaper about a rich Egyptian who had been arrested for trying to poison his elder brother by doctoring his sleeping medication. The prescription drug was the only one that Margot had ever used for occasional insomnia, and it was prescribed by her doctor in West Los Angeles. Ali had never known her to take more than a single capsule once or twice a week, usually on nights when she claimed to be under stress. The vial held thirty capsules, and she would replace it about every four months.

He had been very frightened the day he'd opened that medicine cabinet and shaken out one capsule and slipped it into his pocket. But having that capsule all these months had somehow bolstered his confidence and quelled his frustration and outrage with the American system of justice and with American women who knew how to manipulate the system. Having that capsule made him feel less impotent while he was being ground down by that baffling legal machinery. The capsule told him that he had the power to end it should things ever become intolerable. If she ever made him fear for the safety of his son.

There were a dozen Latino people in the small pharmacy when Ali entered. A young woman working at the forward cash register said something to him in Spanish and smiled. Ali did not understand but smiled and pointed to the lone pharmacist at the rear of the store. Ali was glad to see that there were only two customers waiting for prescriptions. He took a seat in a chair surrounded by shelves full of vitamin bottles and herbal cures and waited. When the second woman had paid for her prescription, he stepped to the counter and smiled at Jaime Salgando, a balding, sixty-year-old Mexican with drooping eyelids, a thin pebble gray mustache, and an air of total confidence.

With barely a trace of a Spanish accent, the pharmacist grinned and said, "Ali! Where have you been hiding?"

"Hello, brother Jaime," Ali said with an insincere grin of his own.

They shook hands and Jaime said, "What's the problem? You need more Viagra to keep up with all your gorgeous employees who fight to take you to bed?"

"God willing," Ali said, maintaining the grin.

"I think I have everything you might need," Jaime Salgando said. "How can I help you, my friend?"

Ali gave him a list of the usual meds: diet pills for Tex and anti-anxiety for Jasmine. And because Margot always had her prescriptions filled at a pharmacy near her doctor's office, her needs were unknown to the pharmacist, so Ali asked for a specific 50-milligram sleep aid, supposedly for Goldie.

When Ali handed the list to Jaime Salgando, the pharmacist said, "Goldie has switched to a different medication?"

Ali shrugged and said, "I pay no attention. You got that one?"

"Yes," said the pharmacist. "And how are you keeping, Ali? Your health is good?"

"Very good," Ali said.

As the pharmacist worked, Ali said, "How is business, brother?"

"Not as good as yours, Ali," Jaime said. "And my employees do not look like your employees."

Twice Jaime had enjoyed dates with Tex, compliments of Ali Aziz for pharmaceutical services rendered. Ali said, "Tex is missing you. When shall you come back to see her, Jaime?"

The pharmacist sighed and said, "Next time I must double up on Viagra. One tablet is not enough when I am with that girl."

Ali forced a laugh that was more nervous than he wished it to be and said, "You tell me when, brother. She is there for you."

"At my age that is very nice to know," Jaime said.

When Jaime Salgando was finished with Ali's entire order, Ali paid him and said, "Jaime, I got a terrible problem and I need more help."

"That is what I am here for," Jaime said.

"I need a capsule of poison. Fifty milligrams."

"What for?" the astonished pharmacist said.

"I got to kill a dog. I must put poison in the meat."

"What dog?"

"My Russian neighbor on Mount Olympus is very rich. He is a very bad gangster. He got this big dog. Fifty kilos. The dog is a killer. Last week the killer dog almost got my Nicky. My son! The housekeeper carried Nicky inside the house just in time. I went to this Russian. He tells me go to hell."

"Did you call Animal Control? Or the police?"

"No, I am afraid of this Russian. He is a very dangerous man. All my neighbors are afraid of the Russian and his dog. All neighbors talk. We say we shall poison this Russian dog. Next time the dog gets out, we give it poison. The Russian must never know who done it."

"I don't know, Ali," Jaime said. "This is not a good idea."

"You read about the Russians in Los Angeles who kidnap and murder the people for money? He is a connection to them. He is a dangerous man. His house is for sale now. He shall be moving away, god willing. We are all scared of him, but right now we are more scared of his dog. Please help us."

"This is a crime."

"Everything is a crime in this goddamn country," said Ali.

"Yes, but this is different. My drugs are to help, not to kill."

"One of my neighbor gave the idea. We put

the poison capsule into the meatball. I do not care what kind of poison."

"Why did you say fifty milligrams?"

"My neighbor thinks we need fifty milligrams of stuff they put into pest poison to kill this big dog. And fast, so the dog don't suffer. We have no wish to be cruel people."

"I think your neighbor might be talking about strychnine," said the pharmacist. "When I was a boy working on a ranch in Mexico, we used to bait coyotes and kill them, but with less strychnine than fifty milligrams. Far less."

"The Russian dog is big like two, maybe three coyotes," Ali said.

"I don't know about this," Jaime Salgando said.

Ali was ready for him. He put five $100 bills on the counter and said, "Please, brother, for me. I'll make the date for you with Tex and Goldie. Both at the same time. You shall never forget the date. You need lots of Viagra for this one!"

Ali felt his chin tremble, but he fought to keep the sly smile in place as Jaime Salgando mulled it over.

Then the pharmacist said, "I'll have to get

what you need from a supplier I know. I'll drop it at your club on Thursday evening at six o'clock."

"That is good, brother," Ali said. "But please make sure, one capsule that we can stick inside the little meatball. I see this Russian many times feed him little Russian meatballs from his hand."

"I'll tell my friend what is needed for the bait," the pharmacist said.

"When you want the three-way date, brother?"

"On Saturday evening," the pharmacist said. Then he added, "Nobody must ever know about any of this, Ali."

"No," Ali said. "Nobody must ever know, or this Russian shall kill me! And thank you, brother, thank you. You have save the life of my son!"

"I'll see you on Thursday with your order," Jaime said. "At the Leopard Lounge."

Affecting a lighthearted farewell, Ali said, "Yes, my brother! And Tex shall wear her cowboy hat and cowboy boot for you on Saturday night, I promise!"

When Ali got to his car, he tore open the

paper bag and was relieved to see that Goldie's sleep aids were identical to the turquoise-and-magenta capsule in his pocket. It had cost him $200 just to be sure that the manufacturer of Margot's sleep aids had not changed the colors or size of the capsule in recent months. He might have to put a few extra capsules of the sleep aid in her vial so that things didn't happen too soon. He wanted her to die when he was ready, and not before.

On his drive from Alvarado Street back to Hollywood, Ali began to fret about Jaime Salgando. But the closer he got to Hollywood, the more his fears seemed irrational. If three months from now Margot were to die, why wouldn't it be considered a suicide over her affair with that new boyfriend, whoever he was? Or, if murder was suspected, why wouldn't the new boyfriend be the object of the inquiry? Who knows what intrigues the boyfriend may have been plotting with Margot. The police might surmise that she had threatened to leave the boyfriend and he was punishing her. Her pig boyfriend would be the target of the police investigation, not Ali Aziz.

Even the most fearful scenario did not hold up

when he looked at it with courage and reason: that Jaime Salgando might have a terrible attack of Christian conscience and inform the police that on one hot summer day he had supplied Ali Aziz with 50 milligrams of poison, ostensibly to kill a dog. But that was the silliest fear of all. If Jaime did such a thing, what would happen to his license, his business, his life? Jaime was a man who had taken money from Ali for years, unlawfully dispensing drugs for dancers at the Leopard Lounge. Jaime, the loving father and grandfather who had bedded a number of those dancers to whom he was unlawfully providing drugs. And how could Jaime ever prove that he gave Ali Aziz a 50-milligram capsule of poison? No, Jaime Salgando had committed too many crimes behind the counter at his *farmacia*. Jaime was the least of the worries of Ali Aziz.

His main concern would be to gain legal custody of Nicky when Margot was found dead. Ali knew that her family, those insignificant people in Barstow, California, would fight for custody in order to have control over their grandson, the heir to Margot's fortune. Or rather, Margot's half of Ali's fortune, the wealth that the bitch had stolen from him through all her trickery. And truth be told, he would let them have everything she had stolen from him — all of it — if only they would not initiate any custody fight for Nicky. All that Ali Aziz wanted was his son.

When Ali got to the Leopard Lounge that afternoon, he went to his office, locking the door behind him. He sat at his desk, turned on the desk lamp, dried his hands, and drank a shot of Jack to steady them. Ali found it absolutely astonishing how, despite his fear, the thought of soon possessing that deadly capsule made him feel extremely powerful. He would have the power of life and death. With the unexpected gifts of drugs that he would be giving to his dancers, he felt entitled to special blow jobs with no complaints. Ali decided to call one of the girls into his office. And he wouldn't be needing Viagra. Not today.

Ronnie and Bix Ramstead's ten-hour duty tour — excluding the half hour for a meal break referred to as code 7 — was to end at eight that evening. But when Ronnie signed out, Bix still hadn't returned. She'd called him on his cell twice but couldn't reach him. She was so worried that she was about to mention it to the sergeant prior to his leaving for a meeting with the Graffiti Committee. Then her cell rang.

"It's me," Bix said when she answered.

"I was getting concerned," she said.

"Sorry," he said. "I got tied up."

Ronnie thought she detected a slight slurring of speech but hoped she was wrong. She said, "You coming in now?"

Bix said, "Check me out, will you? I'll be back later to turn the car in."

Now she was sure of it. She said, "Why don't I come where you are? We could get a bite to eat."

"No, I'm gonna grab a burger with a cop I know from my North Hollywood days. Just check me out. I'll be back soon."

And that's how it was left. If it had been anyone other than Bix Ramstead, Ronnie Sinclair, being so new to the Community Relations Office, would not have complied. She thought about talking to one of the other Crows about it, but she did not. Ronnie liked Bix as much as any cop she'd ever known at Hollywood Station. She was feeling very nervous and worried when she checked out both Bix and herself that evening. Ronnie knew she'd have a restless night, worrying about the possibility of Bix Ramstead and his LAPD car getting involved in a DUI collision.

There was trouble in Southeast Hollywood that evening involving more than fifty Filipino and Mexican men. They had gathered in a warehouse that closed its doors for the day at 6 P.M. but whose back door had been left unlocked by an employee who'd made secretive arrangements with all the other sporting men who worked in the warehouse. One of the storage bays had been roped off, and tattooed workers in company shirts or wife beaters were drinking beer and tequila as they gathered around a fighting pit made of plywood that had been temporarily nailed in place to provide an arena for the grisly spectacle about to take place.

Several trucks arrived and very soon steel cages were being carried into the warehouse and stacked against the wall. Each of twelve cages contained a fighting cock, and every bird was squawking in terror from the commotion.

Mexican music was blaring from an old boom box, and voices of drinking men shouted bets to one another in Spanish, Tagalog, and Spanglish prior to prepping the birds for the bloody fights to the death, scheduled to begin at 8:30 P.M.

It might have gone off as planned except for one young Mexican forklift operator named Raul, who had made the mistake of telling his wife, Carolina, a Mexican American girl born and raised in East L.A., that he would be busy that evening and would be coming home late.

"Busy doing what?" she said.

"I cannot tell you," he said.

"Whadda you mean you can't tell me?" she said.

"I swore a secret," he said.

"You better unswear it, dude," she said. "I wanna know where you're going."

It was always like this. The forklift operator had wished a thousand times that he'd married a real Mexican girl. These brown coconuts, milky white on the inside, were nothing but nagging *gringas* with Hispanic names.

"I have made a promise to my friends," he said.

"I think maybe you're gonna be visiting your old squeeze," she said. "That bitch Rosa with the big *chi-chis*. Well, you can forget about coming home afterwards."

He sat down on the kitchen chair and hung his head and surrendered as he always did and told her the truth. "We are having a bird fight at the warehouse."

"A bird fight?" Carolina said. "You mean you're making roosters kill each other? Like that kinda bird fight?"

"Yes," he said. "I am only going to bet twenty dollars. No more."

"You ain't betting shit," she said. "Because you ain't going to no bird fight. It's against the law in this state, in case you didn't know."

"All my friends will be there, Carolina!" he pleaded.

"You go out this door and I'll call the cops about the bird fight," she said. "It's cruel and disgusting!"

Her husband went into the bedroom and slammed the door. Ten minutes later, while he was in there pouting, his wife picked up the phone and quietly dialed 9-1-1.

* * *

One hour before the 8:30 P.M. cockfight was about to commence, a hastily gathered raiding party had been put together by the assistant watch commander at Hollywood Station. Three patrol units from Watch 3, and two from Watch 5, were assigned to the raid, accompanied by the two teams of vice cops who were available on short notice. A pair of Animal Control employees were to be dispatched to meet the LAPD officers thirty minutes after the raid began, in order to impound the fighting cocks. Everyone was expecting to be writing a lot of citations and maybe booking the event organizers. The animal cruelty code section carried a $20,000 fine and/or one year in county jail.

The Watch 5 midwatch officers tasked were Cat Song and Gil Ponce, along with Dan Applewhite and Gert Von Braun. Most of the cops thought it might be an interesting assignment. There hadn't been many cockfighting raids conducted in the heart of the city, and none of the cops had ever seen a fighting bird.

On their way to the staging area parking lot, from where they would converge on the warehouse, Gert Von Braun made a startling confession to Dan Applewhite.

"As far as big birds're concerned, I look at them like they're nothing but snakes with wings. Thinking of those roosters is creeping me out."

Doomsday Dan was stunned. He didn't think Gert Von Braun was afraid of anything. At that moment, she stopped being this intimidating mass of angry female cop and seemed like nothing more than a sweet and vulnerable girl!

He was absolutely tender when he said, "Don't worry, Gert. If anything should go wrong with the killer birds, I'll be there for you. One summer when I was a kid in Chino, I worked on a chicken farm, culling eggs. I'm a rooster wrangler, is what I am. You just get my back and deal with the drunk Mexicans and Filipinos, I'll do the rest."

"Oh, yeah," she scoffed, "I can just see you there with your pepper spray, telling an insane rooster with knife blades on its feet, 'Okay, birdbrain, *bring* it!' Sure, you will. My hero."

When they arrived at the staging area, the cops turned off their headlights and got out to talk to one another. It was then that they learned of an awful turn of events: The vice sergeant who was supposed to lead the raid was unavailable and had been replaced by a patrol sergeant from the midwatch.

"Chickenlips Treakle!" Cat Song moaned when she got the word.

"Appropriate choice, considering the nature of the event," young Gil Ponce noted.

"He'll find a way to fuck it up totally," Gert Von Braun said. "If a rooster fight can get any more fucked up than they are to begin with."

"I hear *that*," Doomsday Dan concurred. "Treakle in command makes me wanna have a sudden back attack."

And to make matters worse, Sergeant Treakle, shining his new mini-flashlight beam on the raiding party until he spotted his Watch 5 officers, approached Dan Applewhite and said, "I'll be riding in with you and Von Braun."

"Sergeant, don't you wanna drive your own car in case we need extra shops to transport prisoners?" Gert said.

"No, Von Braun," he said curtly. "I want you to drop me fifty yards from the warehouse for a very quick reconnoiter before I give the go command on my rover."

Sergeant Treakle was especially nervous. He kept obsessively rubbing lip balm across his mouth, but he turned his back when he did it. Like he was sniffing coke.

Dan Applewhite whispered to Gert, "Why's he need ChapStick? He's got no lips!"

A bearded Latino vice cop, wearing an Ace Hardware work shirt and kneeless jeans, spoke up then, saying, "Wouldn't it be better if I do the reconnoiter, Sergeant? Your uniform is a tad conspicuous."

"Thanks for the input," Sergeant Treakle said icily. "I'll manage."

"Okay," the vice cop said, "but I hope this caper don't get 'fowled' up." He looked around at the other silent cops and said, " 'Fowled' up? F-o-w-l?"

The others groaned or guffawed, and Sergeant Treakle made a mental note to find out the name of this smart-ass vice cop. He looked at his watch and said, "Applewhite and Von Braun, let's roll!"

"Let's roll?" the vice cop said after Sergeant

Treakle was gone. "Christ almighty. That fucking attack gerbil thinks he's on United flight ninety-three!"

Another midwatch unit, one that had not been assigned to the raid, happened by at that moment after hearing the radio communication setting up the rendezvous. Jetsam was driving, and Flotsam, who had had a very strenuous morning at Malibu, was riding shotgun and nursing an injured shoulder. He was relating the entire tale to his partner.

"Dude, I was ripping on that juicy when I got shut down," Flotsam informed him.

"A total wipeout inside the barrel?" Jetsam said.

"I got pitchpoled, dude. The nose went vertical and I went horizontal, and the board snapped the leash and catapulted straight up in the air. And I'm talking my U-boat. See, I'd pulled the old longboard from my quiver this morning, and there I was, waiting for nine feet of glass to come down on me like a mortar round!"

"Shit, why is there radical surf every time I gotta go to the dentist or something?" Jetsam said.

"The worst part of it is, I swallowed maybe half a gallon of foamy and I'm all coughing and gagging, and what happens? This totally awesome dudette in a white thong bikini comes up and she says, 'Are you okay?' I look at her and I see the most excellent Betty I've ever seen at Malibu. Remember the salty sister we seen at that midnight rager last month? The one that was jumping over the fire pit topless with a tequila bottle in each hand? That one?"

"Are you telling me this one was as cooleo as *that* one?"

"Mint, dude. Totally prime."

"Did you get her number?"

"Dude, I could hardly breathe. I'm all gasping. I'm all choking. Then I'm, like, feeling the IHOP waffles come chugging up my throat."

"Oh, no!" Jetsam said. "You barked the dog?"

"I lunched it," Flotsam said, nodding. "Barfola."

"Don't tell me more!" Jetsam cried but wanted to hear it all.

Flotsam said, "Dude, I blew chunks all over her. She screamed and jumped in the surf to wash off the spooge and I never saw her again. I was soooo bleak."

"Bro," Jetsam said softly. "That is, like, one of the saddest stories I ever heard."

Cat Song and Gil Ponce were the last team to leave the staging area parking lot, when 6-X-46 drove up, flashing headlights at them.

Jetsam pulled close to the other car, facing the opposite direction, and said, "The game's afoot, huh?"

"Yeah, and we gotta go now," Cat said. "Treakle's in charge."

"Aw, shit," Jetsam said. "Sorry for you."

Flotsam looked at the cageless old black-and-white parked in the lot and said, "Which supervisor belongs to that piece of shit?"

"Chickenlips," Cat said. "He's on a sneak-and-peek mission, checking out the target. We can't talk. Gotta go."

"Catch you later," Jetsam said while Cat drove away, following the caravan of police units ready to swoop into the warehouse parking lot.

Flotsam massaged his aching shoulder while Jetsam switched from the Hollywood base frequency to the tactical frequency just in time to hear Sergeant Treakle's high-pitched radio voice.

"All units converge on target!" Sergeant Treakle said, spraying saliva on his rover. "Converge, converge, converge!"

"He gets pretty excited about a bunch of chickens, don't he?" Jetsam said.

"I bet that dude's got women's tits," Flotsam said. "Let's go get a burrito."

While the surfer cops were sitting in their car on Sunset Boulevard enjoying some Tex-Mex, one of the cars that was checked out to the Community Relations Office drove up the hill to Mt. Olympus and into the driveway of Margot Aziz. The driver got out of the car but didn't close the door. He tried to will himself to get back into the car but could not. Then he closed the car door quietly, walked to the front door of the house, and rang the bell. He heard footsteps on the inside marble foyer and knew she was looking through the brass-enclosed peephole.

When the door opened, she threw her arms around his neck and kissed him repeatedly on the mouth, cheeks, and neck as he tried to push her away. Her eyes were bright and wet in the moonlight streaming down, drops clinging to her eyelashes. He felt wetness on her cheekbones, and could taste it when she kissed him, and he wondered why her tears were not salty.

"I was afraid you wouldn't show up," she said. "I was afraid you'd never come again. I left four messages on your cell today."

"You've gotta stop doing that, Margot," said Bix Ramstead. "My partner might pick up my calls sometime."

"But I haven't seen you in twenty-nine days and twenty-nine nights!" She pulled him forward into the foyer and closed the door. She wanted to smell his breath for alcohol, but he kept pulling back when she tried to kiss him again.

"I can't stay, Margot," he said. "I've got a police car here. I've gotta get it back to the station."

"Do it and hurry back," she said. "I'll make some supper for you."

"I can't," he said. "I just stopped by to tell you that you gotta stop calling me. You're gonna get me in trouble."

"Trouble, Bix?" she said. "Trouble? I'm the one in trouble. I'm crazy in love with you. I can't sleep, I can't think. We have something, Bix, and you can't throw it away. I'm almost free of Ali now. Then I'm all yours. Me and everything I have!"

"I can't. I've been going crazy too. Thinking of you. Thinking of my family. I'm no good for you. We're no good for each other."

"You're the best man I've ever known," she said, and then she put her face against his badge and held him hard with both arms.

"I gotta go," he said again, but he wasn't pulling away from her now.

"I've tried to be patient," she said. "The only thing that's held me together is knowing that your family went to your in-laws' for a visit. You see, I've marked my calendar, Bix. You're all I think about. I'm selfish. I want you here with me every night while they're gone. I want the chance to convince you how right we are for each other."

"I can't think straight tonight," he said. "I'll call you tomorrow. I've gotta get the car back to the station."

She released him and he looked at her. Then he kissed her, and for certain she smelled the booze on his breath.

"Tomorrow, darling," Margot said, smiling hopefully. "I'll be waiting for your call."

When Bix Ramstead backed out of the driveway and turned back down the hill, he didn't see the Mustang parked a block farther up. Hollywood Nate had waited since Friday for her call that never came. He too had had a few drinks that evening after getting off duty. And impetuously, he had driven up to Mt. Olympus, intending to knock on her door. Intending to find out just what the hell was going on in that woman's head. But as Nate had approached her driveway, he'd seen a police vehicle. He'd driven past the driveway, turned around, parked, and waited.

Nate didn't have to tail him very long to be sure that the driver was Bix Ramstead. He was tempted to follow Bix to the station for a friendly face-off, to compare notes on Margot Aziz. But he decided that he'd better wait until he was completely sober before trying something like that.

After finishing their burritos, Jetsam and Flotsam drove back in the direction of the cockfight raid instead of toward their beat.

"Where you going, dude?" Flotsam said.

"To take a look at the big chicken caper."

"Why?"

"You ever seen a fighting rooster?"

"No, and I got no desire."

"Might be educational."

By the time they pulled into the warehouse parking lot, everything was under control. All of the Mexican and Filipino spectators were inside being questioned and having FI cards filled out on them. Everyone was being checked for wants and warrants, and a few were being cited. There was nobody outside the building except Gil Ponce, standing by a stack of metal cages containing the fighting cocks, which were still squawking furiously and pecking at the steel confining them.

Jetsam drove up to the young cop and said, "What's going down in there, dude?"

"Nothing now," Gil said. "Just FI-ing everybody and running them for warrants. Gonna book a few. You shoulda been here when we first arrived. One of the organizers of this thing tried to get away, but Gert threw a body block that knocked him flat."

"Yeah, she would," Flotsam said.

Then a lithe figure came through the darkness, carrying a steel crate. When she got close, they saw it was Cat Song.

"That rat dog bastard," she said to the surfer cops. "Treakle's making us carry the birds out here instead of waiting for Animal Control to do it. He wants to lock up the warehouse and go brag to the watch commander about his great chicken raid and leave us to babysit the birds until Animal Control arrives. I've got feathers and chicken shit on my uniform!"

She stacked the cage on top of two others and the fighting cocks made a louder racket at the new arrival.

"How many birds you got?" Jetsam asked.

"I don't know," she said. "Ten, twelve. Haven't counted them." Then she turned to Gil Ponce and said, "Come on, sonny, I'm not carrying these things all by myself."

When they walked back inside the warehouse, Jetsam glanced at Flotsam, who looked like he was about to start whining about his shoulder again.

Jetsam turned out the headlights, jumped out of the black-and-white, and opened the back door on Flotsam's side.

"What're you doing, dude?" Flotsam asked.

He watched in amazement when Jetsam grabbed the top crate and swung it into the backseat of their shop, saying, "You had a bad day at Malibu, bro. I'm trying to cheer you up."

"Just whadda you got on your desktop?" Flotsam said anxiously.

"Now, bro, don't suck the cool outta this situation," Jetsam said, closing the door and getting behind the wheel.

"What situation?" Flotsam wanted to know, and soon found out.

Jetsam drove, lights out, and wheeled into the parking lot, where a lone black-and-white was parked in the darkness. And he said, "You still carry that Slim Jim in your war bag?"

"Dude, this is totally uncool," Flotsam said.

Jetsam got out of the car and said, "Bro, this is fate at work. Look at that old cageless black-and-white sitting there waiting for us. Don't bitch out on me. This is our destiny!"

"Stay real, dude!" Flotsam said, but nevertheless he was fascinated watching Jetsam get gloved up and slide the Slim Jim inside the car window until he unlocked the door.

"Go to sleep, chicken," Jetsam said to the

caged bird when he transferred the cage through the rear door of Sergeant Treakle's car. But when he opened the rooster's cage, he got his finger pecked.

"Ow!" he said. "This ungrateful chicken bit me. And I was starting to like him 'cause he looks so much like Keith Richards."

"This ain't cool, is all I got to say," Flotsam said. But actually he thought it *was* pretty cool. If they didn't get caught.

When Jetsam closed and locked Sergeant Treakle's shop and they drove away looking for a likely Dumpster in which to toss the empty cage, Flotsam said, "Do you think the boot might panic and dime us when that heel-clicking, no-lips little Nazi starts trying to figure out who boosted the chicken?"

"I ain't sure if Ponce's still a probie," Jetsam said. "He might own his pink slip by now. Anyways, Cat Song would shove one of those Korean metal chopsticks in his eyeball if he tries to put us behind the grassy knoll. We're gravy, bro."

Sergeant Treakle was pleased as punch with the raid when all was said and done. Citations were written to three men who had been drinking in the parking lot when the cops swooped in. Five were arrested for public drunkenness or for outstanding traffic warrants. None were cited for being spectators at the cockfight because it hadn't started yet. The two organizers were arrested and booked at Hollywood Station on the animal cruelty charge.

After Animal Control arrived and took custody of the birds, Sergeant Treakle made sure that the warehouse was secured and the burglar alarm set. He was meticulous and proud of the job they'd done. And because he was riding with Gert Von Braun and Dan Applewhite, they had to wait until the bitter end. They were hungry and cranky, and both had soiled uniforms from helping to haul the fighting cocks out of the warehouse.

When everyone was gone or driving away except the two midwatch units, Sergeant Treakle said, "Now, Von Braun, I have a treat for you and Applewhite."

"What's that?" Gert said doubtfully.

"I'm inviting you to take code seven with me. I'm treating. You name the eating spot."

With the odor of the frantic birds and the

chicken shit still in her nostrils, Gert Von Braun said sourly, "Oh, goody. Let's go to KFC, Sergeant Treakle. I want wings and a drumstick."

Gil Ponce suppressed his giggle when he saw that their supervisor was glowering.

"On second thought, you and Applewhite can clear," Sergeant Treakle said with a frosty glance at Gert. Turning to Cat he said, "Song, you and Ponce can drive me to my car."

Gert mouthed the words *Sorry, Cat* when she and Dan Applewhite walked to their car.

"Thanks, partner," Dan said to Gert. "Treakle gives me heartburn so bad I feel like I need a bottle of antacid in my holster with an IV drip attached."

Sergeant Treakle got into the backseat of Cat and Gil's shop and they drove quickly to the parking lot staging area without conversation. Upon getting out of their black-and-white, he said, "Stay here till I get it started. The electrical system in that old car is dicey."

Cat sighed and put the car in park and shook her head at Gil, and they waited. As it turned out, she was eternally glad they did or they might have missed it.

The exhausted bird was down on the floor

in the back, apparently asleep, when Sergeant Treakle unlocked the driver's door and got in, thinking the odor of those horrid birds just wouldn't go away. The bird apparently stayed asleep when Sergeant Treakle pulled the door closed. The bird didn't budge when Sergeant Treakle started the engine. But when Sergeant Treakle tooted his horn to signal to 6-X-32 that they could go ahead and clear, the fighting cock exploded in a whirring tornado of claws, horrifying screeches, and flapping wings!

Gil Ponce heard strange sounds, and he picked up the spotlight and shined it on Sergeant Treakle's car. Then he said, "Cat! Sergeant Treakle's being attacked!"

"What?" Cat Song said, slamming on the brakes.

Then they both gaped, frozen for an instant, as the enraged rooster raked the back of Sergeant Treakle with sharp claws and pecked at his skull, all the time beating powerful wings and screaming like a cat.

But as loud as the fighting cock shrieked, he wasn't shrieking half as loudly as Sergeant Jason Treakle, who fell gurgling from the car onto his face. Cat Song ran to the car and poked her baton at the furious bird, driving it back until she could close the door again.

"Oh, my god!" Gil Ponce said. "Sergeant Treakle, are you injured?"

But Sergeant Treakle couldn't talk. He was making fearful strangling sounds and trying desperately just to breathe.

"Call for an RA!" Cat said to Gil Ponce. "And get that Animal Control truck back here! And then bring me a bag! He's hyperventilating!"

"A bag?" Gil Ponce said. "Where'll I get a bag?"

"Forget the bag! Just make the calls!"

"Okay!" Gil said, running to their car.

When he came back, Gil found Cat propping their supervisor upright, easing him gingerly against the door of his shop. He yelped when his wounded back touched metal, and Cat told him to ignore the pain and try to breathe normally.

"Is Sergeant Treakle gonna be okay?" Gil Ponce asked.

"I think so," Cat Song said. "But he had quite a shock, and he got beat up pretty bad. And he's just *covered* with chicken shit."

By the time the paramedics arrived and treated the wounds on Sergeant Treakle's head, neck, and back, the team from Animal Control had showed up as well. Cat opened the car door for them, then jumped back. But they captured the now docile bird without incident and caged it in the back of their van. The lieutenant was on a day off and the acting watch commander was called to the scene. He happened to be the oldest patrol sergeant at Hollywood Station and was well aware of young Sergeant Treakle's methods and reputation.

Cat was standing near enough to overhear the senior sergeant say to Sergeant Treakle, "Maybe we should keep this outrageous prank quiet. It's just the kind of story that little *L.A. Times* prick who covers the LAPD would love to get on a local headline. The Department would look silly, and so would you."

"*Me* look silly?" Sergeant Treakle said. "I didn't do anything to deserve this! I'd like Internal Affairs to interrogate every officer who was out here and put them all on the polygraph!"

That touched a nerve with the elder supervisor, who had been around long enough to know how unreliable the polygraph is, especially with the overdeveloped superegos of those who make up the police service. He knew that a sociopath's poly chart is essentially flat lines, but a cop's looks like a witch's hat if you so much as ask him if he's jerked off anytime in the last decade.

"I know you don't deserve this," the old sergeant said soothingly. "Nobody deserves this. But everyone who reads the *Times* would laugh at us. Laugh at *you*. If we launch an investigation, it would leak in a heartbeat. Right now, nobody knows about this except Song and Ponce and the paramedics. I'll talk to all of them." When he said it, he turned toward Cat, who pretended to be writing in the log.

"They shouldn't get away with this!" said Sergeant Treakle.

"But we can't go off half-cocked," replied the old sergeant.

"Half-*cocked*," said Gil Ponce, giggling, until Sergeant Treakle scowled at him.

"But I know in my gut who did it!" Sergeant Treakle said.

"Who's that?"

"That smart-ass vice cop. The Hispanic guy with the beard. I just know it was him."

"Look, Treakle," the old sergeant said. "Do you want your family and friends to read a headline that says —"

"Okay, I get it!" Sergeant Treakle said, finding the headline possibilities unbearable to contemplate. "But I know it was that vice cop."

"Maybe you should ask the captain for a transfer to some other division," the old sergeant said. "Get a fresh start somewhere else. Does that sound okay?"

"I can't wait," Sergeant Treakle agreed. Then, for the first time, he was heard to utter an obscenity. He sat and pondered for a moment and said, "Fucking Hollywood!"

Sergeant Treakle refused to be transported for further medical treatment at Cedars-Sinai when Cat Song said they might need to wear biohazard outfits to clean him up. And he drove the cageless shop back to the station on his own — feathers, chicken shit, and all.

The senior sergeant then spoke with Cat and young Gil Ponce about the need to keep the incident quiet for the good of Hollywood

Station. And they indicated that they understood the gravity of a situation where a prank caused injury and terror to the junior supervisor — who would likely be transferring out of the division ASAP. They assured the senior sergeant that they wouldn't breathe a word of it.

Before an hour had passed, Cat Song had phoned Ronnie Sinclair at home, text-messaged Gert Von Braun, and managed to reach Hollywood Nate on his cell phone, knowing how much he loathed Sergeant Treakle. Everyone thanked her effusively for sharing and promised they wouldn't breathe a word of it.

Gil Ponce, being one of the officers who had declined an invitation to participate in Bible study with Sergeant Treakle, whispered all the details to Doomsday Dan in the locker room at end-of-watch — with a theological question attached. The young cop wondered if it was possible that in the first instant of being suddenly enveloped in great dark wings and hearing unearthly screeching in his ears, Sergeant Treakle may have smelled sulfur and believed that he'd been seized by the Antichrist himself!

"It's heartwarming to think so," the older cop replied. Then he added, "The Oracle always said that doing good police work was the most fun we'd ever have. Well, there's a pair of anonymous coppers out there who did some *great* police work tonight. I hope they remembered the Oracle."

THIRTEEN

TWO OF THE CROWS at Hollywood South had worrisome thoughts the next day about Bix Ramstead, but neither was aware of the other's concern. Ronnie wanted to know if Bix had fallen off the wagon and been drinking on duty the night before, and Nate wanted to know what the hell Bix Ramstead was doing up on Mt. Olympus at the home of Margot Aziz. But neither had the nerve to ask him.

That morning, Ronnie and Bix were tasked to do follow-ups to neighbors of various tanning salons, an aromatherapy salon, an acupuncturist, and a chiropractor. All complaints had come from neighborhood residents and businesspeople, and most concerned illegal parking and nighttime noise. There was an accusation of prostitution directed at tanning salons because of an excessive number of men entering and leaving all day and late in the evenings. One of the tanning salons and the aromatherapy salon had been busted in the past by vice cops posing as customers, but both businesses were said to be under new management.

As Ronnie and Bix were getting ready to hit the streets, their sergeant was involved in a peculiar debate with Officer Rita Kravitz about running an errand to the Church of Scientology Celebrity Centre to pick up a generous donation check it had offered for the Special Olympics fund-raiser. Rita gave the sergeant a couple of lame excuses as to why she was too busy to handle the job and suggested he send one of the guys.

"But you might run into John Travolta or Tom Cruise up there," the sergeant said. "Wouldn't that make your day?"

Officer Rita Kravitz pushed her newest and trendiest-ever eyeglasses up onto her nose and with a curl to her lip said, "I might also get taken prisoner by those robots and brainwashed till I turn into a smiley-faced, twinkly-eyed cult cookie. And if you think that can't happen, ask Katie Holmes."

The other Crow with Bix on his mind was having a late-morning Danish and cappuccino at his favorite open-air table in Farmers Market, listening to a former director and three former screenwriters at the usual table railing about the ageism that had killed their careers and promoted mediocrity in Hollywood.

"The last meeting I took was with a head of development who was twenty-eight years old," a former screenwriter said.

"All they wanna do is preserve their jobs," another one said.

"They'd rather have a flop they can blame on somebody else than take a risk on their own that might produce a hit," a third one said.

The first one said, "Every time my stuff gets rejected, they say it's not enough 'outside the box,' whatever that means. Or not enough 'inside their wheelhouse,' whatever that means."

The former director said, "Bottom line, they're terrified of people our age because they think we might know something about making movies that they don't know. And they're right!"

There was a chorus of amens to that one.

Nate wasn't enjoying the show business grousing. All he could think of was how Margot Aziz had looked when he'd first seen her here, and how she had not called him, as promised. He figured that Bix Ramstead might have had a lot to do with that. Nate tried rehearsing half a dozen approaches he could try with Bix to find out the truth. First, though, he'd have to get Bix alone, away from Ronnie Sinclair.

Nate finished his cappuccino and started on his rounds. He had three calls to make on apartment dwellers about chronic-noise complaints. He was already starting to think that this quality-of-life shit was way more tedious and boring than he ever thought it could be. But at least he had last night's adventure of Sergeant Treakle and the rooster to sustain him. He would've loved to share the story with somebody, but so far today, he couldn't find anyone at Hollywood Station who didn't know all about it.

Nine hours into their ten-and-a-half-hour shift, Ronnie and Bix were tired. All they'd accomplished so far was to issue warnings to salon proprietors about the need to screen their workers to make sure that temporary employees were not turning tricks when the boss wasn't around. Of course, they knew that most of the temps were hired precisely because they were more than eager to offer special services to safe and willing customers.

Their last tanning salon was on Sunset Boulevard near Western Avenue and was called Miraculous Tan. This one was larger than the others and seemed to be catering to an all-male clientele. The employees were saline Suzies in short shorts, Miraculous Tan T-shirts, and tennis shoes. When the bluesuits walked into the reception area, two male customers waiting on the sofa dropped their magazines and quickly departed.

The receptionist said, "Please wait, Officers. I'll get the manager."

"Maybe we better take a closer look at this one," Ronnie said. "Seeing us made those dudes run faster than my Sav-on panty hose."

Bix nodded. He had spoken very little all day and his eyes weren't as bright and clear as they usually were. Ronnie had tentatively tried directing conversation toward the previous night, when Bix had asked her to log him out, but each time she did, he'd change the subject.

The manager was as tall as Bix. Her hair was ash blonde and hung over her breasts in two pigtails. She was bulging with saline implants and had heavily rouged apple cheeks, resembling the stereotypical milkmaids from porn flicks they showed at the adult stores on Hollywood Boulevard. She was dressed in a white vinyl skirt, pink long-sleeved cotton blouse, and white wedges.

"I'm Madeline. How can I help you?" she said with a toothy smile that was impossibly white next to her crimson lip gloss.

Ronnie was too tired and it was too hot a day for subtlety. She said, "We're getting numerous complaints from your neighbors that they're suspecting illegal activity is going on here during day and evening hours. Also, we're hearing that your customers are causing noise disturbances at night, and parking illegally."

"Oh, that," Madeline said. "We've changed management. That was before I came here two months ago. One of the girls was doing her own thing and nobody here knew about it. The vice officers arrested her. Your Detective Support Division knows all about it."

"We've gotten complaints more recently than two months ago," Bix said.

"I'll bet they're from the older Asian people who have the tailor shop two doors down, right?"

"We can't discuss who the complainants are," Ronnie said.

"No, of course not," Madeline said, "but they're always complaining about something. You can ask any of the businesspeople around here."

"When we walked in here, two of your customers almost ran over us to get out the door," Ronnie said.

"Maybe they had some problems of their own with the law," Madeline said.

"Mind if we have a look around at your business?" Ronnie said. "I may want to try your services sometime. Especially one of those spritzer tans."

Madeline didn't look happy about it but said, "Of course. Follow me."

The cops followed Madeline into a long hallway with five doors on each side, all of them closed. She led them to an intersecting hallway and turned right, toward a large, tiled room that looked like it was meant for showers.

"This is for sunless tanning," Madeline said.

"As a matter of fact, one of our employees is getting ready to go in now. She has a heavy date tonight and wants to look her best." She turned to Bix and said, "If you would turn your back, Officer, I'm sure Zelda wouldn't mind demonstrating how it works."

Bix walked a few paces farther down the hall and faced the wall.

"Zelda, honey, you can come out," Madeline said, knocking on one of the closed doors.

The shapely, young platinum blonde was wrapped in a towel. A plastic shower cap completely covered her hair, and booties covered only the tips of her toes and the bottoms of her feet. Her eyes opened wide when she saw Ronnie standing there with the boss. She hurried to the sunless tanning room, whipped off the towel, revealing her own implants, and hung it on a hook by the doorway.

"Zelda has cream on her palms, fingernails, and toenails," Madeline explained to Ronnie. "We don't want the tanning liquid to get in the nail beds or on her palms or the bottom of her feet. That would look totally unnatural."

Zelda faced a bank of spigots on the middle

of the wall and pushed a button. The tanning liquid sprayed out, covering her in a mist. She pressed the button again, turned around, and tanned the other side. When she was finished, she was dripping with goop the color of buckskin, and she began patting herself dry.

"We could offer you a police discount, Officer," Madeline said to Ronnie, "if you'd like to make an appointment sometime."

Bix joined them when Zelda was back in her changing room, and they continued their tour of the establishment, looking into one of the little rooms with tanning beds inside.

"Looks claustrophobic," Bix said. "Like getting in a coffin and pulling down the lid."

"Not at all," Madeline said. "We give you tiny dark goggles to cover your eyes, and you're only in there for about eight minutes at any level of tanning power you choose. It's a lot more pleasant than baking in the hot summer sun."

Ronnie said, "Maybe I'd like this kind of power tan better than the spritzer variety. More bang for the buck."

While she and Madeline were talking about tans, Bix continued down the hall, subtly trying doorknobs, but they were locked. Behind the third door he heard a woman moaning. It was loud and unmistakable.

Madeline noticed him listening and quickly came forward, saying, "We can't disturb our clients, Officer. Please follow me and I'll show you —"

"There's somebody moaning in there," Bix said. "A woman."

"Maybe she fell asleep and is dreaming," Madeline said. "Really, I must —"

"Isn't that dangerous?" Ronnie said, exchanging glances with Bix. "Somebody falling asleep under those tanning lamps?"

"They shut off automatically," Madeline said, and now she had Ronnie's arm, trying to guide her back down the hallway.

Then they heard a man in that room cry out, "Do it to me, baby!"

"Got a key?" Bix said.

"I'll... I'll look for one," Madeline said, hurrying back toward the reception area.

Ronnie winked at Bix and knocked lightly on the door, saying, "Hey! The vice cops're here! Split up and get in separate rooms. Hurry!"

Within seconds the door opened and a plump naked man ran out, holding all of his clothes in his arms. He saw the uniformed cops, said, "Oh, Jesus!" and dropped the clothes, his erect penis pointing directly at Ronnie.

Inside the room, an eighteen-year-old honey-haired employee with eyebrow, nose, and lip rings, wearing a Miraculous Tan T-shirt and nothing else, was trying to get her shorts pulled up over her hips.

She said, "I was just trying to tell him his tanning time was up. Honest!"

While Bix got on his radio and asked for a unit to assist, Ronnie pointed to the man's penis and said, "I hope you had plenty of tanning lotion on that thing, sir."

Seeing that the cops weren't about to buy her story, the girl said, "When I went in to wake him up, he was laying there pounding the clown! I didn't have nothing to do with it! Honest!"

"Why, you lying little bitch," the man said, his tumescence deflating.

It was turning out to be a different sort of day for the Crow team, who didn't often get to make a felony arrest. After questioning the customer and the young employee, both of whom clearly implicated the salon manager in soliciting acts of prostitution and signed a report to that effect, Ronnie and Bix arranged for Madeline to be transported to Hollywood Station, interviewed by the vice sergeant, and booked for pandering.

A transporting unit arrived, and it happened to be the surfer cops who'd just cleared from roll call. Jetsam jumped on this one when he realized from the broadcast which Crow needed an assisting unit.

While Jetsam was chatting up Ronnie, Flotsam looked at Madeline's driver's license and said, "Holy crap. Madeline's a man! Name of Martin Lester Dilford."

The manager was standing silent, having admitted nothing, and Jetsam took out his handcuffs, saying, "Well, I guess I'll do the pat-down here, since she's a guy."

"No, you won't," Madeline said. "I'm not a man anymore. And I won't be put into a cell with men. And you won't put your hands on me."

"You're a tranny?" Flotsam said.

"Transsexual, if you please," Madeline said. "I haven't had time to change my name legally yet."

"Pre-op or post-op?" Ronnie asked.

"Post-op," Madeline said. "As of three months ago, and I'll strip and prove it if you like."

"Then I guess I'll be doing the pat-down here," Ronnie said. "Just relax, Madeline."

The desperate situation of Leonard Stilwell had gotten considerably worse. He was failing at every attempt to make a buck, and Ali Aziz had not phoned him yet about doing the job on Mt. Olympus. He had even driven up Laurel Canyon one afternoon and taken the right turn into the Mt. Olympus development, not doubting that there were more Italian cypress planted there per acre than anywhere else in the world. Leonard drove the streets and thought it looked pretty formidable. There were security company signs everywhere, and he saw a few homes where uniformed security people were standing in the driveway. He was not encouraged.

Leonard had been reduced to shoplifting from discount stores, but even boosting small merchandise wasn't so easy anymore. It was at the cyber café where Leonard got drawn into a humiliating plot to commit the most pathetic crime he could imagine.

There were more than a hundred computers for rent in the cyber café, and lots of jackals and bottom feeders whom Leonard knew, tweakers mostly, used the computers to sell stolen items and make deals for crystal meth and other drugs. Leonard had a cheap little CD player with headphones that he'd boosted and nearly got caught with when he'd bypassed the checkout counter. None of the other scavengers in the parking lot of the cyber café would trade him so much as a single rock for the CD player. One of the base heads actually sneered at him. He was about to give up when a tweaker he'd seen before but didn't know by name gave him a nod.

The tweaker was a white guy several years younger than Leonard but in far worse condition. He was jug-eared, with small, close-set eyes and pus-filled speed bumps all over his sunken cheeks. He had only a few teeth left in his grille and he grinned at Leonard. They recognized each other's desperation and that was enough. Names were not needed.

"I need a driver," the tweaker said to Leonard. "I seen you getting out of that Honda. You open for a job?"

"Let's break it down, dude," Leonard said.

The tweaker followed Leonard to his car, which was parked in front of a donut shop in the same little strip mall. After they got in Leonard's car, the tweaker lifted his T-shirt and showed a small-caliber revolver stuck in his waistband.

"Freeze-frame!" Leonard said. "I ain't into guns."

"This ain't real," the tweaker said. And he put the gun to his head and pulled the trigger. It clicked. He grinned and said, "It's a starter pistol. Unloaded."

"I think you better get outta my car," Leonard said.

"Don't flare on me, dawg!" the tweaker said. "You don't gotta do nothing but drop me off on a street. That's it. Drive me around till I see what I'm looking for and drop me off. You don't even gotta pick me back up at the scene of the crime."

"At the scene of the..." Leonard rolled his eyes and said, "Why don't you just call a taxi?"

"We might have to drive around awhile till we spot him. And if something ain't right, we may have to follow him for a little ways. I can't have a cab driver witness."

"A witness to what? You're gonna chalk a guy with a fucking starter pistol?"

"I ain't gonna dump the chump. I'm gonna jack his truck. And afterwards, I'm gonna meet you in the truck and give you two Ben Franklins. You won't even be there when I jack it."

"Lemme track. You saying I'm gonna get fucking chump change for a hijacking?"

"Man, I ain't jacking a Brinks truck."

"What're you jacking?"

"An ice-cream truck."

"There ain't a fucking sane human being left in all of Hollywood," Leonard said to the steering wheel as he gripped it tight.

The tweaker said, "See, this greaser that drives the truck, he brings his cash payment every other week to some other greaser that lent him the money to buy the truck."

"How much cash is he carrying?"

"That's my business."

"Get outta my car."

"I'll give you three Franklins."

"Out."

"Three-fifty, and that's it."

"Three-fifty," Leonard said. "I risk, what? Maybe five years in the joint for chump change?"

"Later, man," the tweaker said, opening the door.

"I'm good with it," Leonard said quickly. "These are hard times."

"Okay," the tweaker said with a gap-toothed grin. "There ain't no risk to you at all. I cased this good. You just drop me near where the guy's selling ice cream. The cash is in the metal box he keeps behind the seat of the truck. I scare the fuck outta him and jump in his truck and drive it maybe six blocks away to some safe place where you're waiting for me. I jump in your car, and you drive me back here to the cyber café."

"Dude, I want my three-fifty no matter what you end up getting from him."

"I'm cool with that," the tweaker said.

"So when do we do it?"

"In one hour," the tweaker said. "In the meantime, could you buy me a Baby Ruth bar? I got the craves so bad I could eat a fishbone sandwich if they'd dip it in chocolate."

Leonard stared for a moment at the "Help

Wanted" sign in the window of the coffee shop. He wanted to tell this lowlife slacker to get a fucking job. He wanted to, but he couldn't. Three-fifty would buy enough rock to tide him over until the fucking Ay-rab called him for the housebreaking job.

He looked at the tweaker and pulled a dollar bill from his pocket. "Go in there and buy yourself a chocolate donut. Tell them to dip it in powdered sugar. It'll get you by for a couple hours."

The hijacking was to occur on a residential street in East Hollywood, one of the few neighborhoods where a vendor could make a few dollars. Rogelio Montez was the driver of the little white truck, which played nursery tunes from a large outdoor speaker attached to the roof as he cruised the streets. He was an immigrant from the Yucatán, and this was the best job he'd ever had in his life.

Rita Kravitz, the Crow who oversaw quality-of-life complaints in that neighborhood, had contacted 6-X-66 at midwatch roll call to help her out with this ice-cream vendor. Rita Kravitz briefed the patrol officers about a chronic complainer who lived on the street, a woman who had nine school-age grandchildren and saw pedophiles everywhere.

"The alleged suspect drives one of those Good Humor sort of trucks," Rita Kravitz had told them, "and he comes by pretty late on summer evenings. Maybe seven o'clock. Just write a shake on the guy and make sure he's not driving the truck with Mister Wiggly exposed. The old lady's already accused her mailman, the meter reader, and one of the presidential contenders of being a willie wagger. Although she's probably right about the presidential contender."

Gert Von Braun said, "Okay, but you should call *Dateline* for this kinda deal. They're the ones with all the hidden cameras and lotsa time to set up on these guys."

Gert Von Braun and Dan Applewhite had gotten teamed again because Doomsday Dan requested it, now that Gil Ponce was just about off probation. Gert told the senior sergeant that she didn't mind at all working with Doomsday Dan, and the astonished sergeant later told his fellow supervisors that there truly is someone for everyone in this world.

When 6-X-66 cleared, they went straight to the neighborhood, found the vendor, and flagged him down, using the excuse that he had only one functioning brake light. Instead of writing him a ticket, they wrote an FI card from the information on his driver's license.

He spoke very little English and seemed contrite about the brake light, and grateful not to be getting a citation. He looked so threadbare and poor that Dan Applewhite insisted on paying for the ice-cream bars that the guy wanted to give to them. Then the cops remained parked at the curb while he drove off, his truck playing merry tunes enticing Latino children from their homes with coins and dollar bills in their fists, all jabbering happily in Spanglish.

Gert and Dan sat, contentedly licking their ice cream and chatting. They were growing ever more comfortable with each other, and the real bonding of police partners had begun. And of course, they'd never heard of Leonard Stilwell and knew nothing of how his life was intersecting the lives of Crow officers. It was quite pleasant to eat ice cream on that hot and dry summer evening when twilight rays of the setting sun cast a magical aura over the land of make-believe, with not a smudge of dark cloud above Sunset Boulevard.

Leonard Stilwell knew he was making a very bad mistake as he drove the tweaker toward the residential streets in East Hollywood, where the ice-cream driver was supposed to be working. First of all, the tweaker kept playing with the starter pistol, twirling it, putting it under his T-shirt inside the waistband of his jeans, and then doing quick draws.

When they were passing L. Ron Hubbard Way, a short street off Sunset Boulevard that fed into the Dianetics Building, Leonard said, "I know you need to smoke some ice real bad, but could you, like, try to chill? You're making me nervous."

The tweaker put the gun inside his jeans again and said, "Get over yourself, dawg, and stay in the game. For my pickup, you look for me one block south of Santa Monica, two blocks east of the Hollywood cemetery. Whatever that fucking street is."

"Kee-rist, dude," Leonard said, "that's the third

time you told me. Your short-term memory's gone!"

"Okay, okay, I'm just sayin'. Don't I gotta, like, keep you dialed in and make sure you got your mind in the day?"

"*My* mind?" Leonard said. "You're worrying about *my* mind?"

They were a block away from the ice-cream truck when the tweaker spotted it. "There it is, man!" he said. "Burn a right!"

"I see it," Leonard said, driving slowly, keeping an eye on the tweaker, who looked like he'd jump out and start running, given half a chance.

When he was six houses away from the truck, Leonard pulled around the corner and stopped.

The tweaker said, "Remember, you gotta meet me at —"

Unable to bear another repeated direction, Leonard interrupted, saying, "Dude, keep this in your fucked-up memory bank. If the cops get onto you, you're gonna have to outrun them in a vehicle that moves at about the speed of prostate cancer. But if you live through it and you bring me less than three-fifty, I'm gonna knock that last corn nut you call a tooth right outta your grille!"

"Chill, Phil!" the tweaker said. "You're gonna get what's coming to you. Now bang a U-ee and split."

With that, Leonard drove off, making a U-turn and watching the tweaker in his side-view mirror. The tweaker immediately began slouching toward the ice-cream truck. The last Leonard saw was the scarecrow jogging, then sprinting, in full attack mode.

Gert and Doomsday Dan were just finishing their ice-cream bars and Dan said, "Okay, we observed the vendor's normal activity and there's nothing abnormal about it. Let's log this and get on with the rest of our lives."

"Yeah, he's clean," Gert said, "but when you think about it, this would be a good job for a pedophile. Selling Eskimo Pies, Push-Ups, and Big Sticks all day long. Like, Hello, little girl, would you like to lick a big stick? Know what I mean?"

"You got a point," Dan said as Gert started the car.

"Man, there's a guy that needs ice cream bad," Gert said.

The tweaker was in an all-out sprint when they saw him in the next block. He ran straight at the vendor, who was giving two ice-cream bars to a girl about ten years old who held a younger girl by the hand. The truck's engine was running and "It's a Small World" was playing noisily.

The tweaker hit the driver hard with his shoulder, sending him sprawling. The children screamed, dropped their ice cream, and started to run. The tweaker pulled his starter pistol, pointed it at the face of the supine Mexican, and said, "Stay down or die!"

Then the tweaker leaped into the truck and drove away.

"Goddamn!" Gert Von Braun said, squealing out from the curb, turning on her light bar as Dan Applewhite got on the radio and said, "Six-X-Sixty-six is in pursuit of a two-eleven vehicle!"

The location and description of the pursued vehicle got garbled by the howling of the siren, and after clearing the frequency for the pursuit car, the radio PSR said, "Six-X-Sixty-six, repeat the location! And did you say an ice-cream truck?"

That was enough to alert a television news crew who monitored police calls. Within minutes, there was a crew speeding toward East Hollywood. Nobody wanted to miss *this* pursuit. An ice-cream truck?

Leonard Stilwell had been sitting with his engine turned off and was worried that it might not start. That would be just his luck. After a few minutes he started it. But then he got worried about overheating the old Honda and switched off the ignition again.

When the police unit was two blocks away but speeding toward him, he heard the siren. It was coming from the direction of the Hollywood cemetery. He figured it might be an ambulance. Yeah, he thought, probably an ambulance. But thirty seconds later, he said, "Fuck this!" started the car, and pulled away from the curb. No matter who that siren belonged to, Leonard Stilwell had just resigned from the hijacking business.

The tweaker was gunning the engine of the ice-cream truck for all it was worth, but it wasn't worth much. The truck was sputtering and the transmission was slipping as the truck headed north on Van Ness Avenue. Driving south on Van Ness in his direction was the tweaker's wheelman, fleeing in his Honda.

The tweaker almost swerved into him head-on and yelled out the window, "You bastard! You chickenshit asshole! Don't leave me!"

The pursued and pursuers, with 6-X-66 still the primary, blew right past Leonard in the opposite direction, and he wheeled west on Melrose, heading anywhere but to the cyber café, where there would no doubt be cops looking for him as soon as the tweaker got busted and spilled his guts. But the tweaker didn't know his name and certainly hadn't written down his license number, and anyway, the loser was so brain fried he probably wouldn't even remember what kind of car Leonard owned. As soon as Leonard got safely back to his apartment, he intended to call Ali Aziz. He needed that job. He needed money *now*.

The pursuit was coming to an end after the ice-cream truck rumbled north on the east side of Paramount Studios, then passed the Hollywood cemetery and turned west on Santa Monica Boulevard. There it caused a traffic collision when a Toyota SUV, trying to avoid broadsiding the ice-cream truck, swerved into the rear of an MTA bus. The tweaker nearly caused a second collision when he pulled a hard left onto Gower Street, nearly rolling the ice-cream truck, and slammed to a stop on the west side of the Hollywood cemetery, abandoning the truck.

Gert Von Braun had almost gotten in a TC of her own at Santa Monica and Gower, where she was stopped cold by a pair of elderly motorists who couldn't tell where in the hell the siren was coming from in the fading twilight and just stopped, completely blocking the intersection. When Gert, red faced and fuming, got around them and squealed south onto Gower Street, the cops spotted the abandoned truck.

A man walking a dog waved at them and yelled, "The guy climbed the fence and ran into the cemetery!"

The mausoleums and tombs on the cemetery grounds contained the mortal remains of Rudolph Valentino, Douglas Fairbanks, Cecil B. DeMille, and many other Hollywood immortals. A pair of security guards opened a gate for Gert Von Braun and Dan Applewhite, and now there were three other Hollywood night-watch and midwatch cars wheeling into the cemetery.

The tweaker had been running frantically through the park, and for no reason anyone could later determine, he ran to the obelisk rising into the blue-black sky with the Hollywood sign visible in the background, to the north on Mt. Lee. He waited while cops and security guards searched the cemetery grounds on foot with flashlights, and with spotlights from the police vehicles. It was there at the obelisk that the tweaker made his last mistake of the day, after being spotted by Gil Ponce, who was teamed with Cat Song.

The tweaker later told a paramedic on their way to the ER that he'd been hanging on to the starter pistol only because he wanted the police to have it if he wasn't able to get away. This, in order to prove that he hadn't used a real gun in the hijacking. The tweaker said that when he saw about two tons of blue running his way, and when a young cop spotted him and began shouting commands, he got worried about the starter pistol in his waistband, scared that the rookie would see it and panic. He said he tried to draw it out with only three fingers, like in the cowboy movies, and drop it on the ground.

But the LAPD hadn't taught Gil Ponce with cowboy-movie training films, and it was too dark to see a three-fingered draw. When the tweaker pulled the gun from his waistband, he saw orange balls of flame and was jolted back against the obelisk, struck in the upper body by two of three rounds fired by Gil Ponce.

Cat was running fast, her nine in both extended hands, when Gil fired the rounds. After the tweaker was on the ground and other cops were running to the obelisk and Cat had gotten on her rover and requested a rescue ambulance, Gil Ponce said, "He pulled a gun, Cat! I had to shoot him!"

"I know you did," she said, putting her arm around the young man. "I would've done the same thing. You did good."

By the time the tweaker arrived at the ER, he was deemed to be in serious but not critical condition. However, after a seemingly success-ful surgery, he died three hours later of a pul-monary embolism. Surgeons reported that one of the rounds had dotted the *i* on the tattoo across his bony chest, which said "Mom tried."

Despite the tweaker's statement, which the paramedic repeated in a TV interview, it

was widely believed that the trapped and surrounded robber had intended to die. In fact, the
TV reporter who covered the incident from the
start of the pursuit came on the eleven o'clock
news and described the events in the Hollywood cemetery. After reciting a long list of film
stars who were interred there, he told his audience that police had withheld the name of the
deceased until next of kin could be located.

Then, in response to a question from the
anchor desk, he said, "It is the opinion of this
reporter that, despite what was said to the paramedic in the rescue ambulance, what we have
here is another tragic case of suicide-by-cop. To
believe that the cornered robbery suspect was
trying to comply with police commands when
he pulled what appeared to be a deadly weapon
from his waistband flies in the face of credibil-
ity. If he'd wished to surrender, he would never
have done something so stupid."

Leonard Stilwell, who was lying in bed when
he saw that newscast, knew from long experience that in Hollywood, things are seldom as
they seem. And he muttered to the TV screen,
"Dude, that idiot's entire brain would fit in a
coke spoon."

FOURTEEN

EARLY THE NEXT MORNING Hollywood Nate got a phone call at home from his CRO sergeant at Hollywood South. The surfer cops had been trying to reach Nate and had left a cell number with the sergeant. When Nate called the number, Jetsam answered, and Nate could hear the sound of crashing surf in the background.

"Why am I being summoned by the headache team?" Nate wanted to know.

"Bro, Malibu is radical today!" Jetsam said. "You should be here. My partner is out there with two little newbies in thongs the size of tire patches."

"I see," Nate said. "You had to give a surf report to somebody and I won the prize?"

"No, bro," Jetsam said. "I gotta talk to you about something."

"Talk," Nate said.

Jetsam said, "I wish I could do it in person

at the station, but our hours and yours don't match too good."

The rest of it faded, and when the signal returned, Nate said, "I can't hear you."

"Shit!" Jetsam said. "Meet us at Hamburger Hamlet at noon straight up."

Then it was Nate who said "Shit!" The signal was gone and Nate figured it was probably because the goofy surfer had failed to charge his cell.

Nate was supposed to meet Rita Kravitz to talk with three members of the Homeless Committee, but he felt obliged to postpone that and meet with Flotsam and Jetsam, who would be at Hamburger Hamlet, expecting him. Hollywood Nate could only hope that Jetsam wasn't in his sleuthing mode again. The last episode had gotten him supper with Margot Aziz, but that was all it had gotten him. She still had not called.

Late that morning Leonard Stilwell dragged himself out of bed without having slept more than two hours altogether. He'd awakened several times with nightmares and had lain awake for hours before falling into a brief but fitful sleep.

For most of the night, he'd contemplated how he had barely survived catastrophe the previous evening as a result of being driven to desperate measures. He was lucky to be alive and free but had no prospects whatsoever, except for the job with Ali Aziz. His weekly rent was due in two days and he hardly had enough money to put gas in his car and enough food in his belly to keep from feeling weak and nauseous. He ate the last of the breakfast cereal right out of the box, since he had no milk, drank a cup of coffee, didn't bother shaving, and got in his car, determined to drive straight to the Leopard Lounge and demand another advance from Ali Aziz.

Leonard had to bang on the kitchen door before one of the Mexican workers looked out and opened it.

"Where's Ali?" Leonard asked.

"He ees een the office," the young guy said, obviously uncertain if he should have opened the door for Leonard.

Leonard walked past him, entered the main room, where another Mexican was vacuuming and cleaning tables, and continued down the long hallway to Ali's office. He didn't bother to knock.

"Leonard!" Ali said, irritated by the abrupt entrance.

"I gotta talk to you, Ali," Leonard said.

"I tell you I shall call."

"Yeah, well, I can't wait no more," Leonard said.

Ali Aziz glared at him. Leonard's freckled face looked blotchy. His blue eyes seemed even more empty and stupid-looking than usual. His rusty red hair was a tangled mess and he hadn't shaved in days. Ali thought he must be a fool to be involved with this thief. If only he himself knew how to open a locked door. He was starting to wonder how long it would take him to learn such a skill and if a locksmith could be hired to teach him.

Then Ali said, "I shall need you soon."

"Well, soon ain't soon enough," Leonard said. "I'm busted, man. I need money now. I'll wait, but only if I get another advance."

"No, Leonard," Ali said. "I give you one advance. We make the deal."

"Four hundred more," Leonard said. "I gotta

pay my rent and I gotta actually take some nourishment once in a while. You ever think of that?"

"We shall do the deal next week," Ali said. "I promise you."

"You said a Thursday. Tomorrow is Thursday."

"This week, no," Ali said. "Next week for sure."

"I'm outta here," Leonard said, turning toward the door.

"Okay!" Ali said. "Leonard, please. Go out to the kitchen and tell Paco to get you food. Eat. I see you in twenty minutes, okay?"

Leonard reluctantly obeyed, wondering what kind of food they'd serve in a joint where all the customers really wanted was to look at bare ass and jerk off.

When Leonard was gone, Ali pulled his worry beads from the desk drawer and fingered them while he dialed the number of the *farmacia* on Alvarado Street.

"*Bueno.*" Jaime Salgando answered it himself.

Affecting a jaunty tone he did not feel, Ali said, "What is happening, Jaime? You do not hire a girl to answer the phone no more. Business is very bad?"

Recognizing the voice and accent at once, Jaime Salgando said, "Ali, old friend! And how are you today?"

"Fine, brother, I am fine," Ali said. "But I must have a very big favor. I must ask my friend to please come for the date tonight and bring what I ordered from you. The girls are very much ready for you. This night is very much better for them."

"I can't, Ali," Jaime said. "My granddaughter is in a school play this evening and I have to be there to see her."

"Jaime," Ali said. "This is most important. I must have it. Another child on my street almost got attacked yesterday. From this killer dog."

"I'm sorry, Ali," Jaime said. "I can't disappoint my granddaughter."

"Can I come to the store and pick up my order today? I do that, okay?"

"But I haven't seen my friend yet," the pharmacist said. "I don't have what you ordered."

Ali thought of how desperate Leonard looked, and now it was his turn for desperation. He worked those worry beads for all they were worth until he came up with a plausible story. Ali said, "Jaime, my brother, I am so sorry. There is another reason that Saturday date is no good."

"What is that?"

"Tex, she is getting married on Saturday. Big wedding. We all shall go to it. She says to me she cannot have fun with old friend Jaime no more after that. Even Goldie shall go to this wedding. I have new girls to work that night. I never meet these girls before. I hire the girls from the agency. I cannot ask new girls to have a special party with my friend Jaime. I am sorry."

The pharmacist was silent for a moment and then said, "Strange. I never think of these girls as doing normal things like getting married."

"But Tex says if her friend Jaime can come tonight, she can give him a very great time. Like, how you say, it is her getting married party?"

"Bachelor party," Jaime said. "Or bachelorette, in this case."

"Exactly!" Ali said. "And Goldie says, 'Oh yes, that is going to be very much fun.'"

Again the pharmacist hesitated before speaking. "All right. I'll make a call and deliver your order to you at seven o'clock. I'd like to watch the show for a while. Then I'd like to have my private party and be home by midnight."

"All shall be as you wish, brother!" Ali said. "The dinner reservation shall be ready and so shall Tex and Goldie!"

"I didn't like that motel last time," Jaime said. "It wasn't very clean. I want to go to that nice one by the Leopard Lounge."

"Anything, brother," Ali said.

After he hung up, Ali scrolled to Tex's cell. When she answered, he said, "Tex. You shall not do the special party on Saturday. You must do the party tonight. Get Goldie. Come tonight, eight o'clock."

He had to hold the phone away when she yelled, "Goddamnit, Ali, I told you I needed tonight off! I got a date I been looking forward to! I ain't doing the old Mexican tonight and that's final!"

Ali felt his blood rising. The planning, the expense, the anxiety, the fear, it was all getting to be too much. He was doing all of this for his son. To save his beloved son from his son's bitch mother. His motives were pure and he was being obstructed by everyone!

Ali heard himself yell into the phone, "I shall

pay you big bonus! I shall pay Goldie big bonus! But you shall come tonight! You are listening to me?"

"Keep the bonus, Ali!" Tex yelled back at him. "You can fuck the old Mexican yourself, for all I care!"

Ali began choking on rage now. His eyes were bulging and he'd broken the strand that held the worry beads. He screamed into the phone: "You do like I say or I fire you! You got to fuck the old Mexican! I am the boss! The boss don't got to fuck no old Mexican!"

He was panting, and he swallowed his spit and felt light-headed and unsteady. He thought he might vomit. The worry beads were scattered all over his desk.

Then Tex's voice said calmly in his ear, "It better be a big fucking bonus, Ali. And I mean it literally."

Four of the eleven senior lead officers at the Community Relations Office were on vacation. Ronnie and Bix were filling in for the Police Explorer Program, which involved kids of both genders ages fourteen to twenty. Many of the former Explorers went on to join the LAPD when they were twenty-one years old. Ronnie liked working with the kids, who were open and eager and idealistic. She hoped they could hang on to some of that if they did become regular police officers. Of course, there was no way she could warn them about the premature cynicism that she and her colleagues had to battle throughout their careers. For these kids, cynicism was not on their desktop.

Bix Ramstead was starting to worry her more each day. Through casual conversation she learned that his wife and two children had left for their vacation, along with his wife's parents, to her parents' lakefront home in Oregon. From what he said and didn't say, Ronnie gathered that Bix's father-in-law, a retired judge and a demanding perfectionist, might not have been a best friend to his son-in-law. In any case, Bix seemed relieved not to be spending two weeks with the judge.

Since his family had gone, Ronnie thought she could see a difference in his eyes, his voice, even the steadiness of his hands. She was positive that he was drinking, and not just a little bit. Ronnie didn't think that Bix should be alone in his house for two weeks.

That day, while the two cops were taking code 7 at a good little restaurant in Thai Town, sharing a spicy, hot shrimp salad, she said, "Must get lonely for you with the family gone."

"I've got our dog, Annie, to keep me company," he said. "How about you? You're always alone."

"I'm used to it," she said. "But you're used to a wife and a couple of adolescents charging around. How're you coping with silence?"

"I get to watch whatever TV program I like," Bix said. "With a big, slobbery dog sleeping in my lap. And I don't have to make the bed."

"You know you're always welcome to join us for our burrito rendezvous on Sunset Boulevard. Sometimes Cat shows up, or Hollywood Nate. Rita Kravitz is usually there, and Tony Silva. The boss comes by once in a while. In fact, we might be going there tonight."

"No, thanks," he said. "I think I'll try for eight hours' sleep, if Annie will let me. She sleeps crossways and takes up most of the bed. She kicks like a mule in her sleep and passes enough gas to launch the Goodyear blimp."

Ronnie hesitated, then said, "Are you still concerned about the, you know, booze thing when you go out with a bunch of coppers?"

"It enters my mind," Bix said, "but that's not the reason."

"How long's it been since you had a drink?"

"I don't count the days like an alcoholic does," he said. "But it's been well over a month."

"Do you miss it?"

He shrugged and said, "I can take it or leave it."

Ronnie Sinclair knew that Bix Ramstead was lying.

"No shoes, no service," the imperious hostess at Hamburger Hamlet — one of the legion of otherwise unemployable liberal arts majors who staffed nearly every nonethnic restaurant and bar in Hollywood — said to the surfer cops when they walked through the front door.

"Bro, I didn't notice you were shoeless," Jetsam said to his partner when they returned to Flotsam's GMC pickup to get his sneakers. "You gotta show some class."

"Why do you take me to fancy establishments where you gotta wear shoes?" Flotsam said. "I'm so used to running around the beach all day, I don't know if I got flip-flops on or not. You think I spend a lotta time looking at my own feet?"

"Since we're not packing, I hope nobody tries to steal our boards," Jetsam said, their guns being under the seat of the locked truck. "Anyways, the wusses that run the consent decree would go all PMS-ey if we capped a surfboard thief."

"Only if they're oppressed minorities," Flotsam said. "If they're white, you can shoot them down like rabid pit bulls and back over them in your truck five or six times."

"Check the city demographics, bro," Jetsam said. "We're the oppressed minority."

When they reentered Hamburger Hamlet, they got disapproving looks from the hostess, this pair of surfers in baggy T-shirts and board shorts, with salt still clinging to their sunburned faces, and sand falling from their hair. They couldn't have looked more like surfers if they'd been wearing half-peeled wet suits, but at least she could now count four sneakers on their sockless feet, so they got seated in a booth to await the arrival of Hollywood Nate Weiss.

They only had to wait ten minutes, and both were hydrating with their second iced tea when Nate entered and sat down.

"To what do I owe the pleasure of doing lunch with you two sand crabs?" Nate said.

"Wanna cold drink?" Jetsam said when the waitress came over to their table. She was an Asian with very nice legs.

"I'll have what they're drinking," Nate said.

"Iced tea coming up," she said. "Lemme know when you want something else."

Nate checked her out as she was walking away and said, "I might just do that." Then he said to Jetsam, "So you wanted face time. What's up?"

Flotsam assumed his "I got nothing to do with this" pose, and Jetsam said, "Last Friday night we wrote a parking ticket to a guy named Leonard Stilwell. The name mean anything to you?"

Nate looked puzzled and said, "Nope."

"Wormy-looking white dude. Maybe a tweaker, maybe a crackhead. Fortyish. Medium height. Red hair, freckles, black Honda with primer spots?"

Nate shook his head and said, "*Nada*. Am I supposed to know him?"

Jetsam said, "I dunno, but he had an address in his car, and just for the hell of it we checked it out, because this dude shouldn't be having an address up on Mount Olympus. Not unless he's going there to clean out their garage or something. He's got a couple priors for burglary."

"Still not tracking," Nate said.

"So we don't find the address," Jetsam said. "The number's off a little bit. But right near there where the address should be, we see a car."

"*His* car?" Nate said.

"Not *his* car," Jetsam said.

That brought things to a sudden stop. Nate frowned slightly and said, "You saw my car?"

"SAG4NW," Jetsam said. "So we thought you should know about this burglar Stilwell, is all."

Flotsam corrected his partner, saying, "*He* thought you should know. Me, I'm neutral in this matter."

Hollywood Nate didn't speak for a moment and then said, "It was the wrong address, you said."

"Yeah, but there was no street address to exactly match the one on the piece of paper. If I remember right, the address you were visiting ended in four eight? His address ended in two six. But then the street turns and the numbers are totally different. The house you were in is closest to the number he wrote down."

Flotsam was sick of this. He said to Nate, "Dude, my pard thinks whoever lives in that house might be a future crime victim or maybe a present criminal if they're connected to this dirtbag Leonard Stilwell. That's, like, the short-hand version of this here drama."

"What's, like, the longhand version?" Nate said.

"The longhand version is that my pard is all goony over Sinclair Squared, and he would love to become a Crow and work with her, even though she don't know a surfboard from an ironing board. But come to think of it, when-ever somebody asks her to iron something, she divorces him. And since she don't marry nobody unless his name is Sinclair, I wish he'd either change his name to Sinclair or stop all this Sherlock shit, because it's wearing me down!"

Jetsam just looked at his partner, astonished. He'd never seen Flotsam so exercised.

"What's his crush on Ronnie got to do with

the burglar?" Nate asked Flotsam, as though Jetsam weren't there.

"He heard that Ronnie and Bix Ramstead were working that part of the Hollywood Hills, kissing ass with all those rich whiners up there, and he's, like, trying to bring the spotlight on this and score points with Ronnie and maybe the Crow sergeant."

Jetsam still stared at his partner in astonishment and finally said, "Bro, why didn't you switch to my frequency? I didn't know you were all vaporized about this!"

"I been trying to for days," Flotsam said. "You ain't been the same ever since you fired off flares over the SUVs in the body shop. You're, like, totally spring-loaded. You just don't listen to body language no more!"

"I didn't know you were all bent, bro!"

"Work out your domestic partnership later," Nate said. "I can tell you that the person who lives in that house is not some kind of crook. As to being a target of this guy Stilwell, I just don't know."

"Is she your squeeze?" Flotsam said with a leer.

"Hey, I don't ask you about your Bettys," Nate said.

"Dude, you are hormonally spirited!" Flotsam said admiringly.

Rebounding from Flotsam's tirade, Jetsam said to Nate, "It wouldn't hurt to ask your squeeze — I mean, the person who lives there — if she knows a Leonard Stilwell. If she don't, it might be something to talk over with the burglary dicks. Trust me, bro, that pus bucket Stilwell is a waste of good air, and he's up to no good."

"I'll give her a call," Nate said, "and see what she knows."

"Is she a hottie or just rich?" Flotsam said to Nate with that same annoying leer.

"She's just somebody with a car for sale," Nate said. "I was talking to her about her SUV."

It had slipped from Nate's mouth before he could stop it, and Jetsam jumped on it. "Hey, bro! That's the SUV from the body shop, ain't it? The one you talked to the guy about?"

Nate saw both surfers looking at him expectantly now. He decided to tell the truth. He said, "Yeah, that's the one. And yeah, she's a burner babe, but nothing happened."

"This is destiny at work, bro!" Jetsam said with a flourish. "There's only a few degrees of separation here. We're all part of some inscrutable plan!"

Nate was speechless until Flotsam said, "He gets like this after we been surfing. He sits out there on the water and gets, like, these visions. They make him go all surfboard simple for the rest of the day. He'll be okay later."

"At least you should bounce for the iced tea," Nate said, finishing his drink.

"Yeah, dude, it's on us," Flotsam said. "But if you want my opinion, you oughtta shine them Hills honeys. All that sculpted flesh and five-karat diamonds look good, but there's, like, better ways to escape your humdrum existence. Grab yourself a log and come to Malibu. We'll be your gurus."

Jetsam agreed, saying, "Bro, it's way wack to go all frothy over Mount Olympus bitches, who think their shit should be gilded and hung on gold chains."

Flotsam concurred, saying, "Yeah, they think their turds should be bronzed and kept in trophy cases, dude."

"Come to Malibu, bro," Jetsam said. "Maybe you'll have a vision too and find your true self."

Nate stood up then, nodded, and said, "Am I ever glad I came here today. All this time I've been buying lottery tickets and stalking talent agents, and the answer was right before my eyes. I just couldn't see it till you sea slugs dialed me in. It all comes down to a surfboard. The stuff that dreams are made of!"

There was no better time of day in Hollywood than twilight, as far as Ronnie Sinclair was concerned. The way the setting sun blasted through the low-hanging summer smog actually burnished the pollution into garish wine-colored clouds. After which, a scarlet glare was cast over the boulevards announcing to all: This place is unlike any other. Here even the toxic gases are beautiful!

After lunch, followed by a perfunctory visual check to see if there were signs of the homeless encampment springing up again, Ronnie drove them back toward Hollywood Boulevard. Bix Ramstead answered his cell phone and the look on his face startled her.

Bix reddened and whispered into the phone, "I'm working. I can't talk. I'll call you later." He snapped the phone shut and said, "My brother Pete. He's a pain. Always borrowing money, never paying it back."

"Yeah, my sister used to be like that till her husband made it big," Ronnie said, looking at Bix, who was smiling but not with those heavily lashed gray eyes she loved. And she knew he was lying again. That was not brother Pete on the cell call.

"Maybe I oughtta join you guys the next time you go up to Sunset Boulevard for a Mexican dinner," Bix said abruptly. "With my family gone, I guess I should get out and mix a bit. Gets lonely talking to a dog, even one as smart as Annie."

"I'll bet she's smarter than most of the people we call on every day," Ronnie said. "I found out that our posse won't be doing our Mexican thing tonight after all, but if you're not busy, I'd be glad to meet you there."

She had never detected a sexual vibe coming her way from Bix Ramstead and she didn't detect it now when he said, "I might do that. When, right after we go end-of-watch?"

"Okay by me," she said. "And I'll pop for it,

since I'm a semiprosperous single copper with nobody to spend my money on but me and two goldfish."

Then another phone call came in, this one on Ronnie's cell. She picked it up and said, "Officer Sinclair."

"It's Nate," Hollywood Nate said to her. "Can I talk to Bix?"

"Sure," she said, handing Bix her phone and saying, "It's Nate."

"To what do we owe the pleasure?" Bix said to him.

Then the smile was gone. His face darkened yet again. His lips turned down and he said, "Yeah, I know the resident at that address." After a moment he said, "I, uh, I'll see you back at Hollywood South and we can talk about it. In an hour, okay?"

When he hung up this time, he felt he definitely owed his partner an explanation, so he said to Ronnie, "Just some Hollywood Nate deal. A person on Mount Olympus that I dealt with on a prior call might be a burglary target. Some guy with four-five-nine priors had the resident's address in his car, or a similar address to that one. It's just bullshit, I'm sure. It's nothing."

The brooding look on his face said that it was not nothing to Bix Ramstead. And Ronnie Sinclair knew that he was lying to her yet again.

Ali Aziz couldn't eat a bite all day. He mulled over his plan a dozen times and he couldn't stop sweating. He even used the shower in the dancers' bathroom and steamed himself clean, letting the hot water pelt his balding dome until it turned pink. He went to the closet in his office and changed into a clean silk shirt. He shaved his face, doused himself with cologne, and flopped onto the leather sofa in his office and tried to nap, but he could not.

He didn't want food or whiskey or women. He only wanted this torment to be over. He wanted Margot to be gone forever. He wanted to have his son, Nicky, and to take him away from this terrible city, from this terrible, godless country someday. Here, there was no respect, no love, no truth. Everything here was a lie.

Jaime Salgando showed up half an hour early at the Leopard Lounge. When he entered Ali's office, he said, "Traffic was light for once."

Ali looked approvingly at Jaime's double-breasted pinstriped suit, wondering if it was a Hugo Boss. And at his starched white shirt with shooting cuffs and gold links and at his sky blue necktie with a perfect knot, and he said, "This is how gentlemen dress. In my country, in your country, men have respect. In this country, no respect."

Jaime said, "Thank you," and sat in the client chair nervously, wanting to get the business finished.

"The girls shall arrive at eight o'clock, like you say," Ali said.

"Yes, yes," Jaime said, "that gives us a chance to do our business. I have an acquaintance at a compounding pharmacy who helps me with these unusual orders."

"What is the meaning of 'compounding'?"

"They mix a lot of drugs and medications for special prescription orders. This employee is from the village in Mexico where I used to spend my summers. He was able to help me, but it cost me six hundred dollars."

Ali looked at him, trying to keep his smile in place. He knew that Jaime was lying to him, but he was powerless. Everyone lied to him. By forcing Jaime to come tonight instead of

Saturday, he was going to pay a price. Ali took the roll of hundreds from his gold money clip and counted out six bills, placing them on the desk.

"Of course, my brother," Ali said. "We got to pay for good service always. That is the American way."

Jaime Salgando picked up the bills and put them in his pocket and withdrew a small pill envelope with his pharmacy's name on it. He opened it and dropped two green capsules on the desktop, then put the envelope back in his pocket.

Ali nearly panicked. "Two?" he said. "I need *two* capsules to kill the dog?"

"No, you only need one of these to easily kill a fifty-kilo dog. The other is just in case the dog does not take the bait or if something goes wrong. Then you can try again some other time."

Ali's relief was palpable. "You are a smart man, brother," he said. "Very smart. Yes, is good to have the, how you say, backdown?"

"Backup."

"Yes, we got the backup now. Very good. Very good."

"I'd like a drink while I wait for the girls."

"Yes, yes," Ali said. "Anything. You want champagne? I got good champagne for special customers."

"I want a bottle of good champagne brought to the motel," Jaime said, very businesslike and matter-of-fact. "Make it two bottles. And an ice bucket. And three glasses, of course. But for now I'd like a double shot of tequila. The Patrón Silver that you serve to your special clients."

"You got it, brother," Ali said, but now his forced smile had turned grim and produced white lines around his mouth. Ali was starting to loathe Jaime Salgando nearly as much as he loathed the other thieves with whom he was forced to do business. Almost as much as he loathed Leonard Stilwell.

By the time the pharmacist had finished his tequila shooter, there was a knock at the door and Tex entered with Goldie.

"Jaime, you rascal!" Tex drawled. "I'm so glad you could make it tonight!"

"Me too!" Goldie said. "This is just too cool for school!"

Both women giggled when the courtly pharmacist rose and kissed their hands. They were both dressed in black Chanel knockoffs with spaghetti straps, as though for one of their nights on the Sunset Strip. Goldie wore three-inch open-toed heels, but because the pharmacist had special needs, Tex did not wear hers. She wore lizard-skin cowboy boots that she used in her act, and a new snow-white cowboy hat with a rhinestone *T* across the crown.

When Jaime Salgando and the dancers were gone, Ali locked the door and took the green capsules out of his desk drawer and looked at them. For what this evening was costing him, he wished he could have put one of them in the pharmacist's tequila.

Ali reached into the back of the drawer and brought out the magenta-and-turquoise capsule he had stolen from Margot's medicine cabinet, along with the coke spoon and razor blade that he used when he had to give the girls a toot in exchange for services. He put the items on a clean sheet of bond paper along with the two green capsules and a funnel he'd fashioned from a sheet of heavier bond. He carefully pulled open the sleep aid and dumped the contents into the trash basket. Then he wiped his hands and held them palms down in front of him to make sure they were not trembling.

He very carefully pulled open the green capsule and poured the contents into the homemade funnel. It looked something like a mixture of cocaine and sugar might look. Then he picked up the empty magenta-and-turquoise capsule with tweezers and funneled the lethal dose into it. The green capsule contained a bit more than 50 milligrams, so there were some granules left over and it concerned him. But the pharmacist had seemed very confident that this would kill a 50-kilo animal, so there must be more than enough to do the job.

He was going to dump the remaining granules from the green capsule into his trash basket, but instead he took the residue into his bathroom and flushed it away. He washed his hands thoroughly and for no logical reason burned the paper he had used. He put the lethal capsule, which now looked like just another of Margot's sleep aids, into an envelope along with the other deadly green sister and stored them far back in his middle drawer alongside the full vial of capsules.

His only concern now was that Margot might only have a few capsules left in her sleep aid vial. And that would mean he'd be afraid to add too many more, for fear of making it obvious. If that was the case, she'd die in the next few weeks rather than in the next few months, after she had gone to wherever it was that she was taking his son. Ali feared that outcome. He wanted her to be found dead in that other place, so that there would be little reason for investigators to look for answers back in Hollywood.

Then he felt his heart go hollow as he thought of where she might go to live when the house closed escrow, those places she had talked about. San Francisco? New York? If the judge permitted this, he might not be able to see his precious boy from the time she moved away until she died. The thought of not seeing Nicky for two months or more made Ali Aziz put his face down on his folded arms and weep.

FIFTEEN

"MAN, YOU AIN'T RIGHT for this work," his neighbor known as Junior said to Leonard Stilwell that evening while Ali Aziz wept and the Mexican pharmacist partied.

Leonard and Junior had been practicing for twenty minutes with a TR4 tension bar and a double-diamond pick that Leonard was planning to borrow from Junior for the job tomorrow. Junior's apartment, three doors down the hall from Leonard's, was about what Leonard had always found in a parolee's crib: Cuervo bottles, porn mags, a half-eaten chocolate cake, candy wrappers everywhere. The room was so small, the giant Fijian would have had to stand in the kitchenette to make the bed, which he never did. He had huge hands and lots of jailhouse tatts that were nearly invisible on his dark skin.

After getting Junior away from the cartoon channel, Leonard was kneeling on the floor with the door open, trying to unlock the double-sided dead bolt with a thumb-turn on the inside. He was interrupted when a fat cockroach crawled up his neck, causing him to yelp and do a roach dance, slapping at his neck and shaking like a wet dog.

"They do not hurt you, bro," Junior said. "Back home we eat them bugs if they too dumb to get off our food."

"I'm scared of roaches," Leonard said. "I grew up in Yuma with six brothers and sisters and a drunk old man that never worked. Cockroaches crawled all over us when we were sleeping, and so did the rats."

"Bro, back home we eat them rats too. No problem."

"Okay, lemme try again," Leonard said.

The tension bar looked to Leonard like a very slender Allen wrench, and the pick, which Junior called a rake, was like a four-inch needle with what looked like a couple of camel humps on the end of it. The fact of the matter was, Leonard had never picked a lock in his entire life and had never bothered to learn from Whitey Dawson, not even once on the dozen jobs they'd done together.

"Man, you was not born for this work," Junior said. "You sure you wanna take the job? You gonna fuck up and get busted."

"I seen it done lots of times when I had a partner," Leonard said. "It looked easy when he did it."

"Why don't you cut that partner in on this job, bro? I don't think you gonna be teachable."

"He's dead."

"Too bad, man. Wish I could help you but I promise my mommy I ain't gonna do no crime no more."

"Show me again," Leonard said. "One more time."

The big Fijian held the tension bar in his massive hand, inserted it, and said, "See, bro, the tension bar turn the cylinder." He slid the pick inside with the other hand and said, "The rake, it lift up the pin." Then he turned the knob easily and handed the little tools to Leonard, saying, "My granddaddy could do this, and he lost one hand to a mako shark."

"Lemme try once more," Leonard said, and he concentrated on copying the big Fijian's finger moves.

He inserted the tension bar and said, "With

this I turn the cylinder." Then he inserted the pick and said, "With this I lift the pin." And he felt it.

"Yes!" he said when he turned the knob.

He did it once more, and again it worked.

"You there, bro!" the Fijian said.

"I'll bring them back to you tomorrow night," Leonard said, putting the instruments in his pocket.

"You get caught, man, you don't know me. You never heard of nobody from Fiji. Not even Vijay Singh."

"I'm good with that," Leonard said. "And when I bring the tools back, you'll get the President Grant, like I promised."

"If you ain't in jail," the Fijian said.

"Later, man," Leonard said, walking out.

"Hey, bro," the Fijian said, "I just remember. Could you gimme a ride to the clinic? I caught the clap from some whore, and the doc say come back for a checkup."

"Yeah, I'll drop you," Leonard said. "Where you being treated?"

The Fijian aimed a fat index finger at his genitals and said, "Down there."

★ ★ ★

When Ronnie and Bix returned to Hollywood South to turn in their car and check out, Hollywood Nate was waiting with his feet up on a desk, reading *Daily Variety*. Bix didn't look happy to see him.

"Go on ahead," Bix said to Ronnie. "I gotta talk to Nate for a minute. I'll meet you at the restaurant, okay?"

"Okay," she said, glancing at Nate, but he just gave her a little wave, betraying nothing.

Ronnie entered the women's locker room to change out of her uniform, more uncertain than ever about her partner. There was something going on other than secret drinking. But what would it have to do with Hollywood Nate Weiss, who was sitting there like a sphinx? If she only knew Bix a little better, she'd just grab him and blurt out some questions she wanted answered. But for now she didn't feel she had the right to intrude.

Bix and Nate walked outside and stood on the step in front of Hollywood South. Traffic was light on Fountain Avenue for such a balmy summer evening. At times like these, old residents of the neighborhood could almost smell the flower gardens and citrus trees that everyone used to cultivate back in the day. But now, in the most traffic-choked city in North America, there was only the smell of engine exhaust.

"Now, what's this about?" Bix said, sitting on the step.

Nate also sat and said, "Like I told you on the phone, the surfers jacked up some dude with four-five-nine priors who had an address in his car. It was a bad address but the closest number to it belongs to someone named Margot Aziz."

Bix Ramstead gave Nate a blank look and said, "What's that got to do with me?"

"Flotsam and Jetsam were wondering if this guy might be employed by the homeowner. His name's Leonard Stilwell. A white dude about forty, medium height and weight, red hair and freckles. He drives a shitty old black Honda with primer spots on it. If he's not working for the homeowner, he might be targeting the house for a four-five-nine. That's what our sleuthing surfers think."

"Again, what's that got to do with me?" Bix said.

Nate had given Bix enough bait, but he

hadn't come close to taking it. So Nate decided to tell a half-truth.

"They drove up Mount Olympus a little later and saw one of our cars up there."

Of course Bix thought that "our cars" referred to police vehicles, and he said, "What night was that?"

"I don't know," Nate said, telling another half-truth. "But they checked and found out who was driving the car that night."

Bix Ramstead looked like he was pondering it and then he said, "Well, if it was the night before last, it was me."

And that was all he said. He looked at Nate as though it was his turn to talk.

Nate said, "I'm not asking you about your business, Bix. It's just that they thought this dude Stilwell is bad news and they just wondered —"

Interrupting, Bix said, "I know the woman who lives there. Last year we met at a Tip-A-Cop fund-raiser, and she calls me with problems occasionally."

Nate would always look back on this moment and regret that he'd not been brave enough and honest enough to show and tell, to compare notes on Margot Aziz. But all he said was

"I don't suppose the problem had to do with somebody who fit the description of this guy Stilwell?"

"No," Bix said, looking less tense, more forthcoming. "Actually, she's worried about her husband, Ali Aziz. Do you know the Leopard Lounge?"

"Topless joint on Sunset?"

"That's it."

"Yeah, I know where it is."

"Ali Aziz is the owner. Anyway, they're in the middle of a raging divorce and custody battle, and she's afraid he's gonna do her harm."

"Is he one of those nightclub-owning gangsters, like the Russians?"

"No," Bix said. "He's just some semi-sleazy operator from the Middle East who found his American dream selling T and A."

Now Nate was the one feeling less tense. It was all in sync with what Margot Aziz had said to him. Of course, the big question tormenting Nate was whether Bix was more than just a professional acquaintance of Margot's. Again he tried to summon the nerve to ask Bix, and to reveal to him that she had almost offered to let Nate move into her house, and that she'd spent an evening trying to pour booze down his throat.

But all he could bring himself to say was "So do you think somebody should ask if she knows Stilwell?"

"I don't see why we should add to her worries. She's paranoid enough about her husband. After all, you said it was a different house number."

"Yeah, but the number he had doesn't exist, and the Aziz address is the only one close to it."

"If it's bothering you, I guess I could call her tomorrow and ask if she knows the guy. Maybe he's giving her a price on window washing or something. She happened to mention the house is in escrow and she'll be moving."

"It's not bothering me. It's bothering those log-head surfers."

"I can call her," Bix said. "Maybe tomorrow."

Nate tried to make it sound casual when he said, "Is she an older woman?"

"Why do you ask that?" Bix said.

"Well, if she's an older woman, I wouldn't wanna scare her."

"An older woman in a custody battle?"

"Oh, that's right, I forgot," Nate said. "She can't be that old."

Bix said, "I'll give her a call tomorrow, just to be on the safe side."

And that was all the nibbling around the edges that Hollywood Nate was prepared to do. He was convinced that Bix Ramstead was more than an acquaintance of Margot Aziz's. Because anybody on the planet, when asked if Margot was an older woman, would have said that far from being an older woman, she was a Hills honey who could stop traffic at noon on Rodeo Drive or anywhere else, no matter how much competition was out there. But Bix hadn't done that.

"Well, I gotta change and meet Ronnie for some carne asada," Bix said. "Wanna join us?"

"Naw, I think I'll go in the workout room and hit the treadmill," Nate said. "I got my physical coming up in two weeks."

"Catch you tomorrow," Bix said.

And suddenly Nate Weiss didn't feel so bad about not telling the whole truth to Bix Ramstead, because he was absolutely certain that Bix had been lying to him.

★ ★ ★

Midwatch unit 6-X-66 was having an uneventful tour of duty so far. Gert Von Braun had written a ticket to a guy in a Humvee who'd been gawking at a dragon hustling tricks on Santa Monica Boulevard. He blew through the stoplight at Western Avenue, almost broadsiding a car full of Asian kids. Then they'd refereed a family dispute involving a soldier just back from Iraq whose wife had moved in with her boss's son and wouldn't let the soldier have personal property that he said belonged to his mother.

Then, two hours into their watch, they'd received a message on their MDC computer that sent them to the bungalow of a ninety-year-old lifelong resident of East Hollywood who claimed that a possible home invader was watching her house. When Gert and Dan Applewhite arrived, they found the old woman sitting in a rocker on her front porch, stroking a Persian cat. A light burned inside and a cable news channel was on.

You could count the old woman's bones through flesh the color of antique ivory, but she seemed very alert and described the suspicious man to Gert and Dan as having black hair and "large, liquid brown eyes."

When Gert asked if she had any idea who the man was, the old woman said, yes, his name might be Tyrone Power.

Gert, who was nearly twenty years younger than Doomsday Dan, said, "Is this Tyrone Power a black man or white?"

"He's white," Dan said to Gert.

Gert looked at Dan and said, "How do you know?"

Instead of answering Gert, Dan said to the old woman, "Was he wearing a black mask, by any chance? And did he carry a sword?"

"No," the old woman said. "Not this time."

"On other occasions?" Dan asked.

"Oh, yes, sometimes," she said.

"Did he ever carve a *Z* on any objects around here?"

"He might have," she said. "He's very handsome."

"I know exactly where this man is," Dan said.

"You do?" the old woman said.

"Yes, and I'll see to it that he doesn't come around bothering you again. You don't have to worry about it. Do you live with someone?"

"Yes, I live with my daughter. She's at work."

"Well, you can sleep tight. We'll take care of that fellow."

"You won't hurt him, will you?" she said. "He's very handsome."

"I promise we will not hurt him," Dan Applewhite said.

When they were walking to their shop, Gert said, "So, okay. Who's this Tyrone Power?"

"You're too young to know, but he was a big movie star."

"And you say you know exactly where to find him?"

"Yes, in a mausoleum at the Hollywood cemetery," Dan Applewhite said.

Gert cleared by pressing a button on the MDC keyboard and they resumed patrol, Dan driving and Gert keeping score. She logged the call and then looked over at Dan.

"You know what I heard about you?" she said.

"What's that?"

"I hear you're a serial groom, that you've been married four times."

"That's a lie," he said. "Three times."

"You don't like to stay married very long, huh?"

"I've been married a long time," he said, "but to three different women."

"Got kids?"

"Only one," Dan said.

"How old?"

"Twenty-six. He's a computer geek, and a whiner like his mother. How about you?"

"Never been married," she said. "This job isn't conducive."

"You've got lotsa time," he said. "You're young."

"Look at me. I don't have anybody breaking down my door," she said.

He turned and did take a good look at her and he said, "Whadda you mean?"

"I'm wide," she said with defiance in her eyes. "Ask Treakle."

"You care what Chickenlips thinks?" Dan said. "I think you look healthy. I'm sick of anorexic women. My last two wives figured out a way to throw up more food than they ever swallowed."

"My dad's a skinny German," she said, "but my mom's Dutch, with big shoulders and wide hips. From picking too many tulips, I guess. I favor her side of the family."

"I like the way you look," Dan said.

Gert smiled slightly and said, "Tyrone Power, huh? I'm gonna have to educate myself. He played Zorro?"

"Long before Antonio Banderas," Dan said. "You like old movies?"

"I haven't seen too many, but yeah, I do."

"I know an art house cinema where they even show silents. You should go with me sometime. I mean, not like a date or anything. I know my sell-by date is way past."

"You're not that old," she said.

"You don't think so?" said Doomsday Dan.

The incipient flirtation was interrupted by another computer message, directing them to an address familiar to Ronnie Sinclair and Bix Ramstead.

When 6-X-66 arrived at that address and knocked, a portly black woman came to the door. She pointed across the street at a wood-frame cottage where two shopping carts were overturned in the tiny front yard.

"I'm Mrs. Farnsworth," she said. "I've called you all about the people over there. About the shopping carts in the yard and about the noise."

"Is that what this is about?" Gert said. "Noise?"

"No, this is about the quiet," she said. "It's too quiet over there. At this time of evening they usually got this weird Somali music blaring. But not tonight."

"Maybe they're not home," Dan said.

"They're home," Mrs. Farnsworth said. "I seen them through their windows an hour ago, but now the blinds are down."

"Maybe they went to bed," Gert said.

"Honey, they don't go to bed till two, three A.M.," Mrs. Farnsworth said. "At least *he* don't. He yells at her all the time. And I know he beats her, but she won't say nothing whenever I get a chance to ask her about it."

"It's pretty hard for us to go knock on people's doors and ask them why they're being so quiet," Dan said.

"There's a young man," Mrs. Farnsworth said, "a young white man. He used to drive her home once in a while. She cleans his house, is what she told me. He lives with his handicapped parents and he has a good job and he's good to her, she said. One day I seen him drop her off, and her husband came outta the house with only his underwear on and he grabbed her arm and started jabbering in their language and dragged her into the house and slammed the door. After that she took the bus home from her house-cleaning jobs. He's a very mean man and she's a very sweet and frightened girl."

Gert looked at Dan and he said, "We can knock and try to think of some reason for doing it. Just to make sure everything's okay."

"The shopping carts," Mrs. Farnsworth said. "He's been warned about that before." Then she went to a bookshelf and removed a porcelain vase with some cards inside. She handed one to Gert, saying, "The officer wrote his personal phone number on the back of the card and said I could call him anytime."

Gert read it and said, "Officer Bix Ramstead." Then she said to the woman, "We'll knock and see what's what."

"Please," Mrs. Farnsworth said. "I'm really worried about that girl. And so was that Officer Ramstead. You could see it in his face."

Gert Von Braun and Dan Applewhite crossed the residential street, needing their flashlights to keep from stepping into the potholes that the city of Los Angeles hadn't the financial resources to repair.

They listened and heard nothing inside. Dan knocked. No answer.

Gert walked a few steps to the window and listened. Dan knocked again. No answer.

Dan said, "There's nothing more we can do here."

Gert put her palm up to hush him and pressed her ear to the door. "I think I hear something," she said.

"What's it sound like?"

"It's very faint. Like a man chanting or something. In their language, not ours."

Dan drew his baton and banged it on the door, good and loud. Gert kept listening after he stopped.

"Anything change in the sound?" he said.

She shook her head and tried the knob. It was locked.

"Maybe we should call a supervisor," Gert said. "To give us an okay to enter."

"And take the chance of drawing Chicken-lips Treakle?"

"Forget the supervisor," Gert said.

Both cops walked back to the street. Gert said, "Put your light on this."

Dan held the business card and lit it for her with his flashlight beam. She took out her cell and dialed the handwritten number on the back of the card.

The Crows were in their street clothes: Ronnie in a striped, tapered shirt, and jeans from Banana, and Bix in a yellow polo shirt and chinos from the Gap. Ronnie thought he was even better-looking out of uniform. LAPD blue seemed somehow unbecoming to him. Ronnie had ordered the chile relleno plate and a margarita. Bix had ordered two carne asada tacos and a cold *horchata,* made of rice water and cinnamon. Ronnie had hesitated before ordering an alcoholic drink in front of Bix but then figured it would make him even more uncomfortable to know she was avoiding booze for his sake.

They were halfway through dinner when his cell chimed. Ronnie wondered if it might be the mysterious caller who'd made him so uncomfortable. The one he'd lied about, saying it was his brother Pete.

He looked at the number and didn't recognize it. "Hello," he said.

"This is Six-X-Sixty-six, Von Braun here," Gert said. "Is this Officer Bix Ramstead?"

"Yeah," he said. "What's going on?"

"I got your number from a Mrs. Farnsworth," Gert said. "It's about some Somalians that live across the street from her. She tells me you know something about them."

"What happened?" Bix said.

"It's weird," Gert said. "Apparently they're in there, but they won't answer the door. The house is way too quiet to suit Mrs. Farnsworth, and I can hear the guy inside chanting some voodoo or something."

"Are you going in?"

"We don't know whether to back off or bang on the door some more or what."

"Did you call a sergeant?"

"No, we're afraid we'd get Treakle. He'd turn it into a fire drill."

"I'll be right there," Bix said.

When he closed his cell, he pulled some bills from his wallet and put them on the table. "That was a midwatch officer. It's the Somalians. Something's wrong and they won't open the door."

"Where're you going?"

"He might open the door for me. I established some rapport with him."

"Bix, you're off duty," Ronnie said. "Let a supervisor deal with it. You shouldn't get involved."

"Finish your dinner, Ronnie," Bix said. "I'll call you when I check it out."

"This is not your responsibility," Ronnie said.

"I feel I should've done more," he said, turning toward the door. "I had a gut feeling."

"We did what we could at the time," Ronnie called after him. "If something bad happened there, it's not your tragedy, Bix!"

She didn't know if he heard that last part or not. Bix Ramstead was running out the door to the parking lot.

Mrs. Farnsworth was standing on the street by the black-and-white. She'd given Gert and Dan each a cup of coffee, which they were finishing when Bix Ramstead drove up and parked his personal car, a family-friendly Dodge minivan.

The cops gave their empty cups to Mrs. Farnsworth, who said, "Evening, Officer Ramstead."

"Hello, Mrs. Farnsworth," Bix said. "I'm glad you kept my card."

"It's real quiet in there," she said to Bix. "And it's never quiet in there. And he got real mad at her last week when a young white man she works for gave her a ride home. If he'd hit her, I woulda called you. But he just grabbed her arm and got in her face and yelled angry Somali talk. And she took the bus home the next day without the young white man. It shouldn't be so quiet in there like it is tonight, Officer Ramstead. I'm scared for that girl."

A moment later, all three cops were back on the front porch of the wood-frame cottage. They stood silently and listened. There was only the hum of traffic on the nearby four-lane avenue and the sound of a dog barking nearby and the whirring of cicadas in the yard next door and faint salsa music from somewhere down the block. Then they heard the sound of a deep male voice, chanting prayers.

Bix knocked at the door and said, "Mr. Benawi, it's Officer Ramstead. I spoke to you last week about the shopping carts, remember?"

They listened again. The chanting stopped.

Bix said, "Mr. Benawi, please open the door. I need to talk to you. It's okay about the shopping carts. I just need to know that everything else is all right. Open the door, Mr. Benawi."

The chanting started again and Gert Von Braun felt a shiver, but it was a warm, dry summer evening with a Santa Ana blowing hot wind from the desert to the sea. Dan Applewhite felt the hair on his neck tingle and he knew it wasn't caused by the Santa Ana.

Bix Ramstead said, "We're not leaving until you open the door, Mr. Benawi. Don't make us do a forced entry."

The chanting stopped again. They heard padded footsteps. Then Omar Hasan Benawi's rumbling voice on the other side of the door said, "There is nothing for you here. Please leave my home."

"We will, Mr. Benawi," Bix said. "But first I need to talk to you face-to-face. And I need to see your wife. Then we'll all go away."

"She will not talk to you," the voice said. "This is my home. Please go away now. There is nothing for you here."

They heard the padded footsteps retreat away

from the door, and the chanting began once more.

"Well, shit!" Dan said.

"Now what?" Gert said.

"This is what the federal consent decree has done to the LAPD," Bix said to Doomsday Dan. "What would you have done back when we were real cops?"

Dan looked at Bix Ramstead and said, "We're white, he's black. We better not do something hasty. I can't afford a suspension right now."

"Answer my question," Bix said to Dan. "What would you have done six years ago, before a federal judge and a bunch of politicians and bureaucrats emasculated us?"

Dan Applewhite glanced at Gert Von Braun and said, "I'da kicked the fucking door clear off the hinges and gone in there to see if that woman is okay."

"Exactly," Bix Ramstead said.

And he took three steps back, then ran forward and kicked just to the right of the doorknob, and the door crashed open and slammed against the plasterboard wall.

Bix Ramstead's momentum carried him into the darkened living room. Gert Von Braun and

Dan Applewhite drew their nines and followed him, casting narrow beams of light around the shabby room. Dan took the lead, trying to illuminate the ominous hallway leading to other rooms at the rear of the cottage.

The chanting had stopped. Now there was no sound at all, except for the traffic on the busy avenue half a block away. The first room was stacked with cardboard cartons, aluminum cans, and refundable bottles. Their flashlight beams played over the boxes, and then the cops advanced one behind the other to the last room, where a dim light was burning. Dan Applewhite pressed his back to the wall, his Beretta semiautomatic in his right hand now, and he crouched and peered around the corner.

"Son of a bitch!" he yelled, and he leaped upright, dropping his little flashlight and holding the Beretta in both hands. "Down! Get down on your belly!"

Gert, holding her light in one hand and her Glock in the other, sprang forward, crouching below Dan's extended arms, and yelled, "Down, goddamn you!"

Bix Ramstead edged into the crowded space and looked in the room.

The Somalian was on his knees then, wearing only the black trousers he wore when last Bix saw him. He was also wearing half-glasses, his eyes looking like tarnished dimes, and he clutched a Koran in his right hand when he slid down into the prone position.

Bix Ramstead mumbled, "In the name of god!"

Lying prone, Omar Hasan Benawi said, "Yes, in the name of the one true god. She did the shameful thing with a white man. Now I give her to the white man."

There was dried white paint spatter on one wall, and puddles of paint on the threadbare carpet had dried and were hardening. Dried paint smeared the other walls and had dried in streaks on the window blinds. The Somalian's hands were white with dried paint and there were smears on his bare torso and on the tops of his bare feet, and the front of his trousers was caked with white paint. A cheap table lamp lay broken on the floor, and an empty five-gallon can of paint was lying on the floor beside the bed alongside an eight-inch paintbrush. There was dried white paint all over the coppery bedspread.

And on the bedspread was Safia, the wife of Omar Hasan Benawi. She had been strangled with the cord he'd jerked from the table lamp, and the ligature lay coiled like a serpent on the pillow beside her head. Naked, she looked tinier, more frail and fragile and vulnerable, than Bix Ramstead had remembered her. And more childlike. She was lying supine on the bed with her head on a pillow, and her arms were crossed over her small breasts, as her husband had posed them. And she was white.

He had painted every inch of her white. From the bottoms of her delicate feet to the crown of her small round head, she had been painted dead white. Even her opened lifeless eyes had not been spared. Dried paint clogged the cavernous orbs that Bix Ramstead remembered so well.

When Dan was handcuffing the Somalian's hands behind his back, the prisoner said, "Now she is yours to bury with other white dogs in your infidel places of the dead."

"Shut the fuck up!" Gert Von Braun said. "And listen while I advise you of your rights."

There were dozens of employees of the Los Angeles Police Department at that crime scene before the sun rose. One of the first was the night-watch detective Compassionate Charlie Gilford, who was about to go end-of-watch when he got the call from Bix Ramstead. He just had to see this one, so he jumped into a detective unit and drove to Southeast Hollywood as fast as he could.

After he took in the grotesque scene in the little bedroom, he walked out on the front step and directed his nuggets of wisdom at a pair of night-watch coppers who'd been called to assist with scene preservation.

"Fucking Hollywood," the disappointed detective said. "You can blame this kinda shit on the movies. I'll bet this fifty-one-fifty was sitting there watching TV and got the idea from *Goldfinger,* where they did the same thing to James Bond's snitch. Different color paint is all. This don't show any imagination. This Somali wing nut's nothing more than a second-rate copycat."

Ronnie Sinclair received a call from Bix Ramstead just before she went to bed. He told her what they'd found in the cottage and that he'd be at Hollywood Station until the early-morning hours, doing reports and being interviewed by homicide detectives. Bix told Ronnie that there was no telling what time he'd get home and would need to take tomorrow off. He said he'd left a long message on their sergeant's voice mail explaining what had happened.

Before the conversation ended, Ronnie Sinclair said to Bix Ramstead, "It was not our fault. It is not our tragedy."

He didn't respond to that.

★ SIXTEEN ★

THIS WAS the thousand-dollar day! Leonard Stilwell awoke before dawn and did something he almost never did. He went for a stroll along the Walk of Fame before the tourists arrived, breathing deeply, even shadowboxing for a few minutes, jabbing and hooking until the midget at the newsstand on Hollywood Boulevard said, "I wouldn't take that pussy jab into a ring, buddy. Even Paris Hilton would kick your ass."

"How would you like me to try it on you, you fucking termite," Leonard said.

But when the belligerent midget scuttled forward, saying, "Bring it, you turd licker!" Leonard got away fast, before the little maggot started gnawing on his leg.

Leonard wanted to go to the Starbucks on Sunset but didn't have enough money. Instead he drove to Pablo's Tacos, where all the tweakers hung out, and he bought a cup of Pablo's crappy coffee and a sweet, greasy Mexican pastry. Then he went home to rest and wait. But first he stopped and stole an *L.A. Times* from the driveway of a house two blocks from his apartment.

The only reason Ali Aziz slept so soundly was that he'd swallowed two of the magenta-and-turquoise sleep aids with a double shot of Jack Daniel's. He did have a slight headache when he awoke, and he recalled that Margot would never take one after she'd been drinking alcoholic beverages. He had a hot shower and then a cold one. Then he sat in his robe with a cup of tea and looked out from the balcony of his condo, where the view encompassed some of the commercial real estate of Beverly Hills.

It couldn't compare with the view from Mt. Olympus, from the house that he loved and that had been stolen from him by his bitch wife. Someday, god willing, when he had his son all to himself, they would live in a place where the boy could have land under his feet, perhaps a dog to run with, or even a horse to ride. There were places like that in some parts of the San Fernando Valley and in Ventura County, but they were disappearing fast with the influx of people clogging the freeways. Still, he would live in a place like that for his son's sake, and he'd make the long daily drive to his Hollywood businesses without complaint. He would do that for his son. He would do anything for his son.

At 2 P.M., Leonard Stilwell arrived at the Leopard Lounge. He found Ali Aziz in his office and he sat in the client chair in front of Ali's desk. Without comment, Ali removed a garage door opener from his desk drawer and slid it across to him.

"How much do I get if this don't work and we have to shitcan the whole plan?"

"It shall work," Ali said solemnly.

"How can you be sure?"

"One day last week when I know my wife was not home, I drove by and pressed on the button. The door opens and closes."

"Okay, gimme the alarm code," Leonard said, and Ali pushed a piece of paper across the desk.

Ali said, "Alarm pad is right inside on the wall. I want these things back to me when we meet later. And my big envelope, for sure."

"Yeah, yeah," Leonard said. "You get all the incriminating evidence and I get my thousand bucks, all at the same time."

"You shall have it," Ali said.

"I better have it," Leonard said. "Or else."

"What is your meaning?" Ali said. "'Or else'?"

"Nothing," Leonard said. "We got to trust each other, is all. Don't we, Ali? And we gotta keep real quiet afterwards."

Ali did not like the words that had just come from the mouth of the thief, but he thought he should say nothing about it. Not now.

"Ten minute after four o'clock, you do it," Ali said. "You park fifty meters past the house, up on top of the hill. No houses there yet. Nobody shall pay attention."

"And I meet you by the Mount Olympus sign down below after I do it."

"That is exactly correct," Ali said.

"I'll see you then," Leonard said.

After Leonard had gone, Ali sat motionless and thought about those words: *Or else.* He wondered if he had underestimated the thief. What if Leonard threatened to tell Margot that he had been paid to enter her house and steal an envelope? It would mean nothing to Margot.

There was no document of any value whatsoever in that house, and Margot knew it, only legitimate file folders with bills and check stubs that they were told to keep for several years in case of a tax audit.

But that would get Margot thinking about why Ali would pay a thief to enter her house. And she would call her lawyer. Ali didn't want Margot to think too much. He hated her, but he admired her mind. Margot was a very clever woman. Look how she had stolen half his fortune. If Leonard ever talked to Margot, it would put Ali in great jeopardy.

He opened his middle desk drawer and withdrew the envelope with the backup green capsule in it. He placed a clean sheet of paper on the desk. He removed the coke spoon and razor blade from the drawer, along with the vial of magenta-and-turquoise sleep aids, and emptied a sleep aid into his trash basket. Then he made another little funnel.

When he had completed his work, there were now two special magenta-and-turquoise capsules in the little envelope. Two deadly sisters side by side. He would carry one of them with him this afternoon and he would leave the other behind. In case there ever was an *or else* coming from the thief Leonard Stilwell.

At 3:30 P.M., moments after Ronnie Sinclair had tried unsuccessfully for the third time that scorching summer afternoon to reach Bix Ramstead on his cell, Leonard Stilwell had just left a drugstore where he'd bought latex gloves. He was driving up to Mt. Olympus a bit ahead of schedule. As his Honda was chugging up the hill, he saw a Latino teenager and an older woman passenger driving down in a smoke-belching Plymouth. He wondered if that was the maid with her grandson. He drove past the house and continued up to a turn in the street where there were no houses because of the steep terrain.

Leonard parked the Honda, got out, and locked it. He remembered Whitey Dawson telling about a time when he and some crack-head pulled a burglary at a supermarket and succeeded in attacking an ATM without setting off any alarms whatsoever. But the crack-head screwed up during their exit and set off the silent alarm, and when they got outside they discovered that their car had been stolen.

They both got caught flat-footed when cops responded to the alarm. He'd learned a lot from Whitey Dawson, but not how to pick a lock.

Just after 4 P.M., Leonard chose a purposefully brisk stride to walk down the steep street to the Aziz home. Whitey Dawson had never believed in slinking around and arousing suspicion. Upon approaching the house, Leonard hit the button on the remote control in his pocket and held it down. When he was in front of the driveway the door opened. He ducked under the rising door and used the remote to stop and close it before it had finished the sequence. When he was safely inside the garage, he donned his latex gloves, took the tools from his pocket, and approached the door.

"Fucking Ay-rab!" he said when he saw that it was not an old knob setup. It was a bronze-handled, single-sided dead bolt, no doubt with a thumb-turn on the inside.

He told himself to stay calm. That shouldn't matter at all. Old knob, new handle, what the fuck was the difference? He found the light switch and turned on the garage light. It was fluorescent and provided more than enough illumination. He knelt in front of the handle and inserted the tension bar, then the pick, and he repeated Junior's words.

"Tension bar turns cylinder. Rake lifts pin."

For a few seconds he thought it felt like the setup on Junior's door. But then he lost it. He removed the tools, took out a penlight, and squinted at the key slot. It looked pretty much like the one at Junior's crib. So why did it feel different?

He tried it again. This time he used all the terminology, mumbling it like a mantra: "Insert TR-four tension bar to turn the cylinder. Then insert double-diamond pick to lift the pin." He moved his bony fingers delicately, gracefully, just as Junior had moved his brown sausage fingers. Nothing happened.

He choked back a sob of frustration. Ten Ben Franklins just to turn a fucking cylinder and lift a fucking pin! A Fijian gorilla with the brain of a cockatoo could do it with his eyes shut. And that gave him an idea.

Leonard shut his eyes and inserted the tension bar and the pick. Blind people develop a special touch, he told himself. He felt for the cylinder and the pin, but he only felt metal scraping metal.

He opened his eyes, and this time a wet balloon of a sob escaped his lips. "Jesus!" he said. "Why can't I get just one fucking break?"

Then he had a head-slapping moment. The gloves! The fucking latex gloves had diminished the feel. The touch.

He peeled off the gloves. He wiggled his fingers. Even though it was a blister outside and ovenlike in the garage, he blew on his fingers and flexed them like safecrackers do in the movies. He held the tension bar and the pick as lightly as he could. Like two delicate bugs he didn't want to harm.

He inserted the tension bar. He inserted the rake. He felt for the cylinder and he felt for the pin. He also felt the sweat pouring down his face. He was tasting it. It was flowing under the neck of his T-shirt. Flop sweat, a Hollywood malady.

He couldn't feel shit! He threw the tension bar and pick onto the concrete floor. If they were bugs, the little fuckers would be dead.

Leonard Stilwell groaned when he stood up. It was over. He was going to blame it on the new door hardware. Maybe that fucking sand nigger would give him something for his attempt. Maybe a President Grant. If not, maybe an Andrew Jackson. But in his heart Leonard knew better. That towel head would want Leonard to return the two-bill advance that he'd already smoked up.

He bent over to pick up the tension bar and pick. His back had stiffened, and feeling unsteady, he grabbed at the door handle for support. And the handle dropped. And the door opened. The maid Lola had failed to set the thumb-turn on the inside handle!

"Holy shit!" he said, stumbling inside, fumbling for the notebook paper in his pocket as the alarm's warning chirp sounded. He couldn't find it! The security breach would show on the computer in the office of the security provider in a few more seconds if he didn't...

He found it in his pants pocket! He looked at it and punched in the maid's code and the warning tone stopped. Then he stepped back out to the garage and retrieved the tension bar and pick. He put on the latex gloves and, for good measure, used the tail of his T-shirt to wipe the door handle that he'd grabbed on to. Nobody was going to *CSI his* ass.

When he got inside, he walked to his right,

entered the kitchen and then the dining room, where he could see the view of Hollywood. He'd never been in a home like this. As scared as he was, he had to admire it for a moment. It was hard to take it all in. The extravagance! Now he wished he'd demanded more for this job. Ali was always poor-mouthing about how his wife had made him almost broke. Look at this! What was an extra thousand to that fucking goat eater? To a man who had lived in a house like this?

Leonard Stilwell believed that was a weakness that had held him back all his life. He was too generous and too trusting in his fellow man, and what had it gotten him? He tore himself away from the sights and got down to business. He found the little office near the kitchen, where Margot Aziz paid her bills. He opened the drawer that Ali had described to him and found the large envelopes, labeled by year. He looked through them until he found the folder for 2004. He tucked it under his arm and returned to the door, setting the thumb-turn that the maid had forgotten to set.

He was into the garage and the spring-loaded hinge on the door was in the process of closing the door behind him when he remembered. Ali said more than once for him to leave the door unlocked. Leonard stopped the door just in time. He unlocked the thumb-turn so that the maid, Lola, would catch hell for not setting it, just as Ali had ordered him to do. Of course Ali would never find out from Leonard that Lola had failed to set it in the first place.

But when he was walking away from the house, Leonard regretted that he hadn't set the thumb-turn. Fucking rich assholes never give working people a break. He didn't want to be responsible for the dumb old Mexican woman getting her ass chewed out. But he figured the divorce was so bitter that Ali's ex would never fire the maid, if only to spite Ali.

On the other hand, the Mexican maid probably had family who would take care of her, and Social Security, and maybe welfare checks, and everything else the U.S. government gives to the millions of wetbacks in this country. The same federal government that turned him down the last time he applied for SSI assistance based on his poor health and addiction to rock cocaine. Some county social worker would always point to some shitty job like dishwasher and expect him to take it. In 2007 Los Angeles, it didn't pay to be a white man.

After being seated safely behind the wheel of his Honda, Leonard opened the big folder to see if he could spot what it was that made this worth so much to Ali Aziz. But all he found were receipts, check stubs, and banking lists of cleared checks. Just ordinary household crap that anyone might keep around for a few years.

As he was driving down the hill to meet Ali Aziz, a lot was going on inside the head of Leonard Stilwell. He kept looking at the file folder. How could it be so important? And then there had been Ali's insistence on the door being left unlocked to get the ex-wife more pissed off at the Mexican maid. But if the house was in escrow and the ex-wife was moving, the maid would be history anyway. It didn't hang together and never had from the first moment Ali had tried to spin it.

When he got down to the Mt. Olympus sign, he saw Ali's Jaguar farther down the road, facing up the hill. He parked on the opposite side of the road, got out with the file folder, and crossed to Ali's car.

He handed the folder through the open window, and Ali said, "Good, Leonard. You done a very good job. Give me the garage opener and the piece of paper with the alarm code, please."

"It wasn't easy," Leonard said, handing both items to Ali. "She has new door hardware. If I wasn't an expert, I never coulda picked the lock."

Ali gave Leonard a roll of hundred-dollar bills, saying, "It is all there, Leonard. Thank you for helping me."

"It was a different lock setup. Not like you said it was," Leonard repeated.

"You leave it unlocked?" Ali said, suddenly concerned.

"Yeah, sure," Leonard said.

"Okay, Leonard," Ali said, starting his engine. "Come by the Leopard Lounge sometime. I shall buy you a drink."

Leonard looked at Ali and said, "Because I had such a lotta extra work to do on the new hardware, it took more time and put me in more danger. I think I deserve a bonus."

Ali pushed the gearshift back into park and said, "We have a deal."

"Yeah, but you didn't get it right and it made

the job very tough and risky. I think I should get another one of them Franklins."

Ali dropped the shift into drive and said, "Good-bye, Leonard."

Then he made a U-turn and drove back down toward the boulevards, as though to return to his business.

Leonard had a hunch then and decided to play it. He took his time getting into his Honda, waiting until Ali's Jaguar had vanished in the Hollywood traffic. Then he started his car, made a U-turn, and drove back up Mt. Olympus, passing the Aziz house, turning onto the street farther up the hill, and parking behind a gardener's truck. Leonard got out and walked back to the corner and watched the house of Margot Aziz fifty yards down the road.

He only waited five minutes until Ali's Jaguar appeared, driving past his former home and parking in nearly the exact spot where Leonard had parked prior to his burglary. Ali got out of his car and walked to the garage and opened it. And Leonard could see the large file folder in Ali's hand. He was returning it, just as Leonard thought he would. This wasn't about a fucking folder full of canceled checks and household shit.

Ali saw for himself that Margot had changed the lock on the garage access door as she had done on the others. He hadn't counted on that, but he doubted that it had presented any difficulty for Leonard Stilwell. Ali was furious that the thief had tried to get another hundred dollars out of him. Ali put on a pair of latex gloves he'd gotten from his nightclub dishwasher, examined the handle, and opened the door.

He used the maid's code to silence the alarm chirp and closed the door behind him, checking his watch. Another thing about Margot was that she was a creature of habit. She went to Pilates every Thursday and stayed until 5:30, no matter what. Then she would pick up Nicky at the home of the nanny and take him somewhere and feed him junk food that he liked, food she would never eat. Ali hated her for that as well. When he got custody of his son after her death, he would see to the boy's healthy diet. Lots of yogurt and lamb and rice and vegetables.

He quieted his fears by remembering the stories in the news a few months earlier about two Los Angeles women who were on vacation in Russia and were poisoned by thallium, the toxic metal that was first suspected in the murder of former spy Alexander Litvinenko until polonium-210 turned out to be the killer. Also, he remembered that Los Angeles County health officials had found that a popular brand of Armenian mineral water contained large amounts of arsenic. And then there was the local and national recall of premium pet foods found to be laced with rat poison that was killing cats and dogs. Poison was everywhere. If it happened after she was gone from Los Angeles, there was no way that anyone could suspect Ali Aziz, no matter how much he gained from her death. Nicky would get her estate and he would get Nicky. In essence, he would have everything back as it should be.

After replacing the large folder in the small office, Ali climbed the stairs to the master bedroom and felt pangs of nostalgia. He had loved this house. He had loved being married to Margot in the early days, and having the most beau-

tiful baby he had ever seen, and making more
money in his two nightclubs — especially the
Leopard Lounge — than he had ever dreamed
possible. He had loved Margot then. Or, more
accurately, had been bewitched by her. She was
the most perfect woman who had ever stepped
on his stage. All natural, no silicone or saline,
not even now, as far as he knew. Before she
became a discontented, scheming bitch, the
sex she had given him was like nothing before
or since. During those early years with Margot
and his infant son, Ali had been a completely
contented man. A devoted husband, a loving
father, a considerate boss who seldom required
blow jobs from employees.

Ali felt the nostalgia more painfully when he
entered the master bedroom. There used to be
a photo of him on the wall by the dresser, but
it was gone. The enormous walk-in closet was
even more full of her clothes than it had been
when he lived there. The bills that came to his
lawyer's office were an outrage and had taken
up so much argument before the judge that Ali
had decided it was cheaper to pay them than to
pay the hours that his lawyer billed to him.

He looked in his former walk-in closet, prepared to see the clothes of the lover Jasmine had told him about, but it was now more than half full of her overflow. He guessed she owned fifty pairs of shoes, maybe more. And those were just the dressy ones. The others — flats, sandals, athletic shoes — numbered in the dozens as well. There was no sign of men's clothing.

He entered the bathroom and was happy to see that there was no trace of any man living in the house. After talking to Jasmine, he'd been afraid that the boyfriend whom Margot had flaunted in her telephone calls might have completely taken over this bedroom suite. He couldn't get his mind around an image of this man in this bedroom, naked with Margot. And where was Nicky during those times?

Ali couldn't put it off any longer. He had to do the terrible job he came here to do. He removed the little envelope from his pocket and then opened the medicine cabinet. But Margot's sleep aids were gone. Panic struck! They should be there. They were always there, high on the top shelf, where Nicky couldn't get to them. He began opening drawers. He opened the medicine cabinet on his side of the bathroom. He opened lower cabinets, even though he knew she wouldn't keep prescription drugs there.

Ali ran back into the master bedroom and started opening drawers in the two massive walnut dressers. Then he went to the upright chests of drawers and opened them. It was hot in the house with the air conditioner timed to come on thirty minutes before she returned home. He was perspiring heavily. He could smell himself. He told himself to be calm, to only look in high places that Nicky couldn't possibly reach.

Ali entered his former closet, the one that now held her overflow. On the top shelf he saw a jewelry box, the one where she kept her costume jewelry. He took it down. The vial of magenta-and-turquoise capsules was there! He was so shaken he had to sit.

Ali went to her vanity dresser and sat down on the padded chair she used when brushing her hair before retiring. He emptied the vial onto the dresser top and took the deadly capsule from the envelope. He put it into the empty vial and then scooped the other capsules on top of it. He opened the new vial that he'd gotten from Jaime Salgando and added six capsules from it to her vial, because hers was half empty. She wouldn't notice the few extra capsules, but they would provide the extra time for her to be living elsewhere when it happened.

He put her vial back in the jewelry box and placed it on the top shelf where he'd found it. He looked around the master bedroom for the last time. He knew he would never see it again, and it brought tears to his eyes. It would all have been perfect if she had not turned out to be such a coldhearted, conniving American bitch who stole his money and broke his heart.

When he got to the garage access door he reset the thumb-turn as he believed it was before Leonard had picked the lock for him. He removed his gloves, opened the garage door, and closed it quickly after stepping outside. Then he walked up the hill, very pleased that there was no traffic passing and there were no gardeners on the nearby properties. When he got in his car, he made a careful U-turn and proceeded back down to the boulevards.

* * *

The gardener had moved the truck behind which Leonard Stilwell had parked, and a woman in the next house watched him when he walked to his car.

Leonard smiled at her and said, "Do you know which house Madonna lives in? I seem to have the wrong address."

The woman looked at him suspiciously and said, "No, I don't. I don't think there's anyone by that name on this block."

"Oh, well, I'll try farther down," Leonard said with a wave.

While driving down the hill, he couldn't get it out of his mind. Ali hadn't hired him to take something out of that house. He'd been hired so that Ali could get into that house. And it had nothing to do with the big folder that Ali had carried back inside. He'd been in there for thirteen minutes. What was he looking for? He couldn't have been stealing something that she'd miss or he'd have wanted Leonard to make it look like a burglary. Yet that's what Ali did *not* want.

Leonard pulled to the curb at the first sewer opening he saw, hopped out of his car, and tossed the latex gloves down the hole. Now let's see them try to *CSI* my ass again, he thought.

When he got back in the car, he took the tension bar and lock pick from his pocket and put them in the glove box. He was two blocks from the cyber café, where he figured to score plenty of rock with some of the Franklins he had, when it hit him: the answer to the Ali Aziz puzzle. Suddenly, he was on it. There was only one thing it could be. That fucking devious Ay-rab had planted a listening device in his ex-wife's house!

If Leonard were to drive up there later tonight, he was sure he'd find somebody parked on that street who shouldn't be there, somebody hired by Ali to monitor what was happening in the little lady's bedroom. Leonard figured that this was the kind of shit that crazed rich people did during their divorces. People who didn't really appreciate what was worthwhile in life.

So it had all been a lie, Leonard thought. Ali Aziz had hired him under completely false pre tenses and had lied to him about nearly everything. Well, he had known something was wrong from the get-go and should have guessed sooner that Ali was a complete phony and liar. That's the way it was nowadays. There wasn't an honest person left in the whole fucking town.

SEVENTEEN

TERRIBLE EVENTS were to take place on Hollywood Boulevard early that evening, events that left tourists screaming and children in tears. And Leonard Stilwell, flush with greenbacks and desperate for rock, walked right into it.

Things hadn't been peaceful along the Walk of Fame in front of Grauman's Chinese Theatre for some time. There was always a Street Character getting busted for something or other by the Street Character Task Force. Arrests had involved the red Muppet Elmo and Chewbacca and Mr. Incredible, to name a few. And the Crows had meetings where they tried to gather the hundred freelancing Street Characters — many of whom duplicated the same cartoon icons, and many of whom were drug addicts — to warn them that laws against aggressive panhandling would be enforced to the letter.

And it wasn't that the Street Characters were only fighting the law, they were fighting one another too. For example, when a tourist was snapping photos of a Superman, a Sponge-Bob SquarePants might hop into the shot and try to hustle half the tip. This caused clashes among the Characters, some of them physical, as well as the forming of cliques. On a given day, one or two of the Spider-Man Characters might align with a Willy Wonka, who might be feuding with a Catwoman or a Shrek. And that might torque off Donald Duck, or the Wolf Man, or one of the many Darth Vaders. It could get ugly when teams like a Lone Ranger and Tonto or a Batman and Robin got hacked off at each other, especially since their tips from tourists depended in no small measure on the partnership itself. What was a Robin without a Batman?

But that was what happened on that Thursday evening, a few hours after Ali Aziz had been so busy perpetrating the future murder of his ex-wife. And shortly after Leonard Stilwell, with a thousand bucks in his kick, could not score at the cyber café or at Pablo's Tacos because of a mini–task force of narcs who were jacking up every tweaker or street dealer anywhere near those two establishments.

It could have been that everyone, including Street Characters, was particularly gloomy from the announcement that there would no longer be a Hollywood Christmas Parade, an event inaugurated by the Hollywood chamber of commerce in 1928. The popular parade had featured Grand Marshal superstars such as Bob Hope, Gene Autry, James Stewart, Natalie Wood, Arnold Schwarzenegger, and Charlton Heston. But as Hollywood had lost much of its glamour in recent years, so did the parade. Recent Grand Marshals included Tom Arnold, Dennis Hopper, and Peter Fonda. And it had finally gotten so bad that they even had to settle for a local politician, Los Angeles mayor Antonio Villaraigosa. That was probably the parade's death knell.

So, on Hollywood Boulevard, on a scorching summer evening when the bone-dry air hit you in the face like a blast from a hair dryer, and the temperature inside Street Characters' costumes was unbearable, the stage was set for riot. And to make things worse, a labor dispute was going on, and a local union had a group of members with signs and pickets demonstrating in front of the Kodak Center because of non-union workers being employed there. A woman officer in plainclothes from LAPD's Labor Relations Section was monitoring, but that was the only police presence.

Just after sunset, when Hollywood takes on its rosy glow, and the hundreds of tourists in front of Grauman's Chinese Theatre feel the buzz that says, anything can happen here, something did. Some said that Robin started it, others blamed it on Batman. Either Robin called Batman "a big fat chiseling faggot" or Batman called Robin "a whiny little sissy punk." Nobody was ever sure where the truth lay, but there was no doubt that Robin threw the first punch at his partner. It was a hook to Batman's ample gut and Batman's plastic breastplate didn't protect him much.

He went, "Oooooof!" And sat down on Steve McQueen's footprints, preserved in the cement of the forecourt.

Then a Spider-Man, one of the larger ones who had been aligned with that particular Batman during a recent Street Character feud, put a hand on Robin's face and shoved him down onto the concrete imprint of Groucho Marx's cigar.

Then Superman and his pal Wonder Woman —

who was actually a wiry transvestite with leg stubble — called Spider-Man a "pukey insect" and proceeded to beat the living shit out of him while tourists screamed and children quaked in fear.

Leonard Stilwell had parked his Honda in the parking lot closest to the Kodak Center. He didn't give a damn about the excessive parking charges, not with all those Franklins in his pocket. He figured to catch up with Junior tomorrow and give the Fijian back his tools, along with a President Grant.

He was surprised to discover that no matter how much money he had, sometimes there were things that money couldn't buy. And so far that afternoon and evening, he could not buy rock cocaine anywhere. He hoped that one of the hooks from South L.A. who hung around the subway station might have a few rocks on him. If not, he could risk trying one of the Street Characters in front of the Chinese Theatre, but only as a last resort. He still remembered clearly what had happened at the Kodak Center to big Pluto when he had the dope in his head.

The woman officer from Labor Relations Section had run to the melee, holding up her badge and yelling, "Police officer!" but Superman and Wonder Woman wouldn't back off and Spider-Man was moaning in pain. And the trouble was far from over.

Batman, having recovered from the blow to the belly, suddenly needed a bowel movement badly. He saw that the labor union pickets had a large trailer parked at the curb, along with an Andy Gump porta-potty attached to it.

Holding his wounded gut, he ran crablike to the Andy Gump, opened the door and stepped inside, and relieved himself with an eruption that could clearly be heard by the outraged pickets guarding the trailer.

When Batman emerged from the Andy Gump, one of the pickets, a diminutive fifty-two-year-old black man, who happened to be the local union representative, said, "Hey, dude, nobody said you could take a dump in our Gump."

"Batman craps wherever he wants," said Batman.

The little union steward said, "Batman is jist some jiveass flyin' rat in a funky ten-dollar cape, far as I'm concerned."

"You're lucky I didn't shit in your hat, you ugly little nigger," said Batman.

The union rep, who had been a pretty good Golden Gloves bantamweight thirty years earlier, said, "Ain't no fuckin' bat gonna front me, not even Count Dracula!"

On the eleven o'clock news that night, the reporter who witnessed the mini-riot showed his audience a Batman cartoon panel and said that what happened next was just like in the comic books: "POW! WHAM! BAM!"

"However," he added, "it was the caped crusader who got clocked and kissed the concrete."

Thus, Batman became the second superhero that day to be taken to the ER for multiple contusions and abrasions.

By then, the Labor Relations cop had put out a help call, and the midwatch units just clearing from roll call, with plenty of daylight left, were on their way. Gert Von Braun and Dan Applewhite arrived first and pulled Superman and Wonder Woman away from Spider-Man, Gert grabbing Wonder Woman by the shoulder-length auburn tresses — which suddenly came off in Gert's hand.

"Mommy!" a young girl shrieked. "Wonder Woman is bald like Daddy!"

Two other night-watch units arrived, and

soon there were hundreds of tourists snapping photos like mad and a TV news van caused a traffic jam on Hollywood Boulevard. Leonard Stilwell decided that this was no place for him. He started jogging around the tourists on the Walk of Fame, heading toward the parking lot, but ran smack into 6-X-46 of the midwatch.

"Whoa, dude!" Flotsam said. "It's him!"

Jetsam grabbed Leonard's arm as he was hot-footing it past the cops and spun him around. "I been thinking about you, bro," he said.

Leonard recognized them at once, those heartless, sunburned cops with the bleached-out spiky hairdos. "I got nothing to do with that ruckus back there," Leonard said.

"Let's see that piece of paper in your car," Flotsam said. "The one with the address written on it."

"What piece of paper?" Leonard said.

"Don't fuck with us," Jetsam said.

"I'm not!" Leonard whined. "I don't know what you're talking about, man!"

"The paper with the address up on Mount Olympus," Flotsam said. "Do you remember now? And you better give the right answer."

"Oh, that paper," Leonard said.

"Yeah, let's go to your car so I can see it again," Jetsam said.

"I ain't got it no more," Leonard said.

"Why did you have it in the first place?" Jetsam said.

"Have what?" Leonard said.

"Screw you, bro," Jetsam said, reaching for his handcuffs.

"Wait a minute!" Leonard said. "Gimme a chance to think!"

"Think fast, dude," Flotsam said. "My partner's outta patience."

"I wrote down an address that I got outta the newspaper," Leonard said. "It was about a job. Somebody needed a housepainter."

"You're a housepainter?" Flotsam said.

"Yeah, but I'm outta work at the moment."

"I been thinking about painting my bedroom," Flotsam said. "Should I use a semigloss enamel on the bedroom walls or a latex?"

Leonard was getting dry-mouthed now. The only latex he knew about involved the gloves he used on his jobs. He said, "Depends on what you like."

Jetsam said, "Do most people use oil-base

enamel or water-base latex on their bedroom walls?"

Leonard said, "Enamel?"

"Let's go visit your car, dude," Flotsam said. "Maybe that piece of paper's still there."

When they got to the parking lot, Leonard led them to his car, parked in the far corner. "You ain't got no right to search my car and you know it," he said.

"Who says we're searching your car?" Jetsam said. "We just wanna see that piece of paper again."

"Then you'll stop hassling me?" Leonard said.

Jetsam looked at Flotsam and said, "He says we're hassling him."

"I'm shocked. Shocked!" Flotsam said.

Leonard opened the car door and got in, reaching for the glove compartment.

"Wait a minute, dude," Flotsam said.

"I'm gonna see if I put it in the glove box," Leonard said.

"Wait till my partner gets around and can see in there," Flotsam said. "That's how cops get hurt."

449

"Me hurt you? Your feelings or what?" Leonard said disgustedly as Jetsam opened the passenger door, his hand on the butt of his nine.

"Now go ahead and open it," Jetsam said.

Twilight was casting long shadows by then, and Jetsam used his flashlight to illuminate the glove compartment.

Leonard remembered where the note was then and reached up under the visor, saying, "Here it is." But Leonard didn't remember that he'd tossed the tension bar and pick in the glove box.

"What's this?" Jetsam said, his flashlight beam on the locksmith tools.

"What's what?" Leonard said. And then he remembered what!

"Those strange little objects in the glove compartment," Jetsam said. "Do you, like, use them to pry off the lids from paint cans?"

Leonard looked in the glove box and said, "They been in the car since I bought it. I don't know what they are. Are they illegal? Like kiddie porn or something?"

"Get outta the car," Jetsam said. "And gimme your keys. I don't think you'll mind if I look for more strange objects, will you?"

"What's the use?" Leonard said. "You'll do it anyways."

When Leonard Stilwell was standing outside the car, and Jetsam was looking under the front seats and in the trunk, Flotsam patted down Leonard Stilwell, felt the bills in his pocket, and said, "What's this?"

"Just my money," Leonard said.

"How much money?" Flotsam said.

"Do I gotta answer that?" Leonard said.

"If you know how much you got, then we'll figure it's your money," Flotsam said. "If you don't know how much you got, we'll figure you just picked a pocket or a purse in front of the Kodak Center. And we'll go look for a victim. Might take a long time."

"A thousand bucks," Leonard said. "Ten Ben Franklins."

The surfer cops looked at each other again and Jetsam said, "You got a thousand bucks in your kick? Where'd you get it?"

"Playing poker," Leonard said.

"And you got locksmith tools," Jetsam said, "but they just happened to be in your car when you bought it?"

"Yeah, that's right."

"And you can't pick a lock?"

"Man, I can hardly pick my nose!" Leonard said. "You guys're harassing me! This is police harassment!"

"Tell you what, dude," Flotsam said. "If you can spell *harassment,* we'll let you go. If you can't, we'll take you to Hollywood Station to talk to a detective. How's that?"

Leonard said, "H-e-r . . ."

Fifteen minutes later, Leonard Stilwell was sitting with Flotsam in an interview room at Hollywood Station, and Jetsam was in the detective squad room, explaining what they'd found to Compassionate Charlie Gilford, who was irritated to be pulled away from his tape of *Dancing with the Stars,* where Heather Mills McCartney hit the floor but disappointed Charlie when her prosthetic leg stayed attached.

"What we got here is some lock picks and a thousand bucks and a guy with a four-five-nine record," Charlie said, never eager to do any work whatsoever. "That's pretty thin for a felony booking. How about that wrong address note? Can't we pull a victim outta that somehow?"

"The burglary dicks might be able to do it tomorrow," Jetsam said. "That's the reason we lock him up tonight, right? To give them forty-eight hours. Come on, this guy's dirty. I just know it!"

"Lemme get a coffee and think about it," Charlie said.

Since the federal consent decree had gone into effect six years earlier, the nighttime detective could no longer approve a felony booking. Now the detective could only "advise" a booking, and then it went to the patrol watch commander for a booking "referral." It seemed that the federal government and its legion of overpaid civilian auditors and overseers didn't like declaratory phrasing and active verbs that sounded too aggressive. Their preferences created a lot more paperwork, as did everything about the consent decree. But in the end, it all amounted to the same thing. A felony suspect went to the slam for forty-eight hours while the detectives tried to make a case that they could take to the district attorney's office.

Jetsam was disgusted. While Charlie was gone, the surfer cop took out his notebook and, sitting at one of the desks, dialed the cell number of Hollywood Nate Weiss just before Nate went end-of-watch.

Jetsam explained what had gone down and said, "Did you ever get a chance to ask that friend of yours on Mount Olympus about this guy Stilwell?"

"No, I didn't," Nate admitted. "But I talked to someone who knows her a lot better than I do and he said he'd ask her about it."

"Did that someone ask her?"

"I don't know," Nate said uncomfortably.

"Look, bro, you gotta help us," Jetsam said. "I was hinked-out by this dude the first time I saw him. He's a burglar. I just know he pulled a job where he stole a thousand bucks, but we got no report on it yet. I think it happened up there on Mount Olympus at the house where you were, or close by there."

The line was silent for a moment and Nate said, "I'll make a call right now and get back to you."

"Thanks, bro," Jetsam said. "That house up there? It gives off bad juju."

Nate rang the home of Margot Aziz, who had just pulled into her garage with her son, Nicky, who was asleep in his car seat. She got Nicky out of the car and was carrying him to the door on the first ring. She tried the handle but the door was locked.

"Damn!" she said. The door was never locked. Lola had forgotten so many times that Margot had stopped reminding her. This had to be the one time Lola had locked it, now, when Margot was hoping for a call from Bix Ramstead, whom she'd been trying to reach all day.

Margot managed to dig her keys from her purse while still carrying her sleeping five-year-old and got the door open just as the phone stopped ringing. She punched in her alarm code to shut off the electronic tone and ran to the kitchen phone, picking it up after the voice message had concluded.

She played it back, but it was the wrong cop. She heard a voice saying, "Margot, this is Nate Weiss. Please call me ASAP. This is about a police matter that might concern you."

A police matter? She picked up his card from the desk in the little office by the kitchen but put it down again. A pussy matter, more like it. After their evening together she had never called him as promised, and now he'd obviously decided to press her. He'd probably tell her that he wanted the job of moving in as her house protector during the remainder of the escrow period.

You had your chance, bucko, she thought. It was too bad he wasn't a boozer like Bix Ramstead. She liked Nate's looks and his sexy manner.

Hollywood Nate made a decision. He was going to do the show-and-tell with Bix Ramstead. He was positive that Bix must have something going with Margot Aziz, and he knew Bix was married with two kids. Well, that was too bad. Nate didn't like embarrassing the guy, but this Stilwell thing had gone on long enough. He was going to tell Bix everything about his evening with Margot, and then either he or Bix was going to find out if anything peculiar had happened around her house lately. Anything that might explain why a lowlife burglar with an address written down that was close to hers had lock picks and a thousand dollars in his pocket. Nate knew from experience that Margot was a smart woman. If the Stilwell business made any sense at all, she might be able to figure it out for them.

Of course, Nate was aware of the Somali murder the prior evening and that Bix had had a long night and was not on duty today. He dialed Bix's home and cell numbers but was taken to voice mail at both of them.

"Bix, it's Nate Weiss," he said on each voice mail. "I've gotta talk to you about Margot Aziz ASAP. It might be very important. Call me."

He looked in the office and discovered that Ronnie had just signed out. He went to the women's locker room, stuck his head in the door, and yelled for her.

He was relieved when she said, "Yeah, I'm here."

A few minutes later Ronnie emerged in her street clothes, and Nate said, "Do you know how I can reach Bix?"

She shook her head and said, "I've tried four times today with no luck. I think that weird murder last night had an effect on him. I'm kinda worried, to tell the truth."

"Doesn't his wife know where he is?" Nate said.

"The wife and kids are outta state, visiting her parents. They won't be back till after the weekend."

"So I won't be able to talk to him till to-morrow?"

"Maybe, maybe not," she said. "He called the sergeant today and took tomorrow off as well. He's got a lotta comp time on the books and said he needed a couple days to do family business."

"You think he went outta town?"

"I don't know, Nate," Ronnie said. "Bix is a mysterious guy. And so are you these days."

"What's that supposed to mean?"

"You and Bix. What's the secret you're sharing? Or is it a guy thing?"

Nate paused for a few seconds and said, "There's this woman who lives up on Mount Olympus. She may have been burglarized today. It's a long shot, but Flotsam and Jetsam got themselves a suspect, and you know how obsessive they are. They want somebody to talk to her right now, but she's not home. I just called."

"What's Bix got to do with it?"

"We both know her and I think Bix probably has her cell number. It's a long story."

"So it *is* a guy thing," Ronnie said, deeply disillusioned. Bix Ramstead, the last of the monogamous cops. An alcoholic in denial. And a womanizer to boot?

"Good luck," Ronnie said. "I gotta go home."

★ ★ ★

Nate found Flotsam and Jetsam in the detective squad room and said to them, "Okay, you guys know that I'm familiar with the woman who lives at the Mount Olympus address, but I'm not as familiar as you guys think I am. I tried to reach her and I left a message. Why don't you just book the asshole and let the dicks sort it all out tomorrow when the lady's at home?"

"Our sentiments exactly, bro," Jetsam said, "but Charlie Gilford's acting all PMS-ey tonight and don't wanna give us a booking approval without an eyeball witness, a videotape, and a confession signed in blood."

Just then Compassionate Charlie came out of the interview room where he'd been talking to Leonard Stilwell. He had a 5.10 report in his hands, which made the surfer cops hopeful. He wouldn't be doing paperwork if he was going to kick the crackhead out the door.

"Okay, I'll five-ten him and advise a booking for four-five-nine," Charlie said. "Book the lock picks and the thousand bucks, and we'll let the burglary team deal with it tomorrow."

"All right!" Jetsam said.

"He said he won the thousand betting on the

Giants against our Dodgers with a stranger he met at a pool hall," Compassionate Charlie said with disgust. "Any resident of this town who'd even think up such a disloyal fucking story deserves to go to jail."

Margot Aziz tried reaching Bix Ramstead yet again. She was acutely aware that his wife and family would be returning home in a few days. That's all the time she had. All the time she would ever have with *that* man, she was sure of it. If it didn't work with Bix, she'd have to come up with an entirely new plan. But would Jasmine hold still for it? Her greed was being overwhelmed by fear and she was already talking about aborting the scheme, even after Margot had put so much time and effort into Bix Ramstead in recent months. Never once in all that time would Bix agree to spend the entire night in her bed. Never once did she have the opportunity to put the plan in motion. It was giving her a headache thinking about it. The stress was getting unbearable.

People thought she could survive forever on a $7 million net worth. Her lawyer estimated that $7 million, more or less, would be her share after all the real property and other assets, including a growing stock portfolio, were divided. But this was before the lawyer's exorbitant fees would be deducted at the end of the ordeal.

The attorney had told her that with proper investments, she and Nicky could live "comfortably." And she'd laughed in his face.

Margot had reminded him that hundreds of homes in the Hollywood Hills were presently for sale for more money than the "comfortable" amount, a few of them for twice that. How could Nicky be raised in his present living standard if she had to spend at least four or five million on a decent house? And did the lawyer know what house maintenance costs were around here? And did the bachelor lawyer have *any* idea what a trustworthy au pair charged? And how about the fees at a good school? Nicky would be in kindergarten come September, and the annual fees would cost more than the Barstow home her parents bought when they'd gotten married. Margot told him that she understood very well what a day-to-day money struggle was all about, but she was determined that Nicky never would.

About Nicky. That's where she and her lawyer had their biggest disagreements. He told her that when he was through with Ali Aziz, the nightclub proprietor would be afraid to ever be a day late with child support payments. She'd told him that was a joke, that she knew Ali Aziz as well as she knew herself. And there was no doubt whatsoever that he would secretly divest himself of his entire net worth and make clandestine plans to convert all his holdings to cash. And then to take his son away from her, away from America, forever.

The lawyer had insisted that Ali Aziz, a naturalized citizen, would never do any such thing. Living in a Middle East country again after having lived a lavish Hollywood lifestyle was beyond the attorney's imagining.

Margot had reminded the lawyer that Osama bin Laden had also been rich and had given it up to live in a cave. And she doubted that Osama would have to spend big bucks on cocaine in order to get his blow jobs. And then she'd asked the lawyer to verify a supposition. She'd asked it casually enough: If Ali passed away at any time during or after the divorce settlement, would his fortune go to Nicky with her as executor?

The lawyer had answered that, as far as he knew, Ali's new will named his attorney as executor, but that, yes, his fortune would go to Nicky. And then she thought about Ali's attorney. He seemed like a reasonable man, as lawyers go. He'd blush when she'd stare at him for too long. She could work with him on behalf of her son. There would be approximately $14 million for her and Nicky. They could get by on that. She was still young, still had her looks. There'd be lots of wealthy men out there after she extracted Jasmine from her life.

And even if she never found the right man, Nicky would come into his inheritance in thirteen years. Margot could not guess what his $7 million, properly invested by Ali's lawyer/executor, would look like by that time. Nicky would take care of his mother then. She'd be forty-three years old and her ass would be falling like a bag of wet laundry, and she'd need someone to take care of her.

Margot looked in Nicky's room and saw that he was sound asleep. She went to her bedroom and undressed, then had a hot shower, and, turning on the bedroom TV, channel surfed. She gave up and switched to one of the easy-listening cable channels, then set the burglar alarm, deciding to turn in early.

Margot went to the closet and brought down the jewelry box where she'd been keeping her sleep aids after catching Nicky one afternoon up on her bathroom sink rummaging through her medicine cabinet looking for cough drops. She got a glass of water from the bathroom and sat in front of her vanity mirror, brushing her hair for a few minutes. Then she removed the top from the vial.

Margot thought of Ali then, of how he didn't like her taking the sleeping capsules for fear that any drugs would cause her to revert to the cocaine use that she'd conquered years before. She turned the vial on its side in order to shake a capsule into her hand. And at that very moment, when she was thinking of Ali, Rod Stewart began singing "We'll Be Together Again." And she felt a shiver jetting through her neck and shoulders.

Margot thought, No, we will *never* be together again. Not in this world, not in the next, if there is one. The very thought of Ali Aziz and what she must do made her hands tremble. She dropped the vial on the dresser

top and all of the magenta-and-turquoise capsules spilled out.

Margot scooped the capsules back into the
vial. One was left on the dresser top and she
put it in her mouth and swallowed it. Then
she swallowed another, despite her doctor's
admonition that one was enough. Tonight she
needed to sleep uninterrupted.

Before retiring for the night, she called Bix
Ramstead's private cell number one more time
and left a message saying, "Bix, I *beg* you to
call me!"

★ EIGHTEEN ★

VIOLENT NIGHTMARES tormented Leonard Stilwell all through the night. He'd been in a cell with three other guys, including a tatted Latino strong-arm robber who'd somehow learned that a prisoner late in arriving — a thirty-two-year-old insurance agent — had been booked for sexually abusing his girlfriend's eight-year-old daughter.

The Latino had been minding his own business until then and hadn't said anything to anyone the whole time that Leonard had been in the cell with him. But when he received the word about the child molestation, he got up and without warning began beating the insurance agent's head against the wall of the tank, causing a laceration on his skull that spattered blood onto Leonard's T-shirt.

When the jailers heard the screams, both men were pulled from the tank. And as the attacker was being led away, Leonard heard him yelling to the jailers, "Me, I'm a robber! That's what I do! Him, he's garbage!"

Later, Leonard was on his bunk, sleeping fitfully, waking often with night sweats. During one of those waking periods, he decided that he was getting too old for this life. He was through doing petty stings and scrounging for rent money. When he got out, he was going to get a stake and begin life anew, and he thought he knew how to do it.

After they were awakened for what Leonard called fried roadkill and fake eggs, he uttered a spontaneous comment to his remaining cellmate, an old con artist with refined features and a mane of white hair who had bilked three elderly women out of their life savings.

"Man, I've had enough," Leonard said to him. "Way more than enough. This ain't what I planned for my life. This ain't what I had in mind."

The old con man replied, "Destiny is pitiless, son. Nobody ever started out in life wanting to be a proctologist either, but shit happens."

The residential burglary team who got the arrest report on Leonard Stilwell had a heavy load that week and were able to devote very few hours to a follow-up. One of them got Leonard out of his cell and interviewed him with much the same result that Charlie Gilford had gotten. The detective's partner, D2 Lydia Fernandez, drove to the address of Margot Aziz and knocked on the door at 10 A.M.

Lola was vacuuming the living room and Nicky was watching *Sesame Street* in the family room, with the volume turned up loud so he could hear it over the vacuum noise. Margot, still in her nightgown and robe after a drug-aided nine-hour sleep, answered the door. A woman not much older than Margot, looking businesslike in a matching summer jacket and skirt, showed Margot her badge and presented a business card, saying, "Good morning, ma'am. I'm Detective Fernandez and I'd like to ask you a few questions."

Margot stepped out on the porch and said, "I'd invite you in but we'd have to communicate in writing. I have a five-year-old in there."

The detective smiled and said, "I'll just need a moment. Do you know a man named Leonard Stilwell?"

"I don't think so," Margot said. "Why?"

"This man?" the detective said, showing Leonard's mug shot.

Margot took the photo and said, "I've never seen this man, as far as I know. Can you tell me what it's about?"

"Possibly nothing," Detective Fernandez said. "He had an address in his car that's close to yours but not right on. He has a burglary record and he had some tools that could be used to enter a locked door. I'm going to check with every resident on this block."

"A burglar?" Margot said. "How scary."

"Was your house or property disturbed in any way yesterday?"

"Not at all," Margot said. "My housekeeper was here most of the day, and a few hours after she left, I came home with my son. The doors were locked and the alarm was set when I entered. Should we be worried about this man?"

"There's no need for alarm," the detective said. "Just be aware that there're always opportunists like him looking for an easy target."

"Thanks for telling me," Margot said.

When the detective was turning to leave, Margot said, "Could I trouble you for just a minute about another matter?"

"Okay," the detective said and stopped.

Margot said, "I'm not worried about burglars, but I'm involved in a very nasty divorce and my husband's made some veiled threats. I'd like the patrol car in this area to drive by from time to time. Would you please remind Sergeant Treakle at Hollywood Station? He was here one night."

"I'd suggest you give him a call," the detective said. "Any note I leave for him might get misplaced in the piles of paperwork at our station."

"I'll do that," Margot said.

She stood on her porch and watched the detective entering the driveway next door. Now Margot had another name to add to the list of police officers she'd apprised of worrisome threats from Ali Aziz.

When Margot reentered the house, she motioned for Lola to turn off the vacuum and said to her, "We have to be more careful about security, Lola. That was a police officer. There might be burglars in the neighborhood."

The Mexican woman said, "I be careful, missus. I always lock doors and set the alarm."

"Yes, Lola, and you'll have to start remembering to always set the lock on the door to the garage. We can't be too careful these days."

"Yes, missus," Lola said. "I am sorry. I forget that one."

"You didn't forget yesterday," Margot said. "So just do it like that every time."

Lola looked perplexed because she couldn't remember setting that thumb-latch yesterday, but since she was getting praised for it, she figured she must have done it for once.

"Yes, missus," Lola said with a fourteen-karat smile.

Ronnie Sinclair made two calls that day to the homes of chronic complainers about trash removal, one of the objects being a twelve-foot sofa with the springs hanging out of it. How it got into the front yard of a vacant house was anyone's guess, and the complainant said it wasn't there yesterday. It was during moments like this that Ronnie thought about becoming a real cop again.

But then she looked on the bright side. She was in street clothes today instead of her uniform because of a dinner meeting she had to attend. And she had no radio calls to answer and got her SLO pay bonus. Moreover, she had time to study for the sergeant's exam. Still, there was a wistful feeling every time she saw a black-and-white roaring to a call with lights flashing and siren wailing.

Ronnie was sure by now that Bix had fallen off the wagon and hit the deck hard. With his wife and kids out of town and with days off, she figured he was binge drinking. After learning that Leonard Stilwell was in jail, she didn't really have an excuse to bother Bix with more phone calls. It was still hard to accept that he might be just another Hollywood Nate, tapping some rich bimbo up on Mt. Olympus. She'd expected much more from Bix Ramstead.

Then she started to wonder why she was so troubled by it. She wondered if there was resentment here because Bix had never so much as uttered a sexual innuendo or shot a suggestive glance in her direction. Was it that her pride was hurt? That Bix might prefer one of those Laurel Canyon stone-washed Crate & Barrel addicts who outgrew their tramp stamps by the age of forty and lived with tattoo remorse or laser scars? Or maybe that he'd prefer one of those Hollywood Hills trophy bunnies in all that distressed second-skin denim, married to middle-aged guys who still dressed like middle school but never in uncool pastels, the lot of them mentally exhausted from trying to think up screwier names for their babies than the movie stars routinely came up with? Is it that I'm a jealous bitch with wounded pride? Ronnie Sinclair asked herself.

The detectives had found nothing on Mt. Olympus or on any report that would marry Leonard Stilwell to a burglary or theft of $1000. The day-watch patrol officers had come in with several arrests that would require extensive investigation, so at 3 P.M. the overworked detectives permitted Leonard to be released from custody, and he was given back his money and his tools. The desk officer at Hollywood Station looked at Leonard like he was nuts when he asked if the officer could break a $100 bill for the pay phone because he'd left his cell in his car.

The desk officer called Leonard a cab, which was driven by a Pakistani, who transported Leonard to the parking lot on Hollywood Boulevard by Grauman's Chinese Theatre. After a raging argument with the parking attendant, they settled on a parking fee of $85 for leaving his Honda parked for twenty-six hours, and Leonard gave the leftover $15 to the cabbie. He was now down to nine Ben Franklins.

Trying to keep all his anger and frustration under control, he dialed Ali's office number and got voice mail. He said, "Ali, it's Leonard. I need to see you at six o'clock. Be there, man."

Then Leonard drove to IHOP and loaded up on pancakes, ham, fried eggs, and hash browns, wolfing it all down so fast the waitress was gawking at him. After that, he drove to his apartment building, wrapped a $50 bill around the tension bar and lock pick, and slid it under Junior's door. Then he went to his room, collapsed on the bed, and fell asleep.

When Ali got to his office, he picked up the voice mail and listened to it three times. There was nothing good going to come of this. He could hear a shaky defiance in Leonard's voice. The "Be there" was particularly worrisome. It had to be about money.

It made Ali open the middle drawer of his desk. It was just a precaution. He would wait until he saw Leonard before he took any action.

Leonard was stupid and he was not. He could outwit the thief and probably reason with him, but just in case, he had to have another option.

Ali had intended to give the vial of sleep aids to the first of his girls who gave him a good blow job, but now he had better use for them. Ali took two magenta-and-turquoise capsules from the vial and emptied their contents into the trash basket. In a few minutes he intended to refill them with powdered sugar from the kitchen. He placed the deadly capsule into the vial near the top. Like in Russian roulette, one could shake a capsule out of the vial and perhaps survive. Or perhaps not. Before Leonard Stilwell arrived, Ali decided he would place the vial on the desktop in plain sight.

Bix Ramstead had a violent headache, as well he should, given the quantity of booze he'd consumed in the last thirty-six hours. He'd woken up in his clothes, sharing the sofa in his living room with Annie, the Lab/shepherd mix he'd rescued so long ago. Annie, staring directly into his face, whimpered and wagged her tail when his eyes opened.

"Hi, Annie," he said and winced.

He pulled himself upright and stretched his back muscles side to side, then limped into the kitchen and rinsed out Annie's dish.

"Want some breakfast, girlfriend?" he said, and Annie sat watching him with the special devotion that rescued dogs were said to possess.

He tossed three aspirin in his mouth and washed them down while mixing Annie's kibble with boiled chicken and a hard-boiled egg. He panicked for a second when he couldn't remember if he'd fed her last night, but then he saw the empty can of dog food on the sink and knew that he had.

After Annie was happily eating, he made sure the doggy door was open, giving her access to the backyard, and he refilled her bowl on the back porch with fresh water. Then he made some coffee and poured himself a bowl of cereal and a glass of orange juice. He got the orange juice down but couldn't manage the cereal.

Bix gathered the two empty bottles of vodka and the dozen beer cans and put them in a trash bag. They'd be collected before he picked up his wife and kids from the airport. He was afraid there would be no way he could hide the drinking from Darcey. She knew him too well and he'd promised her too much. He recalled the last vow he'd made to her: "Even though I do not believe I'm an alcoholic, if I ever get drunk again, I'll go to AA for help, I swear."

And she had said, "As much as I love you, I'll take the kids and leave if you don't."

He brought the coffee cup to his mouth, and a sob escaped him. He put down the spoon and fought for control.

The cell phone sounded and he didn't know where it was. For a moment he forgot that he'd asked for and received a compensatory day off today. He followed the sound and found the cell on the sofa, where it had fallen from his pocket. His hangover prevented him from reading the screen without his glasses.

He managed a painful hello.

"Bix!" Margot said. "Thank god!"

"Margot, why're you calling me?" he said.

"I've got to see you!" she said. "It's urgent!"

"I thought we'd settled this," he said.

"You've got to come. I don't know where else to turn."

"Is it about us?"

"No, I swear. It's about Ali. I think he's insane."

Now the pain was hammering over his right eye. "You've got a lawyer. You've got the law on your side."

"They can't help me if I'm dead. I think I need to buy a gun."

"Jesus, Margot!" Bix said. "Your fears're exaggerated."

"Detective Fernandez from Hollywood Station came by today. There was a suspicious character arrested who had an address in his car that they think might have something to do with me."

Through the fog Bix remembered. "Oh, yeah," he said, "I was supposed to mention that guy to you. His name is Stillwater or something."

"Leonard Stilwell," she said.

"Yeah, that's it," he said. "It didn't sound like much. Frankly, I forgot about it."

"I can tell you about that too if you'll just stop by."

"Margot..."

"Come and talk to me. That's all, just talk. If you think I'm being hysterical, I swear I'll never call you again."

"I'm sick today, Margot," he said. "I'll drop by in the afternoon, but only for a few minutes."

"Wonderful!" she said. "Can I help you? What's wrong?"

"I slipped," he said. "I got blitzed last night. I'm sick today."

"Poor Bix!" she said. "I've got a secret potion for hangovers that I learned when I was a dancer. There were lots of hangovers in the Leopard Lounge, that's for sure."

"How about five o'clock?" he said.

"Can you make it later?" she said. "Lola's here today until five. How about six-thirty?"

"Okay," he said. "Now I gotta go lie down."

"Take some vitamin B and C," she said. "Lots of it. Drink plenty of juice and water, and put a cold towel over your forehead and eyes. Try to catch a nap."

"I'll see you at six-thirty," he said.

Bix thought it over. He felt safe with her in the daytime. The sun was still high enough at 6:30 on these long summer days. It was after sundown that the enchantment always started, the times when he could not resist her.

He'd once admitted that to Margot, and she'd

said cheerily, "Why, Bix, didn't I ever tell you? I'm a vampire!"

Margot Aziz found her go phone and called Jasmine moments after she hung up from her call to Bix. It was difficult not to betray the excitement she felt.

When Jasmine answered, Margot said, "It's me. Where are you?"

"Where am I?" Jasmine said, annoyance in her voice. "I'm home trying to get a little rest after your husband made me dance four sets last night because that cunt Goldie took the night off, claiming she had an ankle sprain."

"Get on your throwaway. I'll call you right back."

In a moment Margot rang the number of the pay-as-you-go phone she'd bought for Jasmine, who answered with a bored, "Yeah, so what's up?"

Margot said, "It's gonna happen!"

"I've heard that before," Jasmine said.

"Tonight!" Margot said.

That got her attention. She said, "Don't tell me that if it isn't true, Margot. I can't deal with it no more."

"Tonight, baby!" Margot said. "Take the night off."

"Ali will kill me!" Jasmine said, and Margot almost laughed.

Jasmine realized what she'd just said and muttered, "Damn! That's sick."

"It's your turn to sprain an ankle," Margot said. "I'll have my friend under control before midnight, for sure. You be ready to do what you gotta do then."

"Midnight?" Jasmine said.

"Right around midnight," Margot said.

"I was starting to think it was like a game," Jasmine said. "Not real, you know?"

"It's real, baby," Margot said. "We'll have it all."

"Will you call me when it's time?"

"You be sitting in your car a block from the club no later than eleven-thirty. Sometime after that you'll get the call, and then you gotta be good, honey. Real good."

"I will be," she said.

"Make that mascara run," Margot said.

"I can do it," Jasmine said. "I just hope you can."

"I love you," Margot said, ending the call.

Margot poured a cup of coffee and called

the nanny in order to have Nicky picked up for an overnighter. The nanny was used to it and got well paid for overnighters. There was nothing for Margot to do now but to prepare herself mentally.

She decided that after a few months she'd kiss off Jasmine with a nice "severance package." Margot figured that $100,000 would be enough for her. Of course, Jasmine would rage and threaten to expose Margot, but what could she really do? Admit to being a co-conspirator and accomplice? And what could she prove if she did make such an outrageous claim? No, Jasmine would take the money and fall in love with someone else. Just like the song, she fell in love too easily, but only if the lover was very rich. That reminded Margot to retrieve Jasmine's go phone in the next few days and dispose of it. Just in case.

Sheer emotional exhaustion kept Leonard asleep for an hour. When he got up, he showered and even shaved. He put on a clean T-shirt and faded Levi's jeans that weren't too grungy and his best pair of sneaks. He smoked a cigarette and amped up on coffee and began a rehearsal. He had to strike the right 'tude going in, was how he figured it. He had to be ready to be just too cool when the fucking Ay-rab started waving the verbal dagger in his face.

The Leopard Lounge had enough dancers in the stable to keep the club crowded in late afternoon, and happy hour prices were not necessary. Leonard counted more than forty cars in the parking lot at 6:10 P.M., and it made him feel more justified than ever in making demands for a decent fee for services rendered.

He once again entered the office of Ali Aziz without knocking, and found Ali seated at his desk with a bottle of Jack and two glasses. Near the bottle were some letters and a blank envelope, along with a vial of magenta-and-turquoise capsules.

Ali, who had also been mentally rehearsing, had the toothiest smile that Leonard had ever seen on him.

"Leonard, my friend!" Ali said extravagantly. "I am very glad to see you. I have got back the important document, thanks to my friend Leonard. Everything is correct again!"

Leonard sat in the client chair and said, "Yeah, well, I'm happy you're happy, because I think we got more business to discuss."

"I wish to order some food for my friend. I feel like a new man. A nice steak, perhaps? T-bone? Rib eye?"

Leonard gave a head shake, not knowing what to make of the new Ali, and he said, "Naw, I ate at IHOP."

"A drink?" Ali said, pouring two hefty shots of Jack Daniel's.

"Okay," Leonard said, picking up the nearest glass.

"You look like you are tired," Ali said. "You are getting enough sleep, no?"

"I get enough," Leonard said.

"I am getting good sleep," Ali said. "I take sleep medicine that one of my dancers gave to me."

"That's good," Leonard said, thinking he might try switching from smoking rock to booze if he could afford good stuff like this.

Ali said, "I am going home in one hour because I was awake at five o'clock this morning to do inventory. My bitch wife no longer does inventory for me, so I must do all things."

"Yeah, life is tough," Leonard said. "You shoulda been with me last night. Even your sleeping pills wouldn't a helped."

"Where you were last night?"

"In jail."

"Oh, god!" Ali said. "What did you do wrong?"

"Nothing," Leonard said. "Except that I did that job for you. And the cops found my tools and rousted me, and I spent the night in jail, even though they couldn't prove nothing and had to kick me out this afternoon."

"Oh, god!" Ali said. "You didn't say nothing about —"

"Of course not," Leonard said. "But I still got popped behind that business I did for you."

"I am so sorry, my friend," Ali said, pouring another double shot for Leonard. "That is why you look so sleepy."

With two capsules full of powdered sugar concealed in his left hand, Ali reached for the vial of capsules on the desk. Ali unscrewed the top and appeared to shake out two capsules onto the desktop, dropping the two that he'd palmed. Then he screwed the top back on and put the vial near the bottle of Jack.

Ali made it very apparent that he was putting

the capsules into his mouth and swallowing them down with a shot of the Scotch, saying, "This is very good sleep medicine. I shall be feeling very peaceful soon. And then, maybe one hour from now, I shall go to bed and sleep for ten, twelve hours. You only want eight hours, you swallow down one capsule. Wonderful sleeping."

"Yeah, that's nice, but maybe we oughtta talk," Leonard said.

Still brimming with bonhomie, Ali said, "You try." Then he unscrewed the top again.

"I ain't ready to go to sleep," Leonard said.

"No," Ali said, "not for now. You try later. You shall thank me. If you like them, I get you all you want."

Leonard had never been one to turn down drugs of any kind, and he gave a nod while Ali dumped the capsules onto the desktop and put the empty vial in the drawer. Then he pushed a plain envelope across to Leonard with his fingernail and, with a mirthless smile, said, "One hour before you wish to sleep, swallow down two."

Leonard scooped the capsules into the envelope, folded it, and put it in his pocket. Then he said, "I been thinking that my pay for what I done for you is pathetic. You just said how much I helped you. But what happened to me? I went to the slam and spent the fucking night with maniacs and child molesters and gangbangers."

Ali stopped smiling then. His brow wrinkled and he said, "I feel great sorrow for you, my friend."

Leonard said, "Yeah, well, I ain't looking for pity. I just want proper compensation."

Ali knew he had guessed correctly. It was blackmail. He'd probably demand another two hundred. Maybe even five. And he'd be back in a few weeks. And a few weeks after that. Ali was glad he had decided to give Leonard the other deadly sister. It would be the only way to stop these petty demands that would eventually get expensive, and even dangerous.

Trying to maintain an attitude of sympathy mixed with puzzlement, Ali said, "How can I help you, Leonard?"

"I think ten thousand bucks will help a lot," Leonard said.

Ali could not remember a time when he needed to control so much outrage. He sipped some Jack and, with a quiver in his voice, said, "You wish for me to pay you ten thousand? Am I hearing the correct words?"

"It's only a loan," Leonard said. "I got an idea for a small business. I need a stake."

"A loan," Ali said without intonation.

"Yeah," Leonard said. "I'll pay you back in maybe a year, eighteen months tops, with twenty percent interest. That's fair, ain't it?"

"But Leonard, ten thousand is very big money," Ali said.

"Not to you," Leonard said. "I seen your ex-house. I seen this club packed to the walls, with money laying all over the bar and the tables and even on the stage. How much did you make on a case of that hot liquor I used to supply you? Come on, Ali, ten grand ain't much for you to lend to a friend."

"I shall have to think," Ali said. "You come back in three, four days. We are going to talk some more."

Suddenly Leonard said, "What would your ex-old lady say if she knew you paid me to steal a folder from her desk?"

Ali knew that his voice might betray the rage welling up from his belly, so he took another sip of Jack Daniel's and said, "My bitch wife? She would say no, Ali has no care about documents in this house. She would not be believing such a thing, Leonard."

Emboldened by Ali's deferential manner and by the liquor warming him, Leonard went for it. With sweat dampening his T-shirt, he said, "What would she say if I told her you planted a bug in her house?"

Ali was genuinely perplexed and said, "A bug?"

"A listening device," Leonard said. "I bet she'd hire a security company to sweep the joint and they'd find it. Where'd you put it? In the bedroom?"

Hanging on to a semblance of a smile, Ali said, "You talk very much shit, Leonard."

"I hung around and saw you go in that garage, Ali," Leonard said. "And you were carrying that folder you never wanted in the first place. And you were in there for thirteen minutes. What would the little woman say about them little nuggets of information?"

Ali Aziz blinked first, unsmiling, his teeth clenched. Then, voice trembling, he said, "I do not put no bugs in the house. I just read the document and put the folder back in the house. That is all."

"I guess you could try to sell that to the little woman," Leonard said. "But she ain't gonna buy it. And after they do the electronics sweep and find the bug, you are gonna be in a world of hurt when her lawyer tells the judge. Actually, what you done was a serious crime, Ali. You committed a felony, entering that house and planting a bug."

For a frightening moment, Ali Aziz thought about the pistol in his desk drawer. He quickly came to his senses, knowing he could never get away with that. Not here, not now. Instead, with a voice hoarse and raspy, he said, "I understand. I shall give you the business loan, Leonard. But I do not have so much money here. Come back next week."

"I want it now, Ali," Leonard said. "We can start with what you got on you. I seen you peel off five grand right outta your pocket one time after Whitey and me got you a load of booze."

Without a word, Ali Aziz reached a trembling hand into his trousers pocket, pulled out his roll of $100 bills, and tossed it on the desktop, gold money clip and all.

Leonard finished his drink, poured another, and removed the money clip and pushed it back to Ali. He counted while Ali sat trying with all of his self-control not to leap across the desk and get the thief's skinny neck in his fingers and squeeze.

After he finished counting, Leonard said, "You let me down. You only got twenty-one hundred here. Go to your safe and get the rest. Whadda you got, a floor safe?"

Ali Aziz could barely get out the words, but he managed to say, "Please go to the bar, Leonard. Have one more drink. Come back and I shall have the money."

"Sure," Leonard said. "But you don't gotta worry about me seeing your safe. I never steal from a friend."

Leonard Stilwell's legs were rubbery when he walked down the passageway to the main room, and he knew it wasn't the booze. He had just pulled off the biggest score of his life! It was scary but he'd stung that fucking Ay-rab with ease, and there was no reason he couldn't do it again before Ali's ex-wife moved out of the house.

What was it Ali had said? Escrow was closing

pretty soon? After that, and after the divorce shit was all worked out, a shakedown wouldn't work anymore. In fact, Ali could retrieve the listening device himself by then, or he might even have somebody else break into the house and get it out of there in order to get Leonard off his back. But Leonard thought he ought to be able to burn Ali Aziz one more time, maybe in a few days, before Ali had a chance to react to what had just happened to him. Leonard figured that in business, timing was everything.

He was so utterly stoked, with more money in his pocket than he'd ever had in his life, that he sat by the stage and stuffed a $20 bill into the G-string of the dancer, a big, busty babe in a cowboy hat who'd licked her lips and winked at him. Then, when he finished his drink, after tipping the cocktail waitress $10, he walked back down the passageway. But suddenly he stopped and felt a wave of fear sweep over him. It was safe enough here with all the people around, but he thought of how Ali's face had gone deathly pale. That swarthy camel fucker had turned whiter than Leonard for a minute there. Whiter than a corpse.

Leonard grabbed the first busboy to walk past him, handed the Mexican a $10 bill, and said, "Come with me to the boss's office."

He knocked this time, then pushed the door open gingerly, holding the Mexican by the arm and saying, "Ali, I brought the help with me."

Ali was sitting at the desk, staring at the doorway, his hands folded under his chin. The look on his face was as grim as Leonard had seen on the strong-arm robber last night after he got the word that their new cellie was a short-eyes kiddie raper.

Ali said, "Please come in."

"I'll leave the door open," Leonard said. Then to the Mexican, "What's your name, son?"

"Marcos," the kid said.

"Okay, Marcos, hang there for a minute," Leonard said, leaving the door open so that Ali knew there was a witness, in case violence was on his mind. Then Leonard hurried across the room to Ali's desk and picked up the stack of currency awaiting him.

"Good-bye, Leonard," Ali said. "I do not want no more loans between us."

"Don't be a drama queen," Leonard said.

"This is what they call squid pro quo. That's lawyer talk and it means we're straight with each other."

When he left the office, he handed the busboy another $10 and said, "Thanks for being my bodyguard, son."

Ali Aziz entered his little half bathroom, closed the door, locked it, turned on both water taps to muffle the sound, and, gripping the sink, screamed until drool ran down his chin.

NINETEEN

BIX RAMSTEAD WAS FEELING much more alive after having had a nap and a shower and shave. He dressed in a pale blue Oxford shirt and clean chinos and swallowed some aspirin to diminish the raging headache. He felt resolute enough to resist Margot Aziz now, while the sun was still high enough over the Hollywood Hills and his resolve had not been shattered by six or eight ounces of booze. That's all it took when he was around her, that alluring young woman so different from his wife.

Bix didn't believe that Margot was truly in love with him, as she claimed. Her miserable marriage made her think so. But to have a woman like Margot Aziz professing her love for him, so passionate for him, had been overwhelming. Margot wasn't shy like his wife, Darcey. She was assertive and sophisticated and always knew just what to say. She was mischievous and funny and made him feel more worldly, more important, than he was or ever could be. And Margot made him feel *young* like her.

When Bix was able to step back and analyze it soberly, none of it made sense. They had been intimate for only five months. They'd had sexual encounters only half a dozen times in those five months, always in hotels, where she'd rented a room and waited for him until he got off duty. And always she had provided drinks to allay his fears and guilt. He'd been besotted by this perplexing young woman who claimed she'd never betrayed her husband before meeting Bix, and who made him believe it.

Bix parked his minivan in her driveway and Margot answered the door very quickly. She was dressed the way she often was when they had evening clandestine meetings. She wore creamy tailored pants that hugged her body, a simple black shell, a delicate gold necklace, no earrings, no bling. Her ears were perfect and she seldom adorned them. Her shoulders were wide and square, her tan was year-round.

Bix was glad she was not wearing low-cut jeans and a rising jersey that exposed her muscular belly, as she sometimes dressed for a day-time rendezvous. That's when she looked most sensual.

"Hello, darling," she said.

"I can only stay long enough to hear the story and offer some advice," he said.

"Of course," Margot said. "Come in."

When they were inside the marble foyer, Margot said, "Let's sit on the terrace and admire the smog, shall we? The toxins are so lovely this time of day."

He followed her through the living room to the sliding doors and walked outside. There was a pitcher of iced tea already there and some smoked wahoo tuna, cream cheese, chopped onions, capers, and a crunchy French baguette, already sliced.

"We'll smell awful after eating this stuff, but what the hell," Margot said.

Bix sat, feeling dry-mouthed, and sipped some tea. Then he said, "Tell me about it, Margot. What's going on?"

"His threats are more overt now," she said.

"Overt how?"

"He talks blatantly to Nicky in my presence when he's picking up our son for his over-

nighter. He makes sure I hear him telling Nicky
how beautiful Saudi Arabia is. Or he tells Nicky
that he'll love seeing the Giza pyramids in
Egypt. Stuff like that."

"He's just trying to goad you," Bix said. "That
guy's locked into America. In fact, he's locked
into his businesses here in Hollywood. He's
going nowhere."

Margot loaded up a slice of baguette with
wahoo and cream cheese and onion, topped
it with a few capers, and handed it to Bix. He
thought she had the most beautiful hands he'd
ever seen, and, as always, her nails matched the
lip gloss she was wearing.

"I always talk to Nicky when he comes back
from outings with his father," Margot continued, "but lately he's clamming up. I know that
Ali has ordered him not to tell me what his
father's planning."

"He's five years old, Margot," Bix said. "Ali's
not gonna be making travel plans with a kid
that young. It's just talk, trying to get Nicky in
touch with his father's culture. That's all it is."

"The last time Ali came for him, my son was
a different child when he came back."

"Different how?"

Margot sipped her iced tea and said, "I took Nicky to bed with me that night and I hugged and kissed him and asked him what he and his daddy talked about. And he said, 'Are you going to come and live with us, Mommy?' And I asked him where, and he said, 'When I meet my gramma and grampa.' And I said, 'You've met your gramma and grampa lots of times. Remember when they came here, and when we drove to Barstow?' And he said, 'My other gramma and grampa. Who live far away across the ocean.'"

"That doesn't imply he's gonna run off with Nicky," Bix said.

"I've got information from a good source that he's put the Leopard Lounge up for sale with a broker. It's all on the Q.T. And he's dissolving every asset he owns that's not part of the divorce action. He's very sneaky. Ali's got secret assets we haven't been able to find."

"That still doesn't mean he's ready to leave the country. Does Nicky have a passport?"

"Do you know how easy it is to leave this country for the Middle East with a child if you have plenty of money? You just hop in your car and drive your child three hours south and cross the border into Tijuana. After that, it's a piece of cake to arrange for passports and flights to anywhere you want."

"Your imagination is getting the better of you," Bix said.

"There's more," Margot said. Then she stopped and said, "Would you mind if I had a drink? It'll make it easier to talk about."

He didn't look pleased but said, "Go ahead."

She returned with a triple shot of premium vodka, on the rocks in a tumbler, just the way he liked it. With a slice of lime hanging on the lip of the glass instead of a lemon twist inside it, also the way he liked it.

She squeezed the lime into it, took a sip, and said, "Oh, that's better. That's much better."

Bix looked at his watch and said, "Get on with it, Margot. I wanna get home before dark."

"Why? Your family isn't home."

"I've gotta feed Annie," he said.

"She can't eat after dark?"

"I can't be here after dark," he said.

"Why?"

"You're a vampire, remember?" he said, smiling just a bit.

Margot chuckled then, a sound he loved to hear, and she said, "Oh, darling, I've missed you so much."

"You were going to tell me more," Bix said, avoiding her amber eyes. "Something you needed my advice about, remember?"

"He said he's going to kill me," Margot said suddenly and took another sip of vodka.

"Who'd he say this to?"

"I'm not sure," Margot said, "but I think it was one of his dancers. I got an anonymous call. My new number's unlisted, but of course he has it. She could have found it in his desk directory."

"Why would he be crazy enough to tell a dancer he was going to kill you?"

"He uses cocaine heavily in his office. He shares it with his dancers for sexual favors. When he's high on coke, he talks way too much. He reveals things he shouldn't. He mixes his drugs and doesn't even remember what happened later. That's what I think happened."

"What did the anonymous caller say?"

"She said, 'Be careful. He's going to kill you and take your son.' Then she hung up."

"You didn't recognize the voice?"

"No, but I'm sure it was one of the dancers."

"You're speculating."

"Based on experience."

"Did you tell your lawyer."

"No."

"Why not?"

"He'd say what you're saying. It's speculation. Someone's trying to scare me. I'm being an alarmist. Et cetera." Then she stopped and her chin quivered, and she put her hand to her eyes, saying, "Excuse me, Bix, I'll be right back."

Margot Aziz left him there alone with the sweating tumbler full of his favorite ice-cold vodka. His face felt fiery hot and he wanted to pick up the glass tumbler and hold it against his cheek to quell the heat. He wanted to hold the glass against his lips.

She was gone for a few minutes, and when she returned, her eyes were a bit moist, as though she'd been crying, and she held a tissue in her hand to prove it. She noticed that the vodka level in the tumbler had dropped. Only a little. But it had dropped.

She said, "Excuse me again, I want to freshen this."

Bix Ramstead felt his heart pounding. This woman. The sight of her. The touch of her skin. Her scent. He had the taste of vodka on his tongue, as he always had when he was with her. This was all so familiar and so frightening.

When she returned, she set the tumbler on the outdoor table with the fresh vodka in it and a fresh slice of lime hanging on the lip of the glass. She looked at him in earnest and said, "Bix, you always carry your gun off duty, don't you?"

"When I come to Hollywood, yeah," he said. "When I'm at home in Studio City, I'm not packing. Not when I go to the market or to the movies with my kids."

She said, "Are you packing now?"

"It's in the car," he said. "Why?"

"I'm gonna buy a gun as soon as possible. I can't stand this fear I'm living under. I want you to tell me what to buy."

"If it makes you feel any better," he said, "then buy one. Just get a wheel gun. A thirty-eight revolver. They're simple. They don't misfire. They're easy to use. Anyway, you're never gonna fire it."

"Any particular make?" she said.

He looked at his watch then and said, "I better be going. I might run into traffic, driving over Laurel Canyon. I don't think I should get on the freeway tonight."

"One drink," she said. "For the road. For old times' sake. In a little while the traffic will be light and you can whiz home and feed Annie."

He hesitated just long enough for her to know she could pull it off. She slid the tumbler full of vodka in front of him and said, "I'll fix myself another."

Then she got up and went to the kitchen. She took her time, and when she returned, she saw that the vodka level had dropped again, but this time more than a little. And she had poured a triple shot into that one.

"Darling," she said, sitting with her fresh drink. "Thank you for coming. There was no one I could turn to. Nobody I could trust but you."

His hand trembled when he picked up the tumbler and drank again. "I've gotta get away from here before sundown," he said.

Margot chuckled again and, yes, he absolutely loved the sound of it. Just as a massive swarm of insects rose like ashes in the sky, tainting his lovely view of multicolored shards of smog over Hollywood.

The crack pipe was red-hot when Leonard Stilwell put it down on the sink counter that evening. He'd finally been able to score some rock at Pablo's Tacos, and he'd driven straight back to his apartment with the rock and with four chicken tacos loaded with guacamole. He'd stayed well away from Hollywood and Highland for fear of running into that pair of cops who looked to him like surf rats.

The crackhead dealer who'd sold him the rock said that he had six grams for sale, and Leonard said, "Wrap it up. I'll take it all."

"Cool!" the dealer said. "Plastic or paper?"

Leonard had been smoking ever since, trying to watch TV but unable to concentrate. When he was feeling both mellow and elated, that combination he loved to feel, he decided to take the advice given to him by Ali Aziz and turn in early for a good night's sleep. The envelope with the capsules was on the cheap little nightstand beside his bed and he shook out three capsules. But then he thought he'd better not push it and dropped one back inside the envelope. He popped two in his mouth and washed them down with a beer.

Then he stripped down, got under the covers, and prepared himself for sweet dreams. Nobody who saw the pile of Ben Franklins he'd stashed inside a pot in the kitchen could say that Leonard Stilwell was anything but a Hollywood success story.

The sun had flamed out unnoticed in wispy clouds of rosy smoke without Bix Ramstead giving a single thought to vampires. Two hours after he'd taken that first sip from Margot's drink, his speech was somewhat slurred, his eyes were 80 proof glossy, and night was on them, light sparkling all over Hollywood.

A large raven flew up from the canyon into the blue-black sky with wildly beating wings, screeching at a mockingbird that was diving at the ebony flyer. Bix Ramstead watched that raven escaping from the feathered tormenter, seeing it fly away from the Hollywood Hills to the safety of its nesting place.

Margot saw him watching it and said, "It's getting too cool and dark for ravens and crows. Let's go inside."

When they were seated side by side on one of the enormous pistachio green sofas, he tried to focus on the glass sculpture hanging from the travertine wall and convince himself that he was not drunk. Mellow music from several speakers surrounded them, and the lamps in the living room and foyer were on dimmers and had been turned low.

"Hope you don't mind that it's all Rod Stewart tonight," she said. "I'm still an old-fashioned girl from Barstow."

"In the oldie song 'Route Sixty-six,' Barstow is mentioned," Bix said, having trouble pronouncing consonants. "You ever heard it?"

"Really?" Margot said. "Don't think I know that one."

"You're too young," Bix said. "Ask your mom and dad."

"I think I will, next time I see them," she said. "By the way, they're as worried about Ali stealing Nicky from me as I am. He's their only grandchild and they adore him. They hate his father, of course, and they hated it when I was a dancer at the Leopard Lounge. They never understood that I did what I had to do to get by. Hollywood is a pitiless place."

"What's your dad do?" Bix said, trying not to gulp this drink. Sip, he told himself.

"He's retired from the post office," Margot said.

"A civil servant," Bix said. "Like me."

"Bix," Margot said, looking more serious, "would you do me a huge favor and bring your gun in here?"

"What? You wanna shoot crows on the hillside? I'm a Crow, remember?" Those consonants again, they were getting tangled on his tongue and in his throat.

But it sounded exceptionally funny to him and he laughed before taking another big hit from the tumbler. He was trying to remember if this was his fourth or fifth drink. He was sure he could handle six, but Margot poured so heavy he was going to stop after five. Was this number five?

Margot said, "I believe I told you that I took a shooting lesson at a gun store in the Valley. And I'm sure you're right about a revolver being what I should buy, but the nine-millimeter pistol I fired in that lesson seemed comfortable to me. If that's a word that applies to a gun. Would you mind getting yours so I can ask you a few questions? Or I can get it if you give me your car keys."

"I'll get it," Bix said with a sigh. "I gotta pee anyway."

It took him two attempts to get up from the sofa, and he weaved when he crossed the living room to the powder room off the foyer. After he'd flushed the toilet, he looked at himself in the mirror, trying to focus on his pupils. Was he drunk? He thought he'd better not have another vodka. Maybe some fizzy water. After that, he was going home.

The second he opened the door to his minivan to retrieve his holstered nine from under the seat, Bix Ramstead felt it: a hint of danger. His neck hair bristled when he touched the gun, and he shivered. Cop instincts that he'd developed over nearly two decades were telling him to get into that van and drive down that hill and never drive back up again. But he decided he was being ridiculous. He was having a pleasant time and would be flying off to his nest very soon. After one more drink.

While he was gone, Margot removed from the drawer in the butler's pantry two magenta-and-turquoise capsules that she'd taken from her jewelry box earlier in the day. She pulled one apart and poured it into the drink, stirring it before dropping in the ice. She didn't like the way it failed to completely dissolve, and she didn't really think it would be needed tonight, but there was no sense taking a chance that he'd somehow summon enough sobriety to drive away from there. The granules were clinging to the ice, and she thought he'd get very little of it into his system, so she took the second capsule and added it, then flushed the empty capsules away. She prepared herself another tumbler of plain tonic, ice, and lime.

When Bix got back inside the house, a fresh drink was waiting for him on the massive glass-and-steel coffee table. He sat down heavily again and withdrew the Beretta from its holster. After taking a sip from the fresh drink, he said, "Is this the kind of gun you fired?"

"Yes," she said. "I just liked the feel of that kind of pistol, but I'm unsure how the safety works. I wouldn't want anything that would be too easy for Nicky to figure out if, god forbid, he ever found it."

"It's your job to see that he never does," Bix

said emphatically. "That's why buying a gun is a bad idea."

"What is that on the frame?" she said. "Is that the safety?"

"No," Bix said with the careful articulation of the inebriate. "It's a decocker. With this gun you don't have to sweep a safety up from the safe position before firing. We can just draw, aim, and squeeze the trigger. The first round is double action and takes more trigger pull. Then the rest are single action while the gun ejects the empty shell casings. Afterwards, we sweep the decocker down to safely drop the hammer, then back up to the fire position, and we're ready again."

"What's the bottom line?" she said. "You only have to pull the trigger, right?"

"Squeeze with the pad of your index finger," he said. "Don't pull, yank, or jerk."

"Got it," she said. "I think I'll buy one of those."

Bix got the hiccups then and Margot got up, saying, "I'll get you some bitters and lime. Works every time."

Bix holstered the gun and took a long gulp

of vodka, but it didn't stop the hiccups. She returned with a saucer. On it was a wedge of lime soaked in bitters.

"Bite on this and suck hard," she said with a grin.

He did as he was told and shuddered, saying, "That tastes awful!"

"Wash it down," she said, and he did, with more vodka.

"Is that better?" she said.

He sat quietly for a moment and said, "My hiccups are history."

"See?" she said. "Would I ever steer you wrong?"

Another Hollywood Crow had too much to drink that evening. Hollywood Nate was enjoying his day off and had gone alone to an early first-run movie in Westwood, later stopping at Bossa Nova on Sunset Boulevard, a restaurant that stayed open until very late and was frequented by cops. He saw a black-and-white in the parking lot, but he didn't know the two cops inside. After he ate, he drove to Micelli's on Las Palmas, thinking he might see a few cops, but there wasn't anyone he recognized in there either. He stayed and had a glass of house red. Then another.

Nate was mellow when he got into his Mustang. And because he was, he again did something that he would never admit having done. Something he would never forget and always wonder about, the thought of which would later fill him with profound regret. He drove up the hill to Mt. Olympus.

He'd never gotten her out of his mind, even though the initial lust he felt for her had subsided. It was the mystery of her. Who was she? What was she about? He didn't know what he'd do if he saw her red Beemer pulling in or out of her driveway. He didn't think he had the gall to walk up and ring her bell at this time of night. To say what? Yes, Margot, I'll take the job as your live-in security guard. And why haven't you called me?

He was a grown man, thirty-six years old, and this was childish and silly, and yet he kept driving up into the Hollywood Hills. Up to Mt. Olympus for no reason that made any sense whatsoever. When he got there, he saw a blue Dodge minivan and he recognized it. Bix Ramstead often parked that minivan near Nate's

Mustang in the south lot, and once he'd told Bix the minivan looked like a vice squad hand-me-down and asked if Bix had to steam clean the cargo area and rake out the condoms after the hookers had been transported to jail.

Seeing that minivan made him face another possibility that he did not like to consider. Was he simply jealous that Margot Aziz could prefer Bix Ramstead to Hollywood Nate Weiss? Nate passed the address, turned around farther up the hill, and stared at the house of Margot Aziz as he drove slowly down past it again. He thought that Jetsam had been dead right. That house had an aura.

TWENTY

"I'M DRUNK!" BIX Ramstead finally admitted.

"You're just a bit tipsy," Margot said, removing the throw pillow between them on the sofa while Rod Stewart sang "You Go to My Head."

"Gotta go, Margot," he said.

Still not touching him, she said, "How about a good-night kiss for the road?"

Quickly, she slid over next to him, and he felt her breath on his neck. She kissed him with lots of tongue, and then she kissed his face and neck and ran her hands all over him while he groaned softly.

"Let's go lie down for a while, sweetheart," she said. "Until you're feeling more alert."

"I can't —," he said, but she cut him off with more kisses.

"You're sweet, Bix," she whispered. "You're the sweetest man I've ever known."

"I can't, Margot," he said without conviction.

"You've never even seen my bedroom," she said. "Let me show it to you."

He would've been surprised by her strength if he'd been sober enough to appreciate it. She half lifted him to his feet, put his arm around her neck, and led him to the carpeted staircase.

"I gotta go feed Annie!" he said, but she had an arm around his waist, and, holding up much of his weight, she started up the stairs.

"Shhhh, baby!" she said. "Wait till you see my bedroom. You can feed her later."

Margot was panting by the time she got him upstairs and into the bedroom. She walked him to the bed, and he stood swaying when she pulled back the spread and top sheet. Then she let him fall back onto the bed. This was not how she had imagined it would happen. She thought she'd have to get him pretty drunk, but not utterly blitzed like this. After sex, sleep would naturally follow. That was how it was supposed to happen, but she'd been too fearful that he'd have an attack of conscience. She'd poured too heavily. The only bonus was that she wouldn't have to ball him after all.

He was up on one elbow, unable to focus,

seeing two Margots, when she quickly peeled off her top and stepped out of her pants.

"See!" she said cheerily, just in case he had any noncompliance left in him. "No underwear!"

He was nearly unresponsive, eyes closed, breathing through his mouth.

Naked, she worked methodically, pulling off his shoes and socks, undoing his belt, unzipping his chinos, pulling them down and off. Then she peeled off his briefs and he seemed barely awake when she unbuttoned his Oxford shirt and got him out of it.

When he opened his eyes, looking past her at the open doorway, she nearly panicked. He couldn't get up now! He couldn't leave now! She climbed on him, sliding along his body, moaning, uttering endearments, running her hands over him, leaning down to kiss him when he tried to raise up.

"Baby, baby," she murmured. "I want you!"

All he said to her was "*Some* angel I am."

"Yes, yes," she said. "You *are* my angel. You *are!*"

It was more of a sex simulation than the real thing, and it required much more effort for her. She was panting from exhaustion by the time he fell into a deep slumber. She gathered his clothes, folded them, and put them in her closet. When she came back to the bed, she strained and pushed and lifted until he was under the covers, his head on the pillow, snoring softly.

She put on a robe and ran downstairs. She retrieved his holstered gun from the coffee table but left the empty vodka bottle and the two glasses on the table, pouring some vodka into her tumbler of tonic to prove that they'd both been drinking heavily.

Then she crossed the foyer to the front door and unlocked the thumb-latch, making sure that the door opened easily. She ran back up to the bedroom and put Bix's holstered gun on the nightstand at his side of the bed, along with his car keys and wallet. Then she turned out all of the lights except a lamp on the second floor at the top of the staircase. She wanted Ali back-lit when he entered her bedroom.

Gil Ponce had gotten back to regular duty in record time after the shooting of the ice-cream hijacker was found to be in policy and the BSS shrink had peeked inside his head. Gil's quick return was probably due to the TV media's being so quick (and incorrect) in calling the incident a suicide-by-cop, thus giving the LAPD bureaucrats plenty of cover.

Six hours into their watch, Cat Song and Gil Ponce took code 7 in a restaurant that Cat frequented in Thai Town. That meant phoning ahead for their dinners so that the food could be served the moment they sat down, giving them the whole thirty minutes to get through the courses.

Cat told Gil that the main course was named for her, and he smiled when they brought out a whole baked catfish. Cat talked to Gil about the satay and the curry, and, using a fork, she flaked off the tender flesh from the fish and spooned it onto his plate. They drank Thai iced coffee, and when the bill came, Cat insisted on paying it, leaving a good tip for the owner.

When they got back out to their black-and-white, Gil driving and Cat riding shotgun, he said, "Why're you being so nice to me? It's not my birthday."

"I'm always nice to everybody," she said. "And you're so close to finishing your probation, I thought we should celebrate. You won't be a probie that we can kick around anymore."

"You've been especially nice," Gil said, driving west on Sunset Boulevard at 11 P.M.

"I hadn't noticed," Cat said, clearing from code 7 and, seeing their MDC blinking, hitting the message-received and display button.

She opened and acknowledged the message, then hit the en route key, and Gil looked at the message on the dashboard screen, saying, "Illegal parking. That's near that nightclub, what's it called? The Leopard Lounge?"

"It's a titty bar masquerading as a fancy nightclub," Cat said. "Somebody's always complaining about the parking around there."

When they were still a few minutes away, Gil said, "There wouldn't be another reason why you've been treating me like you're my —"

"If you say mommy, I'll give you a shot of whup-ass spray," Cat said, touching the canister on her Sam Browne.

"Big sister, I was gonna say." Then Gil added, "Is it about the shooting?"

"You tell me, Gil," Cat said. "I haven't seen you crack a smile since that night in the Hollywood cemetery."

"Well, it was scary with those FID investigators jacking me up. They aren't gentle. The shrink was okay, but I just told him what I thought he wanted to hear."

"Who cares about any of them?" Cat said. "I told you a minute after you shot that guy that you did good. That I woulda done the same."

"I know, but, well..."

"Well what? You shoulda had ESP and known the tweaker was packing a starter pistol? Is that what?"

"I don't know. I just feel...different now."

"Sure, you do," Cat said. "You're supposed to. You took a life — through no fault of your own. He made the choice, not you. I was there, boy. I heard you yelling at him to put his hands on his head and get down and prone out. I heard it!"

Gil Ponce said, "I don't like the other guys slapping me on the back and calling me a gunfighter. I don't like that."

"Screw them too!" Cat said. "Macho dipshits. None of them ever fired their weapons outside the pistol range. Those that have wouldn't go around patting your ass over it."

"Well, I wouldn't want anyone else to know that you and me talked about this," Gil said.

"That's just your Hispanic machismo," Cat said.

"I'm not really Hispanic," he said.

"Let's not go over that again," she said. "Now, listen to me, partner, I don't know how to dial you in except to keep saying you did exactly what any copper woulda done and shoulda done at that moment in that place. And I'd hate to think that my safety could be jeopardized from now on because you're gun-shy."

He said, "Cat, I don't want you —"

"Lemme tell you a true story," she said, interrupting him. "Five years ago, I had a partner for two months. A nice guy. We were working Watch three. He married a woman with four kids who was a peace activist, and pretty soon he decided to resign from the Department. Said he wanted to go into a line of work where he'd never have to use violence on anybody. And on the last day we worked together, he made a little confession to me. Because of his wife's haranguing, he hadn't loaded a round in his nine since before we started working together. It's the closest I ever came to pulling my baton and beating another cop right into the ground."

"Why're you telling me this, Cat?" Gil asked.

"Did you clean your nine after the other night?"

"Yeah."

"Did you reload it?"

"Of course."

"Then I feel safe. Because this is all about me, not about you. I've got a two-year-old at home who needs his momma. I've got a good copper here with a loaded nine who's got my back. So I feel safe. End of story. Any questions?"

After a moment of contemplation, Gil Ponce said, "Thanks, Cat."

"For what?" she said.

Gil Ponce paused, then said, "For the Thai dinner, of course. It was great."

"Don't mention it," Cat Song said.

There wasn't any parking for blocks around the Leopard Lounge at 11:15 on a soft summer night like this one, when a Hollywood moon brought hordes of people out for revelry on the boulevards. Gil parked their black-and-white in a red zone on Sunset Boulevard and they walked south to the source of the call, a large apartment building with parking spaces in front.

The person reporting was a well-coiffed,

well-dressed elderly woman who answered the door at the manager's office and said with a Russian accent, "I'm Mrs. Vronsky. I'm the one who called."

"Yes, ma'am," Gil said.

"At this time of night I should be in bed, asleep," she said, "but if I go to sleep, I'll get woke up when my tenants come home and can't park. A man just pulled into space number two, and when I yelled at him, he said something ugly to me. Then after I called for you, he drove away."

"Then there's nobody for us to cite at the moment," Cat said. "Call us if it happens again."

"Do you know Officer Ramstead?" Mrs. Vronsky said. "He's a friend of mine."

"Community Relations Office?" Cat said.

"Yes, that's right," Mrs. Vronsky said. "He often comes by in the daytime and helps me with the parking problems. It's all because of the nightclub, you know."

"Yes," Cat said, "we sympathize."

"Officer Ramstead is a very kind man and he likes my homemade piroshki," the old woman said. "If I had some, I'd invite you in and pour you some tea, and you could taste it."

"Some other time," Cat said, giving Gil a look that said, Lonely old lady.

"Oh, look!" Mrs. Vronsky said. "Another one."

Sure enough, a four-year-old white Corvette that had been cruising slowly along the street, looking for parking, had wheeled into one of the vacant spaces in front of the apartment building. The driver of the car turned out the headlights but did not get out.

"We'll check this one," Cat said, and both cops walked out to the front of the building.

"Come back when I have some piroshki!" Mrs. Vronsky called after them.

Gil Ponce was surprised to find a young woman sitting in the car when he walked up on the driver's side. A beautiful young woman who looked to be of mixed race, with dark Asian eyes. She jumped when he tapped on her window with his flashlight.

She lowered the window and said, "Yes, Officer?" Then a beam shone along her dashboard and she saw Cat at the passenger window.

"Do you live here, ma'am?" Gil said.

"No, I don't," she said. "Is there a problem?"

"You're parking on private property in a resident's parking space," Gil said, thinking that this girl was smokin' hot!

She blinked, smiled, and said, "But Officer, I'm not parking. I just stopped here because there's no place on the street. I'm waiting for a car to leave a parking space at the Leopard Lounge. I work there."

"May I see your driver's license and registration?"

Jasmine looked in her purse, retrieved her wallet, opened it, and said, "Oh, crap! Today I bought some underwear at Victoria's Secret and paid by credit card. The girl asked for my driver's license too. I must've left my license and my Visa!"

"How about your registration?"

She handed it to Gil Ponce, who shined his light on it and said, "Jasmine McVicker."

"Yes," she said, drumming nervously on the steering wheel, looking at her watch. It was 11:25 P.M.

"Do you have anything else that proves you're Jasmine McVicker?" Gil asked.

She said, "I only have the one credit card. Look, Officer, you can walk across the street to the Leopard Lounge and anybody'll tell you I work there."

Gil looked at Cat over the roof of the 'vette, and Cat gave a shrug that said, Your call.

The fact was, young Gil Ponce wanted to go inside the Leopard Lounge and see what an upscale titty bar looked like. He said, "Let's find a place to park your car and see if you're who you say you are. If you are, I'll give you a warning for driving without a license but no ticket. Fair enough?"

Just then, Jasmine's cell phone rang and she grabbed it from her purse. Margot's voice came on in a whisper, saying, "Showtime."

Quickly Jasmine said, "I'll be delayed. A very nice police officer has detained me for not having my driver's license."

"Goddamnit!" Margot whispered. "Get rid of him!"

"I'll be as quick as I can," Jasmine said, clicking off.

To Gil she said, "Where do I park?"

"Right up at the corner, in the red zone," Gil

said. "My partner can watch your car so you don't get a ticket while you and me run inside for a minute."

"But then I'll have to come back out and move my car to some legal place before I can go back in again! I have to see one of the other dancers about something important and I'm late!"

"Better than getting a traffic citation, isn't it?" Gil said. Then he added, "Are you really a dancer?"

Jasmine was desperate. If there hadn't been a woman cop with him, she'd have given him her address and offered him a late date. Anything to give her fifteen minutes of goddamn parking so she could do what she had to do!

"Okay, okay!" she said. "But let's just leave my car here for two minutes and run across the street. Please, Officer, it'll save time!"

Gil shrugged at Cat, who gave a nod, having figured this one out. Cat had pumped up her young boot's sagging morale to the point where he wanted to stroll into the topless bar with this hottie and check out the other flesh onstage. And who knows? Maybe get Jasmine's phone number. They lose their innocence fast, these male rookies, Cat Song thought.

While Jasmine was locking her car, purse in hand, and Gil Ponce was making a mental list of cliché questions — such as how did such a beautiful girl end up dancing at the Leopard Lounge — Cat Song walked to their shop, opened the door, and listened for radio calls.

After they got inside the nightclub, it didn't take thirty seconds for Jasmine to wave one of the harried, perspiring bartenders to the end of the bar to identify her for Gil Ponce, who couldn't have cared less. He could barely hear the bartender over the erotic, pounding beat from Ali's $75,000 sound system, and he just nodded at everything the man shouted over the nightclub din. Actually, Gil Ponce was preoccupied, gaping at two dancers onstage, pole writhing under strobes, one of whom was Ali's stunning new star, Loxie Fox, her G-string studded with tightly folded $5 and $10 bills.

Cat Song snapped him out of it when she suddenly appeared behind him, saying in his ear, "Excuse me, Officer Casanova. I'm so glad you got your mojo back, but I thought you might like to know, there's a hell of a pursuit coming our way from Rampart Division. Would you care to jump on it, or would you rather just sit this one out for a rainbow drink with an umbrella in it?"

Officer Gil Ponce raced out of the Leopard Lounge without asking for Jasmine McVicker's phone number. Without even saying good-bye to her.

Jasmine hurried to the dancers' bathroom and locked the door behind her. She opened her purse and grabbed the eyedrops she'd bought in a shop on La Brea. It supplied cosmetics to makeup artists working in film and television, drops that helped actors to cry their eyes out on cue. She poured them into both eyes, heeding Margot's admonition to "make that mascara run." When she was finished, her vision was so blurred she could hardly see her face in the mirror, but she knew she looked like hell. She was ready. Showtime.

Ali's office door was locked, and Jasmine figured he was counting the cash. On big nights like this one, he made numerous trips to the bar to retrieve large currency notes, replacing $100 bills with $50s, $20s, $10s, and lots of $5s, which was the smallest tip that customers offered in this upscale nightclub.

Jasmine knew that Ali arranged for private security pickups at the end of the night when the money pile in his safe grew too large. She'd seen that often enough. She also knew that the money he took in at the Leopard Lounge was greater than the IRS, or Margot, or god almighty, would ever know about. And that if Margot thought she was getting half of Ali's assets, she was kidding herself. Jasmine had informed Margot that she believed there was a safety deposit box, but she didn't know where. Margot told her to work on it.

Jasmine banged on the door frantically and yelled, "Ali!"

"Who is there?" he called out.

"Jasmine! Open up!"

She knew he was looking through the peephole at her and then he opened the door, startled by her appearance.

"What has been happening to you?" Ali said, closing the door and locking it. "I thought you were having an ankle sprain?" He was looking weekend sharp, in one of his monogrammed white dress shirts and a charcoal gray Valentino suit, with black loafers.

Through a fluffy blur she could see that on

the desktop there were stacks of currency. She ran to the client's chair and sat while Ali stood between her and the desk, instinctively guarding his money.

"I just left Margot!" she said, wiping the mascara from her face, looking up at him with eyes overflowing.

"What is happening?" he said.

"You told me to spy on her!" Jasmine said, trying to sob.

"Yes, yes!" he said. "What is happening?"

"She's Hoovering cocaine, Ali! She had lines laid out on her dressing table. There musta been three, four thousand bucks' worth of blow! I did one line, sort of, just so I could find out what's happening in that house."

"What? Tell me!" he said.

"They wanted me to do a three-way," Jasmine said. "Her and him, but I told them no way. I told him I don't do kink. He was even more trashed than she was. I was scared of that guy!"

"Nicky!" he said frantically. "Where is Nicky?"

"He was there," she said.

"WHAT?"

It was so loud, she jerked back in the client chair, her head thumping against the tufted leather back.

"I tried to take her aside and talk sense to her. Him, he was just roaming in and out of the house in his Speedo. He'd jump in the pool and then he'd come inside and do a line. Then he'd jump in the pool and swim some more. He kept wanting her to swim, but I kept telling her it was too risky in her condition. I kept telling her to stay in her bedroom and go to sleep."

Ali seemed to forget the money then. He walked around the desk and sat in his swivel chair. He pushed the stacks of currency aside and put his elbows on the desk and his face in his hands. In less than a minute his face was more tearstained than hers.

She worried then that he might be too devastated to act. She was trying to provoke unbridled rage, not debilitating grief. She said, "Nicky wasn't right there when they were doing the lines. He was in his own bedroom."

Ali wiped his eyes with the palms of his hands and said, "Nicky has plenty energy. Nobody is going to keep Nicky in his bedroom."

Deciding to use Nicky as the final card she'd

play, Jasmine said, "The guy's name is Lucas. He's a big, young guy, Margot's age. She met him at a nightclub on the Strip. I think the guy wants to take over Margot and her house, and he supplies her with coke."

"Why is my son in the house tonight?" Ali said. "Please tell me, Jasmine."

"As much as I could find out, this is the way it's been ever since this guy entered the picture. He says she shouldn't waste her money on the nanny. He says the kid should stay at home like other kids."

"Stay home?" Ali said, and she'd never heard him sound so bleak. "Stay home to see his mommy like this? Sex, cocaine, and what more things?"

"I don't know if I should tell you more, Ali," she said.

"Tell me, Jasmine," he said. "I beg you to tell me all. I must know."

"Margot told me they been doing three-ways with other girls on a regular basis, with lots of coke to amp them up. And sometimes they do a lot more than that. Lucas brings girls and guys from the Strip and they all do cocaine, and then they all get weirded out and do one another. Anything they can think of."

"And my Nicky," Ali said. "Where is my Nicky when these things happen?"

"From what I can tell, he's always in the house these days. I guess he's in his room when the really heavy stuff is going on. I don't think Margot would let him be in the bedroom when they start kinking it up. Unless he just walked in on it. I really can't say for sure, Ali. I'm sorry. I tried to find out as much as I could."

"How many people are in the house tonight, Jasmine? Only Margot and this man?"

"Yeah, that's all there was when I left," she said. "But Lucas was talking about calling some friend on the Strip. He's a fucking animal and he's ripped."

"You are a good friend to me," Ali said. "I thank you."

"Are you gonna call your lawyer?" Jasmine said. "I don't wanna get dragged before a judge. I'm telling you what's happening, but I'm not doing a deposition for some lawyer. I'm scared of that man Lucas. And I still gotta work in this town."

"What good is a lawyer?" Ali said. "Margot shall say you lie if we talk to my lawyer. She shall look and talk like the perfect mother when she sits down with the lawyer or the judge. Everybody looks at her and smiles. Beautiful mother."

"I can't see what good it would do to call the cops either," Jasmine said. "They couldn't go in there and check on the kid unless they had a warrant or some kind of firsthand information. And I'm not talking to cops, Ali. You can fire me, but I'm not talking to cops or to lawyers. I did what you asked me to do and now I'm out of it. I want no more to do with your ex-wife and her twisted friend. I'm real scared."

"Yes," Ali said. "I shall pay you the bonus. You are a good girl."

She was losing him again. She had seen the rage rise and fall and rise again. Now it was ebbing. She'd given him too much to process. He was beaten down by it. He looked like he might start weeping and not stop. She was watching it slipping away. All the money she and Margot would share. It was time to play her last card: the ace of spades.

She said, "There's something else, Ali.... No, never mind."

Wearily he said, "What? Tell me all, Jasmine. Please."

"I don't know if I should. I don't have proof of anything, and there's nothing you can do about it anyways."

He raised his eyes from his desk and looked up at her, his dark-rimmed eyes boring into hers. "Tell me," he said.

"Well, there was one point when I heard Nicky hollering for his mom. It's when Lucas was outside in the pool and I was in the bedroom with Margot, telling her she had to get herself together, that her son was calling for her."

"Yes, yes?" he said, his voice pleading to hear, and not wanting to hear.

"She was too into the blow. I couldn't get through to her. Then I heard Lucas come from the pool. I heard him coming up the stairs. I heard him walk down the hall to Nicky's room. I peeked out and saw him, wearing only the Speedo, open Nicky's door and go in and close it behind him."

"Oh, god!" Ali said. And then he began mur-

muring in Arabic. Jasmine guessed it was a Muslim prayer. After a few seconds he stopped.

"I'm not saying anything terrible happened in there, Ali," Jasmine said. "But he was in there for quite a while. Maybe ten minutes. Maybe longer. When he came out, Nicky wasn't yelling anymore."

"Then you did *what?*" Ali demanded.

And there was no doubt about it. This was pure rage. He was scaring her. She said, "Ali, I did what I could! When that man went into Margot's bathroom, I ran down the hall to Nicky's room and I opened the door and looked in."

"He is okay?" Ali said. "Please, Jasmine. My Nicky is okay?"

"The room was dark and he was under the covers, crying. I said his name but he wouldn't come out from under the covers. He knows me, but he wouldn't come out. Then I had to leave him because Lucas was out of the bathroom, asking Margot where I went. I ran back into the bedroom and said good night to both of them and came here as fast as I could."

Ali's fists were clenched so tightly the knuckles were white as bone. He began to rise from his chair, and if he had been looking directly at her, she would have run for the door in fright. He said, "Thank you, Jasmine."

"Are you going there, Ali?" she said. "Oh, I'm afraid. It could be dangerous for you!"

"And for Nicky," he said quietly.

Jasmine stood and said, "Are you taking your bouncer with you? You could, but it might trigger a confrontation."

"Thank you," Ali said, walking stiff-legged toward the door. "I must go there in peace. Alone. I shall only demand to see my son. If they do violence on me, I shall have a reason to call the police."

"Wait!" she shouted, and it caused him to stop. "You can't go there like that. Take your gun with you."

Ali said, "I do not threaten nobody. I shall take my son away. Nobody is going to stop me."

"But, Ali!" Jasmine said frantically. "You can't do it unarmed! That man is big and creepy and young. He won't let you take Nicky. He'll hurt you bad. Maybe Nicky too. Maybe you won't even be able to call the police. Then what? Take the gun as protection for *both* of you. Just in case of emergency!"

Ali stood motionless, then returned to his desk and unlocked a lower drawer and, removing a .32 caliber, semiautomatic pistol, put it inside the waistband of his trousers. And then Ali Aziz did the most amazing thing that Jasmine had ever seen him do. He walked out the door, leaving her in the office with the desktop stacked with money. She went to the door and spoke to him as he was walking down the passageway.

She said, "I had a feeling it would come to this if I told you everything, Ali. So when I went out Margot's front door, I took off the knob lock. And they were both too ripped to have set the burglar alarm. You can just walk in, Ali. But for god's sake, be careful!"

He never turned around but said, "Thank you, Jasmine. You are a good girl."

When she was sure Ali was gone, Jasmine ran back inside his office and scooped all of the money from the desktop into her purse.

★ TWENTY-ONE ★

IT HAD BEEN an uneventful night for 6-X-66, but that was okay with them. Lately, they'd had enough of what Hollywood cops called Star Wars Nights to last awhile. The pursuit of an ice-cream truck ending up as a shooting in the Hollywood cemetery, along with the Somalian woman who'd been painted white, had practically given them carpal tunnel by the time they got through writing all of the reports.

They'd just handled a call that had taken them out of their area and into the Hollywood Hills. It hadn't amounted to much, only a jittery resident worrying about a parked car on Laurel Canyon Boulevard that turned out to belong to a neighbor's nephew visiting from Montana. Gert Von Braun and Doomsday Dan Applewhite were on their way down the canyon, Gert driving, when they saw a Jaguar make a hard right turn onto the lovely tree-lined road leading up to Mt. Olympus.

"That guy almost rolled it," Dan said.

"Let's check him out," said Gert.

She whipped a left and floored it, turning on her light bar. In a moment, the black-and-white had closed on the Jaguar, which pulled over in front of a palatial home halfway up the hill.

Ali Aziz was in the crisis of his life. If the police got him out of his car and spotted the pistol inside his belt, he'd no doubt be arrested for carrying the concealed weapon, even though he had legally purchased the gun several years ago at a gun shop. If he put the loaded pistol on the seat, he'd still have a lot of explaining to do and perhaps be taken to Hollywood Station for further investigation. If he tried to hide it under the seat and they noticed it, he'd be arrested for certain.

In that fateful moment, he even considered telling them the terrible things that Jasmine had said and asking them to accompany him to his home. But he knew that would end with Margot reassuring the cops that everything was fine and that they were in a bitter divorce and custody fight. And the cops would tell him to go home and speak with his lawyer and to the appropriate detectives in the morning. He had learned from experience how the laws of this country worked against people who were trying to do what is right. And in the meantime his son would be left in his bed, weeping in terror, and perhaps from unspeakable harm done to him.

Ali didn't have time and couldn't risk it. He decided in that brief moment to get his emotions under control and to run the bluff of his lifetime. Ali Aziz willed a small smile onto his face when the burly woman cop came up on his side of the car while her male partner stood at the passenger side, shining his light in the window.

"In a hurry, are we, sir?" Gert said.

"I am so sorry, Officer," Ali said. "I am Ali Aziz, proprietor of the Leopard Lounge on Sunset Boulevard. I am in big hurry to the house of my ex-wife to collect my son."

He gingerly reached into his coat pocket for his wallet while both cops shined their flashlight beams on his left hand. He prayed to god that they would not spot the gun when he removed his license for Gert. He also removed business cards bearing the name of the Hollywood Station captain as well as one from the division captain.

"I am always first to give plenty of my time

to the Community Police Advisory Board," he said. "I give always donations to the holiday party for children. Everyone knows Ali."

"Just curious," Gert said. "Why're you picking up your son at this time of night? Won't he be asleep?"

"Yes, you are correct," Ali said. "I work late at the nightclub and this is how I must do. Nicky is going to sleep in my car when I drive with him to my condo."

Gert Von Braun didn't like his plastered-on smile and she didn't like the beads of sweat forming at his hairline. Her blue antenna was sending signals, but the address on his license was up the hill near the top of Mt. Olympus, and everything he said made sense. She looked over the roof of the Jaguar to Dan Applewhite, who shrugged.

"Drive more carefully when you have your son in the car, Mr. Aziz," she said, handing Ali back his license.

"Yes, yes, Officer," Ali said. "I shall drive with great care."

When the cops returned to their black-and-white, Ali drove slowly up the hill to the house on Mt. Olympus.

* * *

Margot had received the two-ring warning call from Jasmine twenty-five minutes earlier. It meant that Ali was on his way. The go phone was on vibrate and she didn't need to answer it. She had been seated naked on the lounge in the darkened master bedroom, on the opposite side of the king-size bed in which Bix Ramstead slept. She got up, went to his side of the bed, and removed his pistol from the holster on the nightstand. She walked back around the bed and out to the terrace through the sliding door that she'd kept open. After she got to the railing, she looked out into the canyon and hurled the throwaway phone into the brush below.

She walked softly to her walk-in closet for a robe and laid it across the lounge. But she would not put it on. Bix had last seen her naked, not that he'd remember. Then she sat back down on the lounge and waited for the sound of a car in front.

Ali Aziz parked in the driveway rather than on the street in case he had to get away fast, with his son in one hand and a gun in the other. He closed the door of the Jaguar quietly and walked to Margot's door, grateful that the security lights in the garden had not been turned on but there was moonlight. He looked up at the bright, glowing moon.

The door was unlocked and Ali blessed Jasmine for it. He entered, leaving the door open for his fast exit. He'd decided to go straight to Nicky's room, take him out of bed, and run with him down the stairs and out. Tomorrow, he and his lawyer, with Jasmine's help — and she would help when he offered her $25,000 — would go to the police, as well as to the judge who'd presided over their divorce proceedings. And if there was any justice at all, he would never have to return Nicky to her again. He prayed that the drug-dealing monster had not harmed his son.

There was a light on. The lamp at the top of the staircase on a marble table under the huge mirror that had cost him a fortune. He ascended, turned left, and crept along the hallway to Nicky's room, finding the door wide open. He stepped inside, but the bed was made and Nicky was gone! What had they done with him? He returned along the hall to the master bedroom. Could Nicky be in bed with them?

The double doors were wide open. He adjusted the gun inside his belt so that it was more accessible. A few more quiet steps and he'd be through the double doorway into the master bedroom.

He stood in the doorway. He could hear faint snoring, but it was very dark in there. He took another step forward. There was only one person lying there, sleeping on what he knew to be her side of the bed. Was it Margot? Was she alone in the bedroom? Where was the man? Where was Nicky? He was confused. He took another step inside. And another, his pupils adjusting to the darkness. And then he heard the loudest shout he had ever heard from the lips of Margot Aziz.

"ALI, DON'T SHOOT! PLEASE DON'T SHOOT! DON'T SHOOT!"

"What?" he said. "What? Margot?"

And Ali Aziz saw three fireballs and perhaps heard three explosions, but perhaps not. He was slammed down onto his back by the fireballs. It was a tight pattern fired from a distance of four feet after Margot stepped from behind the closet door and stood between Ali and the bed, crouching slightly and firing two-handed, just as the instructor had shown her at the pistol range. Ali's chest heaved and began leaking blood, then bubbled from an arterial spurt. His heart stopped almost instantly, pierced by one of the 9-millimeter rounds.

The explosions that smashed Ali Aziz to the floor also brought Bix Ramstead onto the floor, feet first. He leaped from bed and stumbled to his knees, not knowing where he was.

"Bix! Bix!" Margot screamed. "The lights! Turn on the lights!"

But Bix didn't know where the lights were. Bix was trying to decide where *he* was, and he wasn't even sure who was yelling his name. He saw a lamp and reached for it but knocked it from the nightstand.

Margot Aziz did not want light. She had dropped Bix's pistol onto the floor and, with tissue in her left hand, was feeling around Ali's waist and in his pockets. But there was no gun! Where was the fucking gun? Working frantically in the darkness, she managed to get her hand under him but it wasn't there either! Then she accidentally touched his crotch and felt hard metal inside. The gun had slipped down inside his briefs when he'd fallen.

Bix Ramstead figured out that he was in the bedroom of Margot Aziz, and he yelled, "Margot! Where are you! Where's the light switch!"

She saw him lurching naked toward the open doorway, toward the lamp outside, just as she got her hand down inside Ali's crotch and worked the gun up and out, using the sheets of tissue between her fingers and the steel. She picked up the pistol and placed it beside Ali's outstretched right hand.

Margot wadded the tissue in her left hand and, putting her right hand on Ali's bloody chest, smeared some blood on her own chest and cheek for dramatic effect, screaming, "Ali! Ali! Bix, I think he's dead!"

Bix Ramstead found the wall switch by the door, turned on the bedroom lights, and said, "Get away from him! Don't touch him!"

Margot stood up, put her bloody hand to her face, and screamed, "He's dead! Ali's dead! Oh, dear god!"

Bix Ramstead swayed and scrutinized the scene in horror, saying, "Where's my clothes? Where's my goddamn clothes?"

"Ali!" Margot screamed, running into the bathroom, kneeling at the toilet, and making gagging sounds, while Bix found his clothes in the closet and picked up the telephone that had fallen onto the floor beside the bed.

When Margot heard him making the call, she stopped gagging and put the tissues in the toilet and flushed them away. When she came out, Bix was talking to the watch commander at Hollywood Station.

Margot washed Ali's blood from her hands but not from her face or chest. She went to the closet and put on suitable pajamas, a full-length satin robe, and bedroom slippers. Then she walked toward Nicky's room to sit and prepare herself for the questioning.

The last words she would ever speak to Bix Ramstead were uttered when he was downstairs in the foyer, waiting in the doorway for the arrival of police. She was upstairs, standing at the railing outside Nicky's room, and she looked down at him.

"You were right, Bix," she said. "We were very bad for each other. But I want you to know that I'd rather he'd killed me tonight than see you brought into this horrible nightmare. I'm very, very sorry."

* * *

The call was given to 6-A-15 of Watch 3, the morning watch, but when midwatch unit 6-X-66 heard the location, Gert Von Braun said to Dan Applewhite, "Hey, that's the address that was on that guy's driver's license!"

When midwatch unit 6-X-46 heard it, Jetsam said to Flotsam, "Bro, that's the house on Mount Olympus!"

Soon there were four black-and-whites parked on the street in front, one of them belonging to the watch commander. And Bix Ramstead was standing on the porch in front of the house, telling them not to come inside but to keep the street clear for the coroner's van, criminalists from Scientific Investigation Division, and the two Hollywood homicide teams that were coming from home. Only a successful telephonic argument by the area captain, who said that this incident should be contained as much as possible, kept Robbery-Homicide detectives downtown from being called out, as they often are in high-profile cases. With an LAPD cop involved, this was very high profile.

The surfer cops stood in the driveway, and

Jetsam looked up at the moon illuminating the tile roof on the two-story house. For a few seconds, cobwebs of cloud floated across that dazzling white ball high in the velvety black sky over Hollywood.

And Jetsam said to his partner, "The Oracle would have told us to beware tonight. There's a Hollywood moon up there. And bro, this fucking house is *full* of bad juju."

TWENTY-TWO

FLOTSAM SAID TO JETSAM, "One of the corpse cops just arrived."

Hollywood homicide D2, Albino Villaseñor, was the first detective to arrive from home. He parked on the street and emerged from the car with a plastic briefcase and a flashlight, wearing the same brown Men's Wearhouse suit that he'd worn every time Flotsam had seen him.

His bald head glinted under the luminescence provided by the Hollywood moon, and his white mustache looked wild and feline from his having slept facedown in bed. He nodded to the surfer cops and plodded toward the arched doorway in no particular hurry to see another of the multitude of dead bodies he'd seen during his long career.

He turned toward the street when a white van with a TV news logo on the door climbed the steep street and parked as near as it could get to the driveway. And close behind it was a news van from another Los Angeles TV station. The toney Mt. Olympus address on the police band was drawing them from their beds.

After the detective was inside the foyer, Flotsam said to Jetsam, "Dude, do you think a homicide dick gets a secret high when someone else gets laid low? Wouldn't that, like, give you the guilts?"

"It'd creep me out, bro," Jetsam said. "And it looks like there's gonna be an opening in the Crow office, for sure."

By this time, the forensics van had arrived and criminalists wearing latex gloves and booties were in the bedroom, treating the situation like a full-scale murder investigation, even though Bino Villaseñor had been informed by the patrol watch commander that the only crime committed had been perpetrated by the decedent. But with an LAPD cop even peripherally involved, great investigative care was to be taken, per orders from the West Bureau deputy chief. Just in case things turned out to be more dicey than they seemed.

"Here come the body snatchers," Flotsam said when the coroner's van was waved into the driveway by one of the morning-watch officers who'd received the original call.

When Bino Villaseñor got inside, he found Dan Applewhite in the kitchen with Bix Ramstead, who sat staring at his coffee cup, eyes red and ravaged.

The detective, who did not know the Crow personally, nodded at him. Bino Villaseñor, speaking in the lilting cadence of the East Los Angeles barrio where he'd grown up, said to Bix, "Soon as somebody else from our homicide team arrives, I'd like them to take you to the station. I'll get down there as soon as I can."

Bix Ramstead nodded and continued to stare. The detective had seen it before: the unnerving, hopeless look into the abyss.

The detective said to another of the morning-watch cops standing in the foyer by the staircase, "Where's the lady of the house?"

"Up in one of the bedrooms to your left," the cop said. "She's with a woman officer from the midwatch."

Bino Villaseñor climbed the stairs to the upper floor, looked in the master bedroom where lights had been set up, and did not enter while the criminalists were at work, but he could see that blood had drenched the carpet under Ali's body. The detective turned left and walked to Nicky's bedroom, where he found Margot Aziz, still in pajamas and robe, dried blood on her cheek and chest, sitting on the bed, apparently weeping into a handful of tissues. He didn't know the burly female officer with her, but he indicated with a motion of his head that she could leave. Gert Von Braun walked out of the bedroom and down the stairs.

"I'm Detective Villaseñor, Mrs. Aziz," he said to Margot. "We might need you to come to the station for a more formal statement, but I have a few preliminary questions I'd like to ask."

"Of course," Margot said. "I'll tell you whatever I can."

Bino looked around the huge bedroom, at the mountain of toys and gadgets and picture books and the biggest TV set he'd ever seen in a child's bedroom, and he said, "Where is your son?"

"He's spending the night with my au pair," she said. "That's why I...well, that's why Bix and I...you know."

"How long have you and Officer Ramstead been intimate?" the detective asked, sitting on a chair in front of a PlayStation and opening his notebook folder.

"For about five months." She almost said "on and off" but realized how inappropriate that would sound and said, "More or less."

"Do you often sleep together here?"

"This is the first time we've ever slept together anywhere. On the other occasions we went to hotels for brief interludes."

"Tell me what happened after you and Officer Ramstead went to sleep."

"I heard a noise."

"What kind of noise?"

"Ali's car. The window was open and I heard it, but of course I didn't know it was him. It could have been someone visiting next door. There's a Russian man living there who gets visitors at all hours."

"What'd you do then?"

"I've been frightened for some time about my husband. He's irrational... *was* irrational. He hated me and wanted to take my son from me any way he could. I've told my lawyer, William T. Goodman, numerous times about threats my husband made. I can give you my lawyer's phone number."

"Later," the detective said. "Did you tell any-one else about the threats? Did you report the threats to the police?"

"I tried to," she said. "I told it to Officer Nate Weiss of the Community Relations Office, and Sergeant Treakle, and Detective Fernandez, and of course Bix Ramstead."

That surprised Bino Villaseñor, who said, "Did any of the officers talk to you about mak-ing a police report against your husband for making terroristic threats?"

"Nobody seemed to think the threats were explicit enough to qualify as a crime. Everyone seemed convinced that a successful business-man like Ali Aziz wouldn't do anything irra-tional. But I knew he was an insanely jealous and dangerous man, especially where our son was concerned. I knew he'd eventually try to steal Nicky from me. What I didn't know was that he was insane enough to come here to murder me."

"How'd he get in? Did he still have a key?"

"Not that I know of," she said. "I changed

the locks when he turned vicious during our divorce and custody battles."

"How about the alarm? Didn't you change the code when he moved out?"

"Yes," she said, "but...sorry, it's hard to talk about."

"Take your time," the detective said.

"I'm ashamed. So ashamed. But the truth is, Bix and I were drinking quite a lot. He drank a lot more than I did, and I had to practically carry him up the stairs. And, well, we made love. We were both exhausted. I simply could not get up again to set the alarm. I dozed off. I don't know, maybe I felt secure with a police officer...with Bix in bed with me. I'd forgotten that the front door was unlocked."

"Why was it unlocked? Doesn't it have a self-locking latch on it?"

"Yes, but Bix unlatched it when he went out to his car to get something."

"To get what?"

"His gun."

"He went outside to get his gun? Why?"

"I wanted to buy a gun as protection, and I needed to know how things like the safety button work. I asked Bix to show me. You see, I was convinced that Ali might snap one of these days. And apparently he did."

She could see that the detective was very interested now. He'd stopped making notes. He looked her in the eye and said, "Let's go back to where you heard the car in the driveway. What did you do?"

"I tried to wake Bix. I poked him. I called his name. He wouldn't budge. He was out cold, snoring. He was *very* drunk when we went to bed."

"Then?"

"Then I crept to the landing and looked down and I was almost sure I heard the front door creaking on its hinges. And I ran back in the bedroom and shook Bix and said his name, but it was no use. Bix's gun and keys and wallet were on the nightstand. I took his gun out of the holster. You have no idea how terrified I was."

"And then?" the detective said, and his dark eyes under wiry white eyebrows were penetrating.

"Then I didn't know what to do!"

"Did you try to phone nine-one-one?"

"There wasn't time! I could hear his footsteps on the stairs! He was coming fast! I was panicked!"

"Then?"

"I ducked behind the closet door! He came in the room! He had the gun in his hand! He was walking toward the bed with the gun pointed! I thought he was going to shoot Bix! I leaped out and I got between him and Bix and I yelled! I yelled, 'Ali, don't shoot! Please don't shoot! Don't shoot!' But he turned and pointed the gun at me and I fired!"

She buried her face in tissues then, said, "Excuse me," and got up and ran into Nicky's bathroom, where he heard her turn on the water in the sink.

When she returned, the dried blood was no longer on her cheek and chest, and she said, "I'm sorry. I was feeling nauseous. And I didn't know there was blood on me till I looked in the mirror just now. I guess I knelt beside him. I don't even remember that. You'll have to ask Bix what happened then. I don't think I fainted, but I just have no memory of what happened after I fired."

"How many times did you fire?" the detective asked.

"I don't know."

"Had you ever fired a handgun before?"

"Yes, in the Valley at a gun shop. I went there thinking about buying a gun because of Ali. I took a shooting lesson and decided I'd ask Bix about which gun I should buy. I can give you the name of the gun shop. I have it downstairs in my phone file."

"Is there anyone else you told about the threats your husband made against you?"

"I don't have any close girlfriends to confide in. My entire life involves taking care of my son. Let's see, other than the police officers I named..." Then she said, "Yes, two more police officers."

"Who're they?"

"The ones who came the night Sergeant Treakle was here. I thought I heard footsteps outside on the walkway between my property and my neighbor's. I felt sure it was Ali, but the officers looked around and couldn't find anything. You can get their names from Sergeant Treakle at Hollywood Station."

The detective cocked an eyebrow, closed his notebook, and said, "Speaking of Hollywood Station, I think it would be helpful if you would come down to the station now for a few more questions and a more formal statement."

"Are you accusing me of something?" she said.

"No, it's just routine," the detective said.

"I can't possibly go there," Margot said. "I've been through a great trauma. As soon as your people are out of my house, I've got to have my au pair bring Nicky home. There's a lot for me to do, as you can imagine. I'll be here at my house to help you any way I can, but I won't go to the police station unless my lawyer agrees to it and goes with me. And that would happen only after I get some sleep. I'm exhausted."

"I see," Bino Villaseñor said, studying her more closely than ever.

A sergeant from Watch 3 told 6-X-66 that one of his morning-watch units would take over, and the midwatch team could go end-of-watch. While 6-X-66 was heading back to Hollywood Station, Gert Von Braun said to Dan Applewhite, "I wish we'd pulled that guy outta his Jaguar. Maybe we'd have found the gun."

"We had no probable cause," Dan said. "His driver's license had the Mount Olympus address on it, and his registration too. It all checked out."

"I almost always make a guy get out when it's late at night to see if he's DUI. Maybe I got intimidated because he was a big-bucks guy from the Hollywood Hills, with lots of LAPD business cards in his wallet."

"Gert, he wasn't DUI. He was cold sober."

"Maybe we shoulda written him a ticket."

"That woulda delayed what happened by ten minutes, is all."

"I don't feel good about the way we handled it."

"Look, Gert," Dan said, "that guy was determined to kill his wife and he got what he deserved. Stop beating yourself up."

"It's not him I'm thinking about. It's that Crow, Bix Ramstead. How well do you know him?"

"I've seen him around for years, but I never worked partners with him," Dan Applewhite said.

"He's through, for sure," Gert said.

"Bix Ramstead made his choices, just like Ali Aziz," Dan said. "What happened to both those guys has nothing to do with you and me."

"I guess so," Gert said. "But I don't feel right about it."

"We're off tomorrow," Dan Applewhite reminded her. "So how about doing a Hollywood thing? How about going with me to one of those old movies I told you about? Maybe one starring Tyrone Power. If you wouldn't mind going out with a geezer."

"You're not so old," she said.

It was still an hour from sunrise when Bino Villaseñor was seated across the table from Bix Ramstead in one of the interview rooms at the Hollywood detectives' squad room. They had talked for forty-five minutes uninterrupted, all of it recorded.

Bix Ramstead's eyes seemed sunken in their sockets. He still had the unsettling stare when he wasn't directly answering a question, what the detective called "the stare of despair." His mouth was dry and gluey, and when he spoke, the dryness made his lips pop.

Bino Villaseñor said, "You must need a cold drink bad. And so do I."

The detective left the interview room for several minutes, and Bix put his head down on his arms and closed his eyes, seeing strange images flashing in his mind. When the door opened again, Bix could hear voices outside talking quietly.

Bino Villaseñor put two cold sodas in front of Bix, who was dehydrated from so much alcohol. Bix popped one open and drank it down, then the other. The detective sipped at his and watched Bix Ramstead.

"Is that better?"

Bix nodded.

"We've pretty much covered it," the detective said, "unless you have any more to offer."

Bix took a deep breath and said, "No. To summarize: I was stinking blind drunk and I don't remember much of anything after going upstairs. I did hear her yelling 'Don't shoot.' I'm sure of that much. And I damn sure heard the shots. And I saw him dead on the floor, or seconds from death, with blood gushing from chest wounds, and a gun by his hand. Nothing could've saved him. I did not talk to Margot about anything after that and did not contaminate the scene in any way. I told her to sit in her son's room until police arrived. I went downstairs and waited. And I'd give my right arm or both of them if I could set the clock back to seven last night, when I decided I could handle one shot of vodka."

"Okay, Bix," Bino Villaseñor said. "I believe you."

Bix looked up then, the first time the detective could see some life in his eyes, and he said, "Don't you believe *her?*"

"I guess I'll have to," the detective said. "The stories fit like a glove. A latex glove. But I'll always wonder about a few things. That woman told no less than half a dozen cops from Hollywood Station and Hollywood South that her husband was threatening her. She may as well have made a video for YouTube entitled *My Husband Wants Me Dead*. She even took a shooting lesson and wanted to buy a gun. And finally, she managed to get the greatest corroboration in the world. A veteran married police officer, with nothing to gain and everything to lose, was right there as a witness to the event."

Bix looked at the detective and said gravely, "Do you actually think we conspired to murder her husband?"

"No, I don't think *you* conspired with anybody," the detective said. "You wouldn't be dumb enough to put yourself right in the bedroom during a capital murder. There'd be lots better ways for you to get it done. But buddy, you *were* dumb enough to destroy your career. Yet I got this very uneasy feeling about a woman who manages to get her boyfriend in bed for the first time on the very night that her husband decides to murder her in her sleep."

"I'm not her boyfriend," Bix said.

"What are you, then?"

"I don't know what I am anymore," Bix Ramstead said. "Are we through here?"

"We're through, except that Internal Affairs is outside, waiting to get at you next."

Bix gave the detective a bitter smile then and said, "Why would I bother to talk to IA? As you've pointed out, my career is over. My pension is lost. My children will be seeing this filthy story on the news. Their classmates will ask them humiliating questions. And my wife, she..."

He stopped there and Bino Villaseñor said, "You're not gonna talk to them?"

Bix took his badge and ID card from his badge holder, put them on the table, and said, "You talk to them."

Bino looked in those despairing eyes and instantly thought of the Behavioral Science Services shrink. "Okay, Bix, screw IA. But there's a couple of news teams outside, waiting to jump all over you. How about letting me call the BSS guy for you? You need to talk to somebody right now, buddy."

Bix said, "No, I have to go home now and feed Annie."

Before the detective could say anything further, Bix Ramstead stood and walked out the door of the interview room, out of the detectives' squad room, and out the front door of the station, toward his minivan in the north lot, where the surfer cops had driven it.

He hadn't gotten to the parking lot when one of the on-scene reporters, a tall guy with a full head of flaxen hair, wearing light foundation that had smudged the collar of his starched white shirt, leaped from a van, holding a mike. He ran after Bix Ramstead with a camera operator trailing behind.

Bix looked around for a moment until he spotted where the surfer cops had parked his van and was halfway to it when the reporter caught up with him, saying, "Officer Ramstead!

Officer Ramstead! Can you tell us how long you and Margot Aziz have been lovers?"

Bix ignored him and kept walking.

The reporter matched him stride for stride and said, "Do you and Mrs. Aziz have future plans?"

Bix ignored him and kept walking.

The reporter said, "Have you phoned your wife about this yet? Have you spoken to your children?"

Bix ignored him and kept walking.

As they reached Bix's minivan, the reporter asked the ultimate cliché question that Bix Ramstead had personally heard a hundred media hacks ask victims at terrible events.

The reporter said, "How do you feel right now?"

And that got Bix Ramstead's attention. He turned and said, "How do *you* feel right now?" And he swung a roundhouse right that caught the reporter on the side of the jaw, knocking him back against the camera operator and sending them both sprawling onto the asphalt of the parking lot.

As Bix was driving away, the reporter picked

himself up and yelled, "Man, you are *really* in trouble now!"

It was late morning by the time Bix got home. The killing of Ali Aziz had happened too late to make the morning newspaper, but he was certain it would've been on the morning TV news. He had feared that his brother might be waiting for him.

When he unlocked the door, Annie ran from the bedroom and leaped on him with energy he hadn't thought she had at her age. She was bursting with joyful whimpers, licking him and bouncing like a puppy. He knelt down and held her in his arms and said, "Oh, Annie, I didn't feed you last night. I'm sorry. I'm so sorry!"

Then Bix sat down on the floor, his face in Annie's fur, his arms around her neck, and wept.

When he was able to get up, Bix ignored the flashing on his answering machine. Instead, he went to the kitchen and prepared a huge breakfast for Annie, giving her two hard-boiled eggs, several ounces of boiled chicken breast, and her kibble. He mixed some nonfat cottage cheese in the bowl and put it down on the kitchen floor.

While Annie's face was buried in the food, he walked out the back door and filled her water bowl to the brim. But while he was doing it, he heard the flap in the doggy door open, and Annie poked her head out to make sure he wasn't leaving her again.

"Oh, Annie," he said. "I'm here."

Then Bix went back inside, and Annie returned happily to her breakfast while he entered his son's bedroom. Bix looked at a baseball trophy and at photos of Patrick playing ball with Annie when she was a pup, and one of Patrick graduating from middle school. Then he entered his daughter's room and picked up a photo of Janie and his wife, Darcey, sitting side by side on the piano bench. He couldn't remember what they were playing when he'd taken the photo and he was surprised to see that Janie had inherited her mother's lips. How had he never noticed that before?

He entered their bedroom then, his and Darcey's. She'd never liked the photo of her when she was pregnant with Janie, but he loved that photo for the serenity in her face. He was very glad that his daughter's features favored Darcey and not himself.

Bix opened the closet door and reached on the high shelf, back behind a pair of hiking boots he wore whenever they went camping. He opened a zipper case and removed his off-duty gun, a two-inch stainless-steel revolver. When he got to the kitchen, he saw that Annie had cleaned the bowl, so he opened the refrigerator and put all of the remaining chicken into the bowl along with more kibble and cottage cheese.

He went to the wall phone and called the LAPD emergency number, got a PSR on the line, and gave his name and address. He asked that a patrol unit be sent code 2. Then he opened the front door quietly, not wanting Annie to see him leaving again. He walked to the front yard and took the revolver from his pocket.

When Annie heard the gunshot she stopped eating. She ran to the living room and looked out the window. Then she bolted through the doggy door into the backyard and ran along the side of the house to the chain-link fence that prevented her from going into the front yard. She stood up on the fence with her front paws until she could clearly see him lying on the grass.

Then Annie started howling. She was still howling when the first black-and-white arrived.

TWENTY-THREE

HE'D FALLEN ASLEEP watching TV and awoke feeling like Rosie O'Donnell was sitting on his head. He had a humongous headache when he got up that morning. He was looking for something to blame it on besides the two pipeloads of rock he'd smoked, and all those 40s he'd guzzled. Then he remembered those little capsules that Ali Aziz had given him. He vaguely recalled popping two of them before he passed out.

Leonard Stilwell turned on the TV, since he couldn't stand silence, and began drinking ice water. After that he drank a glass of orange juice before going back for more water. He'd never been so thirsty in his life and his head was killing him. It had to have been the sleeping meds. Leonard opened the drawer of the lopsided chest of drawers that contained two pots, a frying pan, two dinner dishes, a bowl, a few knives, forks, spoons, socks, some underwear, and two clean T-shirts. On top of the T-shirts he found the envelope with the magenta-and-turquoise capsules.

He should've known better than to use anything that fucking Ay-rab had given him. He took the envelope into his tiny bathroom and dumped the remaining capsules into the toilet. It took two tries to get them all flushed away.

When he came back into the kitchen, one of the local morning news anchors, a hottie whose heavily penciled eyebrows were used as emphasis, was talking about a killing. Leonard felt like adjusting the TV vertical to keep those bouncing fucking eyebrows in one place. When he turned up the volume to hear if for once she had something sensible to say, he heard "Ali Aziz." Then she went on to the next story.

"Holy shit!" Leonard said, switching to every other local channel. But the news was either over or somebody was talking about some horrible fucking recipe you couldn't get Junior the Fijian giant to choose in place of a bowl of cockroaches.

He quickly got dressed, took four aspirins, and ran downstairs to his car, driving a couple of blocks to a residential street where he could steal an *L.A. Times.* Then he drove back to his apartment and looked all through the newspaper, but he saw nothing about Ali Aziz. He turned on a local channel again and saw an LAPD spokesperson just winding up his brief statement on the suicide of some LAPD cop and the fatal shooting of nightclub owner Ali Aziz by his former wife, who'd been mixed up romantically with the dead cop.

The first thing that Leonard Stilwell thought was, There goes my chance at another Ali Aziz shakedown! The second thing he thought was, How can I make a buck from this by telling the rich widow that Ali bugged her house? The answer was obvious: He couldn't. Not without revealing his own part in it. And he'd seen enough of Hollywood jail.

Leonard Stilwell told himself to look on the bright side. He had ten grand plus. He had the stake he needed to get out of crime and go into the business he'd been contemplating. Still, it was a goddamn shame that the hotheaded Ay-rab had to get himself smoked like that just because some cop was porking his old lady. It was the only time in his life that Leonard Stilwell had found himself right in the middle of a big-time soap opera, and he couldn't figure out how to squeeze a fucking dime out of it!

Late that morning, Detective Bino Villaseñor had nearly completed his reports and was eager to go home, when he got the word that Officer Bix Ramstead had shot himself. Everything changed in an instant. Both the area captain and station captain were in meetings with the West Bureau commander. And the detective knew without a doubt that this thing was going to be discussed with the chief of police himself before Bino Villaseñor ever slept in his own bed.

The detective called the law offices of William T. Goodman, Esq., and was politely told that Mr. Goodman's client Margot Aziz would be making no further comment to anyone unless compelled to do so by court order. Mr. Goodman said that he would accept any subpoena pertaining to this terrible tragedy on behalf of his client at any time in the future.

At 2 P.M. that day, after spokespersons for the chief of police had been badgered and hounded by reporters, Detective Villaseñor found himself in a conference room on the sixth floor at Parker Center with police brass and representatives from the district attorney's office. Bino Villaseñor had been preparing himself for this meeting all day and had expected dozens, if not hundreds, of detailed questions. But by the time he arrived, all of them had already read his reports and seemed satisfied. The questions were few.

A deputy district attorney said, "Detective Villaseñor, is there any doubt in your mind that Officer Bix Ramstead was *not* part of a plot to murder Mr. Ali Aziz?"

"No doubt whatsoever," the detective said. "In my opinion, he killed himself out of shame and remorse. The officer had lost everything and couldn't face the disgrace he'd caused to himself and especially to his family."

The deputy district attorney said, "Is there any doubt in your mind that Mrs. Margot Aziz did not plot to murder Mr. Ali Aziz?"

Bino Villaseñor looked around then at all that brass, everyone expectant. And he said, "If this was a setup and Officer Ramstead was a fall guy needed for corroboration, only Margot Aziz knows how she pulled it off. Getting

Bix Ramstead in that bedroom for the first time might not have been so tough, but getting Ali Aziz in there with his own registered gun in his hand and murder on his mind, well, I just can't imagine how she coulda timed it so well. I'm real sorry that Officer Ramstead is dead, but her story and Bix Ramstead's story are the same story. And every employee of the Leopard Lounge who was there last night has been contacted today. Including a dancer named Jasmine McVicker who popped in the door for a few minutes to have her identity verified for a midwatch unit. And nobody saw Ali Aziz leave the club last night, not even the bouncer, who'd left for fifteen minutes to stop a brawl in the parking lot."

The deputy district attorney said, "Did you speak to Mrs. Aziz's attorney about a family trust or wills involved in this case? As a motive for murder?"

"That was one of my first questions to him," Bino Villaseñor said. "Margot's executor is her father in Barstow, and everything she has goes to her son, Nicky Aziz."

The district attorney said, "And how about the estate of Ali Aziz?"

"His lawyer informed us that he is the executor, and all of Ali Aziz's assets go to Nicky Aziz."

The deputy district attorney said, "As far as you are concerned, then, this is a case of self-defense and not a murder, am I correct?"

"Correct," Bino Villaseñor said. "At least for now."

The deputy district attorney said, "And her lawyer will not produce Margot Aziz for further questions unless by subpoena?"

"Correct," the detective said. "The last thing he said to me was that she's going on an extended vacation to get away from the press, possibly on a cruise. He said that her son has been taken to his grandparents' home in Barstow, and that Margot Aziz would not be returning to Hollywood until what he called the 'ugly scandal' is no longer in the news. He said that she's distraught and mentally exhausted."

The bureau commander said, "You did a good job, Detective. And you look a bit exhausted too. Why don't you go home."

"I got a few good rounds left in me, Chief," said Bino Villaseñor, "but on this one, I'm shadowboxing with ghosts."

* * *

At the end of that long day, the sergeant in charge of the Community Relations Office told all Crows at a very solemn meeting that Bix Ramstead's family was planning to have a private funeral service as soon as the coroner released Bix's body to their mortuary. Then their sergeant told a few anecdotes from happier times he'd had with Bix, and he invited others to do the same.

Ronnie Sinclair had to dab at her eyes several times while others were talking about Bix, and she declined when asked if she'd like to say anything about her partner. Ronnie wanted to tell them about the time Bix became an angel to a dying child, but she knew she'd never be able to get through it.

TWENTY-FOUR

TWENTY-ONE DAYS after the bodies of Bix Ramstead and Ali Aziz were put into the ground at different cemeteries, a cruise ship of Norwegian registry was docked at the port of Istanbul. The entry to Istanbul through the Bosporus, with Europe on one side and Asia on the other, had been thrilling, and Margot Aziz was looking forward to exploring the Turkish port city with other passengers she'd met.

Margot had had no trouble at all finding passengers, especially among the single men, who wanted to be her escort whenever they'd gone ashore at other ports. But none of them interested her very much, and she'd decided to visit the Topkapi Museum and the Grand Bazaar of Istanbul with Herb and Millie Sloane, a married couple from San Francisco.

At the end of their exhausting day, they decided to dine at a highly recommended restaurant rather than return to the ship at the dinner hour. They enjoyed a feast, sampled local wine, and had a very pleasant time. When they got back to the ship, Margot told the Sloanes that she was tired and didn't feel like going to the shipboard nightclub show that her friends planned to attend. The last thing she said to them was that she needed a good night's sleep.

The only thing that had spoiled things for Margot that day was the need to respond to a few annoying calls from Jasmine McVicker, whining about how she should have been invited along as a companion. Margot couldn't make her understand how suspicious it would have looked at this time and decided that the girl was an idiot. She'd have to pay her off and get Jasmine out of her life sooner rather than later. But for now Margot needed rest.

An hour later, Margot Aziz staggered from her stateroom and screamed for the steward. He was a German named Hans Bruegger, who said in his statement that Margot Aziz seemed to be experiencing muscle spasms. He said that her backbone arched and she went into convulsions. She was taken from the ship and rushed to the finest hospital in Istanbul but died of asphyxiation in less than an hour.

The Turkish authorities made immediate inquiries, and at the request of the U.S. State Department, Margot's body was released and flown to California for the postmortem and time-consuming toxicology tests. However, a Turkish pathologist publicly ventured an opinion, based on symptoms and a cursory examination, that he saw indications of something akin to the poison used to kill rats and other pests. The word *strychnine* appeared in news reports. The restaurant where Margot had dined was visited by Turkish health officials, but they could find nothing amiss. And the Sloanes gave statements saying that they'd experienced no ill effects from what they'd eaten and drunk at the restaurant. No rat poison was found anywhere. Nor was pesticide containing strychnine found anywhere on the ship.

When the body of Margaret "Margot" Osborne Aziz arrived home, local reporters engaged in lots of speculation about whether her cruel death could be another case of an American being mysteriously poisoned abroad. It didn't take long for TV reporters to introduce a sinister suggestion that infuriated Turkey's tourist industry, namely that Americans were no longer safe from extremists in any Muslim country, democracy or not.

An angry spokesman for the Turkish Consulate General in Los Angeles said that in his opinion, Margot Aziz's death had nothing to do with Muslims and that suicide should at least be considered as a motive for her poisoning. He suggested that the recent tragic shooting of her husband may have been too much for her to bear. That statement outraged Margot Aziz's lawyer, who called it preposterous, and it brought another furious response from James and Teresa Osborne, Margot's parents in Barstow, California, who were in the process of becoming legal guardians of their wealthy grandson, Nicky Aziz.

There were two people in the city of Los Angeles who were nearly as upset as her parents over the death of Margot Aziz. One was a beautiful Amerasian dancer whose only payday for her nerve-racking work had been the $4700 she'd stolen from the desktop in Ali Aziz's office on the night he was murdered. Jasmine McVicker spent three days in bed grieving after the report of Margot's death appeared on the TV news.

She would forever wonder if somehow Margot could have been a murder victim herself. The thought of it terrified her.

The other Los Angeles resident who was profoundly distressed by Margot Aziz's death was a Mexican pharmacist on Alvarado Street. He had no idea if his former client Ali Aziz could have been a murder victim, but he feared that Margot Aziz probably was. And he thought he knew how it might have happened.

His wife noticed that the pharmacist seemed obsessed with news concerning the case, and she wondered why he had become so diligent about attending Mass, not just on Sunday but sometimes during the week as well. She often saw him on his knees in front of a statue of the Virgin of Guadalupe, his fist pressed to his heart, as though begging forgiveness.

And at Hollywood Station, Detective Bino Villaseñor said to the homicide D3, "When spouses commit murder, the women use poison, the guys use guns. In this case, the woman used a gun and the guy—"

"Is dead," the D3 said. "Ghosts can't poison

people, not even in Istanbul. Let it go, Bino. This case is closed."

"I guess I'll have to," said the old detective. "But something's wrong here, and somebody knows it."

That week, Leonard Stilwell decided that it was time to launch his legitimate business enterprise. He'd also decided that Junior the Fijian was to be his partner, but Junior didn't know it yet. Early in the afternoon, the time when Junior usually woke up, Leonard knocked on the door of his apartment to spring it on him.

"Junior," Leonard said to the still sleepy giant when he got him out of bed. "You and me, babe. We're going into business!"

Junior, who was sitting there barefoot in his baggy shorts and wife beater, said, "Bidness, bro?"

"Yeah, it's time for both of us to start a new life. I'm taking a piece of what I got from that job I done with your lock picks, and I'm setting us both up in legit business."

Junior grinned big, showing two gaps in his grille, and said, "My daddy is gonna be proud! Whadda we do?"

"We're selling something, that's what. And people are gonna buy it."

"Whadda we sell?"

"Happiness," Leonard said.

"You mean like crack? Or crystal meth?"

"No, I said legit business. We're selling goodwill. We're gonna be Characters."

"Everybody say you already a character, Leonard," Junior said, grinning again.

"No, no, I mean Street Characters. Like up at Grauman's Chinese Theatre. That kind of Character."

"I wanna be Spider-Man!" Junior said.

"Jesus Christ, Junior!" Leonard said. "Where the fuck would you get a Spider-Man costume big enough? And would anybody buy into the idea of a spiderweb holding *your* big ass? The fucking thing would have to be made of steel cable."

"Okay. Superman, then," Junior said.

"Right, a Superman that looks like someone who eats missionaries? I don't think so," Leonard said. "What I got in mind is retro. Know what that means?"

"No," Junior said.

"Back to basics," Leonard said. "See, all these

Street Characters are trying to one-up each other. Trying to keep up with whoever's hot right now. That's why there's so many Batmans and Spider-Mans. We ain't gonna go that route."

"Who we gonna be?"

"Mickey Mouse and Pluto, his dog," Leonard said.

"I get to be Mickey Mouse!" Junior said.

"Oh, yeah, a 'roided-up megarodent," Leonard said. "No, dude, I'm the main man."

"You mean the main mouse," Junior said with a giggle.

"I'm Mickey," Leonard said. "You're Pluto the dog. Pay attention!"

Junior stopped picking goop from his toenail with a dinner fork and said, "I hear you, bro."

"Okay," Leonard said. "See, everybody loves Mickey Mouse, but nobody out there on Hollywood Boulevard has ever had a first-class Mickey costume like you see at Disneyland. Well, now I got enough bucks to buy me the best. And we're gonna get a real break on the Pluto costume because the Pluto that was out there had a first-class outfit. But he got busted by the narcs a while back for stashing dope in his head. I know who's taking care of his crib, and we'll buy the Pluto costume cheap. He's gonna be needing bucks for crystal the minute he gets outta jail, so he won't give a shit. Lucky he's a real big guy, so the costume should fit you, no problem."

"What's Pluto do?" Junior wanted to know.

"He barks. He's a fucking dog!"

"How do I make it sound?"

"You just say what a dog says. What's a dog say in Fiji? 'Woof!' Right?"

"No," Junior said. "I seen 'woof' in American cartoons, but in Fijian cartoons, dogs don't say 'woof.'"

"Well, you're an American dog, so you say 'woof,' okay?"

"Okay, bro," Junior said. "Woof."

"Now, here's the deal," Leonard said. "We always go straight to the little kids. The little kids don't really give a shit about Darth Vader and Frankenstein and all those other scary Characters. And the cute Characters, like SpongeBob and Barney? They're boring. But the little kids love Mickey Mouse. Their parents love Mickey Mouse. Their grandparents love Mickey Mouse. You and me, we'll steal the business from all those other jerkoffs by going back to cartoon roots."

"Whadda you do when I say 'woof'?" Junior asked.

"Let's rehearse it," Leonard said. Then, in as squeaky a falsetto as he could manage, Leonard said to an imaginary tot, "Hello! My name is Mickey Mouse! What's yours?"

"Junior," said Junior.

Leonard said, "No, I ain't asking *your* name, for chrissake!"

"Okay, okay, I get it. Do it again," Junior said.

"Wait for your cue," Leonard said. Then, again in a squeaky falsetto to an imaginary tot, Leonard said, "Hello! My name is Mickey Mouse! What's yours?"

"Pluto!" said Junior.

"Oh, fuck," said Leonard Stilwell. "This is gonna take some work."

Hollywood Nate Weiss had occasion to make a call in Laurel Canyon that afternoon. A resident had been complaining to the Community Relations Office about a neighbor's yard sales. They'd been happening at least once a week, and it was, according to the complainant, "unbecoming" to other property owners in Laurel Canyon. After Nate spoke to the neighbor, who agreed to curtail the activity, Nate was driving back when something made him take a left turn up to Mt. Olympus.

He drove to the former home of Ali and Margot Aziz and parked in front. He thought about Margot and about Bix Ramstead. If only he'd obeyed the impulse and gone up to the door and rung the bell on that last night, when he'd seen Bix's minivan in the driveway. He didn't like thinking about Bix. Nate believed the way Bix died had unnerved all of them. But they'd never admit it. It couldn't happen to them. They were tough guys.

Then the front door opened and two young children ran out, a boy and a girl, followed by their pregnant mother. They were heading for the mailbox when they noticed the black-and-white, and the woman said, "Is there anything wrong, Officer?"

Nate smiled and said, "Not anymore. You've got a beautiful house."

"We're very excited about it," she said. "And we know about its history."

"You'll write your own history," Nate said, and they all waved as he drove back down from Mt. Olympus.

When he got to the stop sign at Laurel Canyon, a Porsche 911 flew past him southbound, cutting off a car that had been trying to make a safe left turn. Nate pulled in behind the Porsche, turned on the light bar, and tooted his horn.

She had all the markings of a Hills bunny, with highlighted hair curled and tousled like Sarah Jessica Parker's. She had violet eyes and a sprinkle of freckles across her nose and cheekbones under one of those salon tans like Margot's. Her saline-enhanced bustline reached out and touched the steering wheel.

"Your license, please," Nate said.

"Was I going too fast?" she said with a blazing orthodontic smile. Her license showed her to be thirty-two years old, and she wasn't wearing a wedding ring.

"Yes, and that was a very unsafe pass," Nate said. "We've had several bad traffic collisions on this road."

"I recently got this car," she said, "and I'm

not used to it. I hope you don't have to write me a ticket!"

He noticed her fingers tugging subtly at her skirt until her athletic thighs were exposed. Then she said, "We just moved in. Guess I need someone local to show me the lay of the land."

"Just a moment," Nate said and walked to his shop.

When he returned, the Hills bunny's skirt was almost up to her seat belt, and she said, "I think that if an officer wanted to get to know a girl better, he wouldn't write her a ticket."

Hollywood Nate said, "I think you're right. Sign here, please."

ABOUT THE AUTHOR

JOSEPH WAMBAUGH, a former LAPD detective sergeant, is the bestselling author of seventeen prior works of fiction and non-fiction, including *The Choirboys* and *The Onion Field*. In 2004, he was named Grand Master by the Mystery Writers of America. He lives in Southern California.